# Nicola Cornick

LORD OF SCANDAL

HQN™

ISBN-13: 978-0-373-77211-7
ISBN-10:    0-373-77211-4

LORD OF SCANDAL

www.HQNBooks.com

Printed in U.S.A.

Dear Reader,

In *Lord of Scandal* the glittering worlds of celebrity
and the Regency come together. We tend to think
that celebrity is a modern invention, but historical
figures such as Nelson, Byron and Brummell were the
celebrities of their time, outrageously popular and
mobbed in the streets, until scandal or debt or fickle
public opinion brought them down.

This was the world that I wanted to explore in
*Lord of Scandal*. My hero, Ben Hawksmoor, is a
celebrity in the Regency firmament, a friend of the
Prince Regent, a gamester and self-made man who
has fought his way up from the backstreets of London
and is determined to hold on to fame and wealth at
all costs. Against the backdrop of the Great Frost Fair
of 1814, Ben courts Catherine Fenton, an heiress
whose fortune he covets. But Catherine has a thing or
two to teach Ben about the one thing that money and
celebrity cannot buy…love.

I hope you enjoy Ben and Catherine's story and the
dazzling whirl of Regency celebrity!

Love from

*Nicola*

For Sarah Morgan, fabulous writer,
wonderful friend.

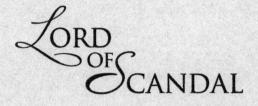

LORD OF SCANDAL

# PROLOGUE

*December, 1812*

LONDON HAD BEEN IN THE GRIP of a hard winter for three weeks and now the question on everyone's lips was whether the ice on the Thames was thick enough to bear the weight of the Frost Fair. The traditional method of testing it was to drive a coach and four out into the middle of the river. Opinion was very much divided over whether or not this was safe. Some said it was; others said that anyone mad enough to put the theory to the test would end up in a watery grave, coach, horses and all. Still others said that anyone who tried it and survived should be locked up in Bedlam anyway, for they were surely insane.

There was only one man wild enough to attempt the feat and that was Benjamin, Lord Hawksmoor.

A frenzy of gambling clutched the spectators as he brought his team down to the riverbank. The carriage was brand-new with the Hawksmoor coat of arms gleaming arrogantly on the door, and the horses were the best that Tattersalls could provide. Some said that Ben Hawksmoor had no right to the title, having been branded a bastard by his own father when he was but a baby, but they said it softly, for had not Hawksmoor killed a man when he was serving out in Portugal with Wellesley—several men, a whole battalion, perhaps—as well as gaining and losing a fortune at cards, seducing a diplomat's wife and daughter, and hacking his way through scrub and forest to escape the bandits? The tales were as wild as the man himself.

The crowds pressed close, calling and jostling. Money changed hands rapidly between the bucks and beaux and even more rapidly slipped into the pockets of the thieves who mingled with the throng.

"A thousand guineas he pulls it off!"

"Two thousand against!"

The air was cold and the wind upriver cut like a knife. The more enterprising of the street vendors had already brought their wares down to the crowds and were making a brisk trade from pea soup and jacket potatoes. Their braziers crackled as the sleety edge of the wind caught their flame.

The crowd cheered frantically as Hawksmoor drove the coach and four down the bank at breakneck pace. It hit the river's edge as though the hounds of hell were snapping at its axles, and skidded across the ice, the horses grappling to gain a grip and the carriage wheels spinning. Up on the box, Hawksmoor brandished the whip like a Norse god, bareheaded, clad all in black, his many-caped driving coat swirling around him.

There was a distant rumble like the roll of cartwheels over cobbles, and then a loud crack like a rifle shot. The crowd fell silent for a long second, then a lady screamed and a frantic babble broke out as everyone surged forward to the river's edge.

"The ice is breaking! Jump, man! Save yourself!"

But Hawksmoor would not leave his horses. The cracks were skewering the ice now, fine as cobwebs but moving faster than a man could run. The back of the carriage lurched and the horses half reared in the shafts as Hawksmoor drove them toward the bank. Then the water was swirling around them and Hawksmoor jumped down, thigh high in dark water, grabbed the bridles and dragged the team the final few yards to the shore.

The crowd fell back, breaking into ragged applause. Ladies were sobbing, or fainting, or both. Men threw their hats in the air. Courtesans cast flowers beneath Ben Hawksmoor's feet as he led his trembling and sweating horses to safety. The printing presses were already turning with the story of his latest exploit. The newspaper hacks were filling their ink pots.

Hawksmoor stopped, turned to the crowd and executed a perfect bow. His buckskins were soaked and clinging to his thighs. His boots were ruined. There was a spark of humor in his hazel eyes. He looked dangerous and disheveled. Those ladies who had not fainted earlier were tempted to do so now.

"Ladies and gentlemen, I fear the ice is too thin. We shall have to wait another year for our Frost Fair."

The throng cheered deliriously and Hawksmoor smiled his wicked smile and continued his hero's progress through the middle of the crowd. Men clapped him on the back and women leaned over to kiss him.

But a few stood apart.

"Only the devil himself could survive that," a passing clergyman observed sourly. "He has sold his soul."

Another man smiled to hear the words, for Ben Hawksmoor traded on that very reputation.

"Thin ice," he murmured. "When did you tread on anything else, my friend? But one day the ice will break. And I will be there to dance on your grave."

# CHAPTER ONE

*January, 1814*

> Never look at any strange man as you approach
> him in passing by, for sometimes a look may be
> taken advantage of by forward and impertinent
> men. It is generally a girl's own fault if she be
> spoken to, and as such, is a disgrace to her of
> which she should be ashamed to speak.
> —*Mrs. Eliza Squire,* Good Conduct for Ladies

IT WAS A FINE DAY for a public hanging.

Above the Newgate scaffold, the sky was a high,
pale blue. The noose swung in the cold winter breeze.
The nobility packed the pavilion behind the gallows.
The victim was a gentleman and that always drew a
good crowd. This was the execution of the Season;
Ned Clarencieux, gambler, adventurer, whose ill luck
at the card tables had led him to pass forged money to
buy his way out of debt and murder his banker in a vain
attempt to cover his tracks. The ladies who packed the
gallery had danced with Clarencieux in *Ton* ballrooms
all over London. Now they came to see him die.

Below the ranks of the aristocracy swarmed the mob, pressing about the foot of the gallows, laughing, joking, good-humored with gin and anticipation. They clambered up the lead drainpipes and onto the roofs of surrounding houses for a better view. They jostled and shouted and drank a toast to Clarencieux, and placed bets on how long it would take the failed gambler to die.

In the press of people behind the scaffold sat Miss Catherine Fenton, pretty, privileged and heiress to eighty thousand pounds, wedged between her fiancé and the squirming body of her six-year-old half brother, John. Despite the coldness of the day, she felt hot and dizzy and sick. She had doused her handkerchief in rosewater and pressed it to her nose, but the faint sweetness of the perfume could do nothing to mask the smell of rank bodies and fetid excitement. To be the only young lady present at a public hanging was no great privilege, but the man Clarencieux had murdered had been one of her trustees, Sir James Mather. Catherine had not wanted to come but her father, Sir Alfred Fenton, could not understand her scruples. He said that she must see justice done. Sir Alfred was a nabob, a man who had lived and worked in India and was accustomed to the sudden and bloody experience of death that living on the subcontinent could provide. He had a cast-iron stomach and an attitude to match. Catherine did not. She knew she was in disgrace because Sir Alfred considered her weak and foolish for begging to be excused the trip to Newgate. Her little brother had begged to be included.

In the event, John had got his wish and she had not got hers. That was no surprise to her. John was loved, spoiled and indulged. She was not.

"Oysters for sale! Whelks ten a penny!" An enterprising street seller was struggling up the steps toward them, a basket of seafood balanced on her hip. Catherine felt her stomach heave as the smell of hot fish mingled with the scent of hot sweat.

"Yes, please!" John said, bouncing with excitement. He proffered his penny to the girl. Catherine turned her head away and pressed her handkerchief more firmly over her nose.

"You are unwell, my love?"

Catherine looked up to see that her betrothed was looking at her with a spurious sense of concern. Algernon, Lord Withers, liked to think of himself as Catherine's fiancé. Catherine preferred not to think of him in any way at all. She hated the relentless manner in which he pursued her and the hold, whatever it was, that he appeared to have over her father. She had been postponing the wedding since the summer, pleading first a mysterious feminine indisposition, then mourning for a second cousin she had not known well but whose death had been providentially timed. Now she had run out of excuses and the wedding date was set for later that spring unless she could come up with a new ruse.

"Oysters are not to my taste," she said, noting that Withers had already lost interest and was now admiring the ample bosom of the street seller instead.

"A shame." Withers's narrow gaze came back to her

with a lascivious gleam. "They are accounted to be the food of love, my sweet. You should indulge. It might make you more…kindhearted…to me."

"I think not!" Catherine snapped. The thought of indulging in any kind of lovemaking with Withers was anathema to her. In her opinion, he would not recognize love if he tripped over it in the street. He would merely grind it beneath his heel.

Plenty of men professed to be *in love* with Catherine, but her fiancé was not one of them. Until her betrothal had been announced, Catherine had been courted and complimented, harassed by poets with bad sonnets, her hay fever exacerbated by the endless flowers delivered by the cartload to Guilford Street every morning. But Catherine was not a nabob's daughter for nothing. She suspected that the gentlemen's affections were reserved for the bags of money she would inherit from her mama's estate. It was tied up in trust until she was twenty-five—or until she married. Algernon Withers's determination to wed her sprang, she thought, from the same source as that of all her other suitors. Greed. And a deeply unpleasant lust that made him determined to possess her.

He had taken her hand in his now and was pressing it tightly until she felt the bones start to crack in protest. Catherine caught her breath. The gleam in Withers's eye had turned to triumph now. He liked to hurt things, particularly pretty things.

With her free hand, Catherine gripped her parasol and drove the spike on the top into the side of Withers's foot. He let her go with a grunt of surprise and she turned her head away, chin raised. She was glad that she had brought the parasol with her now for she had been in two minds earlier. It was sunny but cold. A lady would open the flimsy little umbrella anyway to keep the sun away from her delicate complexion. A nabob's daughter might not bother, however, since she thought such affectations were rather stupid.

Catherine was a cit through and through. Not only was her father a nabob but her mother had also been the daughter of another merchant adventurer, the infamous Scotsman Mad Jack McNaish. His reputation had made men tremble in their shoes but Catherine had adored him. He had told her never to be ashamed of her antecedents. She had no pretense at a pedigree. And the *Ton* had made it clear from the start that she was tolerated in their ranks for her money alone.

John was slurping his oysters with enthusiasm, the juice running down over his chin. His nursemaid fussed about with a cloth.

"What a shocking display," Sir Alfred Fenton said suddenly, raising his quizzing glass to scan the open tavern windows opposite, where a group of Covent Garden bawds romped bare-breasted with a couple of dissolute-looking young men. "Shameful debauchery in a public place!"

"Shameful, Sir Alfred," Lord Withers agreed. "I do believe those are Hawksmoor's set. He was a friend of Clarencieux of course. It is unfortunate the scandal did not bring him down as well."

Sir Alfred grunted. "Hawksmoor is high in the regent's favor. He is safe—for now. But I give less than a fig for his chances if he falls from popularity. They say he owes so much money he would have to flee abroad."

Lord Withers's hot, excited eyes sought Catherine's as the piercing whoops of the courtesans rose over the noise of the crowd.

"Disgraceful, is it not, Miss Fenton? Parading themselves in broad daylight?"

Catherine felt repulsed. She knew that Withers was equally aroused by the lewd nakedness of the women and by the prospect of the hanging. Both disgusted her. *He* disgusted her with his cold, clammy hands, his noxious breath and the increasing liberties he tried to take with her person.

"I consider it more of a disgrace to take pleasure in witnessing a murder than to see public displays of licentiousness," she said coldly, and Withers's angry gaze pinned her in her seat before his eyes slid away from hers and back to the window opposite.

Catherine realized that she was shaking. She hated this, the stench of mingled fear and anticipation, the pleasure that men like Lord Withers took in such hideous depravity and most of all she hated her father for forcing her to accompany him. She had overheard him boasting the previous night at Lady Semple's ball.

"We go to see Clarencieux hang tomorrow. I'll wager he will dance better on the end of that rope than he ever did in your ballroom, madam...."

And people had laughed—*laughed*—at his wit and the thought of a man they had known dying a criminal's death. In that moment, Catherine had hated them all.

She had only met Ned Clarencieux once. The chaperones of the *Ton* were careful to keep men of his stamp away from the debutantes and heiresses, but one day Catherine had been walking in the park with her stepmother and a number of young bucks had come across to accost Maggie, Lady Fenton, with what had appeared to Catherine to be suspicious familiarity. Clarencieux had been charming. He had been the one who had apologized for their forwardness, kissed Catherine's hand, smiled into her eyes and taken his friends away. And though she had known he was a no-good wastrel, he had left her with an irresistible smile on her lips.

Clarencieux, Hawksmoor… They lived very close to the edge and one false step would bring them down.

Catherine bit her lip now to think that her father had warned her away from such men in life but that now Clarencieux was to die he thought nothing of bringing her to the hanging.

Her brother, John, was trying to see past the nodding plumes and parasols that obscured his view, but he was too small. He scrambled onto Catherine's lap, kicking her, clutching at her pelisse, setting her bonnet askew.

"Let me see! Let me see!"

His nursemaid tried to pull him back but he ignored her and after a moment she gave up the struggle and slumped in her seat. Catherine thought the girl looked ill. There was sweat standing out on her forehead and she was the color of starch paste. She put out a hand to the maid.

"Close your eyes, take deep breaths and try not to listen to the crowd."

The girl nodded. A matronly woman in the row in front of them turned her head, smiled indulgently at John and patted the space on the cushion beside her.

"Come and stand here next to me, poppet. You will have a better view."

Catherine glanced at the clock on Saint Sepulchre's Church. Five minutes to the hanging. Her heart was racing and her palms within her kid gloves were cold and clammy. She closed her eyes against the winter brightness of the sun and the seething mass of the crowds, but she could not shut out the pictures in her head. She knew what happened when a man was hanged. They took the prisoner to the Press Room and struck off his iron manacles. They bound his wrists. They prayed over him. And then they brought him through the Debtor's Door and up the steps to the scaffold where the noose was waiting.

Catherine opened her eyes. The romping bawds had vanished from the window opposite and instead a man stood leaning on the sill, his gaze fixed on the gallows below. He was tall and fair and it was his very stillness that commanded Catherine's eyes. It was an intense, concentrated, controlled stillness that never-theless seemed full of violence.

The breath caught in her throat and she stared, transfixed.

Then he looked up and met her gaze, and Catherine recoiled at the anger and passion in his eyes. It was like a physical blow. She felt herself draw back.

"Miss Fenton, Miss Fenton!"

The nursemaid was tugging urgently at her sleeve.

"Master John has gone!"

It was true. The space next to the matronly woman was empty. Catherine looked frantically around. The nursemaid was sobbing.

"I had my eyes shut like you told me to, miss! I didn't do no wrong—"

"Never mind that now," Catherine said. Her heart raced. If John were to get lost in the crowd, they might never find him again. He could be kidnapped or robbed. He had no idea how dangerous a place like Newgate could be. He was just a careless and spoiled child.

Sir Alfred had not noticed anything amiss. He and Withers were deep in conversation and were fortifying their stomachs with brandy from a hip flask.

Catherine stood up. She knew she was going to have to look for John herself. The maid was a broken reed and once her father knew what had happened he would be furious. But there was no need to tell him yet. In all likelihood John had not gone far. She took a deep breath and smoothed her gloved hands down the front of her pelisse.

As she started to edge along the row of seats, apologizing, trying not to step on people's toes, ignoring their grumbles, the clock began to toll the hour. The time of the hanging had come.

SHE WAS SITTING IN THE MIDDLE of the crowd but Ben Hawksmoor saw her at once, as though the sun were shining on her alone. She was dressed in a jonquil-yellow pelisse trimmed with fur. There was a matching fur-trimmed bonnet on her head and beneath it he caught the glint of chestnut-bright hair gleaming in the winter sunshine. She was sitting beside Algernon Withers, the most lecherous man in the *Ton,* which was a fair indicator that she must be a high-class courtesan. Ben had already noted that most of the drabs in London had come to Newgate that day. His mouth twisted with cynical appreciation at the thought of a woman using the occasion of a hanging to find a rich lover. It was a clever idea. Half the aristocracy—the male half—were present, after all, and who would wish to waste such an opportunity?

Not that the girl sitting with Withers looked in need of a new protector. She looked rich and pampered, and Ben Hawksmoor despised her for being so perfect herself and being here to take pleasure in the destruction of another living creature.

Ben straightened and moved away from the window. There was such anger and bitterness seething in him that his hands were clenched in fists of rage. The entire *Ton,* which had once fawned on Ned Clarencieux with the same ardor it now showed to him, had thrown its favorite to the wolves and had come to watch him be ripped apart.

There was nothing Ben could do, of course. Clarencieux had been his friend but he was beyond his help now. Ben had gone to the regent, had spoken up for Clarencieux when every instinct, every principle he lived by, had urged him not to risk his own neck for anyone else. And it had done no good at all. Prinny had not even listened and Ben had seen the flicker of irritation in the regent's eyes and had backed down. He was an adventurer and he could not afford to lose the regent's patronage or he would be back in the gutter where he had begun.

It was too late for Clarencieux, anyway. It had always been too late. The *Ton* was a fickle mistress and Ned had fallen from favor. He had lived by his wits and had no one with money or connections to help him when he fell. Nobody cared. And Ben shuddered because he could see himself so clearly in Ned Clarencieux.

A flicker of movement in the pavilion opposite caught his eye. Withers's demirep had got to her feet and was making her way toward the steps that led down past the scaffold and into the crowd. Ben stared. Was she a fool? He could well understand that the noise, the heat and the stench of a hanging might turn the strongest stomach and make her want to escape, but to go down into so volatile a crowd was madness. They would rob her, rape her, rip her to pieces and count it all as part of the entertainment.

And he really should not care.

He was not certain why he did. He very rarely cared about anyone other than himself. Life had bred that in him. Protect and survive. But he saw the revulsion in the girl's face as she looked about her at the excited crowd and he felt a sudden flash of deep affinity for her. Neither of them wanted to be there. They had that one small thing in common. The girl had probably come only because Withers had insisted. And he... Well, he was there because it was the last respect that he could pay to his friend and the shreds of honor he still possessed had forced him to do that one small thing.

So he could not let the girl go down into the mob alone and unprotected, demirep or not.

With a muttered oath he headed for the door. One of the bawds caught hold of his arm to detain him. He did not know her name as he had not been paying attention when his cousin Sam had introduced them. He had thought it tasteless in the extreme of Sam to bring them to Ned's hanging. And he had never been interested in cheap whores anyway.

He heard the women's laughter as the door slammed behind him. Like everyone else, they thought this was some sort of entertainment, more exciting than wine or hunting or dancing or sexual conquest. He felt a murderous rage. This was life and death and he had struggled against both from the day he was born.

As he descended the tavern stairs, Saint Sepulchre's bell started to ring with a feverish jangling that made Ben's head feel as though it were splitting. Out in the street the sun was cold and bright and the crowd seethed and surged toward the gallows. He started to fight his way through the throng toward the scaffold steps. He could see the girl in the jonquil pelisse. She was on the bottom step, arguing with one of the city marshall's men. Ben saw the man bar her way with his stave and point back up into the stands. The girl's face was pale but her mouth was set in a determined line. She shook her head, ducked under the stave and a second later the crowd swallowed her up. Ben's heart jolted with apprehension as he renewed his efforts to reach her. Even as he struggled with the crowd he felt annoyed at his wayward impulse to chivalry. It was the marshall's men who were there to keep the peace and it was no concern of his if some foolish creature decided to throw herself into the crowd. She was probably far better able to take care of herself than she appeared. No gently-bred girl would ever attend a public hanging. She was probably Haymarket ware tricked out as Berkeley Square. Withers was well known for his low tastes.

A roar went through the throng as Clarencieux came out of the Debtor's Door. The press of people was so dense here that Ben could scarcely move. He saw a flash of yellow and stretched out a hand, but the crowd had surged forward, bearing the girl away, tumbling her over like a leaf adrift on a flood. The bells stopped abruptly and the crowd sucked in its breath. Clarencieux was on the scaffold now. He opened his bound hands helplessly and clasped them together again. His expression was so wild and imploring that Ben felt furious. He was looking up into the crowd behind the scaffold as though begging for someone to save him. His humiliation was unbearable.

Then the hangman pulled the cap down over Clarencieux's face and dropped the noose about his neck.

The priest's lips were moving but the words of the prayers were lost in the sound of the crowd.

Ben's hand closed about the wrist of the girl in yellow and he dragged her out from under the feet of the mob, where she had half fallen in the rush toward the scaffold.

He pulled her into his arms. He felt her body go stiff with shock at his touch and she almost pulled away, but the press of people pushed them together and the resistance went out of her. Her bonnet had come off. Her dark hair was in cloudy disarray about her face. Her eyes were a paler shade of brown than her chestnut hair, a luminous amber. She looked dazed.

"I had no notion it would be like this…." He just caught the whisper of her words through the roaring wall of noise that encircled them.

"You were a fool to come down here." But his hands were gentle on her as he held her tightly, protecting her with his body against the stifling press about them.

"I was looking for someone." There were tears on her lashes now. He saw her swallow hard. "I did not realize it would be so dangerous."

"What were you expecting?" Ben's voice was rough. "A garden party?"

The shout went up. "Hats off!"

It was the only public show of deference to mark the hanging itself. The crowd shuffled and doffed their hats and bonnets. The hangman drew the lever and the trap door fell with a crash. The crowd screamed, a wild and ragged sound with an edge of violence to it, and

Ben felt the shudder go straight through the girl's body. She buried her face against his jacket. His hand tangled in her hair, holding her closer still. He could feel his heart racing beneath the blue superfine of his coat. Her cheek was pressed against his chest and her eyes were closed. The anger and the misery and the hatred swept through him in a vicious tide and he bent his head to blot out the sight of Clarencieux's wicked death and pressed his lips to her hair. She felt sweet and soft and she smelled faintly of roses. Ben could feel the tiny shudders that racked her body. Her tears wet his jacket.

"I met him once," she said, muffled. "He did not deserve this."

"He was my friend. There was nothing I could do." Ben could hear the rawness in his own voice as he faced his failure and loss. Once before he had managed to save his friend from certain death. This time he had not.

She raised her head and looked into his eyes. Her own were dark and innocent, and his heart jolted. It felt as though she could see directly into his soul.

"I am sorry," she said. "It is no more than murder."

The hangman was swinging on Ned Clarencieux's heels to hasten his end. Ben had paid him a lot of money to do it. It had been the only thing he *could* do but at least the promise had been honored. The crowd was cheering now as Clarencieux died. For a moment, Ben stared at the horror of it all and then he gave a ragged exclamation and drew the unresisting body of the girl harder against him. She came without protest and he felt the relief swamp him to feel her close. He needed her. The intensity of his longing baffled him but he could not question it now, not while the darkness raced through his soul and she was the only light. He wrapped his arms about her and pressed his cheek hard against the softness of hers and closed his mind to the demons that swarmed at his heels.

He could not have said how long they stood like that while the violence and the bloodlust swirled around them and, although he knew the girl was terrified, in that moment Ben felt a small sane core of peace.

The tension in the crowd slackened and the noise fell away a little. Ben loosened his grip and the girl drew in a deep, shaken breath. She was still trembling. He could feel it.

"He was a brave lad," someone said. "He died like a man."

People were passing execution broadsides around, with a woodcut picture of the hanging and a report of Clarencieux's alleged confession. They had been printed long before the hanging and Ben ground one underfoot in disgust.

He raised a hand and brushed the tears away from the girl's cheek. He felt exhausted, as exhausted as she looked. Her lashes were black against the pallor of her skin and her eyes looked tired and bruised. His fingers grazed the corner of her mouth and he heard her catch a tiny breath. Her gaze flew to his face, eyes wide and questioning now. Something powerful and indefinable passed between them and the lust slammed through

him. He did not want to want her, not here, not now.
It did not seem right. And yet he needed her. He could
not help himself. It was as alien and as frightening a
feeling as he had ever experienced.

They were cutting Clarencieux down now. Ben recognized the doctor Astley Cooper coming down from
the gallery behind the scaffold, talking to the hangman
and the sheriff. It sickened Ben more than anything
else that day to think that Clarencieux was now for a
surgeon's dissection table.

"Send the body to my chambers as usual," Cooper
said. "I'm for my dinner. Deviled kidneys, is it, as is
traditional?"

Ben felt the girl shudder. In the crowd a small boy
was crying and a disheveled nursemaid was scolding
him in a voice high-pitched with anger and relief. It
seemed to break some sort of spell that had bound the
two of them together, closer than close, soul to soul.
Ben stood back and forced himself to see her as just
another harlot, a pretty girl on the make. Nevertheless
he felt cold inside to let her go.

She pressed her hand against her mouth. "They
will be looking for me. I must go."

Ben was still holding her arm, his grip very light
now. He did not release her but studied her face for a
moment. She was not as young as he had first thought,
maybe twenty or twenty-one rather than the eighteen
he had originally guessed. Her face was free from the
paint that high-class whores normally applied, but
then she did not need the adornment. Her clothes were
stylish, good quality, reeking of money. She must be

important to Withers for him to fund her so well and it was no doubt true that her lover would be coming looking for her very soon….

"Catherine!"

Ben straightened up. As if on cue, Withers had come running down the steps from the pavilion behind the scaffold and had taken the girl's elbow in a deliberate gesture of possession. Ben felt the antagonism he had always held for the other man breathe gooseflesh along his skin. He did not want to think about the things this girl had to do to please the lover who kept those fine clothes on her back.

Withers looked down his nose at Ben, which was quite a feat since Ben was the taller by at least six inches.

"Take yourself off, Hawksmoor," he said.

Ben laughed harshly. He needed to vent his anger and Withers was as good a target as any. "This is a public hanging, Withers," he said scornfully. "Anyone can attend. The clue is in the word *public*."

Withers's pointed features sharpened into hatred. "And anyone can die, can they not, Hawksmoor? You should remember that." His face twisted. "Let Clarencieux's end be a warning. Fate will catch up with you."

Ben laughed shortly. "Are you preaching a moral fable to me, Withers? How very inappropriate."

Withers took a step forward until Ben could smell his rancid breath and feel it on his face.

"Justice was finally done today," he spat out, glancing across to where Clarencieux's broken body was being taken away. "You will be next, Hawksmoor.

I brought Clarencieux down and I will bring you down, too."

Ben heard the girl catch her breath at the threat. "My lord—" she began, putting out a hand toward Withers. He shrugged her off angrily.

"Be silent, Catherine!"

Ben stepped forward, took Withers's lapels in a tight grip and lifted him off his feet. The man's face reddened to a dangerous hue.

"Don't threaten me, Withers," Ben said pleasantly. "I have no notion what your grievance could be but I am not like Clarencieux. I can look after myself." He looked at Catherine whose face was an angry, embarrassed red. "And do not speak so discourteously to a lady. It is conduct ill-becoming."

He put Withers down with exaggerated care and sketched an ironic bow to Catherine. "Excuse this undignified brawl, madam. It was a pleasure to be of service to you." He smiled straight into her eyes and saw the startled awareness leap there, the interest, quickly suppressed, that told him that if he wanted a dalliance with this particular lightskirt she might be more than half-willing.

"I am in your debt, my lord," she said.

"Catherine," Withers said, and there was a clear warning in his tone.

She cast him a faintly contemptuous glance.

"My lord?" ·

"We are leaving. Before this…this *scoundrel* causes an affray—"

Ben took her hand. *Catherine.* He liked the name.

It suited her. Suddenly he wanted to take her away from Withers more than anything else in the world.

"I believe Lord Withers thinks I might spirit you away from him, madam, if he allows you to spend a moment more in my company," he said.

This time her brown eyes flashed with mischief. "Does he so? How...diverting. I assure you there is not the least chance of it, my lord."

Their gazes met and locked in challenge. Ben raised her hand to his lips and pressed a kiss on the gloved palm.

"No?"

She blushed. That was quite an accomplishment. Ben, cynic that he was, still found it was delicious to watch, even knowing it was probably a practiced reaction. She almost managed to convince him that she was an innocent rather than a whore. But the best whores were the most skillful at appearing innocent. He knew all about that. He had lived among them for long enough.

And this one knew her game. She would not sell herself short. She removed her hand very firmly from his grasp, signifying that their brief flirtation was at an end.

"No."

Even so, he saw her fingers curl over unconsciously to trap the kiss in her hand and he smiled.

"It might be worth a thought." He had no compunction about stealing a man's mistress directly from under his nose. It made the conquest sweeter and in this case it would be very sweet indeed to have this clever, tempting little harlot in his bed—and to spite Withers into the bargain.

"I understand that you have nothing to offer a lady." Her tone was cool.

"Not much." Ben conceded it easily. "I have no fortune, as no doubt you have heard. I can only offer my prowess as—"

"*Catherine!*" Withers sounded as though he was about to explode.

"As a gamester," Ben finished smoothly. "I never lose."

Catherine shook her head. "Little enough recommendation, in truth, my lord. You must hold me excused. Good day."

She turned away, evading the proprietary hand that Withers put out to draw her to him. A smile curled Ben's lips to see her defiance. Withers might be able to pay her a fortune but she was still attracted to Ben. He knew it. His body tightened unbearably at the thought.

He watched her as she went up the stairs to the pavilion, her back ramrod straight. Withers was hurrying to catch up with her, scolding, waving his arms about in agitation. Ben waited, but she did not look back. His smile turned rueful. He had a notion that she knew he was watching her and nothing on earth would make her turn around. But he would see her again. He would make sure of it. And then she would not refuse him. He would have her to thwart Withers and for his own pleasure. And he would wager on his success in the conquest. As he had told Catherine, he never lost.

## CHAPTER TWO

We must hope and believe that the liberties thus
taken were owing to no light manner nor indiscreet conduct in your case.
—*Mrs. Eliza Squire*, Good Conduct for Ladies

"WHAT THE *DEVIL* WERE YOU thinking of, Catherine, to
behave like…like Hawksmoor's doxy? No doubt he
and the entire crowd now think you are nothing more
than a whore!"

Lord Withers, like the gentleman he purported to
be, had just about managed to wait until they were
back at the house in Guilford Street, with the drawing-
room door closed behind them, before he finally up-
braided Catherine for her behavior at Newgate.

Catherine had known it would happen. Withers had
been almost bursting with the effort to keep his rage
under control in the carriage, in front of her father. She
knew he would consider himself wronged and think
her fast. And it was true that she had flirted a little.
Withers's proprietary attitude had infuriated her and
her emotions had already been ragged with the experience of being in Ben Hawksmoor's arms. She knew

she had been utterly seduced by the gentleness with which he had held her during Clarencieux's execution. It had been unexpected and frighteningly attractive. And she was so tired of being the obedient young debutante, trapped in a future defined by Withers's cruelty, living a drab life in Guilford Street, the unloved daughter, betrothed to a man who could barely hide his contempt for her.

Ben Hawksmoor had wanted her. She had felt it in his touch and seen it in his eyes. She lived a protected and cosseted life and she knew little of physical desire, but today she had felt its power herself and the feeling had been very, very tempting.

She raised her chin and met Withers's hot, angry gaze with a cool glance of her own. "You know full well, my lord, that I did not seek out Lord Hawksmoor. I only went down into the crowd to find John. If I was at fault in doing so—"

Withers cut her off. "If? Of course you were at fault! What are you? A nursemaid?"

"No," Catherine said, "but I was concerned for my brother."

"Let the servants worry about your brother," Withers said. "You are always doing stupid things to try to help others. You are supposed to be a lady, Catherine! Although I suppose one must make allowances for the fact that your family is steeped in trade—"

Catherine could feel the hot color burning her face. He had brought up the matter of her family's social inferiority so many times in the past. "I make no allowances for it. I was most attached to my grandparents."

"A merchant on the distaff side of the family," Withers said, the sneer of old money in his voice, "and your father nothing more than a nabob, too."

"If you object to my father's company," Catherine said, her voice shaking with anger at his hypocrisy, "you hide it well. I believe you should address your comments to him and not to me, sir."

"And so I shall." Withers took a sharp turn about the room. "I shall speak to him about recalcitrant daughters who behave like ill-bred little cits when they have had plenty of money thrown at their education in order to turn them into ladies."

Catherine's pride burned. It was the cruelest irony that all the luxury and ease her parents and grandparents had struggled for was hers for the taking, when all she longed for was the open horizons and the challenges of the life they had led. She had been brought up to make polite conversation in airless drawing rooms while all the time she itched for excitement and travel and new experiences. Her godmother, Lady Russell, last heard of in Samarkand, was one such intrepid traveler and her letters, received infrequently from far-flung places, gave Catherine huge pleasure and made her long even more to be released from the gilded trap. If her hopes and aspirations made her less of a lady in Lord Withers's eyes, she thought, then that was not something she could regret.

She raised her chin. "Has it occurred to you, my lord, that if Lord Hawksmoor mistook my quality it was because I was in *your* company?" She took a deep, reckless breath. "I hear your reputation is none too sweet, is it, my lord? And you had the ill manners to address me by my given name with a familiarity that suggests a certain lack of respect. You may be a nobleman, albeit one descended from the illegitimate son of a king, but it is *manners* that make a gentleman."

The silence was blistering. Withers's face had turned from bright red to ashen-pale. He took a step toward her and Catherine's heart missed a beat. That very day she had witnessed the pleasure he took in cruelty. Now he looked as though he wanted to vent all that brutality on her.

"I will not tolerate such behavior in my future wife," he said, through his teeth. "You will not reproach me for my conduct, madam, when you are wild to a fault."

Catherine's loathing for him burned in her veins. "And I will not tolerate you as a husband, sir, so we may break this betrothal that neither of us wants and be happy."

Withers took a step forward and caught her arm, pulling her around to face him so brutally that she wrenched her shoulder and could not prevent a gasp of pain. She saw his eyes shine with satisfaction to see that he had hurt her.

"You little jade," he snapped. "You have no choice. I am not letting you go. I will have you and I will break you."

"You will *not.*"

"I said *you have no choice.*"

Catherine closed her eyes. Once again the question of the hold Withers had over her father beat in her brain. When Sir Alfred had told her that he had accepted Withers's offer for her hand, she had been appalled. Plenty of men had asked Sir Alfred for permission to pay their addresses to her. They had all been rejected as unworthy. Withers had not. Her father had blustered something about him being a respected man and a colleague. Respected he was not, for the whole *Ton* spoke of him as a loose fish. As for being a colleague, it was true that he was Catherine's third trustee, appointed by Sir James Mather, her grandfather's banker, after Jack McNaish's death. Catherine had not understood the appointment then and she did not understand it now. Her grandfather, she knew, would have kicked Withers out of the house in disgust.

Even so, there was some truth in Lord Withers's words, painful as it was for her to admit it. A debutante, especially one who still smelled of the shop, had precious little choice if she was not a willing sacrifice to the marriage bed.

She swallowed hard and stared him out. "I could be a governess or a schoolteacher—"

Withers laughed harshly. "You are underage. You have no references. No one would employ you. Besides, we would find you and bring you back."

He was drawing her closer to his body. Catherine resisted and felt his grip tighten. She could feel how aroused he was. His erection pressed against her, swelling hugely. There was a look of pleasurable excitement in his eyes now. She knew her opposition made it all the more enjoyable for him and the thought revolted her.

"If you brought me back I would run away again," she said, through shut teeth. "I will go abroad. I will find Lady Russell and travel with her. You cannot force me to your will! I do not want to live the life of a society lady—"

"Your wishes have nothing to do with it. You will do as I command, on your back, in my bed, whenever I demand it."

His crudeness took her breath away. As Catherine gaped at him, he slapped her hard, across the face.

The dinner gong sounded from directly outside the drawing room and they both jumped. Tench, the Fentons' butler, threw open the door.

"Dinner is served, my lord, Miss Fenton...." Tench's face was arranged into its customary expressionless mask but his eyes flickered nervously. Catherine could have sworn he had heard their raised voices and had interrupted them on purpose, risking Withers's wrath to do it.

Withers bit out an expletive, dropped Catherine's arm and strode past the butler as though he were not there, raising his hand to sweep one of the precious porcelain vases from the hall table as he passed. It fell with a sharp crack and smashed on the floor. The street door slammed, shaking the house.

"That will be one less for dinner, Tench," Catherine said into the silence that followed.

The butler looked shaken. "Miss Fenton—" he said.

Catherine shook her head sharply, her fingers going to the tender skin of her cheek where it burned hot, but not as fiercely as her temper.

She followed Tench silently out into the marble checkered hall. A footman had already scurried off to find a broom to sweep up the broken shards of china. Withers had gone, but Catherine knew he would be back. With each rejection on her part, his determination hardened, became more brutal. She had a disturbing instinct that his revenge, once they were married, would be correspondingly cruel. She shuddered. It could not be allowed to happen. She had to find an escape.

She went into the dining room and took her place at the table. The rest of the family were already assembled. Sir Alfred Fenton was very strict about etiquette, as though it could give his family the aristocratic gloss that they lacked in their pedigree. The room was quiet, as it always was, with the silence her father demanded at dinner. She caught his gaze on her and saw him glance at the red mark on her cheek, but he said nothing and looked shiftily away, and Catherine's heart shriveled a little more. Her father had once been such a strong man. Under Withers's domination he had shrunk like a slug before the salt. There was no one left to protect them now. Catherine knew she was on her own.

They started to eat. The silence was deep. It gave Catherine ample opportunity—too *much* opportunity—to stop thinking about Withers and start thinking instead about the man who had held her in his arms earlier that day. The contrast of Ben Hawksmoor's tenderness with Algernon Withers's brutality was stark. Even now she could not think about the contact of his cheek against hers, the touch of skin against skin, without a hot shiver scalding her blood.

She had heard that Ben Hawksmoor was dangerous. Such information was drummed into debutantes until the more reckless of them longed to elope with the very rakes they were warned against.

*Never be alone with a man.*

*Never touch a man who is not related to you.*

*And,* Catherine thought, *never permit the most notorious scoundrel in the whole of London to hold you in his arms in case you find it impossible to forget his touch and concentrate on your dinner.*

Men like Ben Hawksmoor were far outside Catherine's experience. They inhabited a world so alien from the stilted respectability of her upbringing as to make them seem like a different race. A chaperone could detect a scoundrel at fifty paces and would hustle their charges away before any damage was done or a reputation was imperiled. Catherine knew that in one fateful step that afternoon she had almost undone all those years of vigilance. She had clung to Ben Hawksmoor, had forgotten all the modesty and propriety she had ever known, and she had not cared. He had held her in his arms and for a while it had felt like the most precious thing that had ever happened to her.

Catherine pushed her spoon listlessly around the plate. The only sound was John slurping his pea soup from the best silver. Because they had no guests that evening he had been allowed to join the family for dinner rather than take supper in the nursery. Earlier in the meal he had been full of the excitement of the afternoon.

"A tall man held me up so that I could see better! The noose was so tight and the body was jerking and dancing all over the place like one of Mr. Carew's wooden puppets—"

Maggie, Catherine's stepmother, had made a faint noise of protest and swayed a little on her chair, and Sir Alfred had said, "John…" with a note of warning in his voice. But Catherine had thought that he also sounded rather pleased with his son. She could imagine him boasting to Lord Withers that John was a chip off the old block—no lily-livered die away vapors from him! And now John had a hearty appetite and he seemed to be the only one around the table who had.

Catherine pushed her plate away and the footman came forward immediately to remove it. At times like this she felt as though they were all dining off her expectations. Her future paid for the food they ate, the clothes they wore and all the trappings of wealth that her father liked to display in such opulent show. All he had left of his own fortune was bad debts hiding behind a good name. Naturally the *Ton* did not know that the Fenton fortune was spent and that all that was left was Catherine's trust money. But Lord Withers was a trustee and he would know….

That, Catherine thought suddenly, had to be the true reason for Sir Alfred's tolerance of Withers's suit. They must have come to some accommodation about the money. Her fortune would belong to Withers when they wed, the law taking the somewhat illiberal view that both she and her possessions belonged to her husband. Perhaps Withers had promised Sir Alfred a cut of the money for his agreement to the marriage. The cynicism of such an arrangement made her feel ill. She knew her father had little affection for her but such coldhearted bartering was difficult to stomach.

The silence was beginning to feel oppressive now. There were so many matters unspoken in the Fenton family, from her father's money troubles to Algernon Withers's mysterious power over them, to Lady Fenton's poor health.

Catherine cleared her throat and, ignoring her father's forbidding glare, addressed her stepmother.

"Did you pass a pleasant afternoon, Maggie?" she asked Lady Fenton.

When her father had first married Maggie, he had wanted Catherine to call his new wife *mama* but she had refused. Her mother had died when Catherine was twelve and Maggie Fenton was only six years Catherine's senior, now twenty-seven to her twenty-one. It had seemed ridiculous to call her *mother.* Fortunately Maggie had agreed. Instead they had become friends, very dear friends, and Catherine had loved her new stepmother with an uncomplicated affection.

That was in the days when Maggie could charm Sir Alfred about her finger, the days when she had been an elegant society hostess, not the pale and nervous wreck of a woman she appeared now as she shredded the fringe of her silk-and-lace wrap beneath the table. As she had grown up, Catherine had realized that her stepmother was not strong and their roles had gradually shifted until Catherine had become the protective one, almost as though she were the elder. She still loved Maggie fiercely, and the half brother and little half sister that Maggie had given her, but now she pitied her as well as loved her.

Catherine waited, but Maggie did not reply. Her blue eyes were quite blank. It was as though she had not heard a word. On the mantelpiece, the clock ticked loudly. The room was light and airy, painted in a pale green and white that reflected the sunshine in the summer. The spurious portraits on the walls, which Sir Alfred had bought in pretense that they were his distant ancestors, looked as blank as his wife.

After a moment, Sir Alfred sighed heavily. "Margaret," he said, "are you not attending? Catherine was asking after your day."

Catherine reflected that her father always used a person's full name. She had a vague memory of her mother calling her Kate when she was a child. That time was long gone, along with the warmth and love and laughter that had once filled the house in Guilford Street. These days it was exquisitely decorated—Lady Fenton's taste—but empty and cold. Sir Alfred was seldom there. Catherine suspected he rented another set of rooms elsewhere, where he spent most of his nights. They all knew he had had a series of women in keeping almost from the start of his marriage to Maggie, and probably before. Catherine knew that such things happened in society but it hurt her, for Maggie's sake. Her stepmother had never appeared strong enough to bear such blows and, since the birth of her daughter Mirabelle a year before, she had withdrawn even more into herself and sometimes seemed barely present at all.

"I went to Bond Street," Maggie said, without raising her eyes from her plate, "and then for a drive in the park with Lady Raine."

Silence descended once again. John started to climb on his chair to reach across the table for a piece of bread. His mother said nothing. The footman leaped forward to offer the basket. Cold meats were brought in. Catherine's mind started to wander.

*No man had ever held her close in tenderness before.*

The color burned Catherine's face as she thought of Ben Hawksmoor again. He had held her as though he meant it. There had been an astonishing moment when she had looked into his hazel eyes and seen the pain and the anger in him, and had thought that she understood the demons that drove him. She had felt so close to him. But as soon as he'd let her go, she had been overwhelmed by the strangeness and intimacy of their encounter. And then he had stepped back and smiled that charming smile and something had changed between them and he was as careless and dangerous as the matrons said he was.

"Catherine met Lord Hawksmoor today." Sir Alfred's voice cut straight across her thoughts.

Catherine jumped and her hand knocked the salt dish, scattering the white grains across the polished wood of the table. The footman leaped forward again but was waved back irritably by Sir Alfred. Catherine saw that he was staring at his wife from under lowered brows. His eyes were fierce with something Catherine did not understand.

He repeated, "Catherine met Lord Hawksmoor today. He rescued her from the mob at the hanging when she was foolish enough to go looking for John."

"She need not have bothered," John said, petulantly kicking his heels against the chair legs. "I was not lost!"

No one paid him any attention. Sir Alfred was still staring at his wife and Maggie's face had gone as white as tissue paper.

"We exchanged a few words only," Catherine said hastily. She was aware of a desperate need to deflect attention away from Maggie, whose fingers, shredding the silk shawl, had speeded up their work. Catherine could hear little ripping sounds as the material came apart.

"Indeed," Maggie said. "Lord Hawksmoor is not a suitable acquaintance for a young lady."

"Nor for a married one," Sir Alfred growled. "Just as Edward Clarencieux was unsuitable."

Maggie caught her breath on a painful gasp and suddenly Catherine had a vivid memory of the day that she and Maggie had been walking in the park back in the summer, when Ned Clarencieux had been so charming and Maggie so vivacious. As the gentlemen had strolled away, with many a provocative backward glance, Maggie had laughed and caught Catherine's arm and told her that she should cut men like Clarencieux dead.

"For they are too rakish for you to trifle with, Catherine, until you understand what you are doing. It is the greatest hypocrisy but once you are married you may do as you please."

There had been something bitter in Maggie's face as she had added, "There must, after all, be some consolations for the tedium of married life...."

At that moment Ned Clarencieux had turned and raised a hand in farewell, and Catherine had seen Maggie's face brighten and a smile light her eyes, although she had turned her head away flirtatiously so that Clarencieux would not see it.

Catherine remembered with a cold stab of the heart that Clarencieux had been Ben Hawksmoor's friend, an adventurer, cut from the same cloth.

"Hawksmoor," Sir Alfred was saying viciously, "should not be accepted in polite society. He should never have inherited the title. He is worthless—a gambler and a wastrel."

"Very much like many gentlemen of my acquaintance," Catherine said, stung into responding.

Her father turned his glare on her.

"You know nothing of it, girl."

Catherine bit her lip. She knew plenty. She knew men like Ben Hawksmoor lived on a knife's edge because for all their popularity they could fall from favor at any moment. She knew Clarencieux had died because he had no money and no connections to save him. Society was harsh. It had rules you broke at your peril. Catherine's best friend and fellow debutante, Lily St. Clare, had been married off at seventeen. Four years later she had run away from her husband to be with her lover, but he had spurned her. Lily had ended up living in a brothel, and Catherine was expected never to see or speak to her again, and forget the friendship that had bound them since they were at school, as though Lily had become someone completely different, a bad person whom no one would acknowledge. Society spoke of Lily very much as they did of her.

*Bad blood always tells in the end, you know....*

The injustice of it all made Catherine furious.

She knew that a debutante's role was to marry to advantage and she knew her never-loving father was going to sell her off to Lord Withers like a side of beef.

She also knew that Molly, one of the housemaids, slept with a silhouette of Ben Hawksmoor beneath her pillow. The maid had been laying the fire in Catherine's chamber one day and some cuttings from the scandal sheets had fallen from the box in which she kept the coal and wood shavings for the fire. Catherine had picked them up and handed them back to Molly, but not before she had seen that each of them referred to the outrageous activities of Lord Hawksmoor and his inamorata, Lady Paris de Moine. Molly had blushed and thanked her, and admitted that she thought Ben Hawksmoor a hero because he was so handsome and so dashing, and he had once served in the army and they told tales of his courage and daring. Molly had sat back on her heels before the blackened grate and said that she wanted to be Lady Paris de Moine if only for one night. To have all the excitement and the attention and Ben Hawksmoor for a lover... She had sighed before going back to rubbing her hands red raw with polish.

Later, when Catherine had been out in Burlington

Arcade and seen silhouettes of society figures for sale for a few pennies, she had not been able to resist buying one of Ben Hawksmoor for Molly, who had later confessed that she took it to bed with her every night.

Ben Hawksmoor, the hero. Catherine shivered. The fantasy spun around him was very seductive. How impossible to be so drawn to a man who was everything that a debutante should deplore. How impossible to forget the sweet pleasure of his hands against her back and his heart beating beneath her cheek and his mouth pressed against her hair... How easy to see now just what the chaperones were squawking about when they warned of decadence and pleasure beyond imagining. Catherine discovered that *her* imagination was now remarkably vivid as she tried to picture what it might have been like to let Ben Hawksmoor take his pleasure with her.

Catherine trembled a little as her wayward thoughts took flight, and this time she managed to knock over her wineglass. The ruby liquid spread across the table toward Maggie Fenton, who stared at it as though transfixed.

This time none of the footmen moved.

"Someone bring a cloth!" Sir Alfred ordered, but then Maggie stumbled to her feet, her hand pressed to her mouth. Behind her the dining chair clattered to the ground. With a stifled sob, she turned and ran from the room. John, sensing at last the malevolence in the air, started to wail. Sir Alfred swore. Catherine leaned forward and mopped at the spilled wine with her linen napkin.

"Leave it!" Sir Alfred shouted. John's screams redoubled in volume and he scrambled down from his chair and shot out of the room. Catherine stood up.

"Sit down!" her father barked. "We will finish our meal."

Catherine paused. Maggie had shown her much kindness in the past and now the paper-thin structure of Catherine's family life was under terrible strain. She could not simply watch her stepmother suffering and leave her to do it alone.

"I am sorry, Papa," she said. "Please excuse me. I must go and see how Maggie does."

Sir Alfred waved his fork. A piece of beef wilted on the prongs. "Her maid will attend to her. Sit down, girl." He went back to his food, certain of her compliance.

From upstairs came the sound of John's wailing and above it the descant of the baby crying. The whole house seemed to vibrate to the noise. Catherine hesitated a moment longer, then hurried to the door, ignoring her father's incensed bellows that she return to the table at once.

She found her stepmother lying facedown on her huge tester bed. The room smelled of lavender perfume and was an opulent riot of frills and flounces in pink and green, just as Maggie had been, the opulent trophy debutante, when she had married Sir Alfred. Now she was pale and so thin that her body barely made an impression on the covers.

Catherine placed one tentative hand on her shoulder. "Maggie—"

Maggie jumped as though Catherine had branded her. She rolled over. She had not been crying but her expression was so desolate that Catherine felt chilled. She sat down next to her stepmother on the bed and felt the springs give under her own rather more considerable weight.

"Maggie," she said again, "what on earth is going on?"

Maggie clutched Catherine's hands. Her own were so frozen that Catherine gave a little exclamation.

"I am in a lot of trouble, Catherine," she said.

Catherine raised her brows. The sort of trouble that normally afflicted Maggie involved bills from the milliner and the couturier. Sir Alfred would bluster but he did not really mind. Catherine knew it was more important to him for his wife and his daughter to be creditably turned out than whether they spent beyond their allowance.

"I have a little money left this quarter—" she began, but Maggie shook her head. She pushed herself upright and slid from the bed, crossing the thick carpet to throw open the door of the cupboard opposite and to rummage inside. Catherine waited. Eventually Maggie emerged, pushed the straggles of auburn hair away from her face and came back to kneel at Catherine's feet. Her left hand was clasped tightly about something.

"I stole it," she said. "There was a party and I saw it on the shelf and I thought to have it for myself. A little piece of him…"

Catherine frowned. "A piece of whom? Maggie, you are frightening me—"

Maggie took Catherine's wrist and placed the package in her outstretched hand. It was wrapped in a red velvet cloth. Maggie sat back on her heels while Catherine unfolded the material.

She was holding a miniature of Edward Clarencieux. It was in a silver frame, studded with diamonds. Catherine looked from the handsome, painted face to her stepmother's ravaged one that was now dissolving into silent tears.

"Where did you get this?" she asked.

Maggie's tears fell faster. "I told you. There was a masked ball at Lord Hawksmoor's rooms. I went there—with Ned."

Catherine's heart skipped a beat. *"Lord Hawksmoor?"*

Maggie ignored the interruption. "Such pretty things were exhibited there. Ned's picture—"

There was a heavy step outside the door, Sir Alfred's voice raised in irritable inquiry.

Maggie gave a gasp. She closed her fingers about Catherine's hand, locking the miniature into her grip.

"I loved him," she whispered. "I loved Ned Clarencieux." A tear slid down her nose and dropped, desolately, onto the green silk bedcovers. Maggie looked up and the expression in her eyes made Catherine's heart turn over with pity.

"You have to take it back for me," she whispered. "Your father must never know, for all our sakes. You have to take it back to Ben Hawksmoor but he cannot know where you got it. You must keep my secret, Catherine."

"YOU LET HER GO?" Sam Hawksmoor said blankly. "You met the most beautiful girl in England and you let her go?"

"She wasn't beautiful," Ben said. "She was pretty." He stopped. He was beginning to wish he had not mentioned the encounter with Catherine to his cousin at all. He was hardly the type to confide and unless he spilled his soul in a way he had never done before, he could not begin to explain why he had been so drawn to the girl he had met at Clarencieux's hanging. He could still remember the way that she had trembled in his arms. He could still *feel* it. He was accustomed to passion, to desire, but what he had felt for Catherine in that moment had been an entirely different experience and one that had shaken him to the core.

Ben shook his head slightly to dispel the memories. It would be best to let Sam think this was just a casual lust. Best to persuade *himself* that it was. That moment of affinity between himself and Catherine had been born of nothing more than the anger and guilt he felt over Clarencieux's death. It had meant nothing.

He threw himself down into one of the battered wing chairs in the inn parlor. The whores had been sent packing, Sam's other ramshackle friends had gone to find more congenial company in the clubs, which left Ben and his cousin alone, a fact for which he was profoundly grateful. He did not feel like carousing on this of all nights.

"Pretty, beautiful…" Sam shrugged. "You still let

her go. You could have offered her carte blanche, snapped her up from under Withers's nose!"

Ben loosened his neck cloth. "I did try. She turned me down."

Sam's mouth hung open. "You must be losing your touch. Or you weren't trying hard enough."

Ben laughed. "Sometimes, Sam," he said, draining his glass of brandy, "I think you believe all the things they write about my reputation. This has nothing to do with love and everything to do with—"

"Money," Sam said succinctly.

"Precisely." Ben swung the empty brandy glass gently from his fingers. "Withers has plenty of it. I have none. A courtesan has to calculate such things."

Sam screwed his face up with disapproval. "It sounds very mercenary."

"Life is. Had you not noticed?"

Sam shook his head like a horse troubled by a persistent fly. "I do not have so cynical a view as you do, Ben. Sometimes I think I'd just like to settle down with a nice young lady."

Ben sighed. "I hate to prove my cynicism," he drawled, "but no nice young lady would have you, Sam. You have no fortune."

"I know," Sam said. "But I would like to meet someone to whom that did not matter. Someone I could love."

Ben's lips twisted into a parody of a smile. "Get a dog. They are cheaper than a wife and generally more affectionate."

Sam's good-natured face was disapproving now. "It

has always puzzled me why you do not marry for money since you are so concerned about it," he said. "I know no one would marry me, but they would have *you*."

It was true. While Ben knew that none of the *Ton* chaperones would countenance him as a husband for one of their charges, there were other women—widows, rich merchants' daughters—who would have been only too happy to present him with their fortunes in return for marriage. Notoriety was an advantage and gave him plenty of offers.

"I have thought about it," he admitted, "but I have never met even one woman who does not want something in return, Sam." Cynicism deepened the lines about his mouth. "They would all demand a piece of me in return for their money and that…" He shook his head. "That I cannot grant. I am too selfish a soul."

"You do not like women," Sam said. "I have often observed it."

The brandy glass stilled between Ben's fingers. "You mistake," he said, putting it down carefully. "I do like women. I admire some of them very much. I simply do not *love* them."

"You must love someone," Sam argued.

"I do." Ben reached for the brandy bottle. "Me."

Sam ran his hand through his disheveled fair hair. "No, I mean someone else. Someone you want to care for and protect?"

Ben grinned. "Definitely me."

Sam's lips twitched but he did not allow himself to be distracted.

"There *must* be someone who matters to you." He brightened. "I know—what about Lady Paris?"

Ben laughed. Paris de Moine, his reputed mistress, was a courtesan with the face of an angel and a heart of flint. Falling in love, Ben thought, was almost the worst, most foolish and self-destructive thing that he could ever do and he had never been close to loving Paris.

"Paris does not need my protection," he said. "She can look after herself better than anyone I know."

"Well, at the very least, you must have loved your mother."

Sam was blundering on like a dray horse out of harness and Ben suddenly felt cold. His expression hardened. He never, ever talked about his mother.

"Let us not speak of that," he said.

"But—"

"Sam, I said *no*." He saw his cousin's look of confusion and rubbed an impatient hand across his brow, trying to find the tolerance and the words. "You cannot make me be like you, Sam," he said, a little roughly, "so pray do not try. I know it grieves you that I am mercenary and cynical and shallow but that is simply the way I am."

Sam's face was flushed. "You went down into the crowd to save that girl," he said stubbornly, "so do not pretend you did not care."

There was a silence. Ben knew that what his cousin had said was true. In that moment, he had cared desperately what happened to the pretty girl in her yellow dress. It was inexplicable. It was unwelcome.

And now—happily—it was an aberration that was in the past.

Ben had no time for love, or innocence, or any other quality commonly accounted a virtue. They were not commodities that he valued. He had no use for them. Love led others to take advantage; it saw you fleeced, cheated, discarded…. Once, when he had been a boy, Ben had believed in the goodness of others. But that had been a long time ago. The same boyhood had later seen him stealing clothes from washing lines so that his mother could sell them in the streets to earn enough for them to eat. It had seen him pick pockets, beg and lie to survive. His father had disowned both him and his mother years before, claiming the marriage illegal, calling him a bastard, condemning them both to a life of poverty and degradation. By the time Ben's Hawksmoor uncles had come looking for him to send him to school, Ben's soul was old.

"Acquit me of any chivalrous motives," he said lightly. "I saw her and thought her pretty. And when I knew she was Withers's mistress, I had a fancy to take her away from him. You know I detest the man."

"I see," Sam said. "Worthy motives, all."

Ben laughed. "Worthy of me, certainly."

The thought of seducing Catherine away from Algernon Withers appealed greatly to him. Normally he never wasted his energies dangling after a woman he could not have. Life was too short—and too expensive—to waste time. But Catherine… There he could make an exception. It would be worth it, even for just one night of bliss.

Sam was looking pensive. "Don't think much of her taste if she's with Withers," he said. "The man's a loose fish. No one in the *Ton* gives him countenance. He's…" Sam shuddered. "Deeply unsavory."

"True," Ben said, "but a harlot must make her bed where it benefits her the most." His gaze dwelt thoughtfully on the two empty brandy bottles at Sam's elbow. "And you are scarce as pure as a dewdrop to criticize others, are you, Samuel?"

Sam's good-natured face blushed red. "Unlike Algy Withers, I am not insensible with laudanum every night by nine of the clock."

"No," Ben agreed. "Only with drink."

"Helps pass the time," Sam mumbled. He rallied slightly. "If it comes to that, *I* am not the black sheep of our family, cuz."

Ben laughed. He could never argue with Sam. His cousin was far too easygoing. And he did not really want to lose Sam's regard, anyway. He was the only member of the Hawksmoor family with whom Ben was on speaking terms. In one of his weaker moments Ben might even admit to a slight affection for his cousin. And on a more practical note, to lose him would reduce his family connections from one to none.

"Perhaps, then, I should visit Withers's mistress after nine," he said. "She will have time to spare once her lover is unconscious with laudanum."

"What is her name?" Sam asked.

Ben frowned. "Catherine."

"Catherine what?"

"I do not know. We did not get that far."

His cousin grinned. "Well, I don't suppose it is necessary to get even that far with a whore—" He took a look at Ben's face and added with spurious innocence, "Why do I have the impression that you wish to hit me, Benjamin?"

Ben drove his hands into his pockets. He felt shaken. He could not deny that he had felt a powerful rush of fury to hear Sam refer to Catherine so disparagingly. And yet why should it concern him? He knew she was a courtesan. He had said as much himself. He simply did not like the thought of people calling her a whore.

He moved his shoulders uncomfortably beneath the fine linen of his shirt. He was not himself tonight. Evidently Clarencieux's death had unmanned him. He was turning soft, sentimental. Soon he would be penning sonnets.

"No wonder you weren't interested in Flora and Jane if you were lusting after Withers's mistress," Sam was saying. "You hurt their feelings. And you bored them. That's unforgivable in a gentleman. They were expecting you to be so much more exciting."

Ben had almost forgotten the harlots that Sam had procured earlier in the day. Now the thought of them raised no more than a flicker of irritation in him. His cousin should have known that he would not be interested. He had never been interested in cheap strumpets.

"I am no gentleman," he said, "so they will have to acquit me."

Sam grinned. "True, you are not. But you need not worry. They will not wish to admit that they failed to interest you, so they will tell everyone that you are a marvelous lover anyway."

Ben pulled a face. "I know," he said. The demireps had far more to lose than he had. They would want to boast of an afternoon in his bed rather than confess to the embarrassing truth that he was more interested in the contents of the brandy bottle than in their amatory skills.

He got up and strolled across to the window, leaning on the sill as he had done earlier when he had seen Catherine. Now the square in front of the inn was empty. The scaffold was shrouded in darkness, Clarencieux's body in its rough pine coffin taken away for medical dissection. The thought still made Ben feel ill.

"Clarencieux was my *friend,* Sam," he said over his shoulder. "Those women thought his death was just another sport. They were here to gloat."

Sam's good-humored face fell. "It was disrespectful of me to bring them, I suppose," he muttered. "I didn't think."

Ben gave him a pitying look. "You might have spared yourself their fee," he agreed. His cousin's finances were almost as parlous as his own. Sam belonged to the wealthy side of the Hawksmoor family, but his elder brother, Gideon, kept him on a short rein with an allowance that was barely sufficient to feed him, let alone pay for the pleasures of the town. Ben had the family title, Gideon the family money. Ben wanted money and Gideon would probably have given his left testicle to have Ben's title. They detested one another. Ben could recognize that the irony was the richest thing in the situation.

"I suppose they were Haymarket ware," Sam said, "compared to Lady Paris. No wonder you thought them tawdry. The only thing that astounds me is that you could ever look at another woman with the memory of Paris before your eyes."

Ben laughed. "I have told you a hundred times, Sam, that Paris and I share nothing more than business interests. We do not share a bed."

"Of course not," Sam said, without rancor and without the slightest sign of believing him. "Everyone in town knows you are her lover and you are the only one denying it."

Ben's smile grew. Sam was the only person to whom he had told the truth of his relationship with Lady Paris de Moine, and the only reason he had told Sam was that it amused him to do so knowing that his cousin would never believe him. Every printed scandal sheet in the land reported that he and Paris were lovers. Every gossipmonger in the *Ton* passed on the latest *on dit* that linked their names. Ben had no quarrel with that. Together, he and Paris were more famous, more sought after and more likely to make money than they were separately. It enhanced his reputation to have the most outrageously beautiful courtesan in London on his arm. In return, Paris basked in the glamour that his dangerous reputation shed on her. It was the most perfect charade, as empty as a spun-sugar confection from Gunters.

"Paris and I are not lovers," he said.

Sam's eyes widened. "I see," he said, in a tone that clearly demonstrated he did not. "So when did you last have a woman, Ben?"

"Mind your own damned business," Ben said affably. The truth was that he could not remember. There had been a pretty widow in Spain eighteen months back, when he had been looking to blot out all the twisted horror of the war. And more recently there had been the bored wife of a foreign ambassador whom he had met at one of the regent's soirees. Neither affaire had lasted very long. He was no good for any woman. Before he even met them, he was thinking of how to leave them.

He paused, more than half-surprised to realize that it had been so long. He was no monk, but he was no rake either, despite his reputation. He had lived so long in a world that used sex as just another currency that he had grown bored with it, fastidious even. His lips twisted. That probably made him a hypocrite. Well, he had been called worse.

The sound of voices raised in convivial song floated up from the taproom below. Ben sighed again.

"I am leaving, Sam," he said. "Forgive me, I am not good company tonight."

He looked out into the night. The inn sign creaked in the rising breeze. A crowd of drunken revelers spilled from the inn door out onto the cobbles of the square. A torch flared, throwing the shadow of the scaffold into harsh relief.

Ben turned back to the lit room. He felt blue-deviled and angry with himself for the weakness. Ned

Clarencieux was dead and gone, a fool who had lived by his wits and died when those wits had not proved sharp enough. Ben had no doubt that his friend had been wrongly convicted, but because Clarencieux had had no money, power or status he had not been able to save himself. It was a salutary lesson.

Ben clenched his fists tightly. He was not like Clarencieux. True, he was an adventurer, but he was more ruthless than his friend had been and he had more advantages. He had his title, empty as it was, and the patronage of the Prince Regent—and plenty of enemies who would have been happy to see him swing on the end of that rope.

And as though in an echo of his thoughts, Sam put out a hand. "Ben—" his voice was more hesitant than his cousin had ever heard it "—you will not pursue this matter of Clarencieux's death, will you?"

"Why do you ask?" Ben said.

Sam's face was troubled. "Because when you were in your cups last night, I heard you say that you thought Ned was innocent and that he had been framed."

Ben made an uncontrollable movement. He had not thought he had been so indiscreet even when maudlin drunk on the night before the execution.

"It's all right," Sam said hastily. "No one else heard." He paused. "So was he?"

"You are too persistent," Ben said.

"I know." Sam grinned. "So?"

"I am sure he was," Ben said. He had spent much of the evening thinking about it. "Clarencieux swore he was innocent, and he had not the wit to forge money nor the stomach to shoot his banker."

Sam shook his head. "But why would anyone take the trouble to frame Ned? He was not important enough for anyone to wish to remove him."

"Someone must have had a grudge against him," Ben said slowly. Like him, Clarencieux had been a gamester who had taken money from other desperate men. And Ben suspected that Ned had been engaged in a clandestine love affair. Cuckolded husbands could be extremely vindictive. And then there had been Withers's threats…

Sam was gnawing his lower lip. "But you will not pursue it?"

Ben propped his elbow on the table. "You may be easy. I have no intention of looking for trouble."

Sam looked infinitely relieved. "Thank God! What good would it do, anyway? Ned is hanged and you've never been one to stick your neck out for others."

The words dropped awkwardly into the silence of the room. Then Ben laughed.

"Quite right, Sam," he said. "I care nothing for others, as we have previously discussed."

He stared into the fire. Ned Clarencieux had served alongside him in the Peninsula. They had both been outcasts in their own way, Ben the product of the scandalous match between a lord and a housemaid, Ned the disinherited son of a clergyman. It had been a bond between them. They had been closer than brothers. Ben had saved his comrade's life once when Ned and some of the others had got so drunk on the retreat to Corunna that the commanding officer had ordered they be left behind. Ben had dragged him out and literally carried him until Ned had sobered up. This time Ned had not been so lucky, and Ben had not been able to save him. He knew he should let it go now, but old loyalties were dying harder than he had imagined.

"There is one matter in which I must act, however," he said slowly. "Withers threatened me today. I need to find out why."

Sam was staring like an owl, unblinking. "Withers again? What did he say?"

Ben frowned as he tried to remember. "Merely that justice had been done with Ned's death and I would be next."

Sam raised his brows. "Meaning?"

"I am not sure."

Sam shrugged. "It probably means nothing. Withers is mad and it is true that he has been no friend to either you or Ned, but surely he is not dangerous."

"You mistake," Ben said quietly. "There are men who are nothing but talk and then there are the ones who would knife you in the back in a dark alleyway, and Withers is one of those."

Sam moved away to pour another tankard of ale for himself from the pitcher. "Then let the matter drop, Ben, and keep away from him."

Ben shook his head. "Not until I know if his threats are hollow or not."

Sam paused. "I do not like it," he said obstinately.

"You do not have to."

"At the very least, do not provoke him by stealing his mistress."

Ben laughed. "It might be the very way to smoke him out."

Once again the desire stirred in him, more complex than mere lust. He wanted Catherine. He had held her yielding body against his and now he wanted her with a hunger. He would have to be careful. He would seduce the little jade but that would be all. Anything else would be madness.

He picked up his jacket and slung it over his shoulder.

"I am sorry that I am such poor company tonight, Sam," he said. "Forgive me. I will see you on the morrow."

Sam's face lightened. "Brooks?"

"Brooks," Ben confirmed, with a grin.

He went down the stairs, past the rowdy taproom with its smell of beer and fug of tobacco, and out into the cobbled square. He shrugged his jacket on and turned west. It was a long walk to St. James's but he needed to clear his head.

His thoughts, as it turned out, were relatively easy to clarify. Despite what he had said to Sam, he would look into the matter of Ned Clarencieux's death. His own survival could depend on it. And he would pursue Catherine. He would take her away from Withers and he would take the greatest pleasure in doing so. Now all he had to do was find her.

# CHAPTER THREE

It is not considered seemly for any young girl to
be out alone, not even coming from church.
—*Mrs. Eliza Squire,* Good Conduct for Ladies

"CATHERINE! IT IS SO LOVELY to see you, even though
I know I should not have arranged to meet you here."
Miss Lily St. Clare, her face wrinkled with concern,
drew her friend into the shelter of a shop doorway and
away from the hordes of people milling on the Oxford
Street pavement. It was another cold morning and,
although the sun was rising, it had not yet started to
melt the frost from the London rooftops. The pavement was slippery underfoot. The scent of a thousand
coal fires lingered on the still air.

Catherine submitted to her friend's chiding with a
broad smile, hugging her close. "I wanted to see you
again. It has been an age! Do not worry—no one will
notice us in this crush. How are you, Lily?"

Lily stood back and thrust her hands deeply into her
fur-lined muff. Catherine thought that she looked
pinched and pale, but it was not simply from the cold.
It was as though the months of her social exile had

sapped something from her. Her spirit had died. There was no animation in her piquant face. She was as beautifully dressed as ever, her dark hair peeping prettily from beneath her bonnet, but her outward elegance was a stark contrast to the misery Catherine could sense within her.

"You do not look very happy," Catherine ventured. She felt foolish as soon as the words were out. How could Lily be happy working in a Covent Garden brothel? They were of an age, but now the gulf between them felt immense. Catherine could not even begin to imagine what her friend's life was like, but she knew that gently-bred Lily St. Clare should never have come to this.

They had been the closest of friends from school through to their first London season. Lily had made a conventional marriage to a rich and titled man. Catherine's father had betrothed her to Lord Withers. But suddenly the whole fabric of their parallel lives had started to unravel with Lily's unhappy marriage and her love affair, and the situation had ended with her friend in disgrace, a fallen woman, and Catherine forbidden ever to see her again.

"I am well enough," Lily said, her painted mouth stretching into a smile that did not reach her eyes. "I am only concerned for you, Catherine. You know it is dangerous for you to meet me. Were anyone to see you, or your father hear that you had gone out alone…"

Her voice trailed away as Catherine squeezed her hand. "It is more important to me that we may still see one another," she said firmly. "Besides, no one will notice me in this crush." The crowd on the pavement was growing thicker by the second and now someone trod heavily on Catherine's foot, forcing her to take a farther step back.

"Your chaperone is very lax," Lily said, smiling a real smile now. "You are shockingly bad, you know."

"I know," Catherine said, "but Maggie is sick again—the laudanum, you know—and no one pays any attention to what I do, so I am free to come and go as I please."

Lily was shaking her head, though whether over Maggie's condition or Catherine's own behavior, she could not be sure. The crowd was spilling from the pavement into the road now and Catherine reflected that when she had suggested Oxford Street for her meeting with her old friend she had not anticipated the scrum that would ensue.

"It is monstrously busy today," she said, frowning. "Perhaps we should go to Blake's coffeehouse instead. I have not seen a crowd like this since Papa brought me to see Lord Nelson when I was a child! What on earth is going on?"

"There is to be a curricle race," Lily said. "I confess that I was eager to see it. Lord Hawksmoor has challenged Mr. Lancing to race him along Oxford Street, up Newman Street, along to Cavendish Square and back." She looked closely at Catherine's face. "Are you quite well, Catherine? You have gone very pale. Is the crowd too pressing?"

"I am cold, that is all," Catherine said, through

the sudden chattering of her teeth. She did not wish to admit to Lily that the mere mention of Ben Hawksmoor's name had her shivering as though she suffered an ague. "It sounds like madness," she added. "What on earth would possess them to do such a thing?"

"A love of a wager," Lily said dryly, "and on Lord Hawksmoor's part a reckless disregard for his own life and safety—oh, and a desire to profit by it."

"Profit? How?"

Lily touched her arm. "You see those gentlemen of the press over there? Hawksmoor will already have sold them the story and regardless of the outcome of the race it will appear, suitably embroidered, in tomorrow's scandal sheets."

"I see," Catherine said slowly.

"And he will be taking a cut of the profit from the bets, of course."

Catherine huddled deeper within her thick winter pelisse. "You sound as though you dislike him," she said.

Lily's blue eyes lit with a spark of amusement. "Not at all. I admire his skill." Her tone hardened. "Those of us who have to work to survive do what we must."

Catherine hated to hear the disillusion in her friend's voice. It was as though Lily had gone somewhere that Catherine could not understand; somewhere she could not reach her. It was the same world that Ben Hawksmoor inhabited, as alien to Catherine as a foreign land, where lives were bartered, bought and sold for survival. She hated the thought of it.

Nevertheless she *wanted* to understand. She wanted to help Lily if she could. There was nothing that she could do directly but she had had an idea that might serve.

She put out a hand. "Lily, I was wondering…" She broke off, biting her lip. "I know your current life is hateful to you," she said in a rushed undertone, "and I was wondering whether when my godmother, Lady Russell, returns from her travels, we might arrange something different. You could be her companion, perhaps—"

She stopped as Lily gripped her hands hard. It seemed to Catherine that there were tears in her friend's blue eyes, but it could just have been the keen winter breeze that was making them water.

"Oh, Catherine—" Lily sounded choked "—I love you because you care so much about other people, but you are forever coming up with ridiculous plans! No respectable lady would wish me to be their companion now, with my reputation."

"But Lady Russell isn't respectable," Catherine argued. "That is, she *is,* of course, but what I mean is that she cares nothing for society's opinion. She likes you, Lily! I am sure she would wish to help us."

Lily's mouth twisted. "You are all goodness, Catherine, but I cannot see that it would serve."

"Think about it," Catherine urged. "I do not know when she will be back in London, but when she comes I will send to you." She looked about her. "Now let us forsake this event and retire to Blake's for a proper chat. I am freezing to the spot."

"It is too late," Lily said, shaking her head. "We cannot get through this press of people. We shall have to wait until the race has begun."

For Catherine, it was beginning to seem uncannily like the scene at Newgate. There was the same febrile excitement in the air, the same sense of anticipation and edge of danger. It breathed gooseflesh along the back of her neck and made her tremble down to her toes. Then a hiss went through the crowd like gunpowder catching alight, and Catherine looked up to see a lightly-built scarlet racing curricle drawn by a magnificent matched team of chestnuts pressing its way through the crowded street. Suddenly the whole day seemed more vivid and alive. The seething throng of people pressed forward, pushing and calling. The bookmakers upped the bidding. The newspaper hacks scribbled busily.

"Briggs of Lanchester Square have loaned the curricle to Lord Hawksmoor for the race," Lily whispered. "Is it not fine?"

Catherine could not answer. Her gaze was fixed on the figure of Ben Hawksmoor as he handled the reins with a dexterity that she could see was much envied by the gentlemen in the crowd. He was laughing, his teeth white in his bronzed face as he reached down to shake the hands of the multitude. His hazel eyes were alight with an expression that made Catherine's breath catch in her throat, a mixture of pure uncomplicated excitement and a chilling recklessness.

"Jack Lancing is one of Hawksmoor's set," Lily continued, pointing to the lime-green curricle that was trailing Ben Hawksmoor's down the street. She laughed. "He is another penniless adventurer. Goodness only knows how he scraped together the wherewithal to finance his team."

Jack Lancing was whip-thin and dark, and clearly a favorite with the ladies. Catherine recognized him as one of the men she had seen romping with the half-naked bawds at Clarencieux's hanging.

"They are both penniless?" she questioned. Neither man seemed remotely poverty-stricken. Their carriages, the teams of horses and their own attire were all stylish in the extreme.

"Without a feather to fly," Lily confirmed, "other than what they earn. It's all show, Catherine."

The starter stepped forward to signify that the race was about to begin, but even as he did so another cry went up, and turning, Catherine saw that a high perch phaeton was making its way to the starting line, driven by a florid gentleman whom she immediately recognized as the Prince Regent.

"Glory!" Lily said. "This is high favor indeed! I wonder if the mob will cheer or berate His Highness today?"

But the crowd was clearly in a holiday mood and a ragged cheer went up. The prince raised his whip in acknowledgment and nodded to the two combatants as they sketched a deferential bow in his direction.

"It is almost as though the prince seeks to trade on Lord Hawksmoor's popularity rather than the reverse," Catherine murmured.

"Well, it is certainly greater than his own," Lily agreed

wryly. "Hawksmoor needs to be careful or the prince may turn against him for being the people's favorite."

The starter gestured at the throng to move back to give the carriages some space. The crowd backed off with good-natured jostling and, suddenly, Catherine and Lily were on the edge of the pavement where the two curricles were lining up. There was another delay as Jack Lancing persuaded one of the ladies in the crowd to give him her garter as a good luck token. He was fastening it about his sleeve amid much hilarity. And suddenly the scarlet curricle was right beside them and Ben Hawksmoor was close enough for Catherine to touch. The pavement seemed to shift slightly beneath her feet. She wanted to turn and run but she stood still, rooted to the spot. With a sense of inevitability, she looked up to meet Ben's cool hazel eyes. He was looking at her with disturbing intentness.

"Catherine?" Lily said questioningly, and Catherine jumped and dragged her gaze away from Ben's. He bowed to Lily, smiling.

"Miss St. Clare."

"Lord Hawksmoor." Lily sounded ruffled, but not on her own account. She was looking from Catherine to Ben with a frown on her face. "Have you met? I didn't think—"

Ben turned back to Catherine. His smile was warmer for her, intimate enough to make her stomach clench.

"Madam…" There was the very faintest hint of a question in his tone. Catherine realized that he would think that she, like all the other eager ladies in the crowd, had come deliberately to see the race.

"I did not know you would be here," she blurted out, and blushed at her own gaucheness. "That is, I did not come especially to see you...."

That was even worse. She could feel herself getting hotter and hotter to see the amusement in Ben Hawksmoor's eyes. He had passed the reins to his groom now and jumped down onto the pavement beside her. He took her hand and drew her a little apart, ignoring the calls of the crowd for the race to start.

"I am desolated to hear you did not seek me out," he murmured, the spark of humor still in his voice, "when I would go a deal further than Oxford Street to see *you* again, Catherine."

Catherine closed her eyes for a second against the potent awareness coursing through her. He had the most attractive voice she had ever heard, smooth, mellow and hopelessly seductive. For a moment she felt frighteningly adrift.

"I doubt that," she said, rallying. She looked about her at the throng of people. "You do not need my approval when you have all this."

Ben turned so that his broad shoulders blocked out the crowd. His physical presence was so powerful that Catherine felt a little light-headed. She had his whole attention now. The race, the crowd, the regent himself, none of them mattered. They could have been alone.

"You mistake." He spoke softly. "You are the only thing here that interests me, Catherine."

Catherine's mind went completely blank. She had little experience of flirting or playing games and she knew that was what he was doing. He had to be. He could not be sincere.

"That," she said, "is absurd."

He smiled again and the lines deepened at the corners of his eyes in a way that made her stomach flip.

"You won't flirt with me?"

She took a deep breath. "No."

"A pity. But this time I meant what I said."

Catherine realized that her hand was still in his. She tried to free herself but he refused to let go. He was running his thumb over the back of her hand now in small, distracting strokes. Catherine could feel the insistence of his touch through the material of her gloves.

"You did come here to see me, didn't you?" he murmured.

Catherine's gaze jerked up to meet his laughing hazel eyes. "You have a monstrously high opinion of yourself," she said.

He gave her a rueful half smile and her heart turned over. "Have I?"

She watched his smile fade and another very different, more disturbing emotion take its place. Then someone dug an elbow in Catherine's ribs and she realized they were surrounded by a crowd growing more restless by the minute. She forced herself to look beyond the compelling demand in Ben's eyes.

"You are keeping His Highness waiting," she said.

Ben grinned. "It is worth it."

"You take too many risks."

"Always." He gave her that dangerous, flashing smile, released her hand and swung himself back up onto the box of the curricle. The crowd gave an ironic cheer.

"A kiss for luck!" someone shouted.

Ben leaned down. His gloved fingers touched Catherine's cheek.

"May I?"

She barely heard the words above the pounding of her pulse but she must have made some sound, for he tilted her chin up and then his lips brushed hers, lightly, a brief but insistent pressure. He was cold and tasted of fresh air and her mind reeled. "Thank you," he said. Catherine opened her eyes to see the blaze of triumph in his.

The winter sky was too bright. The light hurt her eyes. She felt shaky. The crowd roared its approval.

The starter dropped the flag; there was a clatter of hooves and the race was on.

"Gracious," Lily said, grabbing Catherine's arm to gain her attention, "what was *that* about?"

Across the street, Catherine suddenly spotted Lord Withers in the crowd. He had his arm about a woman she did not recognize. Fortunately he was looking the other way. Catherine gave a gasp and shot off hastily down the pavement, a startled Lily hurrying behind.

"Catherine—"

"Withers," Catherine puffed, diving into Blake's coffeehouse. "With some female."

"Emily Spraggett," Lily confirmed. "She is a terrible old strumpet. I am sorry, Catherine."

"Do not be." Catherine subsided into a seat well

away from the window. She gave a sigh. "It is not as though I care for him. Nor does it surprise me."

Lily was frowning. "Then I am sorry for that, too. You do not have many illusions left, do you?"

A waiter brought them hot chocolate and Lily smiled her thanks. Catherine stirred her chocolate slowly, head bent. She knew her friend. In a moment Lily would start asking awkward questions.

"Catherine," Lily said slowly, "have you met Lord Hawksmoor before?"

"Yes," Catherine said. "We met at Ned Clarencieux's hanging a few days ago."

Lily was momentarily distracted. "A *hanging?* What on earth were you doing there?"

"Papa insisted I attend," Catherine said. "Sir James Mather, Clarencieux's victim, was one of my trustees."

"I remember," Lily said. She fixed Catherine with a stern blue gaze. "So you met Lord Hawksmoor there. How did that happen? I cannot imagine your papa introducing the pair of you."

"Lord Hawksmoor…um…" Catherine hesitated, feeling the blood scald her cheeks at the memory. "John ran off into the crowd and I went to look for him," she said. "I had not realized it would be so dangerous. Lord Hawksmoor rescued me."

Lily's eyebrows shot up into her hair. "He *rescued* you?"

"Yes."

"Gracious," Lily said again, faintly. "How out of character. And such prior acquaintance was enough for you to permit him to seduce you in the street just now?"

The color flooded Catherine's face. "He was not seducing me!"

"I apologize for contradicting you," Lily said dryly, "but that was precisely what he was doing, Catherine. In fact you could not have done anything more dangerous had you set a match to a barrel of gunpowder!"

Catherine bit her lip. "I did not flirt."

"For a debutante even to *speak* with Ben Hawksmoor is a truly imprudent idea," Lily said.

"He does not know I am a debutante," Catherine said after a moment. "He doesn't know my name. I think he believes me to be a demimondaine. I think he assumed that no gently-bred female would attend a hanging, and to be fair that is very much the case. And also Lord Withers addressed me by my name with a certain lack of respect, and we have seen the company he keeps. Who could blame Lord Hawksmoor for taking away the wrong impression of me?"

"And now he has seen you with me and so his suspicions that you are a courtesan will be confirmed." Lily groaned, putting her head in her hands. "Oh, Lord, Catherine. No wonder he thought it a small matter to kiss you in the street!"

Catherine did not reply immediately. It had not felt like a small matter to her. Oh, she had known the kiss had been done for nothing but show. She knew it was part of Ben Hawksmoor's charm, part of the legend he spun. She should feel used. If it had not been her, it would have been some other pretty girl in the crowd.

And yet the memory of what had happened at Newgate was still with her, confusing her. She had thought then that she understood Ben Hawksmoor, all his hatreds, fears and longings. She had felt so close to him. And she could not shake off that feeling, even though in her heart of hearts she knew it had to be false.

For a moment, out there in the street, she had even believed that she might be able to seek him out and confide in him the truth about Maggie—and return Clarencieux's portrait without need of deception. But common sense had prevailed. For Maggie's sake, she had to be so very careful. She could not trust him no matter how she felt.

"I know the kiss did not mean anything," she said. "And doubtless he will have forgotten me the next instant."

Lily was shaking her head. "I do not think so. Did you see the expression on his face when he was looking at you?" She put her spoon down with a clatter. "Perhaps it is better if you did not. Ben Hawksmoor wants you. And what he wants he usually takes."

Catherine bit her lip. "You speak nonsense. With Lady Paris de Moine as his mistress he would never be interested in me."

Lily frowned. "You understand nothing. I am certain Lord Hawksmoor and Lady Paris have no more than a business agreement. I have suspected it for some time. He squires her about town and she appears to advantage on his arm but there is no more to it than that."

"I don't understand," Catherine said.

"Precisely. That is what I have just said." Lily sounded cross. "You are well beyond your depth, playing games where you have no concept of the rules." She sighed. "Well, if he comes asking after you, I shall simply have to deny all knowledge."

Catherine gulped her cooling chocolate. "Asking after me?"

"At the bawdy house. It would be the first place that I would go to find you if I were him."

Catherine's mouth dried. "I had not thought of that."

"Which," Lily said, placing some coins on the table, "is exactly what I have been trying to tell you." She stood up. "Come along. I shall procure you a hackney carriage before you cause any more trouble."

Out in the street, the crowds had moved away to the finishing line. The gutters were full of discarded scandal sheets wilting in the cold breeze. Catherine gave Lily a hug and climbed into the hack her friend had found for her.

"Write to me!" she said, hanging out of the window. The carriage began to move away and Lily waved, but suddenly Catherine had the strangest feeling she was slipping away from her again, back to the life she had stepped out of for a few hours.

The house in Guilford Street was very quiet when she got back. Tench confirmed that Lady Fenton was sleeping and Sir Alfred was out at his club. Catherine took a book and curled up in a chair in the library. She had no engagements that afternoon, though Withers was due to dine with them at seven before they all attended the opera. No doubt he was with his mistress now. Catherine rested her book on her lap and thought about her future as Lord Withers's wife and his as her unfaithful husband. Why was life so weighted against the woman in such a situation? It seemed so harsh. She thought of Lily seeking solace with her lover and paying the ultimate price, and that inevitably led her thoughts to Ben Hawksmoor and the sweet seduction of his kiss.

It was a bare two hours later that Tench knocked at the door and brought in a scrap of paper on his silver tray.

"A message, Miss Fenton," he said, somewhat superfluously.

Catherine unfolded it. It was brief.

*He came asking after you. I told you he would.*
*Be careful. L.*
*PS He won the race.*

After that, Catherine found it impossible to concentrate all the way through dinner and the long, long opera that followed, and as she tossed and turned in the night she would have even been prepared to try some of Lady Fenton's laudanum to help her put the troublesome memory of Ben Hawksmoor's kiss from her mind.

"WHAT MAY I DO FOR YOU, Lord Hawksmoor?"
Ben was sitting before the desk of the most

shadowy and discreet information broker in the whole of London. The office was on the top floor of a tall building down by the docks and on this January afternoon it was lit by candlelight even though the hour was only just past two. A cheerful fire burned in the grate and Ben had been offered one of the best cups of coffee he had ever tasted, rich and smooth. That alone almost justified Bradshaw's fee in his opinion.

"I need you to find out about someone for me," Ben said.

Tom Bradshaw inclined his head. "Of course. Whom?"

"Algernon, Lord Withers." Ben hesitated. "Specifically, I wish you to discover what connection, if any, he had to Edward Clarencieux, and what grudge, again if any, he may bear against me. He has threatened me and I require to know if it is a genuine threat or not."

It had been Ben's first instinct to hunt Withers down himself, but it was at times like this that his notoriety was a drawback rather than an advantage. If he started to ask questions, people would become curious. Withers would hear of it and Ben would achieve nothing other than to put him on his guard.

Bradshaw had been taking notes and now his pen stilled for a moment.

"Withers," he said reflectively. "I see." He sketched a few idle drawings on the paper. "I assume you know of no connection between Clarencieux and Withers already?"

"None whatsoever." Ben shifted. "But if I were to

speculate then I would say it would be something to do with money or with women."

"That scarcely narrows the field," Bradshaw pointed out.

"I suppose not," Ben said. "And similarly there is no obvious connection between myself and Withers other than that I covet his mistress."

He coveted Catherine so much, in fact, that he had been tempted to ask Bradshaw to find her into the bargain. When he had seen her with Lily St. Clare in Oxford Street that morning, the wicked excitement already coursing through his blood at the prospect of the curricle race had soared. He would have counted it fair exchange to forfeit the race to Lancing and carry Catherine off there and then to make love to her. One kiss had scarce been enough. And later he had gone to the high-class brothel where Miss St. Clare worked, confident that he would be able to persuade her to disclose Catherine's identity and her address. But Miss St. Clare had been surprisingly reticent, open to neither persuasion nor, unusually, to bribery. So he was still at an impasse and he burned all the more to possess Catherine as a result.

Bradshaw had smothered a grin at his words. "Men have died for less," he said. "You know of no other link between yourself and Lord Withers?"

"No," Ben said.

"The army, perhaps?"

"He did not serve, to my knowledge," Ben said. He reflected that his army career had been littered with hard decisions. If Withers had a grudge relating to one of them he would scarce know where to start.

"Then since your return to town?"

"I have fleeced him at cards a few times," Ben said, "but if all the men I had taken money from sought my death, I would be cold in the ground by now."

Bradshaw's smile widened. He stood up. "Leave the matter with me, my lord. I shall be in touch when I have some information for you."

They shook hands and Ben went out of the office and down the narrow wooden stair to the street. The wind was fresher now with an edge to it that promised snow soon, but despite the cold, Ben turned on impulse toward the docks rather than seeking the warm fug of an alehouse. The river was partially frozen but the stevedores were still working and the clatter of freight sounded above the clanking of the masts in the rising wind. Ben leaned on the river wall and looked out across the Thames. He had grown up in this warren of streets, he and his mother occupying one dark room in the basement of one of these houses. He could see her now, her face gray with exhaustion, her hands red raw from the laundry she took in to scrape a living. In the winter, the walls of their tenement had run with water and in summer, the stench of rotting humanity had been appalling as fever rampaged through the packed houses and carried off all but the strongest. He had been strong. He had survived. So had his mother, for a little. But in the end, the unremitting cold and toil and sickness had taken her and there was nothing he had been able to do about it. The poverty had worn her down. Even thinking about it now turned his blood to ice. He knew he could never, ever allow that poverty to touch him again.

Ben drove his hands into his pockets and walked slowly along the quay. A group of ragged children paused in their game on the street corner to watch him, fanning out behind him like a wolf pack as he passed. He knew what happened next. It was dangerous for a rich man to walk alone in the shadow of the docks, and to these people he would look richer than their dreams. So one of them would bump into him and lift his wallet, or they would knock him to the ground and pick over him like vultures, taking the very clothes he stood up in. He should know. He had done the same so many times in the past.

He turned abruptly to face them, seeing the wary aggression in the young faces that confronted him. Then the recognition flickered in the eyes of the ringleader and suddenly they were pressing close in hero worship rather than violence.

"It's him! The famous cove… Hawksmoor… One of us…"

*One of us… The one that got away…*

His mother had wanted him to open orphanages for the poor children when he'd finally come into his inheritance. She had had such charitable plans. And he had disappointed her. He had done nothing for those he had left behind.

And of course he had never really been one of them. He was the son of a lord. His Hawksmoor uncles, intent on fulfilling their Christian duty even to a bastard, had plucked him from the obscurity of his childhood, sent him to school and restored him to his place in society. It would have been like a fairy tale if only it had not damaged him so much in the process. He had never fit in at Harrow. It had been far too late. The other boys, following his father's example, had taunted him for his birth. He'd run away. The uncles had found him and sent him back. He'd refused to go to Oxford or Cambridge. In the end, the uncles had bought him a commission and for a while it had seemed to solve everyone's problems as he'd tried wholeheartedly to get himself killed. But then his father had died, sustained only by the hatred that had kept him company all his life, and Ben had come home to claim the Hawksmoor barony in a scandalous court case. He had won, and gained the title and with it a tumbledown house in Yorkshire that he never visited but milked for every penny it could yield. He had restored his mother's good name, proved his legitimacy, but in the end she had still died.

He knew he would never really be accepted by the *Ton* because of the scandal of his childhood, but for the moment the Prince Regent held him in favor and the mob loved him, so he would take that and use it and earn enough money to guard against the future.

So he shook hands with the gathering crowd, fended off the scissors they were waving in an attempt to cut a lock of his hair as a souvenir, and signed the scraps of paper that they brought for his autograph even though he knew they could not read his name and would probably sell the memento for a few pennies. It did not bother him. He would have done the same thing himself.

All the same, he was not sorry to see the back of

Angel Alley and wished that his impulse had not taken him back there. He did not belong there. He belonged nowhere. And he had a living to earn since his father had run through the family fortune and left him penniless. It was time to hit the gaming tables.

THE HOUSE IN GUILFORD STREET was quiet that evening with the uncomfortable peace that Catherine had come to expect in recent days. Her father was from home and Maggie, who had become distressed once again at dinner, had been dosed up with laudanum to a point where she did not know whether it was day or night and cared even less. There were few invitations on the drawing-room mantelpiece, for town was quiet in the winter months before the Season began. Nevertheless, Catherine would have appreciated the distraction of a trip to the theater or a small evening party with friends. With her chaperone insensible in a drug-induced sleep, she could go nowhere and had already run through all the books she had taken from the circulating library the previous day.

It was as she was somewhat listlessly preparing for bed that night that there was a knock at the door and she turned to find Alice, Maggie's personal maid. Alice had a face like a rusting hatchet and a manner to match. Sir Alfred had appointed her when he and Maggie were first married and Catherine wondered now if her father had always known of his wife's wayward tendencies and had set this watchdog to guard her. Yet somehow, Maggie's insouciant kindness had charmed Alice, too, so that within six months she was eating out of her new mistress's hand. Now she was fiercely loyal and Catherine could tell from the wasp-chewing expression on her face that she was also fiercely concerned.

"Madam's in trouble," she said bluntly. She came into the room and closed the door behind her. "She went out over an hour ago, as soon as your father had left the house, Miss Catherine."

Catherine stared. "But that's impossible! She was sick—I thought she had taken laudanum?"

Alice shook her head. Her hands were working in the folds of her gown, creasing the material.

"Sometimes she does not drink it. She pretends…." The maid looked away. "I was sitting with her but she sent me down to the kitchens for a cup of chocolate. I was only gone a moment!" Her voice wobbled, perilously close to losing control and she gulped a breath. "She told Jeremy footman that she was going to Crockford's!"

Catherine shook her head slightly. "Crockford's?"

The maid looked at her, her eyes widening. "God bless you, miss, I wouldn't expect you to know of it. It's not the sort of place for a young lady of quality to go. They call it the Pandemonium—"

"The gaming hell in Piccadilly," Catherine said, remembering. "I have heard of it."

Alice nodded. "Madam goes there to gamble. The deepest play in town. She has no money but she will bet the very clothes she stands up in when she is in a mood like this."

Catherine pressed her fingers to her temples. "My father—"

"Gone to his fancy woman in Chelsea, begging your pardon, miss." The maid looked suddenly shifty. "He mustn't know about this. He would banish her!"

"Yes," Catherine said slowly. "I think he probably would." She let her hands fall to her sides. Her father was with a mistress in Chelsea and her stepmother was playing deep in the most notorious hell in London. For a moment she was swamped with despair. But she could not shrug the matter away as being of no concern to her. She had a loyalty to poor, frail Maggie and a desperate need to keep the shreds of her family together.

"Well," she said, "we will just have to get Lady Fenton out of there then. I will go now. You had best come with me, Alice. Bring my cloak."

The maid stared at her for a long moment but she did not demur.

"You cannot go into the Pandemonium dressed like that," she said at last. "You need a mask and a domino." And it was then that Catherine realized the extent to which Maggie's duplicity had trained her servants in the art of deception, and her stomach lurched again with misery.

Alice was striving to be practical. "No one must see your face, Miss Catherine, or you'll be ruined. Madam has several outfits you could borrow. I will fetch them." Her expression crumpled suddenly with fear. "Oh, miss, you *can't* go there, not you, a young lady—"

"Yes, I can," Catherine said. "Someone must. Fetch the domino." She was shivering with nerves. Any hesitation on the part of the servants and she knew she would be lost. "Have Jeremy footman call a hackney. He must come with us, too, for protection."

While Alice scurried off to fetch one of Maggie's dominoes, Catherine stood before the mirror and stared at her reflection with a kind of horrified despair. She knew that there was no one else to go after Maggie. If she did not act, then her stepmother would very likely gamble away an enormous fortune, or cause some scandal so terrible that Sir Alfred would be obliged to divorce her and mire the family in so much misery that they would never recover. She thought of John and of baby Mirabelle in the nursery. The way that matters were tending, Mirabelle was set fair never to know the warmth of her mother's love. Catherine remembered the way that her own mother had held her and comforted her and protected her against the world, and a very hard lump formed in her throat.

"Here—" Alice was thrusting a midnight-blue domino into her hands. Catherine slipped it over her head and the material slithered down over her gown, transforming her at once from a young woman in a demurely-cut dress to a siren in shifting silk. She stared at her image in perplexity. Alice was tying the mask now and Catherine could see a stranger gazing back at her, a stranger swathed in secrecy, whose expression was enigmatic behind the mask's disguise. She pulled on her gloves and drew the hood of the domino close about her face. She knew she had to go before she lost her nerve.

The night was dark and foggy. The weather had turned icy that afternoon, with a freezing mist that wrapped the whole of London in its white shroud. It was not possible to travel far. The fog shifted and ran in pale strands as the hackney carriage picked its slow way along the London streets. It was no night to be out. From time to time, Catherine caught sight of a glimmer of light from behind shuttered windows. She ached to give the order to turn the carriage around and return home but she kept her lips firmly closed. She felt cold and shaky and alone. Alice's face was in shadow. Jeremy footman shifted nervously and cleared his throat so many times that Catherine wanted to snap at him to be quiet. But she needed them both. They were the only people who could help her.

The hack lurched to a halt and the servants scrambled down. Jeremy put out a hand to help Catherine alight.

"Wait here," Catherine said, resisting the urge to cling to Jeremy's hand like a lifeline in a stormy sea. Her teeth were chattering from cold and nervousness. Ahead of her the lights of the gaming hell blazed through the mist. She could see a huge chandelier in the entrance hall throwing out light to draw her in. She gathered the folds of the domino in one hand and hurried up the steps to the door. The bag of gold she had taken from the drawer in her father's desk weighed down her pocket and bumped against her knee. Catherine had no idea how the rules of the gaming hells worked but if Maggie was in deep debt, Catherine might need to buy her out of there immediately.

A liveried servant bowed her within and Catherine passed through the doorway and into the hall. She was not sure what she had been expecting but it was not this opulent splendor. It was like walking into the most richly furnished aristocratic house in London. Another liveried footman threw open the doorway at the end of the hall for her and she stood still in the opening for a moment, and viewed the room before her. It was thickly carpeted in plush-red that was so soft it sank beneath her slippers as she moved forward. In the center of the room stood a big hazard table of mahogany, covered in green baize, a box and dice standing temptingly in the center. A croupier, as elegantly attired as any footman to a great family, was leaning forward and raking the counters toward a woman sitting directly opposite Catherine. It was Maggie Fenton.

No one looked up as Catherine came in. No one glanced in her direction at all. The room was very quiet with a strangely intense silence that Catherine understood at once. Gambling was so important here that it brooked no interruption. She imagined that the house could catch fire and they would still insist on staying to finish the game.

Maggie did not see her until she stepped up and touched her on the arm, and then she jumped like a startled cat. There was a feverish glitter in her eyes and her fingers were trembling.

*"Catherine!"*

"Good evening, Maggie," Catherine said. Suddenly she felt completely out of her depth. How was she to persuade her stepmother to leave voluntarily when on her face was an expression as fervent as that of the most hardened gamester?

"You have come to take me home," Maggie said. Her lower lip quivered just like John's when he was thwarted. "You can't. Look!" She gestured to the pile of rouleaux. "I am winning!"

"Maggie—" Catherine said hopelessly.

Maggie hunched a shoulder against her.

There was only one other player at the table, a blond woman who was dressed in white satin and diamonds. Catherine recognized her from the penny prints as Lady Paris de Moine and her heart plummeted into her slippers, for where Paris was there, surely, would Ben Hawksmoor be also. She wondered why it had never occurred to her that she might meet Ben at the most exclusive gaming hell in town. Where else would he be, unless it was in Paris's bed? But then her concern for Maggie had made her blind to all else.

The pencil sketches had not been able to do anything near justice to Paris's shallow and glittering beauty. It was difficult not to stare, for there were jewels cascading down from Paris's hair to adorn a truly staggering bosom that looked cantilevered to within an inch of its life. Catherine marveled at the engineering involved and found herself hoping that Paris's stays were horribly uncomfortable.

Paris had been watching her and now she laughed

and took up the dice box. She kept her hard blue gaze fixed disdainfully on Catherine and Catherine could feel her face heating beneath that contemptuous regard.

"Your little friend doesn't approve of us, Maggie," Paris said. Her voice was husky. "What is she—a Methodist? You shouldn't invite *children* to join you at play."

"She's not my friend, Paris," Maggie said petulantly. She turned sharply on Catherine. "Go home, Catherine. This is no place for you."

Catherine tilted her chin up. "You are coming back with me."

"I am *not!*"

Paris threw two fours and looked suitably disgusted. Maggie snatched the dice box. Her hands shook and the dice shot away, spinning across the table, settling with two ones. Maggie groaned.

"Ames-ace," Paris said, smiling. "The girl brings you bad luck, Maggie. Send her away."

She nodded and the croupier raked Maggie's pile of counters toward her. Maggie gave a wail and scrabbled after them.

"How much?" Catherine said. "How much does she owe you?"

Paris looked down her nose. "Only a thousand guineas. It's a trifle." She looked at Maggie. "Pay or play, Maggie." She yawned, shrugged one voluptuously rounded shoulder. "It makes no odds to me."

"Maggie—" Catherine said, pulling her stepmother's arm with increasing desperation. A thousand guineas was already lost and she did not know how to begin to stop Maggie from wasting even more.

Maggie grabbed a fold of Catherine's domino and pulled her close. "Listen, you little fool," she hissed into her face. "I have no money. I *have* to play. I have to win it back!"

Paris yawned again and started to stack the counters in an idle pile. "Make your mind up, ladies." Her bright blue gaze fixed on Catherine again and she smiled.

"What about you, little Miss Mystery? Do you have any money?"

Catherine took the red velvet bag of guineas from her pocket and plonked it down on the table. It made a satisfyingly expensive thud. Paris's blue eyes opened wider.

"I see," she said. "Then you are welcome to play."

"I want to pay Maggie's debt," Catherine said stolidly, but Paris shook her head. Her eyes were bright with amusement.

"No," she said. "Play me and win. Then I'll cancel it. Those are my terms."

The croupier stood silent, waiting, his face as impassive as a well-trained servant's should be. Maggie had laid her head on her folded arms now and was humming softly to herself as though she were almost asleep. Paris cast her a single contemptuous look.

"She never could hold her wine and now she is half-mad with laudanum, too."

Catherine felt her fury rise in a scalding tide. This woman's disdain was so insulting she wanted to slap the scorn from her painted face.

"I'll play," she said recklessly. "If it is the only way to get Maggie out of here, then I will play."

She heard the croupier catch his breath in surprise. Paris smiled.

"Will you indeed? Then call a main."

"A moment," Catherine said. She beckoned to one of the club servants. "Pray help Lady Fenton out to the carriage," she said. "It is waiting at the front door. And tell my servants I shall join them shortly."

The man bowed. He helped Maggie to her feet. She was laughing and trying to flirt with him as he and a colleague steered her toward the door. Catherine turned aside from the pitiful sight to where Paris was waiting with barely disguised impatience.

"Nine," Catherine said. "I call a nine."

Paris's eyes opened wide. "You are ambitious, my little miss. Either that, or you know how to cheat."

Catherine laughed. She took the dice box. It felt smooth beneath her fingers. The dazzling lights swung overhead. She took her time, took a deep breath. She had played dice with her grandfather many times, the old man taking great pleasure in teaching his grand-daughter the sorts of skills that had made her mother blanch with disapproval.

"Show no fear," Jack McNaish had always told her. "If you have confidence in your throw, then the dice will fall as you wish them to."

Catherine straightened her shoulders and threw. The dice spun and settled. A five and a four.

Suddenly Paris was not smiling.

"Devil take it!" she snapped.

"Fortune favors the bold."

Catherine looked up sharply. Ben Hawksmoor was leaning on the back of Paris de Moine's chair, his hands resting on her bare shoulders in a gesture of casual possession that made Catherine feel hot and naive and envious all in one uncomfortable moment. He was dressed with magnificent understatement in black, with a snowy-white neck cloth in which glittered a diamond pin. Together, he and Paris looked so striking it was difficult to tear one's gaze away. Catherine felt a furious rush of jealousy that almost choked her.

She looked down, trying to get a grip on her feelings. This was foolish, like a silly schoolgirl having a crush on her dancing master. Ben Hawksmoor had shown her some kindness a few days before, had kissed her on a whim, and she was about to fall for all that studied, superficial charm. Lily had been right; she was in as much danger from her own foolish fantasies as she was from Ben Hawksmoor's legendary lack of scruple.

She saw him watching her, his gaze straight, his hazel eyes bright. It was the most unsettling look that she had ever received from a man.

Her heart lurched. For a moment, brown eyes and hazel met and held. Catherine's chin came up. She knew he had already recognized her. The domino and mask did not fool him. But at least he did not know her identity. All she had to do was get away....

"So, Catherine," he said slowly, "who taught you to play hazard like that?"

"Who cares?" Paris shrugged pettishly, shaking him off. She put a hand out toward the bag of money. "I'll take the debt, and you—" she gave Catherine a less than friendly look "—can go home."

"I thought," Ben said gently, "that I heard you say that you would cancel the debt if Catherine won, Paris." There was a hint of laughter in his eyes.

Paris gave him a distinctly un-lover-like look. "So I did," she said sweetly. She yawned. "This company gives me the headache. Excuse me."

She rose gracefully and stalked off to the other side of the room, where she took a seat at a faro table.

Catherine looked at Ben. He had made no move to follow Paris and now he leaned on the back of the chair, his gaze moving thoughtfully from the bag of guineas to Catherine's face. He smiled a challenge.

"Another game?" he suggested softly.

His words breathed shivers down her back. For a long, long moment she held his eyes. There was a disturbing intensity in his bright stare that made her breath catch in her throat. Something almost painful tightened inside her. Her lips parted and she saw his eyes go to her mouth in a sudden, dangerously sensuous glance that made her alive with memory. Time seemed to slow down, stop, wait forever.

She cleared her throat. "I think not," she said huskily. "You told me you never lose."

The lines around Ben's eyes deepened as he smiled. "So I did. How careless of me to throw away my advantages."

He was turning the dice box between his fingers

now. "We need not play for money," he added, with a silky emphasis that made his meaning crystal clear.

The shock brought a gasp to Catherine's lips. Suddenly she was grateful for the concealment of the mask, for the color had faded from her face and then rushed back in a scalding tide. Her heart hammered. So here she had the proof of what she had suspected all along. He had assumed she was Withers's mistress, he had seen her in company with Lily, and so he thought she was a courtesan who might be prepared to grant him her favors for a night. He wanted to seduce her. Of course he did. All he sought was a little dalliance with a pretty girl. Perhaps Lily was right and his arrangement with Paris was purely a business one. Whatever the case, she had been foolish ever to entertain the thought that she could trust him.

"I do not think I understand you, my lord," she said coldly. She got to her feet. Ben did not move. He was still watching her, a faint smile playing around his lips.

"Oh, but you do understand me," he said. "You have understood me from the very first, Catherine. You know what I want and I dare swear you want it, too."

The ground shifted like sand beneath Catherine's feet. She felt trapped. She wanted to disabuse him at once and tell him who she really was. But for a debutante to visit a gaming hell meant ruin to her reputation. The repercussions for herself and for Maggie if the truth came out did not bear thinking about. She would be ruined and her father would hear of Maggie's financial profligacy and banish her, and it would be intolerable, even more intolerable than matters already were in the Fenton household....

Catherine swallowed hard. She had to keep her name a secret, so she was caught in a dangerous identity she did not want. The only thing that she could do was run away.

She swept the bag of money up in one hand and was glad to see that for all the turmoil inside her, her hand was still steady.

"Excuse me, my lord," she said. "I must go. Truly I must."

It was no real answer but Ben did not challenge her, merely stood watching her with that look of speculative inquiry still in his eyes. Catherine knew that he was prepared to wait. That patience, that calculation, was what made him such a master player when she barely understood the game at all.

"I will escort you to your coach," he murmured. He took her arm and his grip seemed to brand her through the thin silk of the domino.

"There is not need—"

"I insist."

The room was a blur of color and dazzling light as they crossed to the door. Catherine was aware of nothing except his hand on her arm, the warmth and the strength of it. When they went out into the hallway and down the carpeted steps to the door, she shivered as the cold, foggy night air enveloped her.

The hackney carriage had gone.

Catherine stopped dead. For a moment she could not believe the evidence of her own eyes. Surely the servants had not simply driven off and left her? Had Maggie countermanded her orders to wait and told the driver to take them home? She ran down a couple of the steps, staring out into the night. No reassuring lights gleamed in the fog. She was quite alone.

She turned back. Ben Hawksmoor was standing on the steps behind her, arms folded, one brow raised in amused inquiry.

"Oh, dear," Catherine said, inadequately.

He laughed and turned to the doorman, who had been watching with ill-concealed interest. "Call my carriage, please," he said. He smiled at Catherine. "I am most happy to offer my escort."

Catherine looked at him sharply. She knew she could not accept his offer. The panicky feeling in the pit of her stomach warned her that being in an enclosed space with him—a dark, enclosed space— would be beyond irresponsible and straying into reck-lessness.

"You are most kind," she said politely, "but I would hate to take you away from your evening's engage-ments."

Ben shrugged. "There is nothing that cannot wait."

"But Lady Paris—"

"Is well able to shift for herself. I am more con-cerned about you."

Catherine saw the club servant smile meaningfully.

"I will take a hack," she said and, turning to the doorman, "if you would be so good as to call one."

The doorman looked to Ben for confirmation, which made Catherine furious.

"If the lady wishes," Ben said with a whimsical smile.

"Thank you," Catherine said. "But I do not require your permission!"

"Of course not." Ben had stepped closer to her and in the coldness of the night he seemed to emanate a warmth that made her want to draw closer still. She folded her arms protectively about herself and kept quite still.

"It would be safer to travel with me," he added in an undertone.

Catherine's brows arched sarcastically. "Do you think so?"

His lips twitched in a smile. "Nights like this bring out the most dangerous elements in society."

Catherine looked him up and down with pointed regard. "Indeed they do."

Ben sighed. "I am merely trying to point out that a woman traveling alone is at risk of attack."

Catherine looked at him. She knew he was right. There had been a spate of assaults in the street recently, people had been dragged from their carriages and robbed, and traveling alone was very foolhardy, particularly when she had a bag full of gold guineas in her pocket and carried no pistol with which to protect herself.

"I appreciate your offer," she said carefully, "but it is not one that I would be wise to accept."

Ben's smile was devastating. "I understand your

scruples, ma'am, but if you wish, I could promise to behave as a gentleman should."

"Could you?" Catherine said.

Ben bowed. There was laughter in his eyes. "If that is your desire." There was a dry note in his voice, as though he was already challenging her truthfulness. Catherine shivered and turned her face away from him, aware that her expression gave too much away. She knew that there was a part of her that did not wish him to behave with honor. There was a heat in her blood that reminded her of how tempting, how seductive, it had been to be held close in his arms. She knew exactly how dangerous he was and yet she was struggling against this perilous attraction.

"I cannot trust you," she said. "You trade on the very reputation that puts me in danger."

Ben inclined his head. "You will be quite safe. I assure you that no matter what they say of me, I am not so lost to propriety as to ravish any woman who crosses my path. Apart from anything else, it has never been necessary."

Catherine could not repress a slight smile. "I told you that you have a monstrously high opinion of yourself."

"That's true."

He said nothing else to persuade her and Catherine sighed. Could she truly trust him? It was rash and imprudent of her in the extreme but she kept remembering the gentleness he had shown her at Newgate and thought that perhaps he would keep his word. Besides, what was the alternative? A knife in the throat, robbed, raped, beaten in the streets?

"Well, then," she said a little awkwardly, for all her attempts at town bronze, "I accept your offer with gratitude, Lord Hawksmoor."

The carriage came, all gleaming black panels and high-stepping horses. Catherine looked at it dubiously. The team was barely under the coachman's control, shying at shadows.

"Where to?" Ben asked, and Catherine realized with a shock of relief that he did not know her address. He might have recognized her behind her mask, but he still did not know her true identity. She had to keep it that way.

"Millman Street, if you please," she said hastily. It was only a step from her front door but it would help preserve the fiction.

"I do not think the horses like the fog," she added, as Ben helped her up into the precariously rocking carriage. "I hope they do not overturn us. Did you choose the team yourself, my lord?"

"I did," Ben said. He settled himself opposite her.

"And the coach?" Catherine could see little of the interior but it felt decadently opulent. She sank so far into the seat cushions that it was like falling into a feather mattress.

"That, too."

"They are both as I would have expected."

The coach set off with a sudden jerk, almost decanting Catherine into Ben's lap. He helped her back onto the seat—and removed his hand from her arm immediately.

"And what did you expect?" he asked.

"They are very ostentatious."

"All display and no substance?" He seemed amused rather than offended at her candor.

"Well…" Catherine had not intended to be quite so blunt. The carriage blinds were down and the darkness felt intimate. It emboldened her. It was odd, but she felt as though she could say anything she wanted to Ben Hawksmoor. She struggled against the impulse to be too open.

"You wish to give the impression of wealth," she said slowly, "and you do not do it discreetly."

"You think me flamboyant?"

"I think you wish people to see you so," Catherine said. "Whether it is true is another matter."

She saw him smile in the darkness. "Why should I do that?"

Catherine thought of the penny prints and the newspapers and the silhouettes and the gossip and the scandal.

"I assume you find it profitable, my lord."

"You are quite right. One must give the impression of wealth to generate more."

"But you are not showy in your personal attire."

Ben laughed. "You think that I dress well?"

Catherine thought of what he looked like in the elegant evening clothes. "Tonight you dressed deliberately," she said, "as a foil for Lady Paris."

"You see a great deal."

"It worked," Catherine said.

She felt a strange sensation of anger and it puzzled her. She could not quite understand the feeling, but it was part jealously and also something to do with the perfect counterfeit that he had created.

*All display and no substance…*

"You look well together," she said colorlessly.

Ben laughed. "Thank you."

Catherine remembered what Lily had told her. "Is that all a fiction also?"

There was a pause before he replied. "Are you wishing to discuss my mistress with me?"

The casual amusement in his voice caused Catherine to go hot with annoyance at her own gaucheness. "No," she snapped. "I do not know why I asked."

"You asked because you wanted to know the answer," Ben said. "You wanted to know if Paris really *is* my mistress."

The darkness was thick with tension. It caught at Catherine's throat, silencing her. She could feel her heart slamming in hard strokes and the blood scalding her veins.

"Didn't you?" Ben said softly.

"I… No! Not at all. It is none of my concern." Catherine's mind was a scramble of thoughts. How had she strayed onto such treacherous ground?

"It could be your concern if you wished it to be," Ben said.

The silence burned between them. "I do not wish it." Catherine's voice was a little husky. "Do not ask this of me, my lord."

She heard Ben sigh in the darkness. "It seems you are determined to be proper, sweetheart. And though I promised to be the soul of propriety, I find myself wanting to change your mind about that. What could I do to persuade you? Kiss you again, as I did in Oxford Street the other day?"

Catherine gulped. "But that was just for show, was it not, my lord, as everything is with you? All show and no substance?"

There was a long pause as she realized that had probably been the most downright provocative thing she could possibly have said and cursed herself for her naivety.

"I... I did not mean—" She stopped. "I did not intend..."

"I know." Ben's voice was very quiet. "You do not flirt, do you, Catherine, despite what you said the first time we met."

"That was a mistake," Catherine said, remembering her foolish impulse to thwart Algernon Withers.

"Because of Withers?"

"Amongst other things."

"Forget him." Ben's voice was hard now. "There is nothing but the two of us, Catherine, here and now."

Catherine's breath caught as he leaned toward her and started to untie the ribbons of her masquerade mask. She could feel his fingers in her hair. The sensation held her still and silent for a moment. His hands were gentle, their touch so soft she could barely feel it and yet it seemed to send the blood singing through her body. She put up a hand to protest, but he caught it in one of his and returned it to her side. In the dim light she could see his expression was still and serious. It made her stomach flutter.

The mask fell. Catherine made a grab for it but he whisked it from her.

"Oh no! Someone might yet see me."

Ben's fingers touched her cheek, turning her face to the faint light. "Do you then have a reputation left to lose, Catherine?" he said. "You surprise me."

Yes, she had a reputation to lose. She was shocked to realize that she had almost forgotten it herself.

"I have to be careful," Catherine said.

"Because of Withers again," Ben said, "I understand your situation—"

"I doubt that," Catherine said truthfully.

"I understand what it is to be obliged to do something that makes you unhappy because you have no choice," Ben said. There was a wealth of bitterness in his voice and it caught Catherine off guard. She turned her head to look at him. Some stray beam of light from the lanterns outside shimmered on an expression in his eyes that was so remote it made her want to reach out to him. It was like the moment at Newgate when she had looked into his face and seen all the anger and the pain there and had wanted to hold him and ease the hurt. Her foolish impulse to save people…

"I am sorry," she said.

She heard him swear quietly under his breath and then she was in his arms. His mouth touched hers softly at first, then with deliberate intent. It was Catherine's first real kiss, so different from that brief embrace in the street and yet just as perilously seductive. The strangeness of the sensation was all she could think of for a moment. The feel of his lips on hers was unfamiliar and new but it was not in any way unpleasant. It felt warm and sweet and insistent. She instinctively eased a little closer.

"Catherine..." Ben's mouth left hers for a moment. His voice was ragged and when she heard it, Catherine's mind caught up with her body and the shock exploded in her head. This was Ben Hawksmoor and he was kissing her. Her mind reeled at the mere thought of it, but then she forgot to think rationally, forgot everything as his tongue parted her lips and a deep pleasure coursed through her, all the more startling for its wild and wicked edge.

Ben shifted slightly to draw her closer into his embrace. His tongue tangled with hers, she felt as though she were falling, and then she found herself lying on the soft cushions of the seat, pinned there by his body as the kiss became deeper and more intimate still. He held her there with his body against hers and kissed her for a long time while the carriage rumbled through the foggy streets and the sound of the wheels on the cobbles was lost in the sheer sensations that held her captive.

When Ben finally released her, Catherine felt utterly adrift with no idea how much time had passed. She felt his weight on her ease, felt his lips brush the corner of her mouth and drift with a feather-light touch across her cheek, and then she was free; free, breathless and utterly lost.

For a moment she lay still, shocked and bemused. Then the monotonous rolling of the wheels came back to echo in her head and she opened her eyes and looked up at Ben. There was a hard, heated expression on his face that half frightened, half excited her.

"I promised," he said roughly, "and I was within an ace of breaking my word. You would tempt a saint, Catherine, and I am nowhere near sainthood."

The carriage drew to a sudden and abrupt stop, and Ben pulled the curtain aside.

"We are in Millman Street," he said. His voice was still a little uneven. "I am certain it is not your precise destination but I doubt I can persuade you to vouchsafe your real address any more than I can convince you to tell me your real name."

Catherine gathered up the skirts of her domino in one shaking hand. "I can give you neither," she said. "Good night, my lord."

She was surprised that he opened the carriage door for her himself and jumped down to help her alight. His hands about her waist were firm and hard as he swung her to the ground and for a moment he stood there, holding her, and then he stepped back, raising her gloved hand to his lips in an old-fashioned gallant gesture and her heart almost melted where she stood.

"Good night, Catherine," he said.

In the hall at Guilford Street, Alice's strained expression eased into relief when she saw Catherine come through the door.

"I sent the hackney back for you, miss," she said. "I sent it straight away. Madam was ill. We had to get her home—"

"It does not matter," Catherine said. She felt bone-tired all of a sudden. "Lady Fenton is asleep?"

"Yes, madam. One of the maids is sitting with her."

"And my father?"

Alice's mouth turned down. "He will not be home tonight, Miss Catherine."

Catherine nodded. Yawning, she made her way to the study and replaced the bag of guineas in the drawer of the desk. Maggie was safe for now and she was home unscathed. Except that Catherine could never feel quite the same again.

She pressed her fingers to her lips. Her first kiss.

Ben had thought her a courtesan, yet he had still treated her with tenderness. And she, silly little fool that she was, was half in love with him for his gentleness—and because of that moment when she had looked in his eyes and seen the loneliness there. She had wanted to reach out and ease that isolation in him. It was what she had been doing all her life with Maggie, and Lily, and those she cared for. And the knowledge terrified her because in her own way she knew she was equally alone and that was why Ben felt like a kindred spirit.

Alice bustled in and pressed a beaker of hot choco-late into Catherine's hands and she drank urgently, drawing nearer to the study fire to try and quell her shivering. The simple truth was that she did not belong in Ben Hawksmoor's world and she had best remember that. She might be a changeling, caught between the world of trade and the world of the *Ton,* but the rich decadence of the regent's circle was another matter entirely. She did not understand it and it could ruin her.

The warmth of the fire was starting to dispel her chill now and the hot chocolate soothed her, making her sleepy. But one thing nagged at her mind. How to get Maggie's miniature back to Ben Hawksmoor without him knowing or being able to trace it back to her. Once that was over then the entire charade would be at an end. She would take it back as soon as she could. She wanted fiercely to be rid of the picture, rid of the whole situation and the need to deceive Ben Hawksmoor as to her identity. When she had become Miss Catherine Fenton, debutante, once more, she would never meet him again. It would be better that way.

She placed the empty beaker down on the desk next to Sir Alfred's copy of the *Times.* It was open at page four and a small paragraph at the bottom of the page caught her eye.

Benjamin, Lord Hawksmoor, has confirmed that he has called in the Bow Street Runners in the matter of the silverware stolen from his house several months ago. Lord Hawksmoor is offering a reward of one thousand

pounds for any information leading to the
arrest of the thief.
We are assured that a resolution of the case
is close....

The *Times* was the least sensational of newspapers
but those stark words struck cold into Catherine's
heart. She put the paper down slowly. The net was
closing on Maggie now. She had to act.

# CHAPTER FOUR

You are strongly advised to accept nothing from
a gentleman; considering how familiar they fre-
quently are we strongly advise you to decline
any advances.
—*Mrs. Eliza Squire,* Good Conduct for Ladies

ST. JAMES'S WAS NO PLACE for a lady to walk alone
after midnight, nor was a ball hosted by the most notorious man in society the kind of event that a debutante should ever consider attending.

Catherine paused outside the door of number
forty-three St. James's Place before she took a deep
breath and dived through the scrum into the hallway
beyond. Now that she was here she did not want to
go ahead with her plan, but loitering on the doorstep
was an invitation to every last libertine in the neigh-
borhood, and of those there were plenty. The road
in front of the house was thick with carriages.
People jostled on the pavement, shouting, waving,
wild with excitement. The light poured out of the
house into the foggy night beyond. Ben Hawksmoor
was hosting a ball for the Prince Regent and anyone

who was anyone in the demimonde was in attendance.

Catherine still could not quite believe that she had ventured out in the foggy London night one last time to return Maggie's portrait. It was cold. The sounds and smells of the city swirled about her. There was the scent of smoke and excitement on the air. London felt restless. It never slept. And Catherine had felt restless and excited, too, as well as more nervous than she had ever been in her life.

"No one must know," Maggie had said, clutching Catherine's hand so tightly that the diamonds in the miniature's silver frame had scored her palm. "You must take it back and no one must ever know…"

In the days since Maggie had consigned the picture to Catherine's care, it seemed she had forgotten all about it and Catherine was now left alone to deal with the problem. That was Maggie all over, Catherine thought. No doubt she *had* forgotten in the midst of her laudanum-induced stupor, or else she knew that her stepdaughter would not let her down and was taking advantage. Catherine sighed. The trouble was that Maggie was right. She knew she was too kind. But she could not change the way she was.

In the hackney carriage on the way to St. James's Catherine had seriously considered consigning the whole miserable package to the bottom of the Thames were it not for the fact that the river was still partially frozen. She knew that now that the hunt was on for the miniature, she could not sell it or even give it away without suspicion. Nor could she involve anyone else in the affair. She was trapped.

It was a week since she had met Ben at Crockford's, and not a day had passed that Catherine had not chafed against the delay in getting rid of the painting. She had not had a free evening in all that time, for first there had been a ball, then a musical soiree, then a trip to the theater with Withers, then Maggie had apparently recovered her spirits and wished to attend a concert. But then Catherine had seen in the *Court Circular* that the Prince Regent was attending a masquerade at Lord Hawksmoor's invitation on the seventeenth, and she had felt a huge relief. It was a way into Ben's house and, in a crowd, she was so much more likely to be able to evade his attention. She need only be there a moment. He would never know.

There was a black-clad butler inside the door. He looked impassive and terribly, terribly discreet, as though the discovery of a masked and cloaked lady on the doorstep was a commonplace occurrence, as no doubt it was at this particular address.

"I am a friend of Miss Lily St. Clare," Catherine said, hoping that her teeth were not chattering too loudly. "She was not able to attend tonight but suggested that I come in her place."

The butler smiled a discreet smile. "Of course, madam. This way please."

It was warm inside the house, luxurious, wonderfully relaxing. The air was scented with flowers and was full of the clamor of voices. Catherine walked slowly down the long corridor toward the ballroom.

This was not the type of event where a starchy butler announced the guests. Being incognito was part of the fun. The reception rooms were already overflowing with people drinking, gossiping, flirting, kissing and much, much more. Two men were entwined intimately together behind a group of statuary. Catherine looked, and felt her face flame. She was feeling hotter and hotter as Ben Hawksmoor's guests turned their blank masked faces toward her. Behind their disguise, the eyes followed her, avid and curious, malicious and sly. They were whispering about her. Someone put a hand out to draw her in, but she hurried past, her heart racing. This was all much, much more licentious than she had imagined. Indeed, her imagination could only take her so far and now she realized how little she knew or understood of life outside the confines of the debutante's world.

Not everyone had chosen the anonymity of a mask. Catherine was astonished to recognize a duchess, whom she had thought the very epitome of respectability, with her gown around her waist and her breasts being caressed by two gallants at once. Several gentlemen of the *Ton* who had always struck Catherine as rather staid were indulging in riotous horseplay with ladies clearly not their wives. Catherine drew her domino closer, intent on remaining unseen. Once she had worked out the design of the house, she could find the room that Maggie had described and leave the miniature where her stepmother had found it.

The ballroom door gaped before her and Catherine peered inside.

It was like no ball that she had ever witnessed before. They were dancing the waltz, a dance that Catherine had performed at Almacks the previous summer. The chaperones disapproved and whispered that it was improper but Catherine had seen little that was indecorous in the slow and stately circuits of the floor that the waltz had demanded. Until now. Now she could see how the waltz could be considered utterly licentious and abandoned, for in Ben Hawksmoor's ballroom the figures swooped and spun in each other's arms, shrieking with delight and taking every amorous opportunity that the dance offered.

Catherine froze. The Prince Regent—a very drunk Prince Regent—was swaying toward her, leaning heavily on the arm of a highly painted and huge-bosomed lady. He raised his quizzing glass and ogled Catherine as they passed until his inamorata pulled crossly on his arm to regain his attention. Then a ripple went through the crowd and Catherine caught her breath, for Ben was strolling toward her down the corridor. Clearly he had not bothered to dress for his own ball and amidst the overblown splendor of his guests his casual attire was more eye-catching than any evening dress could be. His buckskins shaped to his muscular thighs so closely that Catherine felt another wave of heat roll over her. He still wore his top boots and they had a mirror polish. He looked elegant and shockingly self-assured.

Catherine shrank back against the wall and was profoundly grateful as others surged forward in front of her. She saw Ben lean down to kiss the cheek of a lady in scarlet satin and whisper something in her ear, and the cyprian clung to his arm and her lips curved in a provocative smile and Catherine felt a little sick. She turned her head away as Ben walked past and waited until he and the crowd had vanished into the ballroom, then she seized a moment when there was no one about and hurried to the bottom of the stairs. It was quieter now, although she heard a door close down the corridor and the sound of a female giggle, cut off rather abruptly. No doubt Lord Hawksmoor's guests sought the seclusion of the other rooms for a little private dalliance and no doubt she should be long gone from the house by the time the party turned wilder still.

Catherine stood at the bottom of the stairs and gazed upward. The landing and the upper floor were shrouded in shadow. Maggie had been maddeningly vague in her directions, as she was in most things.

*"Up the staircase... The second door on the left... No, was it on the right? It was the room with the glass sculptures from Mr. Vane's studio—such pretty things, you know, Catherine—glass animals and flowers and all so delicate... Anyway, it was on the shelf in the chamber beyond.... You will find it easily enough...."*

Catherine untied her mask and tiptoed up the stairs, hoping that the treads would not creak. Tiptoeing quickly was a great deal more difficult than she had imagined. Her heart was hammering and she could feel her hands shaking. She had never trespassed in anyone's house before, least of all a house where a near-orgy was taking place. She could not recommend the experience to anyone but the most hardened thrill-seeker. It was far too nerve-racking.

The vision of Maggie's face was before her still and it was the only thing that drove her on to see this mad errand through to the end. Maggie had looked lost, distraught, baffled somehow, as though someone had struck her a grievous blow.

"No one must know…" she had said, but Catherine suspected that her father already knew—knew that his young wife had betrayed him with Ned Clarencieux. Kneeling beside Maggie that night as Sir Alfred's steps had come ever closer, as his voice had grown louder, as his presence had filled the room with fear, Catherine had known she had to help her stepmother or matters in the Fenton household would go terribly awry and never be well again. For John's sake, for Mirabelle's, for her own, to preserve the fragile peace that held them all together… She had no choice.

The hall landing was light and airy, lit by a single lamp, and painted in white with an artful arrangement of flowers on a table at the top of the stairs. One painting hung against the blank wall. It was a scene of the river at sunset in bold red and gold. Catherine remembered Maggie mentioning once that the Royal Academy had loaned a number of paintings to Ben Hawksmoor. Apparently they had paid him for the privilege of exhibiting in his home. As had John Vane, to display his glass sculptures, and Jasper French to show the exquisite silverware that Maggie had taken such a fancy to. The delicate silver miniature of her lover that Maggie had been unable to resist felt as though it were burning a guilty hole in Catherine's little silver reticule.

She opened the second door on the left and found that she was in a study. It was a very masculine room with a leather-topped desk and matching chair and a profusion of bills and letters tumbling to the floor. It did not look as though Ben Hawksmoor cared overmuch about paying his debts. No matter. She did not have time to stand here and deplore his extravagance. Anyone might discover her here at any moment.

Catherine crossed the landing surreptitiously and opened the second door on the right. This time she was in a drawing room. There was a sofa and matching chairs that were striped like a dowager's ball gown and some fine cherrywood tables. The carpet felt thick beneath her shoes. Ben had not lied when he had told her that ostentatious show was his aim, no matter the cost.

Catherine took the silver miniature from her pocket and slid it beneath the corner of the sofa so that its corner stuck out a half inch. Any maid worth her salt would spot that now and assume that the piece had fallen from the shelf and accidentally been swept beneath the sofa to lie undiscovered for the last few months.

Catherine rubbed her damp brow with the back of her hand. She felt almost light-headed with relief. Maggie was safe and no one would ever know, just as she had wished.

Catherine turned the doorknob and slipped out onto

the landing and in the same moment she heard the sound of hurried steps on the stair and a low masculine voice edged with anger.

"Get rid of everyone, Price. I am retiring. I do not care to entertain tonight. They are all so drunk they will not notice if you throw them out into the street."

There was a pause. "Yes, my lord." The butler sounded strained. "Was it the messenger, my lord? Is there anything amiss?"

"Nothing." Ben Hawksmoor was closer now and Catherine thought he sounded in a particularly bad mood. "Just get rid of them, Price. I will be upstairs."

"But the Prince Regent, my lord! I cannot simply turn him from the house—"

"He can go to his club," Ben snapped. "They all can. They can go to hell for all I care."

Catherine stopped dead. She had taken too long. She had known it. She should have been out of the house by now and away without needing to make explanations. And now Ben was here and she was trapped. She pressed her sticky palms against the cool white wall and tried not to panic.

Ben came round the corner of the corridor. He had what looked like a letter in one hand and, as she watched, he crumpled it into a ball and sent it spinning away. He looked absolutely furious. Then he raised his hand to loosen his neck cloth, leaving the neck of his shirt open. Catherine drew back on a gasp. There was something wild in his eyes, the same controlled violence that she had seen in him that day at Clarencieux's hanging.

It was only a matter of seconds before he realized

that she was there. Catherine's trapped mind ran desperately over whether it was better to step forward and reveal herself or wait and hope against hope that he might not notice her. And then it was too late. Ben saw her. And stopped dead.

He paused, drawing the crisp white stock between his fingers. For a moment Catherine was puzzled by the expression she saw in his eyes, for he was looking genuinely surprised, and then, fleetingly, so angry she almost flinched. But a second later she thought she must have been mistaken, for he smiled at her, that same brilliant smile that made her heart jump with fear and wayward excitement.

He was looking at her quite differently from the way he had done that night at Crockford's. Then there had been speculation in his eyes as well as desire. Now, it seemed, he was sure of her. She suddenly realized that in coming to his house she had confirmed his belief that she was a courtesan. He would think that she had fallen for temptation at last and taken advantage of the ball to seek him out because she wanted to make love with him. She was in all probability standing outside his bedroom door. By her presence she had just borne out everything he believed about her.

The heat flooded Catherine's body at the thought and receded equally quickly, leaving her shivering. How to get out of this tangle now? She had a fanciful idea that she could hear a trap closing. Instinctively she glanced behind her. The long corridor ended in a blank wall. There was only one way out—and Ben Hawksmoor was blocking it.

His lazy gaze raked her from head to foot. Hard, insolent, amused, his hazel eyes brought the hot color into her face and left her trembling. She knew he had every reason to think the things he did. She had flirted with him at Newgate out of sheer recklessness, had played the part of a courtesan to thwart the possessiveness of Withers, whom she detested. He had seen her with Lily and sent to the brothel to find her. Even when she had met him at the gaming hell, she had not revealed her true identity. How completely disastrous it was turning out to be. Because now came the reckoning.

"Good evening." Two words, and Catherine could actually feel her knees weakening. She leaned against the wall for support.

"I did not expect to see you here," Ben added. "Nor—" his appraising gaze raked her again "—to meet you like this, Catherine."

He took her hand. The impact on Catherine's senses correspondingly increased. A cool shiver ran along her skin. She tried to ignore it; tried to concentrate. Panic filled her. This man thought she was a demirep. She should tell him the truth at once, before this masquerade went too far. But how could she explain her presence in his house? If she stepped out of character, Maggie's secret would be revealed. Everyone would know she had been Clarencieux's lover. She would be divorced, disgraced, ruined.

Ben was standing very close to her now and Catherine found she was powerless not to look at him.

*Consorting with a gentleman is ruinous to a*

*young lady's reputation. If you seek out a gentleman
in his chambers you will no doubt reap the outcome
you deserve....*

It was not particularly helpful, Catherine thought, to
remember the words of one of her conduct manuals at
this late and rather hopeless stage in the proceedings. She
needed no book to tell her that she was in very big trouble
indeed. In that moment, she realized that Benjamin
Hawksmoor was a threat not simply because he was sophisticated and in control and she was not. He was dangerous to her because despite all she knew of him and
despite all she had seen, she still could not convince
herself that he was no more than an amoral scoundrel.
She wanted to believe that he was better than that.

Nevertheless she knew that this was not the time to
discuss it. She had to come up with a halfway decent
excuse for her presence in his house. And then she had
to run away.

Could she continue to carry this off? She was the
world's worst actress. In school plays at Miss Minsham's
Academy in Bath, they had usually given her the part of
prompter because her acting had been more famously
wooden even than the scenery. To continue to act the part
of a fashionable impure seemed impossible and yet she
had some advantages. She saw the expression in Ben
Hawksmoor's eyes and felt slightly dizzy. He already
believed she was a courtesan. He wanted to believe it
because he wanted her. That much she understood.

Downstairs the music had stopped and she could
hear the sounds of voices raised in protest at the abrupt
end of the ball.

"Has Lord Hawksmoor been taken ill, Price?" one lady was demanding.

"No, ma'am," Catherine heard the butler say. "He is merely being boring."

There was general laughter at this. Catherine could imagine the headlines in the paper the following day: Lord Hawksmoor Cancels His Own Ball on a Whim Because He Is Bored

Somehow, as always, he would get away with it.

The voices faded, the shadows shifted. Ben had not taken his eyes from her the whole time and Catherine's heart started to slam in long, hard beats.

"Well, Catherine," Ben repeated her name like a caress and Catherine's throat dried at his tone. "What are you doing here?"

"I…I came to thank you for the service you rendered me that night at Crockford's, my lord," Catherine said quickly. It was a poor excuse but it was all that she could think of in a hurry. "If you had not come to my aid that evening…" She stopped as she saw the flash of amusement in his eyes.

"I would have done a great deal more for you, Catherine, had you permitted it." Ben's voice was smooth, the smile still in his eyes. The implication of his words was crystal clear, even to someone of Catherine's limited experience. He was not talking about helping her into her carriage or some other blameless activity suitable for debutantes. He wanted to make love to her.

Catherine closed her eyes as the implications of the thought hit her and made her feel slightly faint. She opened them again quickly. Her wits were going a-begging just when she needed them. It was most unhelpful.

"So I understood, my lord," she said. "I told you when we last met that you could not tempt me."

"And yet you came here tonight," Ben murmured.

"As I said, I came to thank you."

Ben nodded, but Catherine knew he did not believe her. He thought they were engaged upon some kind of game, of which both he and she would know the rules. Except that she did not.

"Most people would send a note," Ben said, "rather than appear outside my bedroom door." He stepped in close. "Shall we set your gratitude aside now, Catherine—and speak of what we both want?"

Catherine's heart seemed to leap into her throat. Her fingers gripped her reticule tightly. So now the game was at an end and he had decided it was time to be direct. Perhaps that was how a gentleman conducted business with his inamorata. There was no need for pretty words or declarations of love because it was business after all.

Nevertheless, the look in his eyes practically robbed her of breath. It did not speak of business. It was very hot and very intense and it spoke of desire. It called up an answering tug of feeling within her that made her feel dizzy.

"I…" She cleared her throat. "It is not so simple…."

Ben rubbed his thumb thoughtfully over the palm of her hand and the caress sent tremors coursing through her whole body.

"There is always a way to get what one wants," he said. "Is it a matter of money? It generally is."

"No!" Catherine's exclamation was out before she could help herself. She blushed and cast her eyes down.

"No need to sound so indignant, sweetheart," Ben drawled. "It cannot be a matter of love—not with Withers—and everyone has their price. So what is yours?"

Catherine started to edge along the corridor toward the top of the stairs. He followed her, still amused, still predatory.

"Would you like a carriage and pair?" he suggested. "A pearl-and-diamond bracelet? Or are you more ambitious than that?" He considered her thoroughly and his scrutiny made color burn along Catherine's cheekbones.

"Yes," he said. "I think you might well be expensive. A town house and a diamond necklace at the least."

Catherine thought of the piles of jewelry her mother had left her, locked in the bank, and could not quite repress a smile.

"A lady would tell you that a diamond necklace requires ear drops to match," she said. She shook her head. "But no, my lord, I do not require such things."

Ben saw the smile and raised a brow. "Then you are unusual."

"That is certainly true," Catherine agreed.

He stretched out a hand and took the material of her domino between his fingers. It was a deep ruby velvet, very simple but very expensive.

"Perhaps you are right," he said slowly. "I may tell you plainly that I cannot afford such luxury anyway. But maybe that does not matter. Perhaps you came to me for something else? Revenge?" He smiled. "Or pleasure…"

Catherine's breath locked in her throat. This was getting very dangerous. Revenge on Withers… She could see that he might make that assumption. She had shown her disdain of Withers's possessiveness before. It had been that very defiance and her decision recklessly to flirt with Ben himself that had got her into this pickle in the first place.

As for pleasure… She swallowed convulsively. She only knew in the vaguest possible terms what he might be offering but still it was sufficient to make her catch her breath. The memory of his kisses clouded her mind, filling her with a strange longing. To be held by him, to be loved by him. It was well nigh irresistible.

"You do not understand," she said, drawing away.

He let her go. "Then explain to me," he said softly.

*Explain.* She could not. Not if she were to keep Maggie's secret safe. John, baby Mirabelle… Their future depended on her keeping the family together and covering Maggie's deceit.

Ben cast a look over his shoulder. "Although my guests have gone now, I would rather speak with you in private, Catherine. Come with me." He pushed the door of a room open and drew her inside.

Catherine's first wash of relief that it was not the drawing room where she had planted the painting was quickly superseded by shock as she realized it was a bedroom. She was in *Ben Hawksmoor's bedroom* now.

In one mistaken move, she was in a place that half the women in London aspired to visit.

Her fascinated gaze was drawn to an immense tester bed with a peacock-blue and silver cover. All of a sudden she remembered the words of the priest who had conducted the Sunday services for the students of Miss Minsham's Academy:

*The downward path is easy but there is no turning back.*

It seemed so long ago that she had sat in that hard pew, wriggling with both physical discomfort and moral unease. She had not really understood then what the priest was talking about but she knew it was something bad, something to do with hellfire and eternal damnation. But she understood now. Oh yes, she understood perfectly. It was just a pity that eternal damnation could sometimes appear so tempting….

She closed her eyes, opened them again, and determinedly blocked temptation from her mind.

"We cannot talk here!"

Her voice came out like a bat's squeak and she saw the amusement dance in his eyes.

"Are you nervous, sweetheart?" He shrugged his broad shoulders beneath the fine linen of his shirt. "I swear you have no cause to be."

He was slipping the velvet domino from her shoulders as he spoke.

"Yes, but I…" Catherine licked her lips. She was very bad at this and he was very good, and it was proving to be a fatal combination.

"There is no need to be afraid." He gestured toward

the table where a couple of fine crystal glasses reflected the light and a bottle full with red wine stood beside them.

"A drink, perhaps?" he said. "It might help you decide what you really want." A wicked smile curled the corner of his mouth. He gave her another long look. "You must be new to this. That would account for much."

Catherine drew in a deep breath. She had never really seen herself cut out for a harlot's progress before, but now she could see just how easy it might be with a man like Ben Hawksmoor. Maggie's desperate longing for a little excitement in a loveless marriage was no longer incomprehensible. There was something so seductive about being wanted. Her own affectionless life suddenly seemed like a wasteland. She had been brought up to repudiate every last thing that this man stood for yet the attraction she felt was ruthless.

Ben was close enough to her now that she could smell his skin and the faint scent of lime cologne. Her head spun. An icy chill swept through her veins, followed by a warmth that stung her blood.

"No… No drink, thank you," she said. Nothing but the truth would do now. "I must go. I am sorry but I fear I have made a mistake. I am quite out of my depth."

There was a smile lurking at the back of Ben's eyes. It was a smile that was intimate and sensual. Catherine trembled. Damn the man and his charming, dangerous ways.

"I see," he said. He laughed and straightened. His hand came up to capture her chin and tilt it up so that her eyes met his. His touch was gentle. "I do believe you are," he agreed, and there was something close to surprise in his tone.

Catherine cleared her throat. "The truth is that I am not accustomed to dealing with men like you," she said.

Ben's eyes danced. "What sort of man do you think I am?"

"You are what my schoolteacher would have called *a detrimental*," Catherine said. "You are too dangerous."

He accepted the assessment with an inclination of the head. "But you like that, do you not, Catherine? It is what attracts you to me. You cannot be here to bargain your favors for my money since I have none. So…" He paused. "You must want the danger I offer."

The shocking truth of his words hit Catherine and silenced her for a moment. He did not know the real reason for her visit, of course—he could never be permitted to know—but there was still much more than a grain of truth in what he said. She had always thought herself to be a sensible young lady but the contradiction lay in her response to his touch. She ached for him with a need that was neither sensible nor respectable. And, here in his bedroom, she was beginning to fear that convention could not overcome her desires.

While she hesitated, Ben put out a hand and caught her wrist. The sudden contact took her by surprise. It brought the palm of her free hand up against his chest so that she could feel the heat of him through the linen shirt. His fingers came up to touch her cheek, smoothing back the strands of rich brown hair, lingering in the feather-soft curls.

"I understand that you are having second thoughts about what we are doing," he said. His voice was slightly husky. "I would not hurry you."

"Yes," Catherine said. She swallowed hard. "I mean no." She was getting well beyond second, third or even fourth thoughts now.

"If you have changed your mind," Ben murmured, "I am going to have to let you go. A pity, but as I said before, I would never force myself on you."

Catherine's first flash of relief was lost as he bent his head and brought his mouth down on hers. She stiffened with surprise but she did not resist. The memory of the kiss in his carriage was with her now, mingled with the new sensations evoked by the touch of his lips. She thought that she should pull away but she did not, and he groaned and slanted his mouth against hers hungrily, searchingly. The pleasure curled down to her toes and swept back through her whole body and she felt weak with excitement. And then it was over and Ben was standing back.

"If we meet again I won't let you go," Ben said, a rough edge to his voice. "I do not want to." He gestured toward the door. "Take your chance, Catherine. Before we both let this go too far."

"We will not meet again," Catherine said. Her voice came out as a thread of a whisper. The miniature was returned, the secret kept. She was going to leave. It was all over.

She felt his hands slide caressingly down her arms from shoulder to elbow, and she tried not to tremble. She was not successful. She could feel herself shaking and she knew he could feel it, too.

"Then," he said, his lips a mere inch from hers, "if I am never to meet you again I shall have to kiss you one last time. I shall always wonder what might have been."

Catherine raised her lips the last inch to meet his. She was lost as soon as they touched, lost and adrift, the cold fire burning in her veins. This time her lips parted instinctively and his tongue touched hers slowly, stroking deep. His hand tangled in her hair, tilting her head up so that he could take all he wanted from her mouth, plundering its sweetness. Catherine gasped against his lips and he took advantage to deepen the kiss further still.

"Are you sure," Ben said softly, as he released her, "that you would not prefer to stay after all?"

Catherine pulled away from him. There was a hard, bright light of desire in his eyes. She felt hot inside, and faint and hollow with longing. She felt appalled that Ben Hawksmoor could do this to her when she did not really know him and yet she wanted to feel the touch of his hands on her body. She wanted it more than anything else in the entire world. And though Ben made no move toward her, he kept his eyes on her face and she felt the powerful tug of need between them with an almost irresistible force.

For a second, Catherine saw a different world, the world that Maggie knew, full of sensual excitement. It was vivid with color and it shimmered with temptation. She was twenty-one years old and her life was empty of warmth, barren of love since she had been a child. She was betrothed to a man whom she detested, duty-bound to a marriage she could not bear even to think of. But she made herself think about it now; made herself concentrate on all the empty tomorrows that stretched ahead of her into an icy-cold infinity. It made her heart ache with loneliness.

She could walk away from Ben Hawksmoor now. She knew he would let her go. And if she did, she could spend tomorrow and all those empty days reminding herself of her good sense and trying to blot out her loneliness. She would always wonder what might have happened. She would always regret that she had been too afraid to find out.

She had reached a point where she longed for something different. This was the moment and this was the man.

She looked at Ben and saw the naked desire in his eyes and felt the fear and longing explode within her. He was waiting. He did not move. It seemed that the moment spun out between them forever, so weighted with significance that he would not do anything to influence her one way or the other. Except that he already had.

She wanted him desperately.

She closed her eyes for a second and stretched out a hand to him and when she felt him take her hand in his she almost fainted with relief.

He did not pounce on her as she had thought he might, but drew her to him gently, into his arms, and for a moment his cheek rested against hers as it had done when he had held her at the hanging. Something broke within her then, something dangerously like love, and she turned her mouth up to his in blind need. He kissed her softly, her lips, her cheekbones, her eyelashes, and with each touch she could feel her resistance weakening further until it was all but gone. Her heart was slamming in long hard strokes but all she could think of was that she did not know what to do to accomplish her own seduction and he would have to help her or she would die with longing. Then he spoke.

"I need to get you out of these clothes."

His voice was hoarse and Catherine felt another stab of pure desire to hear it. Her breasts felt tight against the material of her bodice and there was a hot quivering need low in her stomach that she realized with a shock must be the physical signs of the desire that was turning her heart and her mind inside out. To be rid of her clothes seemed imperative. She turned obediently and felt his fingers among her buttons and laces. His hands slipped, and she heard him swear softly with a note of impatience in his voice.

The material gave suddenly and the air touched the skin of her back, a shocking counterpoint to the warmth of Ben's hands as they caressed her. He eased the dress away from her and bent to kiss her bare shoulder, his hair brushing her skin. His hands lingered, stroking her gently. Then the gown crumpled to the floor and Catherine's stays fell away, leaving her standing in nothing but her shift and her stockings.

Ben moved away from her and she turned to look at him, watching with fascination and awe as he tore his shirt off to reveal a strongly muscled chest and broad shoulders. His skin was golden in the candlelight and the sight of him stole the last of her breath. She felt fearful for a moment, afraid of the barely restrained sensuality that she could see turning his hazel eyes dark with passion. The intensity of the awareness between them seemed to hang on the air like lightning. It was too late to change her mind now but she found she did not want to. A part of her was afraid but the stronger part was excited, too, drawn to him and to the warmth and promise of his embrace.

He picked her up and placed her on the bed, following her down into its softness. His fingers were busy in her hair—she had not pinned it up, merely confining it with a ribbon that he now pulled free. She heard his breath catch as he spread her hair across the pillow and raised a strand to his lips.

"You are very beautiful."

No one had ever called Catherine beautiful before. She had not even thought of the word and of herself as having any connection. She started to smile in wonderment but Ben dipped his head and kissed her, and suddenly the gentleness was gone and his kiss was hungry and demanding. Before Ben, no one had ever kissed Catherine, and she had certainly never dreamed of such an embrace but now she recognized it instinctively as a statement of possession. She made a soft, sweet sound against his mouth and heard him groan in response.

His lips left hers and brushed her throat with a feather-light touch.

"Catherine… Kate…"

Her heart jumped to hear that name on his lips. She had not been called Kate for so long. It belonged to a past time, a time of warmth and love, a time she had lost. Now it felt as though she might regain it. She savored the thought for a moment but then forgot it as she felt his hands on her shift, drawing it over her head, discarding it.

She was naked. For a moment she felt too exposed, too apprehensive, but his mouth was at her breast and she forgot everything else in the splintering sensation of need that consumed her whole body. She arched upward to the demand of his lips as he suckled, flicking with his tongue at her nipple until it was so hard and sensitive that she could scarcely bear the feeling. She writhed beneath his hands, her own sliding down his back until they reached the barrier of his breeches. The material felt smooth to her fingertips but she wanted to be rid of it, wanted to touch him. The instinct no longer startled or shocked her. She was driven by pure need now and no sense of shame or convention could restrain her. When he left her for a moment to remove the remainder of his clothes, all she wanted was to have him back, skin to skin, his nakedness against hers.

He lay back down beside her and she opened dazed eyes to look at his body, now revealed in all its hard and muscular perfection. She was not entirely ignorant of the male physique—in the past when Withers had held her and tried to kiss her she had been aware of his arousal and the thought of what it had meant had sickened her. Now, however, she could not resist stretching out a hand in awe and curiosity to touch Ben. He felt silky soft but when she ran her fingers tentatively along his erection he caught her wrist in a grip that made her gasp.

"Not this time," he said, "or I shall disgrace myself. I want you too much."

*Not this time...*

Catherine trembled to think of doing it again. Her mind was a dark spiral of sinful, erotic thoughts that clamored for release. Ben slid one palm down over her bare stomach until it reached the soft hair at the top of her thighs. As though he sensed the last shreds of her uncertainty, he leaned over and kissed her again, wooing her to relax and open to him.

The muscles low in Catherine's belly jumped and contracted as he caressed her. He stroked her thigh with slow persuasion and she parted for him, and then he was touching the moist hot core of her, slipping inside. Catherine moaned. It was exquisite but it was not enough. It was nowhere near enough.

With a sudden movement, as though he could wait no longer, Ben rolled over and pressed her thighs more firmly apart. Catherine opened her eyes. There was a look on his face that she recognized as a mirror of the emotions within her, a look of vulnerability and hunger and desire that turned her heart inside out.

And then he took hold of her hips and she felt him thrust inside her and the penetration was sharp and uncomfortable and almost made her cry out. Catherine's exquisite pleasure dissolved into pain far more quickly than she could ever have imagined.

She lay still, half her mind grappling with the discomfort and the other half reeling from the sudden, cold realization that she had lost her virginity. How could such pure pleasure turn into such disappointment? It seemed most unfair. All the thoughts flew through her head in a split second and then Ben moved slightly, and this time she did catch her breath on a gasp of mingled pain and frustration. She felt him go very still.

"Damn it to *hell*—"

He was not thinking she was a courtesan now. The weight of his body on her was withdrawn, he moved away, and suddenly Catherine felt sore and lonelier than she ever had done in her life before. The stark contrast with what had been happening a moment ago was too much to accept. The emptiness flooded back into her heart. For one dreadful moment she thought she was going to burst into tears as everything she had longed for seemed to vanish from before her eyes. All the intimacy, all the warmth, all the comfort she had thought she could find seemed a hollow sham and suddenly she was no more than yet another foolish debutante who had been betrayed by her own naiveté and her desperate search for love.

*Love.* She could not bear the thought now of how close she had come to thinking herself in love with

Ben Hawksmoor when the truth was that she did not know him at all. She had been desperately attracted to him and had mistaken her fascination for something deeper, something he did not, had not ever, reciprocated. She had thought he had a tenderness for her beneath that practiced charm. Now she realized that he was every bit as cynical and ruthless as he had appeared. The humiliation of the deception she had played on herself burned her throat with tears.

She tried to slip from beneath the covers but he was too quick for her, catching her arm and pulling her back over to face him.

He looked utterly furious and she quailed at the rage in his eyes.

"Oh no you don't," he said coldly. "You do not run away from me now, *Miss Catherine Fenton*. Not until you tell me what the *devil* that was all about."

BEN RELEASED HIS HOLD on Catherine's arm, swung himself over the edge of the bed and searched rather irritably for his clothes. He felt tired and no longer aroused, although his body felt cheated. That made him still angrier. He was furious with Catherine but he was far more furious with himself. Without the dangerous seduction of desire to sway his judgment, he could see perfectly well that the girl in his bed was a virgin; or at the least she had been until he had made love to her. Her eyes were wide with apprehension and shock now. She held the sheet right up to her chin and she was biting her lip in a gesture that made him want to kiss her. That feeling alone, after what had just happened, was enough to irritate him almost beyond measure.

The anger and frustration slammed through him again in a physical wave, as it had done earlier in the evening when Tom Bradshaw's message had arrived in the middle of the ball. Despite the presence of his guests, he had stepped aside to read it at once. It was too important not to.

There had been various pieces of information in the letter relating to Algernon Withers; dates, places, details of relatives, his fortune, his business interests and a warning that he was involved in some very crooked dealings indeed. Bradshaw had noted Withers's mistress as one Emily Spraggett, a raddled old doxy who no doubt catered to Withers's lowest desires. At the time, Ben had been briefly amused, re- membering what he had told Bradshaw about coveting Withers's mistress. No doubt the man would think him even more depraved that he already did.

And then his eye had fallen on the next lines that Bradshaw had written:

Lord Withers is betrothed to a Miss Catherine Fenton, daughter of the merchant Sir Alfred Fenton. It seems that he and the Fentons are involved together in criminal dealings although at present I do not know the extent of these because they keep close counsel. I also believe Miss Fenton to be a fashionable impure who may have been involved with Mr. Clarencieux. Certainly he was engaged in an affaire with a lady late last year thought by my informers to be Miss Fenton, and this would be a link between Clarencieux and Lord Withers. More information when I have it. Yours, Bradshaw.

Ben had been possessed by a blistering fury when he had read those words. He knew that it was not unknown for the daughters of the merchant class to become cyprians if they thought it would profit them. However, the thought of Catherine being betrothed to Algernon Withers and he acting as some sort of complaisant procurer was distasteful even to a man of Ben's broad experience. Worse was the suggestion that she had been involved in a love affair with Ned Clarencieux. Withers must have known. Probably he had orchestrated it. The thought of Catherine implicated in Withers's criminal dealings, as corrupt and venal as he, caused a red mist to rise before Ben's eyes. Something had snapped in his mind then. He thought of Catherine flirting with him and no doubt laughing with Withers afterward over every little detail. Perhaps they planned to use him and bring him down as they had Ned Clarencieux. He thought of the way Catherine had clung to him at Newgate when Clarencieux might well have been swinging on the end of that rope because of something that she and Withers had arranged between them. Bradshaw had implied as much and his intelligence was the best in town.

The desire had flooded back into him, sharper than ever before, to take Catherine and use her and throw her back to Withers in contempt. It would be an uncivilized revenge, but one that they both thoroughly deserved.

The anger had been enough to send him storming out of his own party. And then he had seen Catherine, there in his house, and he had been astounded at her brass-faced audacity and had lost his temper and his self-control comprehensively for the first time in as long as he could remember. He had acted out the game then by the rules she set, playing along with her pretense at hesitation and modesty, and all the time intending to confront her once they had made love and he had slaked his need for revenge.

Only it had not been like that. The hell of it was that she had seemed so sweet and so innocent that he had all but forgotten his original intentions in the bliss of making love to her. Until he had taken her virginity and realized in that one terrible, catastrophic moment that Miss Catherine Fenton was not, in that respect, at all what he had thought her to be. She could not be the fashionable impure that Bradshaw had claimed.

"I did not realize that you knew my name." Her voice was very quiet.

Ben swung round on her, his anger—with her, with himself—so great that he could barely keep his voice from shaking.

"I knew who you were all along."

He saw her close her eyes briefly and open them again, and the pain that shimmered in them made him feel vaguely sick.

"I do not understand," she said. "If you knew I was no courtesan, why—"

"Why did I treat you like one?" Ben shrugged. "You threw yourself at me so I took you. How was I to know you were still a virgin? You have behaved like a whore since we met."

He heard her catch her breath and thought for a moment that she was going to cry but she did not. He admired her for that. He also knew that he was blaming her when he was at least partially culpable. He had believed her to be a cyprian but only because he had *wanted* to believe it. He should have recognized from the first time they had met that she was a lady of quality, an innocent, but he had overridden that instinct in his desire to bed her.

He thought about what Bradshaw had said in the letter, implying that she was implicated in all Withers's unscrupulous schemes.

"Did Withers make you play the whore for me?" he asked, deliberately cruel. "Was it part of his plans?"

Her eyes went blank with shock. "Of course not! I do not understand what you mean—" She broke off, her face bleak with disillusionment. "I see," she added after a moment. "That is what you think of me—that Lord Withers and I had some plan afoot?"

"Withers threatened me," Ben said. "And you are his fiancée, and involved in all his business dealings, so I understand."

"You understand incorrectly." There was temper in her voice now. "I know nothing of Withers's grubby dealings, nor do I wish to."

So she had been innocent of that as well. How could Bradshaw have been so wrong? Damn, and damn and damn it all to hell and back.

Ben picked up his crumpled shirt and shrugged himself into it, then drew on his breeches.

"Then I hope," he said bitingly, turning back to look at her, "that you have another, particularly good explanation for this situation, Miss Fenton."

Her head was bent, the soft fall of chestnut hair hiding her expression from him. Ben remembered the silken slither of it through his fingers and almost cursed aloud. Hell, it had been months since he had bedded a woman and now that he had broken his self-imposed celibacy, it was to find that the knowing courtesan he thought he was seducing was nothing but a virginal debutante.

Conscience flicked him. He tried to ignore it. It was the first time in years that his conscience had troubled him at all. He had almost forgotten that he had one.

"If your aim was entrapment I fear you have chosen the wrong man," he said. "You will have to make do with Lord Withers. I never offer for debutantes regardless of what I have done to them."

In truth he never offered anything to any woman, debutante or otherwise. But this was the first time he had seduced an innocent.

He saw the color drain from her face at his words. "I did not seek to entrap you, Lord Hawksmoor," she said. She looked down her nose at him, which struck Ben as rather comical. There was a dignity about her despite her lack of clothing that only served to emphasize that she was a lady.

"I had heard that you never do the decent thing, so why should you start now?" she said. "Besides, you are the last man on earth I would choose to marry. You are far from ideal."

Ben could not argue with that. "Then if you were looking only for some excitement to boast about to your debutante friends and it went too far—" He broke off. The look on her face told him she was not the type to go foolishly seeking adventure and then cry about it later. She had too much character for that.

"You are far out in your assumptions," she said, "and I owe you no explanation."

"Yes you do!" Ben moved suddenly, grabbing her arms. The sheet slipped, revealing the upper curves of her breasts. He tried not to look. He could not help himself. Her skin was pale and soft and he felt the same shocking desire for her that had possessed him earlier. He let her go as quickly as he had grabbed her.

"You used me to relieve you of your virginity," he said slowly.

Her lashes flickered. "It was not like that. I did not intend…" She stopped, then raised her chin. "I should like to get dressed now, if you please."

It did not please him. He wanted to keep her there, naked, in his bed but he knew he could not. He stood up and made a slight, ironic gesture.

"Please do so."

She glared at him with defiance in her dark eyes. "Kindly turn your back."

Ben laughed. "A pointless exercise in modesty."

She held the sheet scrunched beneath her chin and her gaze was dangerous. "Please do as I ask."

Ben shrugged and turned away. His senses seemed unnaturally alert. He heard the rustle of the bedclothes as she put them aside and caught a flash of her pale nakedness out of the corner of his eyes. He could tell she was dressing as quickly as possible. He knew she wanted to be away from him and the thought flayed him alive.

"I cannot do up my top buttons," she said, and at last he heard a hint of something approaching despair in her voice.

Ben turned around. The effect of her dressing herself without a maid was naturally haphazard and she looked adorable. He realized it and felt annoyed all over again. From the start he had wanted her with an emotion more complicated than mere lust. He should have recognized his danger and left well alone.

"Come here, then," he said.

She came, reluctantly. He brushed the tousled hair away from the nape of her neck and set to fastening the remaining buttons. When his fingers touched her skin accidentally, he heard her quietly gasp and the anger dug into him again like a spur. Could she not bear for him to touch her now? He finished and caught her by the arm, spinning her around to face him.

"A moment. You will tell me why you came here tonight."

Their eyes locked.

"No," she said after what seemed an hour to him. "I cannot. I will not." She turned away to pick up her domino and her hair fell forward, shielding her expression from him once again, shutting him out. His frustration mounted.

"I do not understand," he said.

She turned back and for a moment Ben thought he saw a flash of pain in her face beneath the defiant smile.

"You do not need to understand, Lord Hawksmoor," she said. "You made no promises and I asked for nothing. And we will not see one another again. I swear I will not seek you out." She slipped the domino about her shoulders. "It was no more than a mistake, and a disappointing one at that. Good night."

*A disappointing mistake.*

Ben stood quite still as the door of the bedroom closed behind her. He could hear the faint tread of her footsteps fading away down the corridor and then silence.

He had been walking away from situations like this for all of his adult life, he realized, yet when Catherine walked away from him it was deeply unsatisfactory. Rather like Catherine's first experience of lovemaking. A self-deprecating smile twisted his lips. She had not been wrong. In the end it had been very far from pleasurable, although before that it had been absolutely exquisite....

His body responded to the thought but he ignored it and tried to concentrate. He had robbed a young woman of her virginity yet she had sworn she had no wish to entrap him into marriage. Perhaps the morning would give the lie to that when an angry father or intemperate brother arrived on the doorstep with a shotgun. He shrugged. If that were the case, it would cause a huge scandal but in the end Catherine would be the one to suffer. The *Ton* expected such behavior from him. The lady was always the one whose reputation was ruined.

Ben went over to the table and poured some wine into one of the crystal glasses, drinking deeply. To his surprise, he found he did not like the thought of Catherine's reputation being ruined, of some other man spurning her as a fallen woman. He hated the hypocrisy of society in such matters. Yet now he had put her in precisely the situation where that might happen. And if she were to bear a child, she would be utterly destroyed. He froze as the possibility struck him for the very first time. It was unlikely, but it was not impossible.

It was so long since Ben Hawksmoor had suffered the twin torments of guilt and responsibility that he barely recognized them. He had done plenty of things in his life that would have caused another man to lose sleep but he had always been able to forget them. Until now.

He put his glass of wine down slowly. He needed brandy and he needed it now. He rang the bell for Price, his butler.

*I had heard that you never do the decent thing, so why should you start now?*

Catherine's words echoed in his head. Ben winced. She had an uncanny knack for getting to the point of things.

Price arrived with a bottle. His butler knew his tastes.

In fact, his butler generally knew everything. Ben had always found it essential to have good intelligence at his disposal. It kept him a step ahead of the game.

Ben saw the butler's gaze take in his state of undress and the tumbled bedclothes, but although Price's lugubrious expression deepened, he made no comment. Ben was accustomed to Price's disapproval from twelve years experience. He could still visualize the expression on Price's face when he had been assigned as his batman when Ben had joined the regiment all those years ago. Price had looked like a man who had just realized that fate was punishing him for some terrible wrong he had not even been aware that he had committed. His mournful face—fatter then, but still with its pursed lips and sucking-on-lemons expression—had fallen ludicrously before he had recovered himself, given a slight, precise bow and muttered, "Very good, sir," to the commanding officer. And Ben had not been particularly surprised at his new manservant's reaction. Serving the hell-raising, outcast son of a wastrel baron was nothing to boast about in the barracks.

Since then, Ben had inherited the wastrel baron's title, but he suspected that Price thought that this was very little to boast about either.

The butler placed the tray on the table and unstoppered the brandy decanter.

"I secured a hackney carriage for the young lady, my lord," Price said suddenly. "This is no night for a lady of quality to be out alone."

Ben looked at him. The thought of Catherine flee-

ing his bed and Price calmly calling a hack for her
made his mind boggle. There was a tone of reproach
in the butler's voice that made him wince a little. He
had enough disapproval of his own conduct not to
wish to tolerate his butler's disapprobation.

He turned the brandy glass idly around in his hands.
"Did you hear where Miss Fenton instructed the hack
to take her?"

Price's mouth turned down at the corners. "Yes, my
lord."

There was a short silence. Ben raised a brow. "I beg
your pardon, Price. Clearly I did not explain myself
adequately. Do you know the lady's destination *so
that you can tell me?*"

The butler looked haughty. "I understand, my lord,"
he said. "The lady asked for Mrs. Desmond's House
of Enchantment, in Covent Garden."

Ben felt shocked. It was another emotion so alien to
him that for a second he failed to recognize it. So few
things shocked him these days. But suddenly nothing
was making any sense anymore. It was true that he had
seen Catherine in company with a Lily St. Clare, a
cyprian from Mrs. Desmond's brothel. It was one of the
things that had misled him as to her quality. But what
was irrefutably true was that she had been no whore
herself. He knew that now, now that it was too late.

The questions hammered at his mind. Why had
Bradshaw thought her guilty when she was surely no
more than an innocent caught up in Withers's intrigue?
And if she was innocent, why had she come to his
house that night?

He put his brandy down abruptly, repelled by the smell of alcohol, and ran a hand through his hair.

"I do not understand," he said slowly.

"No, my lord." Price sounded very lugubrious indeed.

Ben frowned. He was accustomed to young ladies of good family conceiving a *tendre* for him, although none of them had ever taken matters this far. Plenty of them sent him love notes drenched in lavender water and proffering impassioned declarations of naive worship. He threw them in the fire. Then there were the women who sent him their unmentionables—a variety of underclothes from wisps of lace to bodices the size and consistency of sacks, to suit every imaginable sexual taste—and wrote of all the things they would like him to do to them in bed. He usually threw those letters in the fire as well. Debutantes and harlots did not interest him. Nothing interested him.

Nothing except Catherine, who had stepped into his bedroom hiding her innocence behind a facade of semi-sophistication and had ended up being ruthlessly seduced, as much by her own desires as by his. And yet despite what had happened, Ben's instinct told him that she had not come originally either to seduce or to compromise him.

"Do you know why she came here tonight, Price?" he said slowly.

"I think I may do, my lord." Price reached into the pocket of his coat and held out something in the palm of his hand. "I found this in the drawing room, my lord. It was not there earlier. It *was* there after the lady left. Thus the conclusion is inescapable, my lord."

Ben took the silver miniature from Price's outstretched hand and stared down in shock at Ned Clarencieux's smiling face. The theft of the painting had caused him an inordinate amount of trouble. It had gone missing after one of his riotous parties the previous year and at first he had hoped someone had merely taken it as a joke. But then the silversmith had insisted on being reimbursed for the whole sum, picture and silver frame together. Ben could not afford to pay, but nor could he afford to lose French's patronage nor that of his colleagues. In the end he had had to extend his debt with Henshalls, the moneylenders, and he had called in the Bow Street Runners, although he'd had little hope of them discovering the piece no matter what they claimed in the papers. And now here it was. Catherine Fenton had brought it back.

Bradshaw had said that she was connected with Clarencieux, had suggested that she had been his mistress. But that could not have been true. Ben had the irrefutable proof. Further, she had disclaimed all involvement in Withers's affairs and he had believed her because her shock and horror at his accusation had been so acute it could not have been feigned. Some debutantes did become involved with unsuitable men. In Ben's experience, men and women alike had strong feelings and emotions that would lead them into all manner of behavior whether that behavior happened in the bordellos of Covent Garden or the drawing rooms of Berkeley Square. His own blatant stupidity had just proved it. But it had also proved that Ned Clarencieux had not been Catherine's lover. And in that case, how had Clarencieux's miniature come into her possession?

Suddenly Ben wished heartily that he had paid more attention to Clarencieux's amours. His friend's affaires had been as numerous and varied as his own were not, and he had never really been interested in Ned's fleeting fancies.

Of one thing he was certain. He had an absolute conviction that he had never met Catherine before the day of the hanging. If she had been to his house with Ned, even for a masked ball, he would have seen her, spoken to her, felt her presence....

He shook his head sharply. It was madness to imply that he would have known her, recognized her on some deeper level. She was no different, no more important to him than any other pretty girl. He had some guilt over the way he had treated her but that was all.

He realized with a sudden flash of intuition that on all the occasions she had met him, Catherine had never wanted him to know her full name nor guess her identity. She had never told him, nor had he seen her in her true persona. When he had addressed her as Miss Fenton that night, she had been shocked. And with the discovery of the miniature, her imposture suddenly made perfect sense. She had not wanted him to know her true identity because she had a secret to keep.

"I must find her and get the truth from her," he said softly. "This has something to do with Ned and Withers, and I cannot simply let it lie."

"Will that be all, my lord?" There was a gruff note of disapproval in Price's voice.

"Yes, thank you," Ben said.

"Very good, my lord." The old soldier's tone was still grumpy.

Ben gave him a quizzical look. "Disapprove of me, do you, Price?"

"Not my place, my lord." Price was stiff.

"But if it *was* your place…"

Price drew himself up. "That lady was no piece of Haymarket ware, my lord. Nor is she guilty of whatever it is you seem to suspect of her. Have you lost all judgment that you treat a lady with such contempt? Your behavior has been despicable."

There was a long pause. Ben glanced from the disheveled bedcovers to his butler's furious face. "I see. Thank you for your observations, Price."

"My lord." The butler's tone had eased slightly now that he had got his feelings off his chest, but he made no move to leave. Ben raised a brow. "Was there something else, Price? Some further strictures on my behavior, perhaps? Be assured that I can take it. My shoulders are broad."

"You sail too close to the wind, my lord." Price sounded more resigned than critical now. "This matter of Mr. Clarencieux, my lord… He had powerful enemies. You will overreach yourself."

Ben nodded. "I do believe you are correct, Price. Thank you. That will be all."

The butler hesitated. "You came through Bussaco and Salamanca, my lord," he said, "and since then you have done nothing but attempt to get yourself killed. Why throw your life away drowning in the Thames or challenging some fellow to a duel over a trifling gambling debt, or digging into matters that can only lead to trouble?"

There was a pause. Ben felt nothing but coldness where his heart should be.

What was the answer to Price's question? *I will throw my life away because there is nothing better to do with it?* All he knew was that he could never go back to the filthy streets and the hungry days and the desperation of poverty.

"I said that will be all, Price."

"My lord."

The door closed behind Price with a reproachfully quiet click and Ben reached automatically for the brandy bottle. He poured for himself, but then stood with the glass untouched in his hand as he stared into the fire. Tonight was unsettling. Price had raised questions he would rather not face and Catherine had stirred emotions he did not even know he possessed. Perhaps that was why his feelings about her seduction had turned out to be so much more complicated than he would ever have imagined. This did not feel like something he could merely walk away from. It had been a betrayal of innocence, unpardonably cruel. It was unforgivable.

Ben shifted uncomfortably. He had done a number of unforgivable things in his life and had still managed to forget them. Perhaps in time his conscience would be stilled on this matter, too.

Except that he had to go after Catherine. He wanted to know how she had come by the miniature and why she had brought it back.

There was a knock at the door.

"I wished to remind you that Mr. Hilliard will be here to paint you early in the morning, my lord." Price was at his most formal.

"Thank you," Ben said. "I will make sure I am available." He sighed as the door closed once again. No doubt Price disapproved of portrait painters as well as everything else. When the project had first been mooted, he had thought Price was going to have an apoplexy. His face had reddened and swelled with outrage, and Ben had thought he was going to tell him that no red-blooded man would ever act as an artist's model. It simply was not British.

He threw himself down in the armchair. He could not afford to turn down good money on a commission like this. Hilliard needed a model and he needed cash. He was perpetually short of it. He had a mouldering mausoleum of a country house that was mortgaged to perdition, and it cost a fortune to sustain his lifestyle. And he would never, *ever,* go back to the poverty he remembered from his youth. The thought brought him out in a cold sweat. He could feel it prickling between his shoulder blades. The fear of financial ruin stalked him like a malign ghost. Sometimes he thought that he would never be free of it. Sometimes he thought he would be better off dead.

The sound of Price's measured tread in the corridor outside raised him from his reverie. Tomorrow Price, bless him, would help Hilliard to carry his easel, canvases and paints, no matter how much he despised the man's profession. For a moment Ben felt something dangerously akin to affection for his old servant. Then, more practically, he prayed that they would not dislodge any of the statuary on display in the hall when Hilliard arrived. He had borrowed it, the shop being flatteringly eager to have their wares exhibited in his home. He could not afford actually to pay for it.

And after he had sat for Hilliard, he would track down Miss Catherine Fenton, debutante, and demand that she tell him the truth about Clarencieux's portrait. He would concentrate on that sole matter and refuse even to think about the sublime pleasure he had found in taking her to his bed. He tried to dismiss his recollection of the softness of her skin beneath his hands and the warmth and sweet taste of her as she had parted her lips to allow him in, but the memory of her stubbornly refused to be dislodged. Suddenly the thought of posing through an interminably long sitting with Hilliard seemed intolerable. He would be thinking about Catherine the whole time and then—he looked down in exasperation—he would have an erection of monstrous proportions again, which simply would not do when Hilliard was supposed to be painting him in the guise of King Edward the Confessor. He doubted that the saintly monarch had ever felt the sort of earthly lust that was troubling him now.

With an oath, he reached for his jacket and flung open the bedroom door. He could not simply sit here while Catherine was in some Covent Garden bordello. He had to find her now. He had to ask her what was going on. He had to find out about the miniature.

He passed Price in the hallway.

"I am going out, Price," he said. "To Covent Garden. Pray do not wait up for me."

And as he strode past, he had the strangest impression that Price was actually smiling. He turned quickly to check, but the butler's face was impassive once more.

"Of course, my lord," Price said, as though he had known all along that this would be the inevitable course Ben would take.

# CHAPTER FIVE

If you are engaged to another man and accept the attentions of anyone other *than* your affianced husband, your conduct is reprehensible and disgraces you.
—*Mrs. Eliza Squire*, Good Conduct for Ladies

LADY PARIS DE MOINE WAS sitting in front of her dressing table in a state of extreme *déshabillé*. She had returned early from a dinner engagement because she was once more suffering from a headache brought on, she was sure, by the maddening inability of the Duke of Beaufoy to propose to her. To think that she had turned down the opportunity to attend Ben Hawksmoor's ball—in company with the Prince Regent—only for Beaufoy to hum and haw and waste his opportunities! It was insupportable. And as if that were not bad enough…

The fine satinwood surface of the table was cluttered with pots and potions. The air in the boudoir was rich with the mingled scent of lily of the valley and musky rose. The satin ribbons on Lady Paris's peignoir were trailing in the face cream, but for once she did not notice. She was staring into the mirror—it was an extremely large mirror—with a look of abject horror on her beautiful features.

"What," she said, stabbing a finger toward her reflection, "is that?"

Edna, the maid who was the only person in the world who knew all Lady Paris's secrets, wrinkled up her nose and peered into the glass.

"It is a pimple, my love."

"No," Paris said. She pointed at another part of her face. "That is a pimple, Edna. This is…it is…a carbuncle! A monstrosity! How can I possibly attend Lord and Lady Askew's breakfast tomorrow when I look like this? I will be a laughingstock."

Edna peered closer. "We can hide it—"

"With what? A marquee?"

Lady Paris got to her feet and flounced away across the room. "I have had the headache for days. I feel sick and I look like a freak show. I am going to bed. Cancel all my engagements."

The maid bent and started to pick up the first of a huge mound of discarded clothes that littered the floor.

"Of course, my lady."

"For tomorrow and the next day."

The maid paused. "All of them, my lady?"

"All of them." Paris's voice was muffled. She had put a large pillow over her face. "Close the drapes, Edna. And the window. It is too cold in here. Fresh air is very dangerous to the complexion."

"You do remember that you were intending to visit the theater with the Duke of Beaufoy tomorrow night?"

A humphing noise sounded from beneath the bed-covers. "Beaufoy can wait," Paris said. She was very annoyed with the young duke. He was fathoms deep in love with her but when she had told him she would settle for nothing but marriage, he had turned very white and muttered something about his trustees disapproving.

"It will do him good," she added. "He should have had the courage to elope with me by now. I have had my portmanteaus packed this sennight past."

Edna smiled. "Indeed, madam. But you do remember that Wednesday night is the ball at Carlton House?"

Lady Paris shot up in bed. "The Prince Regent's Ball? Damnation!"

Edna placed a soothing hand against her forehead. "You are running a temperature, pet. Lie still. I shall call Dr. Long."

Paris pushed her away and swung her legs over the side of the bed. "I cannot miss the Prince Regent's Ball. I have been angling for an invitation these five months past. I must be seen there! Everybody who is anybody will be present." She hurried back to the mirror. "If it is a masked ball perhaps we may do something about this excrescence—" She stopped on a wail of anguish. "Oh! Look!"

Her flimsy peignoir had fallen open and there, on Lady Paris's famously ample bosom, was another large spot exactly like the first.

Edna pursed her lips. "Perhaps if you were to wear a high-necked gown…"

"Do not be absurd," Paris snapped. "I never wear

anything like that! People must be able to see my—"
She broke off again and this time her wail was more
muted, almost resigned. "There is another one, and
another… I am infested! Do we have fleas in this
house?"

"I do believe," Edna said, head on one side, "that
you have the chicken pox, my poppet."

Lady Paris stared at her. "That is impossible. I
simply cannot afford to be ill."

Edna pulled a face and carried on stolidly folding
the garments.

Paris swung back to the mirror as though to
convince herself that the spots were not there. For a
long moment she stared at her reflection and then she
gave a small whimper.

"How long does it last, Edna?"

"Two weeks," the maid said. "Maybe three if it's
really bad."

"And does it hurt?"

"It itches like a torment but you cannot scratch," the
maid said cheerfully, "for if you do, you will be left
with ugly scars."

Paris stared at her creamy-white skin, which
seemed to be erupting before her very eyes. "I must
not cry," she said between her teeth. "Crying lines my
face."

Edna patted her arm. "Go to bed, madam. I will send
for the doctor and fetch you a soothing cup of milk."

Paris's big blue eyes were still full of unshed tears.
"But the Prince Regent—"

"I'm sure he will understand that you are indisposed."

Paris shook her head fiercely. "No, Edna! We cannot tell anyone I am ill. It is too embarrassing." She gripped the maid's arm. "Can you imagine the scandal sheets—Lady Paris de Moine has the chicken pox! That is not the sort of story I can permit to circulate."

For the first time, Edna looked dubious. "But madam, how will you prevent it?"

Paris rubbed her aching head and then remembered not to spoil her hair. If she was to receive anyone— even in her bed—she must look her best.

"Never mind the doctor," she said. "He charges too much anyway. First thing in the morning I wish you to send for Ben Hawksmoor. I need him. He will know what to do." She frowned, bit her lip, then released it as she remembered that it was disfiguring. "That is, if he can manage to tear himself away from that puling chit he seemed taken with at Crockford's," she added viciously. "I cannot be certain, but I think he meant to bed her."

"Who is she, madam?" Edna inquired.

Paris made a sharp gesture. Truth to tell, she was worried. She had been ever since Ben had disappeared from Crockford's in company with the girl he had addressed as Catherine.

When Catherine had first arrived to take Maggie Fenton home, Paris had barely been interested. She knew Maggie slightly from the occasional social event where their paths had overlapped. She had heard that Maggie was flighty and lived dangerously, cuckolding her rich husband and seeking excitement wherever she could find it. Paris felt no sisterly interest and no compassion for her. She had very little time for women.

But Catherine had been a different matter. Catherine was dangerous. Paris could feel it.

Paris had never repined over the fact that Ben was her lover in word but not in deed. They had met in Portugal when she had been down on her luck and Ben had helped her find a rich protector. When they had first met, Paris had propositioned Ben to sleep with her and he had turned her down. He had done it lightly, charmingly, but very finally. Paris had eventually conquered her anger and had had the sense to see that Ben's friendship was too valuable to lose. Unlike her lovers, he was always there when she needed him and he never tried to tell her what to do.

Ben had been injured two years before at Salamanca, and Paris had been tired of an itinerant life by then and had just parted from her latest protector. She and Ben had planned a dazzling return to London together. They had woven a wonderful fiction about themselves. The pretense had been worth as much to Paris as the substance of an affair would have been.

Paris was not particularly interested in sex and certainly not interested in love. Once, when she was young, she had thought herself in love with her husband, Alex de Moine. She had been swiftly disillusioned, had left him, and later heard that he had gone missing in the wars, presumed dead. These days, sex was just a means to an end for Paris—the way to achieve riches and security. Paris knew that she and Ben looked good together. They were feted, courted, flattered, two halves of a dazzling whole. It mattered nothing that the whole thing was an invention. She would use it until she could persuade Beaufoy or another nobleman to marry her and then she would kiss Ben goodbye.

But now she feared she might lose everything prematurely, because Ben had been looking at Catherine in a way Paris had never seen him look at a woman before.

She turned her head to see that Edna was watching her with a curiously pitying look. Paris glared at her. "She is a nobody! She is a friend of that featherhead Maggie Fenton, that is all. But I…" Paris hesitated. "I need to make some inquiries. I will find out who she really is."

"A rival, madam?" Edna spoke softly.

"Don't be stupid," Paris snapped. She snatched up one of her fans and started to rip the colored feathers from its tips, dropping them to the carpet. "You know as well as I that I have the upper hand. If I can land Beaufoy then I will tell Ben Hawksmoor to go hang!"

"So—" Edna prompted.

"So there is nothing to fear." Paris was speaking so softly now it was as though she spoke only to convince herself. "All the same I will find this little trollop who catches his eye. And I will bring Beaufoy to heel. But not—" she looked down in disgust at the spotty expanse of her bosom "—not like this! Damnation!"

And she swept the pots from her dressing table in a fit of rage.

Mrs. Desmond's House of Enchantment was one of the more salubrious brothels in Covent Garden. Catherine went up a shallow flight of steps to an imposing door flanked by two bay trees in pots. On the doorstep, she hesitated, but there was a gentleman ascending the steps behind her who seemed particularly interested in making her acquaintance, so she knocked twice, decisively, and prayed hard for the door to open. She was shaking, breathing quickly and lightly, and she was not at all sure what she would do—something very violent, though—if the gentleman actually laid a hand on her.

When she had run past the butler in Ben Hawksmoor's hall and out into the street, the cold, foggy air had been like a slap across the face and had made her gasp with shock. She had stopped then, confused, utterly disoriented by everything that had happened to her that evening. She had wanted to run away somewhere and hide but she knew she could not go home. The emptiness of the house in Guilford Street would be too much to bear. She needed to talk to someone.

She had become vaguely aware that the butler had come out of the house and taken her arm gently. He was speaking to her but she was not aware of his words. And then the hackney carriage had appeared, wrapped in a shroud of fog, and she had given Lily's address and climbed inside. She had huddled into a corner for the whole journey and she had tried to think about nothing at all. But her perfidious body, still aching with the aftermath of her discomfort, had reminded her of the pleasure that had preceded it and she quivered a little with sensual discovery.

Then she had remembered Ben's words and had closed her eyes to blot out the harsh and painful truth. He had known who she was all along. He had thought that she had thrown herself at him like a whore so he had treated her like one. He had believed her to be involved in some scrubby little plot with Withers to bring him down so he had used her for revenge and for amusement and then dismissed her, thinking her Withers's harlot as well as his own. And even though he now knew the truth, it meant nothing to him. All the tenderness she had thought she had seen in him had been part of his calculated seduction. She had been caught up in the fantasy of her feelings for him while he had merely been amusing himself. *That* was his opinion of her. That was what she could not bear.

What was done was done. She could not undo it but she bitterly regretted the feelings that had led her astray that night. She was a fool. She faced the fact squarely.

She was a grown woman, and though she was inexperienced she was not usually so stupid. She knew enough of the ways of the world to know that if one strayed into a gentleman's chamber and showed little interest in retreating he might show scant regard in behaving as a gentleman arguably should.

As the hack had made its tortuously slow journey through the foggy streets, Catherine had opened her eyes and stared into the dark. She knew she had stayed with Ben because she had wanted to. Curiosity, attraction, fascination and that damnable desire to fill the void in her life with an intimacy she craved… Those had all been her undoing.

Her fingernails had dug into her palms. She wanted to escape the match with Withers even more now. Intolerable to think of submitting to his kisses when her mind was full of another man entirely, a man whose merest touch could completely seduce her, whose kisses had been so tempting. But Catherine knew she was a fool to think of Ben Hawksmoor in that way, and no doubt, she had reflected bitterly, she was not the first woman to think it. Nor would she be the last.

The door of the brothel opened and a huge man stood in the aperture. He was at least six foot tall and almost as wide, and looked built to withstand a military siege. Catherine gulped.

"I wish to see Miss Lily St. Clare, if you please," she said.

The man seemed unimpressed. "Do you now?" His voice had a faint brogue. He opened the door a little wider to permit the gentleman who had followed Catherine to enter the house with no more than a nod of acknowledgment. Then he turned back to Catherine and shook his head.

"I'd say you were in the wrong place, miss. Best to go home. Good night, now."

Catherine peered past him into the hall. The light hurt her eyes. There were candles flaring in all the sconces, illuminating a scene of tasteful opulence. It could be any house in the most respectable part of town, except that upstairs Lily and her colleagues plied their trade.

"Wait!" she said, as the door started to close.

The man paused, then laughed. "I said go home, little girl."

Catherine put her foot in the door. "I can pay."

The man paused. This was a currency he understood. He opened the door wider. "Is that so? Then you had better come in."

Catherine perched on one of the tall gilt-colored chairs in the hall. The house was quiet. The candlelight illuminated the high white walls and threw shadows across the marble-checkered floor. She could hear the faint sound of voices and masculine laughter from behind one of the closed doors. The air smelled of cigar smoke and fresh flowers. Catherine's hands were clenched very tightly in her lap. She was seeing everything as though it were a long distance away and held herself upright, tense, tight as a drawn bow.

There was the tap of heels on the marble of the floor and then Lily was coming toward her, pulling a gauzy spencer about her shoulders over a gown of quite staggeringly low décolletage. Catherine had been troubled about disturbing her friend at work and now was relieved to see that Lily looked exactly as she had always done, aside from the décolletage. Her blue eyes were worried and she rushed forward, hands outstretched.

"Catherine!"

Catherine tried to smile but it came out in a rather wobbly way. She stood up. Behind Lily was the burly man and a statuesque woman with striking auburn hair and hard green eyes, who was arguing fiercely with him.

"This is a schoolgirl, Connor. What the devil are you doing, allowing debutantes into my house?"

"Catherine?" Lily said her name again, her tone troubled as she surveyed her friend's face. "What has happened? What are you doing here?"

"I'm sorry!" Catherine gulped. "I needed to talk to someone—" She caught Lily's hands. "Lord Hawksmoor—" She was finding it increasingly difficult to put the words together.

Over her head, Lily's startled eyes met those of the other woman. A strange, rather watchful silence fell over the group. The huge man shifted uncomfortably.

"Hawksmoor?" Lily repeated. "Oh, Catherine, I warned you—"

"In here," Sarah Desmond said, bundling them both through a doorway as another knock came at the front door. "Connor, make sure no one comes in."

After the bright lights of the hall, the drawing room was dimly lit, the candles throwing long shadows. There was a merry fire burning in the grate but Catherine could not feel its warmth. She was shivering and shivering.

"She is suffering from shock, Sarah," she heard Lily say, and she pulled away abruptly, dimly aware that she did not want anyone thinking Ben Hawksmoor had physically hurt her.

"No I am not!" The words came out far too loudly and Catherine collected herself with an effort. "That is, I have done such a *stupid* thing—" Her anger at her own folly burst out. "Oh, Lily, I am such a fool!"

Lily put her arm about Catherine and guided her to the sofa. "That is enough of that," she said, pulling

Catherine down to sit beside her. "Tell me what has happened, Catherine."

"Your little friend looks as though she could do with a drink," Sarah Desmond said, walking over to a beautiful cherry escritoire. Catherine heard the clink of glass. Sarah Desmond put it into her hand. Her teeth chattered against the rim.

"I have done such a *stupid* thing," she repeated.

Lily smiled. "You always did."

"Those were schoolgirl things. This is serious." Catherine's hands shook. She spilled some of the liquid in the glass.

"Drink up," Sarah Desmond said. "You look as though you need it."

Catherine obeyed. She did not recognize the spirit but it was so strong it almost took her throat out. She coughed, felt it burn her stomach and then, miraculously, everything seemed to settle down.

"That's better," Sarah said with satisfaction. "So what have you done, Miss—"

"Fenton," Catherine said. "My name is Catherine Fenton."

Sarah raised her brows. "Lily's schoolmate."

"That's right."

Lily took Catherine's cold hand in hers again. "Tell me what has happened, Catherine."

"I seduced Ben Hawksmoor," Catherine said bluntly.

She heard Lily catch her breath and Sarah Desmond give a low whistle of surprise. "No one does that, Miss Fenton," the courtesan said. "It just doesn't happen."

"Well," Catherine said, "I did it."

Sarah sat down with a soft swish of midnight-blue silk. "Well, upon my word, if it's true you can have a job here whenever you want, darling."

"Don't," Lily said quickly. "Can't you see she's not one of us, Sarah?" She turned urgently back to Catherine.

"Kate…" The pet name was an unconscious echo of what Ben had called her, and Catherine flinched a little.

"Are you sure?" Lily said. "I mean, you may think that you did, but—"

Catherine was torn between a desire to laugh and a strong urge to cry. "I know what happened, Lily. I am not a complete innocent."

"Not anymore, by the sounds of it," Sarah said.

Lily shot her a look. "But… But how? I mean, I thought you were going to keep out of his way?"

"I went to his house tonight," Catherine said, and saw the despair and the horror deepen in Lily's eyes. "It wasn't what you think!" she added quickly, unable to bear her friend believing that she had been stupid enough to throw herself in Ben's way.

"Then what was it?" Lily asked quietly.

"It was for Maggie," Catherine said, the tears thickening her voice. "She had an affair with Ned Clarencieux and took a picture from Lord Hawksmoor's house as a memento."

"The miniature mentioned in the paper?" Lily said.

"That's right." Catherine bit her lip painfully. "She asked me to take it back for her. So I did."

Lily was shaking her head. "Oh, Catherine, why? Why must you do these foolish things for other people?"

"Maggie was afraid that Papa would find out," Catherine said. "I had to help her, Lily! For the sake of our family… And the runners were on her trail…."

"Your family is not what you think it, Miss Fenton," Sarah said, in a hard voice. "Your father keeps another establishment in Chelsea and your step-mother is given to affaires with handsome young men. There is nothing to save other than appearances. You must open your eyes."

Catherine felt sick. The world she had wanted to preserve was splintered already and only the surface remained. Her family life was as empty and meaning-less as a puppet show.

"One hears things in our profession," Lily said softly, apologetically. "I am sorry, Kate."

"Maggie is ill," Catherine said defiantly. "She would not behave so if she were well."

"She is sick with laudanum," Sarah Desmond said harshly. "So is that blackguard, Withers, with whom your father is closer than two thieves. He is an opium eater."

Catherine stared, distracted for a moment from her own affairs. "Is he? But surely it could be he who gave laudanum to Maggie?"

The question fell into an awkward silence. She could tell that both Lily and Sarah Desmond thought that that was exactly what had happened.

Sarah got to her feet. "I will leave you to talk, Lily." She checked the elegant little clock on the mantel. "Do not forget that Faulkner may call—"

Catherine saw Lily blush. "I won't."

Sarah nodded to Catherine. "I like you, Catherine

Fenton, God help me. But I don't want debutantes in my house. Gives the place a bad name." She smiled suddenly. "Good luck."

She went out and closed the door softly behind her. Catherine looked at Lily.

"I like her, too."

Lily smiled. "She has been more than good to me. She took me in when no one else would help me."

Catherine nodded. "Thank you for seeing me," she said.

Lily sighed. "You should not have come here, Kate. If anyone finds out, you will be ruined."

Catherine gave a laugh that was a half sob. "After tonight, Lily—"

"Do not say that." Lily's hand tightened on hers. "Tell me what happened."

Catherine told her. She explained about Maggie's trip to Crockford's and how Ben had kissed her in the carriage on the way home, and about the miniature, and how she had attended the ball that night, and she only stumbled when she came to relate what had happened with Ben after his guests had left.

"You do not need to tell me about that, Kate," Lily said. "I understand. Truly I do understand how painful it can be to believe oneself in love and then discover…" She broke off and Catherine remembered the painful shock of Lily's own betrayal at the hands of a man who had sworn he loved her and then abandoned her publicly when she had taken the scandalous step of leaving her husband for him.

"I am not in love with him," Catherine said. "I barely know him." But her heart betrayed her even as she spoke.

Lily looked at her. "Love can happen in a year or an instant, Kate. There are no rules."

Catherine shook her head stubbornly. "I made a mistake, Lily. I thought that what I felt was more important than it really was." She looked up. "I daresay I am not the first young lady to…to lose her heart to Ben Hawksmoor."

"No," Lily said, with some of Sarah Desmond's dryness, "but you are probably the first to lose her virginity to him. Lord Hawksmoor does not have any interest in debutantes."

"He took me out of revenge," Catherine said bleakly. "At first I thought it was because he believed me to be a courtesan, but he told me he knew who I was tonight." She knitted her fingers together hard to still their shaking.

Lily was looking appalled. "He knew you were a virgin but he despoiled you anyway? The actions of a blackguard!"

"No," Catherine said. "It is worse than that. He believed that I was in league with Withers against him, that we had planned the whole thing together. He seduced me to spite Withers, I think."

Lily was white. "Kate!"

"I know," Catherine said. "I do not know why he should think it of me but that is what he said."

Lily put her hand over Catherine's closely clasped ones.

"I am so sorry, so sorry that you had to be disillusioned in this way."

Catherine was silent. Everything she had ever

wanted had been offered to her on a plate in her life. Everything except warmth and love, and when she had reached out for those, she had made a dreadful mistake.

"Everything that a debutante is taught," she said slowly, "suggests that to give oneself to a man out of wedlock is the most disgraceful of crimes. If people knew what I have done I would be ruined."

Lily's serene face set in hard lines. "That is true, Kate. Those are society's rules."

"And yet," Catherine pursued, "once one is married and—preferably—has provided the heir, one is free to do as one pleases."

"Also true," Lily said. She was smiling slightly now. "Unless one breaks the rules again—as I did."

"Yes," Catherine said. She looked at her friend. "And yet you are the same person that you were before, Lily. So am I. I regret what I did but I am not a lesser person because of it. Neither are you."

Lily gripped her hand and Catherine suddenly saw that her friend's eyes were brilliant with tears. "You are very strong and very wise, Kate," Lily said. "It has taken me months to see that I should not let the opinion of others diminish me." She looked around. "Yet the reality is that because of the opinion of the world, I am now obliged to earn my living as a courtesan, which—" she looked away "—is not a profession that suits me." She blushed. "There are those who are temperamentally suited to such a life, those such as Lady Paris de Moine, perhaps, who can profit from it. But I did not want this."

A wave of fury took Catherine unawares, breaking through the cold misery that had trapped her since she had fled from Ben's room. Society had treated Lily badly. She had no intention of allowing it to do the same to her.

"No," she said. "You wanted a home and a family and someone who cared for you. Not so much to ask."

"Do not allow it to happen to you, Kate," Lily said, and suddenly Catherine saw the lines of fatigue deep in her face. "Put this behind you. Marry Withers—"

"Well, I certainly won't do that," Catherine said, "since that would be worse than anything. I am lucky." She tried to keep the bitterness from her voice. "I am blessed with fortune and therefore have no need to marry. And I shall try to forget." She stopped, thinking that perhaps for all her life she would be haunted, not by a sense of shame at what she had done, but by the ghost of what she had wanted, what might have been. But it was foolish to think on that. Ben Hawksmoor had never been hers. He could not give her the warmth and the love that she craved. Their tragedy was that they had both thoroughly misunderstood what the other had wanted, she looking for love in the wrong place and he thinking she was someone very different from the real Catherine Fenton.

There was a silence. "Well," Lily said, "whatever the case, we must decide what to do now. You should go home, Kate, and try to put this behind you if you can. I will see you soon."

The bell jangled with an earsplitting peal, making them both jump. There was the sound of the front door opening followed by a sudden outburst of voices in the hall—Connor's threatening, Sarah Desmond's smooth and placating, then masculine tones that Catherine recognized all too well. They were low and hard and menacing.

"I know she is here, madam, so do not trouble yourself to deny it."

"Lord Hawksmoor!" Lily whispered.

Catherine looked around. Her first instinct was to hide, her second to climb out of the window and run away. But it would not serve. Money had bought her entry to Mrs. Desmond's House of Enchantment. The same inducement would no doubt buy Ben Hawksmoor all of her secrets. As he had said earlier, everything—almost everything—had a price.

She smoothed her skirts down in a nervous gesture, threw Lily a smile and walked across to the door, opening it quickly before her nerve failed her.

Out in the hall, Ben Hawksmoor was adjusting the set of his jacket and smoothing his cuffs. Catherine could see Connor sprawled on the marble floor behind him, knocked out cold. Sarah Desmond was looking both impressed and slightly put out by this high-handed behavior. Ben turned slowly and his eyes met Catherine's. She felt the heat and anger in his gaze like a physical touch.

"Lord Hawksmoor," she said, and she was proud of the steadiness of her voice. "I did not expect you to seek me here."

Sarah Desmond took one look at her face and stepped between the two of them.

"Lord Hawksmoor," she said, "we are naturally delighted to have the pleasure of your custom tonight, but what can I interest you in?"

There was a dark and dangerous look in Ben Hawksmoor's eyes. They pinned Catherine to the spot. "There is only one thing of interest to me in this house, madam." He put a hand into his pocket and withdrew a pile of guineas.

"An hour of your time," he said, directly to Catherine. "I want to talk to you now."

THE DOOR OF THE DRAWING ROOM was firmly shut behind them but when Ben turned the key in the lock, Catherine was moved to protest.

"My lord, I should be more comfortable were we not imprisoned together."

Ben shot her a look. Very deliberately he placed the key on the cherry table and beside it, the pile of gold coins. "I should not wish you to feel constrained, Miss Fenton. The key is here and you may leave at any time." He drove his hands into the pockets of his jacket. "I would ask that you stay a little and speak with me."

"Because you have paid for my time," Catherine said coldly.

He gave her another look, dark and unreadable. "Because I ask it, Miss Fenton."

Catherine nodded slightly. "Very well. But how did you find me?" She swallowed convulsively. "Oh, I remember—the butler. He told you…"

Ben shrugged. "Price heard you give directions to the hackney and I remembered that Miss St. Clare was your friend. I confess that it surprised me, though. You are no whore, are you, Catherine, no matter what you did tonight?"

Catherine felt cold at his words. She wrapped her arms about herself for comfort. What had she expected from him—a declaration of love? She had already realized that the deep emotions that had moved her had had no similar effect on him. He had wanted her, had shown her a man's lust, and that was all. She was the one who had made the mistake here.

"Lily and I were at school together," she said colorlessly. "I do not forget my friends, no matter what befalls them."

Their eyes met but he said nothing.

"Why did you come?" she asked. It seemed difficult to force the words out when he was standing watching her with that pitiless gaze. Never had the gulf between them seemed so wide.

"I came because I wanted some answers," Ben said. He held out the silver miniature in his palm. "I want to know where you obtained this, and why you thought it necessary to bring it back to my house."

Catherine felt a wave of sickness sweep over her, part fear, part disillusion. He had found the miniature already. A tiny part of her heart had hoped he might have sought her out for herself alone. Would she never learn? She had stumbled into a game where the rules were far more sophisticated than she could ever have imagined. It was no wonder that she had got hurt. She allowed the last of her hopes to be extinguished. Even if he accepted that she had no part in Withers's schemes, he still did not care for her. In his eyes she was a foolish debutante who had played with fire and been burned as a result. But he did care about the theft of the miniature and what was behind it.

"I cannot tell you that," she said. She knew it would anger him but she thought it was better than to prevaricate.

Ben's hazel eyes narrowed on her face. "You are protecting someone."

Catherine did not reply. Her heart was tripping with quick, light strokes. He was not stupid. He would guess soon enough, put the evidence together, remember seeing her with Maggie…

He came across and sat beside her on the sofa. "Listen to me, Catherine—"

Her eyes flashed at his use of her name and she saw him smile, that wicked smile that had been the undoing of her foolish heart. "I beg your pardon. Miss Fenton. Please listen to me."

Catherine set her jaw. "Pray continue, my lord."

Ben shifted. "Very well, then. If you do not tell me the truth, Miss Fenton, I shall have you arrested for theft."

The brutality of it took her breath away. Her eyes flew to his face. "You would not!"

He shrugged. "I need to know who gave you the miniature and why. So tell me."

Catherine pressed her fingers together to stop them from shaking. She felt sick and giddy with fear.

She looked up and saw that he was watching her implacably.

"You did not take it yourself," he said.

"No." The first admission felt like a step on a slippery downward path.

Ben inclined his head. "When we met at Ned Clarencieux's hanging you told me that you had met him before. But you were not the one who was his mistress, were you, Catherine? Who are you protecting?"

His perception was frightening. He had deduced at once that one of Clarencieux's mistresses had taken the miniature as a memento. Catherine tried not to panic.

"I…" Her voice was a whisper. "I did it for a friend…."

Ben's expression eased to have his suspicions confirmed. "How unconscionably naive of you to be so helpful. I cannot conceive why anyone would go to all that trouble for someone else."

"No," Catherine said. "I do not suppose that you could."

Ben frowned. "So you have a friend who was Ned's lover."

Catherine trembled. "I… Yes. Yes, I do."

"What is her name?"

Catherine straightened. That night at Crockford's he had seen her with Maggie. If he remembered for one moment…

"I will not tell you that," she said. "She swore me to secrecy."

Ben shook his head. "Either you are lying to me and this is another of Withers's schemes, or you are too kind for your own good. Such generosity of spirit is only for fools."

Catherine thought of the fragility of her family. She had already fought so hard to protect those she cared for. "I would expect a man of your stamp to care for nothing but himself," she said. "You would not understand."

She saw Ben's lips tighten into a thin line. "Tonight you came to my house solely to put the miniature back on behalf of your friend."

Catherine raised her chin sharply. This was the moment to restore some of her lost pride. "Solely for that," she said. "Nothing else, my lord."

There was some expression in his eyes that she could not read and it was gone before she had time to be certain of it, but for a moment it had looked like pain.

"I see," he said. "And what followed—"

"Was a mistake," Catherine said, "as I previously mentioned."

"A rather large one," Ben said, "for a virginal young lady." His hands bit into her shoulders suddenly. "Why, Catherine?"

Catherine stared into his face for what seemed an age. It was the first time that she was seeing the man himself rather than the handsome adventurer she had longed for. But although she could see him now without illusion or pretense, it made little difference to her feelings and with a pang of despair she realized that maybe it never would. There was something about this man that drew her. She knew that whatever happened to her in the future, for all her life, memories of him would come to her, unbidden, catching her unawares, making other men appear dull in comparison. But she had to learn to live. She could not nurse a broken heart forever. She had to teach herself to forget and she had to start now.

"I went too far," she said honestly. "I did not do it deliberately. I was misled by my feelings and I was not experienced enough to know how or when to stop."

*Nor did I want to. I thought I loved you....* Her perfidious heart whispered the words but she kept them locked up within.

Their eyes held and he was the first to look away. "I am sorry," he said.

Catherine thought he had probably never said that to a woman before, but as his hands fell from her shoulders, she saw the pity in his face, and felt glad that she had at least withheld a small part of the truth from him. He did not know that she thought she had loved him—and he would never know.

"I cannot tell you whom I am protecting," she said again. "I promised."

His expression was hard again. "Do you think I cannot find out?" Ben got to his feet and strode over to the cherry table where the guineas gleamed dully in the firelight. He picked them up then stacked them again. The coins clinked together.

"There are any number of people in this house who would sell me that information," he said softly. He glanced at her over his shoulder. "I suppose you have told your friend Lily the whole story? And Sarah Desmond?" He saw how her face paled, and nodded. "I thought you would do. You are too trusting."

"Lily would never betray me," Catherine said defiantly.

"But Sarah would if the price was right." Ben smiled, a parody of a smile. "Or I could simply save time and take you to Bow Street and have done with it."

Catherine jumped up. "You would not dare! That would be abduction!"

He shrugged carelessly. "Abduction, seduction… You have learned little of me if you think I would stop at either."

Catherine thought of the prone body of Connor sprawled untidily in Sarah Desmond's hallway. Physically it would be easy enough for him to do but she did not believe him. Despite all he had said and all he had done, she did not believe that he would lay violent hands on her. He was not like Withers, who had thought nothing of hitting her in his fury. Ben had seduced her and broken her heart but he had never physically hurt her.

"I won't tell you," she repeated stubbornly.

He turned on her with barely repressed fury. "You do not understand! This is important. You said that you were not implicated in Withers's plans."

Catherine drew herself up. "I am not. I detest the man and I cannot imagine why you would believe it of me!"

Something shifted in Ben's face. Regret again? She could not bear for him to pity her.

"I was misinformed," he said.

"How unfortunate for you," Catherine said coldly. "And even more so for me."

She saw him take a deep, steadying breath. "If you

hate Withers so much then help me," he said. "This is to do with Ned Clarencieux's death. Clarencieux was no forger and no murderer either. Oh, he was foolish and reckless and spendthrift, but—" He broke off as though he was catching himself on the verge of some admission. Catherine understood. He was revealing vulnerability and he did not want for her to see it.

She looked at him. "So you do at least care for someone?" she said.

Ben shot her a look of dislike. His whole body was rigid with tension. "Clarencieux was framed," he said. "He was set up and I think that Withers did it. I do not wish that to happen to me. That is all."

Catherine stared as his words started to sink in. The murder of Sir James Mather had been an unpleasant surprise to her. He had been her trustee, a man she had known for a long time, appointed by her grandfather. When she had heard that Ned Clarencieux was involved, the reasons seemed perfectly clear. Mather was a banker; Clarencieux, like her, was one of his clients. Clarencieux had become embroiled in financial trouble and had started to try to pass counterfeit notes to buy himself out of his difficulties. Mather had discovered the fraud and Clarencieux had killed him to stop him exposing the truth. He had been seen running from Mather's chambers after the shot had been fired. His pistol was discovered beside the banker's body. And counterfeit notes had been found in his rooms….

Catherine shook her head. She did not want to believe what Ben was saying. Why would Withers frame him? And if Clarencieux was innocent, who had killed James Mather?

"You must be mistaken," she said. "Mr. Clarencieux was surely guilty! Besides—" She stopped, looked at him. "Why would Withers wish to frame him? Or bring you down, for that matter?"

"That," Ben said grimly, "is what I am trying to discover. But you heard him, Catherine. You were there when he made the threat."

That gave Catherine pause. "I did," she allowed. "But I did not think he meant anything by it." Unconsciously she fingered her cheek where Withers had hit her that time. "He can be violent," she said, "but I thought his threats were no more than words."

Ben caught her hand in his. "Has he hurt *you?*"

For a moment Catherine stared at him, unable to decipher the expression in his eyes.

"He hit me once," she admitted, and heard Ben swear violently.

"But this has nothing to do with me or to do with—" Catherine stopped herself just in time before she betrayed Maggie's name. "I promise I know nothing of this," she began again, but Ben interrupted her, his face hard.

"You can promise all you wish but until I find out your link to Clarencieux, I do not intend to let you go."

Suddenly Catherine was tired to her bones with an aching, empty exhaustion that made her long for a hot bath and her own bed. She wanted to go home, no matter how chill and barren the house in Guilford

Street. She flung out a contemptuous hand and scattered the pile of golden guineas across the floor.

"You may buy information from whomever you can persuade to betray me, my lord," she said, "but I will tell you nothing more. I took the portrait back on behalf of a friend who was Edward Clarencieux's mistress. I did it because she was terrified her husband would find out and denounce her. As for Withers's threats, I understood nothing of them. And that is all I know." She glanced ostentatiously at the clock.

"You paid for an hour, I believe. Your time is almost over."

Ben took her arm, swinging her around to face him. Catherine's breath caught in her throat. She felt so vulnerable. She had wanted to be indifferent to him now that was all that was left to her, but the moment he touched her, she was undone. Her body still responded to his touch and her heart betrayed her.

"Then since talking has been so unprofitable for us," Ben said pleasantly, "perhaps we should spend the rest of our time employed in something we found more enjoyable."

Catherine saw the flash in his eyes but read his intentions a second too late. He had put a hand on the nape of her neck and now he pulled her close enough to kiss her. She was taken by equal parts of shock and desire. His touch reawakened all the painful longings she had so recently discovered. She felt the hot stroke of his tongue, urgent and deep, and then her knees threatened to give way and he swept her up into his arms and carried her to the sofa.

"Ben…" It was the first time she had called him by his name, but instead of a reproach, it came out as a plea and he groaned, drawing her closer, as close as she could get, so that she lay along the hard length of his body. She could feel every ragged breath that he drew, every beat of his heart. Her body was softening again at his touch, wanting him. She felt ripe and ready to fall. Her mind struggled to control the sensations but then he was kissing her again, savagely, hungrily, and she let go of all thought and returned the kiss, unable to resist. His mouth left hers and brushed the lobe of her ear, sending delicious shivers down her spine. Her nipples hardened beneath the material of her shift and when his hand came up to cup her breast, its heat branded her through the silk. Her head fell back against the sofa cushions and she felt his mouth trace the line of her throat down to the neck of her dress, and linger where the swell of her breasts strained against the cloth. His teeth nipped at one tight peak where it rubbed against the silk and Catherine caught her breath on a scream. Ben tangled his fist in her hair and turned her head so that her mouth met his again. Catherine felt as though she had a fever. She could not understand the desperation between them, but she knew with an instinct deeper than time that Ben felt it, too.

She opened her eyes and saw the golden guineas scattered across the floor and something shriveled in her heart, turning it to ice. Ben Hawksmoor had paid for an hour of her time and now he was making love to her in a whorehouse. There was precious little romantic in that. A short while ago she had promised herself never to make the same mistake twice, yet here she was doing precisely that. Ben did not love her, did not even care for her beyond the desire he so evidently felt for her. To forget that, to allow herself to be deceived by his touch, was madness.

She struggled to sit up and he let her go immediately.

"Catherine?" His voice was unsteady.

"Do not think to seduce the information you want from me," Catherine said, wanting nothing more than to strike out and hurt him as he had hurt her. "I am not so naive as I was a few hours ago. You have seen to that."

Ben released her so suddenly she almost fell to the floor. She had thought that her taunt would have been as ineffectual as the scratching of a kitten, and was taken aback. She scrambled to her feet, but by then he was already halfway to the door.

"You are correct, of course," he said. "I had better go."

Catherine sat braced upright upon the sofa until she heard the sound of the front door closing and then she curled herself up tightly, her knees to her chin. She had been a child starved of affection and had become a woman whose natural sensual instincts had been locked away, stifled, until Ben Hawksmoor had released them. She had learned so much of herself in one night that she could scarce believe it.

She had given herself to a man who desired her but did not care for her one whit.

And that, she thought, was the bitter end to her first lesson in love.

THE WATCH HAD ANNOUNCED the hour of four and the night was darker than pitch when a closed carriage left Mrs. Desmond's House of Enchantment and rumbled through the frosty streets to Guilford Street.

At the same time, a messenger was knocking on the door of Lady Paris de Moine's house in Cheyne Gardens. The night porter took the letter and went, yawning, to wake Edna. He knew that such an action would prove unpopular but the messenger had insisted that the matter required the utmost urgency.

Edna was not happy to be disturbed. She rubbed the sleep from her eyes, took the missive and when the porter told her unhappily that it was for Lady Paris's eyes only, she told him sharply to get back to his post. She knew better than to trouble Paris with anything that was not a matter of life and death, especially now that my lady was so poorly.

Even so, when she had broken the seal and read the contents, she leaped from her bed as though someone had applied a hot coal to her feet. She was down the corridor and knocking on Paris's bedroom door before the night porter could do more than splutter in amazement.

And a bare two minutes after that, the whole house was awoken by the sounds of breaking china and glass, as Lady Paris de Moine gave vent to her feelings with an intensity that none of them had previously heard at all.

# CHAPTER SIX

An inefficient chaperone is a great drawback to
a young lady.
—*Mrs. Eliza Squire,* Good Conduct for Ladies

SIR ALFRED FENTON WAS ASLEEP in his armchair, the
*London Chronicle* sliding farther from his lap with
each rhythmic rise and fall of his chest. He had dined
at his club that night with Algernon Withers, who had
been anxious to acquaint him with the latest faults he
had to find with Catherine's behavior. These were
legion, and Withers's complaints had been sufficient to
put Sir Alfred in a black mood; so bad, in fact, that he
was glad to see the back of the man when Withers
finally took himself off for some low gambling den or
other.

He knew that he should never have got in so deep
with Withers. When it had all begun he had thought
that he needed someone with the brand of ruthlessness
Withers possessed. Too late he had realized that the
man was not only ruthless but undisciplined, too. He
never knew when to stop. And in his arrogance he
would bring them all down.

Already matters had spiraled far, far out of Sir
Alfred's control. He had only wanted someone to help
him break the trust fund, a fellow signatory to help
him deceive Sir James Mather. Sir Alfred had been
running short of money and Catherine's fortune was
like a prize that glittered just out of his reach. Catherine's grandfather, that old rogue McNaish, had arranged it so. McNaish's only weakness had been his
love of his family—his daughter, Violet, Sir Alfred's
first wife, and his granddaughter, Catherine, whom he
had adored. He had tied up his fortune so that Catherine should inherit and Sir Alfred would have nothing
but the interest on the principal. Sir Alfred knew
McNaish had done it on purpose. It was almost like a
taunt.

At first Sir Alfred had not cared. His own business
interests had prospered and he did not need his
daughter's money. But gradually a series of reversals
had reduced his wealth until he could no longer
maintain the style to which he had become accustomed.

It had been easy to persuade Mather to take Withers
on as the third trustee when McNaish had died. Sir
Alfred had vouched for Withers, and Mather had been
an honorable man who had not suspected dishonor in
others. The deed had been done, the papers signed,
and Withers and Sir Alfred had been fleecing the fund
ever since. But then Withers had turned to funding
criminal excess, gangs of body snatchers who worked
the graveyards of London. It had sickened Sir Alfred
to hear of it, but Withers had just laughed and said
there was money in old bones. And then Mather had

discovered the fraud of the trust and had had to be silenced....

Sir Alfred twitched and groaned as his sleep was riven with images of greed and violence. The paper fell from his lap to crumple on the floor.

Sir Alfred's dream quieted and now he was imagining the haven of the house in Chelsea where his mistress waited patiently for his visits. She would have known by now that he was not planning to come to her this night and would have taken to her bed in the peach-scented boudoir where he had known such pleasure.

She would not be waiting for him once she knew he was bankrupt, even less so if he were under criminal investigation, as surely he would be if Withers continued in his current ways. She would be gone to another protector, taking his refuge and his diamonds with her, leaving him with nothing but cold memories and a wife who was colder still.

Sir Alfred snored so loudly that he woke himself up and sat up with a start, staring about him. The clock registered fifteen minutes past four. The fire had died and the house was cold and silent.

At first, when Sir Alfred had returned home, he had not been concerned that both his wife and his daughter were missing. He had assumed that they were attending some social occasion and had retired to his study with the newspaper. But as the hours ticked by, he had become irritated to be sitting at home alone in the early hours and had called for the butler. Getting information from Tench had been on a par with pulling teeth from a hen, but eventually he had ascertained that Catherine had gone out at a little before midnight, and that Lady Fenton had left separately, just before he had arrived home. Neither lady had vouchsafed their destination.

Sir Alfred had digested the information in silence. He had left Catherine's chaperonage very much in his wife's hands since such matters bored him and it was only now that it was becoming apparent just how inadequate Maggie Fenton's sense of responsibility was. Sir Alfred supposed that his wife might have arranged for another matron to chaperone Catherine if she herself had a separate engagement, but nevertheless, his uneasiness persisted. He had known for some time now that Maggie was deucedly dependent on her laudanum bottle and how attached she was to certain rackety young men about town. He had known, but he had not wanted to confront the truth. And then the business of Ned Clarencieux had forced him to face matters. Withers had told him about Clarencieux. And had promised to deal with it just as he had sworn to deal with Mather.

Sir Alfred stood up a little stiffly and marched over to the door, but stopped with his hand on the knob. What good would it do to call Tench now and make a scene? The butler had already told him all he knew. The situation would only serve to emphasize how little Sir Alfred was in control of his own household, with an errant wife and a daughter who mystified him.

Sir Alfred stared at his reflection in the pier glass above the mantel. He looked old and tired. In Chelsea,

Rosabelle would have caressed him into contentment and told him he was a fine figure of a man. He would have known she was lying, of course, but he would have liked to believe her.

He flung open the door of the study and at the same moment heard the sounds of a carriage pulling up outside the house. The front door opened and Catherine walked in, drawing off her gloves as she did so. She wore no bonnet and her hair was down. Sir Alfred, no expert when it came to women's fashion, was still able to discern that his daughter was not dressed for a ball or a social occasion. Indeed, she looked as though she were hurrying home from an assignation.

Catherine looked horrified to see him. Her face was so pale with exhaustion that she was almost translucent. There were dark marks beneath her eyes and smudges on her cheeks from dried tears. She dropped her gloves and stooped automatically to pick them up.

Sir Alfred found his voice. "Where the *devil* have you been, girl?"

Catherine did not answer immediately. They stared at one another and Sir Alfred was suddenly keenly aware of the close resemblance Catherine bore to her mother. Violet had had that stance; the courage, the defiant tilt to the chin. He had never loved her. He had married her for the connection to McNaish, just as he had later married Maggie Arden because she was the daughter of a baron. Acquisition was his way of life.

And even as they stared at one another, and Sir Alfred realized how little he knew his daughter and how thoroughly he had failed her, the door opened again and Maggie stumbled inside. If Catherine had looked disheveled, Maggie looked abandoned. Her hair was in rats' tails and she was wearing her gown inside out, and she appeared neither to know nor care. Her eyes were wild.

For a long moment, the three of them stood captured in the silence, as though they knew that whoever spoke first would finally break the code that had held the Fenton household together in uneasy truce for all these long months. Then Maggie opened her mouth and the words started tumbling out, and everything was changed forever.

"I know," she said. "I know that you had Ned Clarencieux killed. You did it because of me."

For a moment, Sir Alfred did not understand what she was talking about. There was a rushing sound in his ears and a mist before his eyes. He shook his head slowly.

"What the deuce are you talking about, Margaret?"

Suddenly Maggie started to pummel his chest with her fists. "You knew I loved him!" she shrieked. "You were jealous! I know you killed him! Withers told me this evening. He told me everything!"

Sir Alfred grabbed her wrists and held her from him at arm's length. Catherine had not moved. She was standing still and stiff, her face a white mask. Maggie was kicking and wriggling in Sir Alfred's grip but she was tiring now. He looked her up and down, at the gown that was inside out and only half-fastened, and all he could think of was the frightening truth that

Withers had betrayed him twice over. Withers had told Maggie that he was responsible for Edward Clarencieux's death and then—Sir Alfred swallowed convulsively—Withers had slept with Maggie, carelessly, casually, for no other reason than that he wanted to and that it demonstrated his power. There was a mist of fury before Sir Alfred's eyes. Withers must have gone from taking dinner with him to taking his wife.

"You come back to me from Withers looking like *this?*" His fury burned higher. He was angry with her and with Algernon Withers, but for the most part he was despairing at his own weakness. He should have stopped Withers long ago but now it was too late. The man had despoiled everything that was important to him.

"You trollop!" he snapped. "How could you do this to me?"

Maggie did not answer. She was drooping in his grip now like a cut flower. She was weeping softly. He shook her again and from the pocket of her cloak fell a bottle of laudanum. It rolled back and forth, coming to rest by Sir Alfred's left foot, as though a mute answer to his question. He let Maggie go and she dived to pick the bottle up, but Sir Alfred was too quick for her. He splintered the bottle beneath his foot, crunching the glass into the floor, even as his wife was down on her hands and knees in a desperate attempt to get there first, and her wail of loss filled the room.

"I need that!" Her voice disintegrated into a moan. "I only did it for the laudanum…."

Her hands were cut now from the shards of glass,

the blood streaking her palms. Catherine knelt beside her, coaxing her to her feet, putting an arm about her unresisting body.

"Come to bed now, Maggie," she said gently. "Everything will be all right...."

Sir Alfred did not move. He watched his daughter help his wife toward the stairs, still talking softly to her as though she were a child.

He thought about Algernon Withers.

He thought about the pistol in the drawer of his desk.

He thought about his shocking inability to take matters into his own hands and deal with Withers as he deserved. Someone else would have to do that. Someone strong, not a broken reed such as he had become.

"Tench!"

The door to the servants' quarters opened so quickly that Sir Alfred realized the entire house must have been listening to the confrontation he had just had with his wife. No matter. He suspected that the whole of London had heard about his errant wife by now. They said that the husband was always the last to know.

"Fetch me brandy," he said. "Then leave me alone. I do not wish to be disturbed."

BEN HAWKSMOOR STROLLED UP the steps to Lady Paris de Moine's front door and threw a greeting to the press hacks who were chewing their pencils and waiting patiently on the pavement below. They brightened when they saw him and told him sympathetically that Lord Askew had arrived before him but had been turned away. They begged for a piece of news, gossip or anything that might make the presses later that day. Ben duly obliged. Since publicity was his lifeblood he was not going to bite the hand that currently fed him.

Paris's messenger had arrived at eight o'clock that morning when Ben had had no more than three hours sleep. The messenger had stated that the matter was important, but then when Paris wanted something it was always urgent. She had not changed in the ten years since Ben had first known her. Her name had been Patience then and she had hated it. Ben had suggested she choose something she preferred. He promised to keep quiet about Patience. She had paid him a lot of money to do so.

If it came to that, Ben thought, he had been plain Captain Hawksmoor when they had first met, with little to be proud of either. At that stage no one had imagined that he would inherit any title other than that of spawn of the devil.

Ben had had a bad night. He had not dreamed of Catherine, although she was the first thing that he thought of when he awoke alone in the bed that they had so briefly shared. In the darkness he had been plagued by nightmares of his time in the Peninsula and the horrific retreat to Corunna in particular. In his dreams, the French were cutting down the laggards while Ben watched, and one of the dead men had been Ned Clarencieux, holding out a hand and begging Ben to save him…. Ben had shuddered awake, bathed in sweat, to find the cold, foggy light of morning creeping around the curtains and the bed equally as cold and desolate beside him. Once again he had found himself wanting Catherine with a longing that baffled and disturbed him.

"Lord Hawksmoor!" One of the reporters had elbowed his way to the front of the crowd and his shout stirred Ben from his reverie. "I heard that Lady Paris is minded to wed the Duke of Beaufoy. What do you think of that, my lord?"

Ben paused with his hand on the door knocker. Truth was he did not care who Paris inveigled into marriage. If she chose to wed one of the royal princes, he would do no more than wish her luck. Paris was scarcely exclusive in her affections and no one expected her to be. But the papers all thought he was her lover, so he had to appear vaguely interested.

He laughed. "Then I would admire her exceedingly," he said, "for getting past Beaufoy's guardians. Why, the lad is scarce out of the nursery!"

There were raucous guffaws at this from the crowd, for they knew that the twenty-year-old duke had been languishing after Lady Paris for weeks like the lovesick youth he was, while his formidable guardians watched from the sidelines to make sure he did not commit the cardinal folly of eloping with a lightskirt. Ben hoped for Beaufoy's sake that Paris failed to persuade him. She would ruin him within three months.

Edna opened the door to his knock, her mouth turned down at the corners. Like her mistress, Edna had also been a camp follower, but had recognized her own limitations and Paris's potential, and had turned her undoubted skills to the organization of Paris's career.

"Madam's sick," she said bluntly, as Ben shed his coat and gloves. "It's bad. She's asking for you."

She made it sound as though Paris was at death's door, but Ben found this highly unlikely. After all, he had seen Paris only a few nights before and she had been in fine fig, feeding grapes to the regent.

"Too much to drink, was it?" he inquired, following Edna up the stairs. "I did warn her."

The house was stiflingly hot and when Edna threw open the door to Paris's bedroom, Ben could barely see or breathe. The whole room was plunged into darkness and was thick with the overpowering smell of Paris's latest perfume. Ben tried not to cough.

"Where the devil are you, Paris?"

"Ben, darling?" Paris's voice was plaintive. "Over here. I am in bed."

He caught sight of a pale arm waving imperiously at him, and then it disappeared back under the bedclothes rather swiftly.

"Can you not open the curtains a little?" he asked Edna, but she shook her head.

"Madam does not wish it."

Ben reflected that if Paris invited all her lovers to join her in this less than welcoming fashion, it was astounding that she was a successful cyprian at all. He trod gingerly through the mountainous piles of discarded clothes and by the time he finally reached the bedside, his eyes were starting to adjust to the gloom. Even so, Paris was nowhere to be seen.

"Paris," he began, "for pity's sake—"

He stopped as Lady Paris de Moine poked her head

from beneath the covers. Her normally immaculate hair was tumbled about a face that was almost unrecognizable. Her eyes were puffy and her skin was blotched with spots of fiery red. Ben felt a completely unchivalrous urge to laugh.

"Dear me," he said mildly. "So it is true. You are sick."

"I have the chicken pox," Paris said grumpily.

"I see." Ben sat on the edge of the bed and looked at her thoughtfully. He had never seen her looking anything less than perfect since the day he had pulled her out of a waterlogged trench in Portugal. He remembered the time with some affection. Matters had been much simpler then.

"Don't stare," Paris said crossly. "I know I look a fright."

"You do." Ben started to smile. "Who would have thought you could look as bad as this?"

Paris slapped his arm. "Stop it! I only allowed you to see me because…" Her voice trailed away.

"Because you do not need to impress me," Ben said, without resentment. "And, I suspect, because you need my help."

Paris looked at him. He could see the fear in her blue eyes now. She remembered their pact as well as he did. If they could be of use to one another, then that was all well and good. If one of them became a liability, then it was each for themselves.

"I have to go away," Paris said urgently. "No one can know what has happened to me."

"Yes." Ben understood the problem. While it was

essential to see and be seen in society, Paris would be a laughingstock if it became known that she had succumbed to a childish ailment such as chicken pox. She lived so precariously in the fashionable world. One slip and everything would be gone, and her fame and future with it. Paris had even less in the way of family or fortune to fall back on than he did. At least he had his title and a tumbledown house, even if he had no money to support it.

"What do you want from me?" he asked.

The fear in Paris's eyes intensified. Her fingers dug into his sleeve. "Firstly you must promise not to tell anyone what has befallen me, no matter what happens."

Ben shrugged. "Agreed."

"You must help me to concoct a story that will satisfy people," Paris continued, "and you must not take up with any other woman whilst I am on my sickbed. I could not bear to be supplanted."

"I see," Ben said.

"I shall be better within the fortnight," Paris said, "and then I am not certain I shall forgive you if you do not help me now."

The threat was implicit. If he let her down, she would simply cut him adrift. She would cast him out to make or lose his fortune on his own. Her eyes were as cold as ice.

Ben laughed. "You will cut me dead anyway if you land a proposal from Beaufoy, Paris darling. Do you think I do not know that?"

Paris's eyelids flickered down. "That would be different. His family may pay me off and then there will be rich pickings for you, Ben. That was what we agreed. And even if I do catch Beaufoy in parson's mousetrap, I will still pay you. I always honor my promises."

She did. It was one of the things that made it hard to dislike Lady Paris de Moine. She had her own sense of fair play.

"But," Paris continued, her tone hardening, "I cannot promise that I will feel so generously inclined if you break faith with me. I will cut you loose."

Ben stood up. Although they had never been lovers, he sometimes thought that he and Paris knew each other too well. When they had thrown their lot in together, they had given too much away. He knew that she was afraid of losing her looks and ending in the poorhouse, condemned as a lonely old whore who had never had the sense to secure her future. And he had been born into abject poverty and had inherited nothing but debt. Paris knew the thing that he most feared was finishing back in the gutter where he had started. She would not hesitate to use that knowledge to her advantage.

He walked across to the window and drew back the drapes slightly.

"There are a dozen newspaper hacks on your doorstep," he said softly, "and any one of them would sell his mother for the story I could tell them now. So do not seek to threaten me, Paris." He turned back toward her. "We should both accept that we can inflict equal damage on the other and seek instead to find a compromise."

Paris struggled to sit upright. Her nightgown slipped from one rounded shoulder. The sight of her in déshabillé did not arouse Ben and it never had. He knew she would not attempt to seduce him to her point of view.

"Normally I would agree with you, Ben darling," Paris said. She reached across to her bedside cabinet and slid the drawer open. Ben heard the wood scrape and the rustle of parchment. "Normally I would trust you," she repeated, "but I feel very…anxious…at present." She looked up. "So I wish to tell you that if you betray me, I will tell the whole town that you have debauched a debutante and then both you and your little light of love will be ruined."

Ben was so shocked that he actually jumped to hear the words. Across the room, Edna had paused in her tidying of Paris's clothes and stood still, a silk petticoat dangling from her hand. Her expression was a mixture of sympathy and speculation. Ben looked in blank horror from the maid to the mistress and saw that Paris's eyes gleamed with a triumphant light.

"I know all about it," she said. "I know about you and Catherine Fenton."

Ben caught his breath sharply. For a brief moment, panic swamped him, all the more shocking for being utterly unexpected. Paris knew that he had seduced Catherine. Catherine's reputation was in the hands of the most dangerous harlot in London. He felt sick to think of it, stunned and confused to find he cared.

He let the curtain drop into place and crossed to the bed. Paris was sitting bolt upright, the letter clasped tightly in her hand. He reached out to snatch it from her but she whisked it out of sight beneath the covers.

"It is anonymous," she said defiantly.

Ben stared down at her. "I do not believe you, Paris. Information like that is never free. Your informant must have asked for a reward in return—or a favor, at the least."

Paris held his gaze. "I tell you, it is unsigned. No name, no fee."

Ben's lips thinned. "Show me."

"No!"

Ben shrugged. "It is nonsense."

Paris shook her head. "I think not. I saw it in your face when you first heard the charge, Ben darling. You are as guilty as sin."

*As guilty as sin.* Catherine was in serious trouble now and it was indeed his fault. All the thoughts that Ben had been repressing since the previous night surfaced with sudden and terrifying clarity. What would Algernon Withers say when he heard the tale? What would he do to Catherine? Ben felt the cold sweat trickle between his shoulder blades even to think about it.

He drove his hands into his pockets and turned away so that Paris could not see his expression. The only thing he could do now was to try to trick Paris, bluff his way out of it. He was a skilled gambler. He could surely carry it off. If only Catherine's reputation, her very future, did not depend upon it....

"I am not certain that I understand what you are trying to blackmail me with," he said casually. "So it is true. The silly little chit threw herself at me so I took her." The words seemed to stick in his throat but he made them as convincing as he could. Paris was watching him like a snake watches a mouse.

"If you tell everyone, it will do no more than damage her reputation," Ben continued. His mind was full of pictures of Catherine; Catherine defiant, courageous, beautiful; Catherine tumbled in his bed with her hair spread about her, her expression innocent and wondering, her touch... He cleared his throat. "You cannot hurt me. It is always the woman who suffers."

Paris's expression was stony. "Her father will lynch you when he finds out. And she is betrothed to Algernon Withers. He will put a bullet through you."

The name sent another slither of revulsion down Ben's back. It was all too possible that Withers would call him out but he found he was more concerned about what the man did to Catherine. The thought of Withers wreaking a revenge on her appalled him. Worse, it frightened him. He felt a terrible compulsion to protect her, he who had seduced her without compunction and then thought he could just walk away.

He shook his head abruptly to stop this worrying trend of thought. From the start, he had wanted Catherine. It was impossible to deny. Now he realized in some complicated way that his feelings ran deeper than that. He had been slow to recognize it, but he needed her. He wanted her to belong to him and to none other, to take her away from Withers.

But he could not think of that now, or Paris would divine his true feelings and use the knowledge to blackmail him. He turned back toward her and kept his expression studiously blank.

"You mistake," he said lightly. "Neither Fenton nor Withers will call me out. They will want to hush the matter up rather than publish the girl's ruin all over town. Your threats are worth nothing, Paris."

Paris was looking at him with a curious mixture of admiration and aversion.

"You are a coldhearted bastard, Benjamin Hawksmoor," she said.

Ben smiled. "So I am told." He sensed that Paris was weakening and felt a huge relief.

"I was afraid," Paris said lightly, "that you might be about to do something foolish, such as make the chit an offer."

Ben raised his brows. "Why on earth would you think that? You know that I detest the very idea of marriage."

Paris shrugged. She looked evasive. "So you do."

"So," Ben said, "shall we forget your misplaced attempts to blackmail me, Paris, and continue to search for some sort of compromise?"

He saw her smile. "A good solution, Ben darling. I should hate—positively detest—to fall out with you."

Ben smiled a little grimly. "Of course. Now, as you said, you must go away. It is impossible for you to stay here for two weeks out of the public eye. People will talk and the less you tell them, the more they will make it up. It will not serve."

"But someone will recognize me wherever I go,"

Paris objected. "They will see that I am spotty and then they will tell the papers what has happened."

"Not if you leave in secret and travel somewhere no one will find you."

Paris looked horrified. "Are you speaking of the *country?* That is impossible! I cannot go to the country. I would rather die."

"Do not be so stupid, Páris," Ben said bluntly. "If you stay in London all you will achieve is social death. It would be rather more painful and long-lasting for you than the other sort."

Paris's lower lip quivered. She looked like a tragic if blotchy heroine. "You are so cruel—"

"I am trying to help you."

"By packing me off to the country?"

"It is the only way. My cousin Gideon has a place in Surrey, just beyond Richmond. He never goes there. You and Edna will travel there and stay until you are better."

"Surrey?" Ben thought Paris could not have looked more horrified if he had suggested she sail for the Americas. "But that is miles away! We will never get there in this fog!"

"Yes you will. It is not far and you will travel tonight."

Paris gave a wail. "But Surrey is the back of beyond!"

"All the less reason for people to guess where you are. The Lady Paris de Moine that the world knows would never consider staying in a farmhouse in the middle of the country. Meanwhile we shall concoct a story to cover your absence. A sick mother, perhaps—"

"I cannot possibly have a mother! It does not suit my image at all. Mothers are so out of fashion!"

Ben shrugged irritably. "Then a sick retainer, or a sick dog, if you prefer. Once you have left London we will put the story about that you are gone on a mission of mercy and will be absent for a week or two. When you return you will be even more of a mystery."

There was a misty look in Paris's eyes as she contemplated this possibility. "I will own that it would be preferable to staying here and being the butt of spiteful gossip." She looked at Edna. "But how are we to manage, just the two of us?"

"I will send Sam to keep an eye on matters for you," Ben said. "I cannot come myself because I am too easily recognized. It would give the game away if I were to be seen."

Paris gave a little shriek of horror. "Sam Hawksmoor? That oaf? I would rather fend for myself!"

"Very well," Ben said, shrugging. "You can chop your own wood and build your own fires and fetch your own food."

Paris looked sulky. "I suppose you may send Sam to run errands for us, but he is not to speak to me." Her gaze narrowed thoughtfully on him. "But what will you be doing whilst I am withering away in the country, Ben darling? Not pursuing debutantes, I hope."

Once again, danger threatened. Ben gave her a smile that had broken a thousand hearts. "You do not trust me."

"Of course not."

"That is too bad. You will have to pray for a swift recovery and the means to secure Beaufoy—or another duke. I am sure you will succeed since you are far too clever and pretty to remain a courtesan all your life."

Paris chewed her lip. "Well…"

Ben laughed. "Our relationship has always worked so well, Paris, because neither of us trusts the other one further than we could throw them."

Paris smiled reluctantly. "You are no more than an adventurer, Ben Hawksmoor. I know, because I am one, too."

For a moment they looked at one another, then Paris said, "It is a shame that we can never wed, Ben darling, for I do love you."

Ben suspected that in Paris's own way, this was probably true. It was not a type of love that most people would recognize, for Paris's emotions had been tainted with self-interest all her life. She loved herself far more than any other living thing. He understood her because he was exactly like her.

"Touching as such sentiments are," he said, "I must be gone. If you will prepare to remove to Saltcoats, Paris, I shall make sure that a carriage is ready for you tonight."

Paris nodded.

"And no more threats of blackmail," Ben continued, "or I shall have it reported across town that you have left London because you have the pox." He smiled pleasantly. "I do not think that Beaufoy will be so anxious to wed you after that."

Paris glared at him. She snapped her fingers. "Show

Lord Hawksmoor out, Edna. He gives me the headache. His manners are worse than those of a barrow boy."

Ben laughed and blew her a kiss and followed the maid down the stairs. When they reached the hall, Edna grabbed his arm and drew close to him. She smelled of sweat and patchouli, and Ben tried not to grimace.

"The letter," Edna whispered. "It was from Sarah Desmond."

Ben looked at her. He did not feel remotely surprised. "I see. I am uncertain why you are telling me something that I do not care about, Edna."

The maid scowled. "You have been good to us in the past and I am trying to help you, my lord. You are aware that Miss Fenton is an heiress? To eighty thousand pounds?" She paused, scanned his face and smiled with satisfaction. "*That* is the bit of the letter my lady did not want you to see, my lord."

Ben nodded. He understood perfectly Paris's refusal to hand over the letter now. He reached into his pocket, extracted a coin and pressed it into her hand. "Thank you, Edna."

"Edna!" The screech from above would have done credit to a fishwife. Edna shot him an apologetic look.

Ben went out into the wintry sunshine. The hacks on the doorstep looked hopeful, so he smiled broadly and told them that Lady Paris was in good looks and high spirits. The clock on Saint Day's church chimed the hour, reminding him that he was late for his sitting with the artist Hilliard. Now Price would be disapproving of him again.

He walked back to St. James's but he barely noticed the passing streets. He and Paris understood one another. He knew she would not go through with the blackmail about Catherine for fear of reprisal. He thought about Sarah Desmond. Paris had spies in brothels all over London ready to tell her who was plump of pocket and might be worth her time and her charms. He could not really blame Sarah. Except that Catherine, in her innocence, had probably thought her to be a friend.

He also thought about what Edna had told him about Catherine's fortune. Eighty thousand pounds was a hell of a lot of money, enough to tempt a saint never mind an unregenerate sinner such as himself. He had told Sam that he had never sought to wed for money because he was too selfish—he could not tolerate what a wife would demand of him in return. Now he was inclined to reconsider. He needed money and he wanted Catherine Fenton. And with the advantage he held, he could force her to break her despised engagement to Withers and marry him instead. Her father would not kick up a fuss. If he did, she would be ruined.

Fate had delivered Miss Catherine Fenton, heiress to eighty thousand pounds, into his life and his bed, and he was not a man to turn down so generous a gift. His need for Catherine was like a fever in his blood. She and the money together were an irresistible combination. With Catherine in his bed and her money in his bank, the terrifying specter of poverty would recede a little. It was the ghost that had haunted him all of his life, but Catherine's fortune would give him the protection he needed.

He would make Catherine Fenton an offer she could not refuse.

He would propose to her and tell her that unless she accepted he would tell every scandalmonger in London how he had compromised her.

She would have to marry him. It was marriage—or ruin.

## CHAPTER SEVEN

If a young lady should have the melancholy duty
of refusing a proposal of marriage, she should
do so gently, courteously and with no injury to
the gentleman's feelings.
—*Mrs. Eliza Squire,* Good Conduct for Ladies

WHEN TENCH, THE BUTLER, received the summons to
Sir Alfred's study the following morning, he was a
little concerned. After all the disturbances there had
been in the Fenton household of late, it was only
natural to wonder whether he would shortly be looking
for a new position. Tench had no concerns over his
qualities as a butler and his ability to find a new post,
but he did dislike the idea of approaching the domestic
employment agency. It was very demeaning for an
upper servant of his stature to be obliged to seek work
in that fashion and he hoped to be spared the ordeal.

When he saw Miss Catherine Fenton seated at the
desk beneath the picture of her grandfather, Jack
McNaish, he smiled spontaneously, for she looked
extremely businesslike and disconcertingly like her
grandsire. She greeted him warmly and gestured him

to a seat, a kindness that Tench had not been expecting. Sir Alfred tended to make him stand.

"How is my father this morning, Tench?" Catherine asked, fixing him with a direct brown gaze that brooked no avoidance. "I know that he was drunk for the entire day yesterday. Is he merely foxed today, disguised or totally cast away?"

Tench permitted himself a small grimace. "I fear that he is totally cast away, miss, and likely to remain so for the rest of the day. Jeremy footman and I took the liberty of removing him from the library yesterday and putting him to bed."

"And of airing the room as well, I hope," Catherine said, wrinkling her nose. "It stank like a tavern in there."

"Indeed, miss," Tench said. "It is being cleaned now."

"Good," Catherine said. "I will speak to my father later in the day if he sobers up. Please see that he does not go out without consulting me, Tench, and please lock the cellar and make sure that my father does not have access to the drink."

"Yes, miss," Tench said with respect.

"In the meantime," Catherine continued, "I have written to Lord and Lady Arden at Winterstoke, to suggest that Lady Fenton might go to visit them for a space. Although they live much retired, they still have their health and I am sure they would be willing to give a home to their daughter for a while." Catherine tapped the parchment in front of her with the tip of her pen. "It seems to be for the best. Lady Fenton is not well, Tench, and must leave town as soon as it can be arranged. I thought tomorrow."

"Indeed, miss," Tench said fervently, remembering the scene in the hall the night before last. The scrunch of glass and the smell of the laudanum had set his teeth on edge. "I will tell Manners to prepare her ladyship's portmanteaus. Are the children to travel with her?"

Catherine nodded decisively. "Yes, they are. I am sure that Lord and Lady Arden will be delighted to see their grandchildren."

"Then I will acquaint the nursemaids with the plan as well," Tench said, "and see that they have the young master's bags made ready, and Miss Mirabelle's, too."

"Thank you," Catherine said. "Now, I should also be obliged if you would send a man to Lord Withers with this letter, Tench." She held it out. "I am breaking my betrothal to him." She frowned. "There is another letter on the tray for the offices of the *Morning Post*. I require that notice of the termination of the engagement be published in its pages."

Tench sat up a little straighter. He had always detested Algernon Withers and thought that Catherine's actions were long overdue.

"Very *good,* miss!" he said and was rewarded when Catherine smiled.

"You never did care for him, did you, Tench?" she observed.

"No, miss," the butler said. "Not fit to touch the hem of your gown, begging your pardon, miss." He nodded toward the portrait. "*He* would not have approved."

"No," Catherine said, glancing up at her grandfather, "I do not think he would."

There was a final letter on the desk in front of her. She picked it up thoughtfully and weighed it in the palm of her hand. Tench saw her bite her lip.

"This letter—" She colored slightly, looked away but then recovered herself. "This letter is to go to Lord Hawksmoor, Tench. It does not require a reply."

"Very good, miss," Tench said again. He exercised all his butlerly restraint to keep his eyebrows from shooting into his hair. He knew about Hawksmoor. Half the housemaids and all of the scullery maids fancied themselves in love with the man, handsome scoundrel that he was. What he did not know about was Miss Catherine's involvement with the man. He was not sure that he approved.

Once again Tench caught Jack McNaish's eye and stared hard. He had been another scoundrel, cut from the same cloth. Would he have approved of Ben Hawksmoor?

"That will be all for now, Tench," Catherine said. She stood up, indicating that the interview was at an end. "Thank you very much for your help. It is time that certain matters were resolved once and for all."

"Quite so, miss," Tench agreed. He took all the letters and went out into the quiet hall. The house was gloomy with the press of fog still wrapped about the city, and yet under the silence it felt as though something was stirring. Tench speeded up as he strode toward the servants' quarters. He found that he was whistling under his breath, a sprightly air in time to the tap of his footsteps. He found Jeremy footman and confided the letters to him. When he burst into the housekeeper's room, Mrs. Bunting looked up from her account books in lively surprise.

"Good gracious, Mr. Tench, you look as though you have lost a groat and found a guinea!"

Tench beamed at her. "Celebrate, Mrs. Bunting! The house has a new mistress!"

Mrs. Bunting sniffed. "I hope Sir Alfred has not brought that doxy of his over from Chelsea or I'll be leaving."

Tench was genuinely shocked. "Good gracious, no, Mrs. Bunting! I only meant that Miss Catherine has taken charge. Just like old Mad Jack, so she is. There'll be no nonsense now."

There was a suspicious hint of moisture in Mrs. Bunting's eyes. Despite a starchy exterior that frightened the maids, she was as soft as soap inside.

"Has she so?" she said. "Well, bless her! It was time someone sorted out Sir Alfred's drinking and her ladyship's—" Mrs. Bunting paused delicately "—her ladyship's habit of young men and laudanum."

"Miss Catherine has sent to Lord Withers to give him his marching orders," Tench said, giving a happy sigh as he eased himself into the chair by the fire. "A joyful day, Mrs. Bunting, a joyful day!"

Mrs. Bunting smiled. "A cup of tea, Mr. Tench, to celebrate the good news? Or perhaps—" she glanced meaningfully toward the corner cupboard "—a glass of the Madeira?"

"Don't mind if I do, Mrs. Bunting," the butler agreed. "Don't mind at all."

CATHERINE PACED ACROSS to the window, turned on her heel and paced back again. How long had Jeremy been gone? An hour? Two? Lord Withers would certainly have received her letter by now and she was on tenterhooks, uncertain whether he would simply accept the ending of their betrothal or whether he would force an interview with her. She straightened her back. If he demanded to see her then she was prepared. He could bluster and threaten all he wished but she would not relent. She had been looking for an opportunity to break the betrothal for months and now at last she had her chance.

When Maggie had stumbled in two nights before and it had become apparent that she had prostituted herself to Withers for the sake of a bottle of laudanum, Catherine's strongest emotion had been an overwhelming pity. Maggie was so sick and so broken now that Catherine did not know how she would ever recover, nor how Sir Alfred would deal with this latest blow. His retreat to the brandy bottle had not been unexpected, but neither was it promising. Catherine could see that the household had fallen apart now. And so for the sake of them all, she had put aside her own distress and had focused very practically on what she had to do to save them all. She had laid her plans carefully.

Withers was banished finally and forever. She fully intended to confront her father when he was sober and ask him about their joint business dealings, especially now that Ben Hawksmoor had intimated that Withers was involved in criminal activity. But in a way, it was irrelevant anyway. No matter what the hold was that Withers had over Sir Alfred, she was determined to break it. She would not carry on with this sham of a betrothal or allow fear to dictate to them any longer.

She glanced up at her grandfather's portrait as though drawing strength from him. She wished fiercely that he were here now to help her. But she recognized that he had given her his spirit even if it had taken the events of the last few days to awaken that in her.

Her second letter had been to Ben Hawksmoor and in it she had laid bare the whole history of Maggie's relationship with Ned Clarencieux and her own involvement in returning the miniature. She had done it because she felt very strongly that the whole matter needed to be made plain between them so that there could be no further misunderstandings. It had been a painful decision and she had blocked out her feelings for Ben the whole time that she was writing, but as with Withers, she knew it had to be done for everything to be finished between them.

The door knocker sounded once. Catherine drew herself up. She heard Tench's voice and low, masculine tones too deep for her to discern the words. Then the study door opened.

She was not sure whom she had been expecting, but it was Ben Hawksmoor, not Algernon Withers, who stood in the entrance. He held her letter in his hand.

Catherine stared. She had thought—hoped—they might never have to see one another again. The letter had been intended to ensure that very aim, to tie up all loose ends, to finish matters. And yet...

"You were not supposed to come here," she said. She looked at the letter again, as though to confirm he had actually read it. "I asked you not to."

Ben inclined his head. He was unsmiling.

"I know," he said.

Catherine looked at him. She put her hands on her hips. "Then why are you here?"

It was incredibly difficult to face him with any degree of equanimity after what had happened between them the night before last. She had tried to pack her feelings away, discard them even, by writing the letter and telling herself that the whole episode was closed. Yet now she found herself noticing the little things about him, such as the fact that he was bareheaded and there were tiny drops of water in his hair from the fog outside. He smelled of the fresh air and some pine cologne that was refreshing and heady. She noticed that he appeared to have dressed with even greater care than he normally did. His boots had a high polish and he looked very formal in a coat of dark green superfine and fawn pantaloons.

"First of all I came to thank you," he said, "for explaining the connection between your stepmother and Ned Clarencieux. I promise to keep it a secret."

Catherine closed the door gently in Tench's fascinated face. She felt very tired. "It matters little now. My father is aware of her indiscretions and I believe…" She stopped. "It does not matter," she repeated. "If that is all that you have come for then I thank you and wish you good day, my lord."

"It is not all," Ben said. "I wanted to explain that I thought that you were she. I thought it was you who had the affaire with Ned."

Catherine's head jerked up and the color spilled into her face. "Is that supposed to be an apology for what happened between us?"

"It is an explanation." Ben ran his hand through his hair. "I had been told that you were a fashionable impure and that you were involved with Withers's plans—"

"So you thought to take me and use me as you believed I had used Clarencieux," Catherine said, "and by the time you had realized the truth, it was too late. I understood as much, though I did not know why." The anger flickered within her. "I do not see that it profits us any to speak on this further. I have terminated my betrothal to Lord Withers and I wish you joy in discovering the true nature of his criminality. But I have no desire to speak further with you."

Ben shook his head. "I beg your pardon for persisting, Miss Fenton, but there is another matter I wished to discuss with you."

Catherine raised a haughty eyebrow. "And what could that possibly be?"

She saw Ben take a deep breath. "I wish to pay my addresses to you, Miss Fenton. Specifically, I am asking you to marry me."

*"To pay your addresses…"* Catherine grabbed the back of a chair to steady herself.

"Quite so, Miss Fenton."

"What in God's name would induce you to do such a thing?" Catherine demanded.

Ben smiled, that slow, wicked smile that made her weaken at the knees. "Two nights ago I compromised your reputation."

Catherine remembered all too well. It was not something she would forget in a hurry. She pushed the memory firmly aside. This morning, she had promised herself, marked a new beginning. She was not going to let Ben Hawksmoor change that.

"And I told you," she said, "that I would not dream of trying to entrap you into marriage, my lord."

"I know." Ben turned her letter over in his hands. "I fear that the boot is on the other foot, Miss Fenton. I am here to entrap *you*."

Catherine stared at him. "Because of that night—" She stopped as a blinding wave of disillusionment hit her.

"Because of the money," she whispered. "You did not know before that I am an heiress."

She looked up into his face. There was the smallest shadow of something in his eyes. Was it shame? She doubted it. An adventurer like Ben Hawksmoor would not regret the good fortune that had dropped such a gift into his lap.

"You have heard that I have a fortune." She managed to force the words out past the pain that was building in her throat. "And you are a man who values money above all else."

"I am." He looked at her very straight. "I would not lie to you, Miss Fenton, and pretend that I had proposed for any other reason."

Fury and disenchantment ripped through Catherine. "You are an unprincipled fortune hunter," she said bitterly.

Ben shrugged. "Is there any other sort?"

Catherine glared. "I will *not* marry you, sir. I will not wed a man who is an arrogant, opportunistic adventurer without a single shred of honor."

She saw Ben wince. "Your opinion of me is lower than even I had imagined."

"That is only the start," Catherine said sweetly. "I have plenty more opinions should you wish to press your suit!"

Ben took a step toward her. "Then what is your opinion of the passion that was between us that night, Miss Fenton? Do you deny that you wanted me as much as I wanted you?" His hands bit into her shoulders suddenly. "You know full well that you respond to me," he said softly, "or we would not be where we are now."

Catherine was silent. She could not blame him for her seduction, not when she had so wholeheartedly compromised herself. But there was a heat and a dark desire in his eyes now that frightened her because it demanded a response from her. And she had no wish to prove him right. Not now, when he had shown himself clearly in his true colors as no more than an adventurer.

"You said it was a disappointing mistake," he said. "I promise you that the reverse will be true when we do things properly. Or indeed improperly."

"That is just male pride talking," Catherine said. "You were offended because I insulted your prowess.

I am sure the impulse to set matters right on that score will pass."

She saw the corner of his mouth twitch in a smile and his hands gentled on her shoulders. "You do not know enough about men and sex to make that assumption, Kate."

Her gaze flew to his. He had called her Kate again. It felt too intimate. It felt *right* to hear the name on his lips. It reminded her of that night in his bed. She struggled with the memories and managed to subdue her feelings.

"I may know little of such matters," she said coolly, "but I do know that I have no desire to give you a second chance, nor to wed a man who wants my money first, my body second, and has no concern for my feelings at all."

To her surprise, he just smiled. "Liar," he said. "You want me, too."

The pink color stung Catherine's cheeks. "I do not!"

He leaned closer, his lips brushing her cheek, touching the corner of her mouth. "Admit it," he whispered, his breath stirring her hair. "It is not just about the money."

Before Catherine could respond, he kissed her, his tongue moving against her own with deliberate demand, deliberate possession. She felt the earth tilt beneath her feet and clung to him, unable to conceal her response.

"Make the deal, Catherine," Ben said when he released her. "You are a nabob's daughter. You understand about business."

"No," Catherine said. "There is precious little in such a deal to please me."

"Is there not?"

He kissed her again. Her body flamed to life, the heat pooling low in her stomach. She knew she lied in denying him. There was pleasure here for her. There always had been. But it had been her downfall once and she was not going to let that happen again.

"So," Ben said, when he let her go, "say you will wed me. It will not be a poor bargain—for either of us."

"No," Catherine said. "I will not wed you simply because some…some accident of attraction creates this feeling between us. I'll wager it is my fortune that tempts you even more than I do!"

There was a spark of humor deep in Ben's eyes. "Both tempt me equally, Miss Fenton." He drove his hands into his jacket pockets and the humor died from his face. "Miss Fenton, I do not think that you understand." There was a thread of steel in his voice now. "When I said that this was a case of entrapment…" He shrugged elegantly. "What can I say? If you do not agree to the match, I shall tell everyone that I have seduced you. You will be ruined."

Catherine stared into his hazel eyes. "Lord Hawksmoor," she said, "you are an unmitigated scoundrel."

"Agreed, Miss Fenton."

Catherine squared her shoulders. She walked away from him. "Lord Hawksmoor, in your rush to the altar, you have perhaps not taken sufficient time to learn of my family," she said. She gestured toward the picture of her grandfather.

"That is Mad Jack McNaish," she said. "He was my grandfather. He was a legendary nabob. He taught me the value of everything, not just money." She leaned her hands on the desk and looked at him. "To understand me, you need to know about Mad Jack, Lord Hawksmoor. He and my mother were the only people ever to teach me about love." She paused for a moment. Even though she had sworn never to tell Ben her feelings for him, she wanted there to be absolute truth between them now so that there could never, ever be any more misunderstandings.

"I thought I loved you," she said. It was hard to get the words out but she forced herself to do it. "I told you before that I allowed you to seduce me because I went too far and did not know how to stop. That was true, but the reason it happened was because I thought I was in love with you. That was my mistake, and a bad one."

Ben made an involuntary move toward her and she shook her head sharply, warning him to keep his distance.

"I will never marry unless it is for love," she said. "The fortune that you covet now was amassed by my grandfather for my future welfare and not to satisfy the greed of an unprincipled rogue."

There was a silence. "I am sorry," Ben said. "I am sorry that I cannot give you what you want—"

"Do not be," Catherine said. She, too, felt regret, regret that he could be so honest and yet not be the man she wanted him to be.

"As I said, it was my mistake," she said bleakly.

"But you can see now why I would never entrust myself—or my money—to a self-confessed fortune hunter."

Ben smiled, the laughter lines crinkling the corners of his eyes. "From what I have heard of him, Miss Fenton, Mad Jack McNaish was just another such adventurer as I. He might well have approved of me."

Catherine paused. There was some truth in that. She knew that her grandfather would have far preferred Ben's outspoken honesty to Withers's slimy half-truths and deceptions. Even so, she would not accept him. She could not and still be true to her own principles. Her instinct told her to seek the comfort of his arms. She would find passion and excitement and all the things she had discovered that she craved. But her mind told her that such things were worthless without love.

She shook her head.

"You mistake, Lord Hawksmoor, if you think that my grandfather would have entertained your suit for a moment," she said. "What do you really think he would have done if he knew you had seduced me and then tried to force me to marry you?"

"He would have called me out," Ben said, without hesitation.

"Precisely," Catherine said. She smiled. "Not for nothing am I his granddaughter. Name your seconds, Lord Hawksmoor. I challenge you to a duel."

"YOU CANNOT DO THAT." Ben had responded before he even thought about it. Challenge him to a duel to defend her good name? It was unthinkable. He could not believe that she genuinely meant it.

He saw Catherine stiffen her spine and her chin came up.

"Why can I not challenge you?" She arched her brows at him. "Because I am a female?"

"No." He admired the spark of fury in her brown eyes. It called to everything that was primitive and masculine within him and made him want to sweep her into his arms there and then. Ben shifted a little, keeping his hands firmly at his sides. He was beginning to get the measure of Miss Catherine Fenton now. There was no doubt that he had underestimated her. He thought that if he touched her now, she would probably hit him with the poker.

"Dueling is illegal," he pointed out.

Catherine snapped her fingers dismissively and swept away from him with a soft swish of silk. "No one observes that," she said over her shoulder. "Why, only last week Lord Granville challenged Lord Belk. And you of all people—" he could hear the derision in her voice "—are hardly going to respect the law."

There was a silence. Ben thrust a hand through his hair in a gesture of frustration. "I refuse," he said.

"You refuse my challenge?" Catherine had stopped beneath the portrait of Jack McNaish and had turned to face him. The resemblance between her and the picture was striking; the strong, determined planes of the face, the cool calculation in the dark eyes.

"You cannot do that in all honor," she said.

"Catherine…" Ben spread his hands in a pleading

gesture. He could not believe she was doing this. "I understand that you are angry with me," he said, "but this is folly. I am a crack shot. I don't want to hurt you."

He saw her smile. "Whereas I would take pleasure in hurting you very much, Lord Hawksmoor. That probably gives me the edge."

Ben rubbed his brow. "Catherine—"

Her jaw set hard. "Name your seconds, Lord Hawksmoor, or I shall have it said in every club in London that you are too much of a coward to take my challenge."

Ben reached her side in one stride and grabbed her by the upper arms. "Catherine, this is madness. Even if I were to meet you, I would delope. I could not fire on a woman."

He could feel the tension in the body beneath his hands. She held herself very stiff and straight away from him. There was no chance that he could persuade her now with caresses and soft words. He admired her for it even as it frustrated him. Oh yes, he had underestimated Miss Catherine Fenton and now he was paying the price. He had thought he could persuade her into marriage with the threat to her reputation, or seduce her with the passion that he knew they could conjure between them. But she was too principled for that. He began to see that he did not really know her at all.

"It would be very foolish of you to delope, Lord Hawksmoor," she said, "for then I would shoot you in cold blood." She laughed. "Have I offended your male pride? Challenged by a mere woman! How will you live it down?"

Ben shook her. "Catherine, you would be creating

the greatest scandal, dragging your *own* name through the mud, ruining your own reputation—"

Her eyes flashed defiance. "Is that not what you would be doing, my lord, if you stoop to your blackmail?"

"There need be no blackmail and no scandal if you agree to accept my hand in marriage," Ben argued. "Devil take it, Catherine, withdraw the challenge!"

"I shall not," Catherine said, "unless you withdraw the insult of your threat to compromise me."

Ben stared down into her eyes. He found he wanted her even more now than he had at the start of their interview. He wanted to crush that soft mouth, now set in such uncompromisingly firm lines, beneath his own. He wanted to take her back to his bed, where she belonged, and take her until they were both exhausted. He felt a primitive possessiveness he had never experienced before. It drove him and he knew he would have no peace until he could claim her again.

"I will not withdraw my offer," he said. "I want to wed you and I will ruin your reputation if that is what it takes to achieve our marriage."

She bit out each word of her reply. "Very well. Then you will answer to me for that insult at a time and place of my choosing. I give you one week, Lord Hawksmoor. You will meet me at Harington Heath at dawn, seven nights from now or I shall have you denounced as a coward."

Ben released her. They stared at each other for what seemed an eternity. Then he nodded.

"Very well," he said. "I accept."

SAM HAWKSMOOR'S HORSE PICKED its way through giant snowdrifts on the Twickenham Road. It had been snowing for the best part of two days and Sam had been unable to leave London to check how Paris and her maid were faring. On the third day, the sky had cleared and a brisk, cold wind had sprung up, so sharp that Sam now felt as though he were frozen in his saddle. He thought of Gideon's drafty old farmhouse, currently housing a most unexpected and secret tenant, and hoped to goodness that he would not arrive to discover that the most famous courtesan in London had frozen to death in his absence. That would create a wonderful news story, but not the sort that Ben would want to see in the papers.

When Ben had first told him what he required him to do with regard to Paris, Sam had refused point blank.

"No," he said. "No, no, no. Not Paris. She frightens me."

Ben had laughed and told him that Paris was easy to manage when one knew how and that Sam would have to be firm with her, but that, Sam thought, was easy to say. He would rather deal with a basket of scorpions than with Paris de Moine. On the night that he had escorted Paris and her maid to Saltcoats, she had refused even to acknowledge him.

"Don't look at me, don't speak to me," she had said, before turning away from him and spending the rest of the journey in silence.

Sam turned down the lane that led to the farm. The most recent tenant farmer had left a month ago and Gideon had not yet installed a new one. Sam shuddered to think what Gideon would say if he found out that his detested cousin Ben was housing his mistress at the farmhouse. Sam sighed, wishing that Ben would not play such dangerous games.

There was no one about. The fields were a blank, white snowscape. Sam relaxed a little. At least no one was likely to find Paris in such a benighted spot and Gideon would not be making any unexpected trips out of the city when the weather was so inclement. The horse's hooves crunched on the deep snow. Heavy overhanging branches scattered little shards of ice on the track. Then the trees opened up and he was at the entrance to Saltcoats drive.

The house was set well back from the road with stables and a walled garden to the side. Sam rode up the drive, tied his horse to the mounting block and un-latched the gate leading to the gardens and stables. Then he stopped and stared.

There was someone—or something—out in the garden. After one astounded second, Sam identified the creature as human, although it was rolling in the snow rather like a dog desperately trying to rid itself of fleas. Back and forth the creature rolled, making a strange squeaking noise and sending the snow flying in all directions. Then it stood up and Sam realized with the biggest shock of his entire life, that it was Lady Paris de Moine. She was entirely naked.

Sam stared at Paris. Her body was stung pink with blotchy red patches and snow melting all over her. She looked… Sam swallowed. She looked quite ridicu-lous. The most sought-after courtesan in the kingdom had ice stuck in her hair—in all her body hair—and looked like a madwoman from Bedlam.

Then Paris reached for the robe that was draped on the nearest branch and said crossly, "What are you gawping at?"

Sam found his voice. "What on earth are you doing?"

Paris looked even crosser. "The spots itch. This is the only way I can scratch them. Don't just stand there," she added. "Stable your horse and bring the food in."

Sam did as he was told. In the stables he found that the wood he had been expecting to chop was already cut and neatly stacked ready for use. He filled a basket and took it inside with him, wondering whether Edna had been resorting to manual labor or whether Paris already had some poor unsuspecting local farmer under her thumb. The house was warm with a good fire burning in the parlor. Paris had disappeared upstairs and Sam took the saddlebags with their food and wine into the kitchen. It was a huge room with a long table and worn stone flagged floor. There was a pan of vegetable broth bubbling on the stove and a half-plucked chicken on the slab.

"Paris wrung its neck," Edna said cheerfully, in answer to Sam's question. "She was feeling blue-deviled and we needed to eat. We were not sure when you would be able to get through to us because of the snow. The rest of the brood are safe in the shed," she added.

Paris came in then. She was wearing a simple high-necked gown and had her startlingly pretty fair hair tied back in a bow. Her face had several large chicken-pox spots on it. She scowled at Sam.

"Still staring, I see," she said.

"I haven't seen you without your makeup before," Sam said. "You look nice," he added foolishly and waited for Paris's wrath to descend on his head.

Strangely, though, she said nothing at all. Sam thought he saw Edna hide a smile as she bent over the vegetable pot.

"I brought wine," he rushed on. "And meat and cheese."

"There is some very good elderberry wine in the pantry," Paris said, giving him the cool blue stare that conversely made him feel very hot.

"I made that," Sam said. "I lived here for a few months in 1809. I was recovering from diphtheria," he added.

"Diphtheria! Chicken pox! The place is a positive plague house!" Paris snapped. She glared at him. "There is some plum jam, too, from the trees in the orchard. Did you make that as well?"

"No," Sam said.

Conversation faltered. Over at the stove, Edna hummed softly as she stirred the broth. Sam felt warm and ran a finger around the inside of his collar. He watched Paris out of the corner of his eyes, as though she were some unpredictable animal. She was looking at him with a calculating expression that gave him deep misgivings.

"Can you make bread?" she asked suddenly. "Neither Edna nor I know how to do it."

"No," Sam said.

"You're useless," Paris said disagreeably, turned on her heel and stalked out of the room.

Edna sighed. "I am sorry," she said. "The spots make my lady very bad-tempered."

"I don't think it's just the spots," Sam said. He looked at the slaughtered chicken lying hopelessly on its slab.

"Do you wish me to chop any more wood before I go?" he asked.

Edna shook her head. "We have plenty. My lady has done it herself."

The thought of Paris with an ax in her hand made Sam feel quite queasy with fright.

"Stay for some broth," Edna said. "Don't mind her." She jerked her head toward the parlor. "You get used to it."

Sam sighed. He went into the parlor, where Paris was sitting huddled by the fire. There was a book on the table, a pile of embroidery and a stack of playing cards. Paris glanced up when he came in but said nothing.

"Edna has asked me to stay to eat," Sam said.

Paris hunched her shoulders even more. "Do what you like."

Sam threw another log on the fire. "Is there anything else you need me to do for you?" he asked.

Paris shook her head. "No."

"Is that your embroidery?"

Paris gave him a scornful look. "Is that likely?"

Sam looked at her. She stared straight back.

"Right," he said. "I will be back tomorrow."

Paris frowned. "That is not necessary."

"Nevertheless—"

"I forbid it."

It was not often that Sam lost his temper. When they had been children, Gideon had sought to provoke him on many an occasion and received such a bland response that he had taunted his brother for being simple. Not even that had roused Sam's anger. But now, looking on Paris's pretty, sulky, spotty face, he felt his temper stir.

"Paris," he said, "I will be coming back tomorrow." He saw her open her mouth and carried straight on. "I don't want to come here," he said. "I don't like you, I don't want to help you, and I would far rather spend my time doing something more congenial. In fact, if it comes to that, I never have liked you. You are spoilt and rude and not even a very nice person. But I promised Ben I would do this so I will."

He turned on his heel and made for the door. "Until tomorrow."

"Sam." Paris had waited until he was almost out of the room before she spoke. He turned. She did not look in the least apologetic. She was holding the pack of cards in her hand.

"Yes?" he said.

"There is something that you can do for me," Paris said. "You can play piquet with me. We will play for pennies."

Sam paused. This was the moment, he knew, when he should just tell her to go to hell. She had made no attempt to apologize. She did not even look particularly bothered whether he stayed or not. He suspected that *sorry* was, for Paris, the hardest word to say.

After a moment he sat down opposite her. Paris dealt. Sam picked up his cards and set about fleecing her.

TWO FULL DAYS AFTER CATHERINE had issued the challenge, she was still waiting for Ben to name his seconds for the duel. It infuriated her. *He* infuriated her. Catherine knew he had deliberately failed to react in order to see what she would do. He was testing her, raising the stakes. And she knew she had to respond because she simply would not give him the upper hand.

A half hour after breakfast, Catherine was in her father's study, trying to decide what to do. The house was quiet. Maggie and the children had been gone a couple of days and Sir Alfred had not left his room since the night of the terrible confrontation with his wife. He was sober now but had contracted a fever, which the doctor had told Catherine had been brought on by excessive alcohol and a disorder of the nerves. In the meantime, Algernon Withers had neither written nor appeared in person in answer to Catherine's letter. It was as though he had simply vanished. And although Catherine found this most satisfactory, she still felt sick at the thought of eventually confronting him. His casual cruelty, his blatant debauchery, the way he had used poor, broken Maggie for his own ends... The thought made her blindingly angry.

Catherine poured herself another cup of coffee

from the cooling pot and rested her chin on her palm as she tried to think. She needed to know precisely how matters stood in regard of her business affairs. She was not sure how to achieve that given that one of her trustees was dead, a second was ill and a third had disappeared.

And she needed to bring Ben Hawksmoor to heel. This unsatisfactory state of affairs could not continue. She would go to St. James's and oblige him to name his seconds for the duel.

She was halfway to the door, intending to go upstairs to dress to go out, when the door knocker fell sharply and she heard Tench make his way across the floor to answer. Callers were rare in Guilford Street these days, for with Maggie absent they could neither entertain nor go out. Lily St. Clare had been the only caller the previous day, visiting in answer to Catherine's plea that she act as one of her seconds in the forthcoming duel. Catherine thought that Tench had dealt very well with an accredited courtesan calling at the house; not by a twitch of a muscle had he expressed any emotion whatsoever except pure courtesy. He was, Catherine thought, a gem among butlers.

Now, however, it sounded as though Tench was dealing with a very different kind of caller. Catherine opened the door a crack and heard an imperious feminine voice.

"Perch, Plaice, Tench, whatever your name is, tell Sir Alfred that Lady Russell wishes to see him!"

There was a pause as Tench replied that Sir Alfred was indisposed.

"Indisposed?" the voice said incredulously. "Arrant nonsense! You mean that he is foxed?"

Catherine rushed out into the hall. "Aunt Agatha! Oh, Aunt Agatha, I am so pleased to see you!"

The elderly vision removing her hat in the hall paused with the pins in her hand. A smile creased her face, which was as brown and wrinkled as a walnut. She was small and round and clad in a startlingly scarlet cloak.

"Kate, my dear!" she cried. "Well, at least one member of the household seems still to have her wits about her. I came as soon as I heard. I thought you might need me."

Catherine slipped her arm through her godmother's and drew her toward the library. She glanced back at the butler who was turning Lady Russell's strangely shaped bonnet around in his hands as though he was not quite sure what to do with it.

"Tench," Catherine said, "may we please have some refreshment served? Thank you." She turned back to Lady Russell. "You mentioned that you had heard of my father's indisposition, ma'am? Is it then common knowledge?"

"All over town," Lady Russell confirmed gloomily, subsiding in a chair with a heavy sigh. "Heard all about it at Grillons Hotel and you know what a dashed respectable place that is! Did your father not tell you that I was back from Samarkand?"

"No," Catherine said. She wondered why Sir Alfred had seen fit to keep the news from her. Perhaps it was because he knew she would immediately enrol Lady

Russell on her side in her attempts to discover what had happened to the trust fund. And Lady Russell was a dangerous adversary. Just to have her godmother by her side now made Catherine feel inordinately more cheerful.

"I hope that you enjoyed your trip," she said. She looked at her godmother, tiny, wrinkled as a prune and resplendent in a vivid gold-and-scarlet gown. "You are looking very well indeed, Aunt Agatha," she added. "Positively radiant."

Lady Russell beamed. "Travel agrees with me. But I will tell you about that later. First, I need to know what is going on. Seems to me there is some devilish coil here, Kate, and you are all caught up in it."

As well as being Catherine's godmother, Lady Russell was an old acquaintance of her grandfather's and widow of a fellow nabob. The shared past of the Russells and McNaishes in distant lands had seemed to the young Catherine to be as richly furnished as a fairy story. Lady Russell's presence in Catherine's life had been fitful given her predilection for travel overseas, the more exotic and far-flung the destination the better. After her husband had died, she had followed the trade routes of Asia and India in some sort of final pilgrimage, and Catherine had not seen her for several years. But now she was back and Catherine was delighted to see her. She sat down opposite her.

"It seems that you have already heard that Papa has taken to the bottle," she said. "He has a fever at present. And Maggie is sick with the laudanum and has gone to her parents and I have broken my betrothal to Algernon Withers."

Lady Russell made a disgusted noise that sounded like a camel snorting. "Withers! That wastrel! Well done, my dear! I knew his father, of course, and his younger brother. Both very bad *Ton!*"

"He is still one of my trustees," Catherine said.

"Appointed at your father's instigation," Lady Russell said, nodding ominously. "And then there is that curious matter of James Mather's death. The whole matter smells as strong as the fish market to me, Kate. I will ask my lawyer to make inquiries if you will, and see if we might find out what is at the bottom of this."

Catherine nodded. "Thank you, Aunt Agatha. I have asked Papa before but it gets me nowhere. I am certain that Withers has some hold over him."

There was a pause while Tench came in and distributed pastries and tea.

"So," Lady Russell said, head turned to one side as she viewed her goddaughter, "your papa is a broken reed, Maggie is sick and you have dismissed your betrothed…. Is there aught else that I have missed whilst I have been away, Kate?"

"A little," Catherine said cautiously. "I have rejected a proposal of marriage from a gentleman who threatens to ruin my reputation and…" She gulped. "I have challenged him to a duel!"

She waited but Lady Russell merely observed her with a distinctly shrewd expression.

"Well," her godmother said after a moment. "A young gel should be permitted to put a bullet through a man if she don't like him. I remember once back in

India there was a fella in the company who insulted me and I called him out." She shook her head regretfully. "The fool was too much of a coward to meet me! He called off!"

"Well, Lord Hawksmoor has agreed to meet me," Catherine said. "At the very least he is not a coward."

Lady Russell tilted her head thoughtfully. "Hawksmoor, you say? The chap who was in the Peninsular? I met him once. Shocking scoundrel, very dangerous." She was smiling. "Fatally attractive, of course. That type always is."

Catherine blushed. "What was he doing at the time you met him?" she asked. "Seducing all the local beauties?"

"No," Lady Russell said, eyes twinkling, "he was rescuing a comrade from behind enemy lines. Plenty of courage, that boy."

Catherine frowned. "What were you doing behind enemy lines, Aunt Agatha?"

For the first time in their acquaintance, she thought that Lady Russell looked shifty. "Ah," her godmother said, "best not to ask." She cleared her throat. "So he compromised you, did he?"

"I compromised myself," Catherine said a little bleakly. Although Lady Russell was famous for her tolerance, Catherine did not intend to tell her godmother just how thoroughly she had ruined herself.

"Lord Hawksmoor, realizing that I was an heiress, decided that I should be forced into marriage with him," she explained. "I refused and when he threatened to tell everyone, I responded by challenging him to a duel."

Lady Russell nodded slowly. "Seems reasonable to me. Not the required behavior for a young gel, of course, but needs must. Have you named your seconds?"

"I have asked Lily St. Clare to act for me," Catherine said. "You remember Lily, Aunt Agatha?"

Lady Russell nodded. "Sweet gel," she said. "You were at school with her as I recall. How does she do these days?"

Catherine swallowed hard. "She is…um… She was obliged… That is, she is a courtesan."

She saw Lady Russell's eyes bulge slightly. "Good God," she said faintly. "I have been away a long time. London is gone to rack and ruin!"

"It was dreadful," Catherine said. "Lily's husband was a cad and used to beat her and when she turned to a lover, he betrayed her…. Poor Lily, she is in the most desperate straits. She is not happy."

"Don't know what society is coming to," Lady Russell said gruffly, selecting another scone with a look of relish. "There are some good men out there but where are they when you need 'em?" She fixed Catherine with a gimlet gaze. "Left us all at the mercy of rakes and wastrels! Best be sure Ben Hawksmoor is not a good man before you put a bullet through him, miss."

"I won't kill him," Catherine said, "but I do feel most strongly that he deserves to be taught a lesson."

She paused, drumming her fingers thoughtfully on the arm of the chair. Was Ben Hawksmoor a good man? Conventional judgment said not, and yet he had been a war hero. People spoke of his courage. And she herself had seen the loyalty he had for Ned Clarencieux. She sighed.

"I know it is not at all appropriate to ask you, Aunt Agatha, but do you think you might act for me as well? I realize that the whole matter is most unconventional—"

Lady Russell beamed. "Thought you'd never ask, Kate. I'd be delighted. Need a bit of excitement in my old age. Thought London was going to be dashed dull after Samarkand. Seems I was wrong."

Catherine breathed a sigh of relief. "Oh good. Well, thank you, Aunt." She glanced at the clock. "In point of fact, I was about to call on Lord Hawksmoor when you arrived. He has refused to name his seconds, you see, and I know he does it just to taunt me. I am determined to make him meet my challenge."

Lady Russell put down her teacup. "Then by all means let us call upon him, my dear."

They took a hack. The snow had been swept from the main thoroughfares now, but it was still slow going.

"There have been the most dreadful accidents out in the country, you know," Lady Russell confided. "They say that coaches have been overturned in the snowdrifts and an entire company of soldiers frozen to death near Shrewsbury!"

Catherine shivered. "I hope that Maggie and the children reached Kent in safety. We had not had word, but with the weather being as it has…"

"Difficult conditions under which to fight a duel," Lady Russell observed.

"I will find a way," Catherine said.

At number forty-three St. James's Place, they found the same discreet-looking butler who had admitted Catherine the night of the masquerade and subsequently found her a hack to take her to Covent Garden. Catherine felt slightly embarrassed but the manservant gave no sign of recognizing her at all.

"His lordship is at home," he confirmed, "but he is currently occupied. If you will wait in the drawing room, ladies, I will let him know that you are here."

Catherine stood before the fireplace, fidgeting with her gloves. She felt very on edge and irritated to find herself feeling that way. In the two days since she had issued her challenge to Ben, the blinding fury that she had felt at his blackmail had not abated. It had hardened into a fierce determination to teach him a lesson for his arrogance.

"Once he knows I am here, he will creep out the back door, or tell the butler not to admit us, or pretend that he is occupied," she said fiercely. "I know he does it only to annoy me."

"It seems to be working," Lady Russell commented. She opened the door and peered out into the corridor. "I can see that close-looking fellow in the doorway of a room at the end of the hall," she said.

"The ballroom," Catherine said, without thinking, and saw her godmother's eyebrows shoot up into her hair.

"I see," Lady Russell said. "You have been here before."

Catherine cleared her throat. "Oh, I am going in there. I cannot be doing with all this waiting about."

She marched down the corridor before her god-mother could protest. The door of the ballroom was ajar and she could hear the butler within, speaking to someone—presumably Ben—who was out of sight.

"...I have asked the ladies to wait in the drawing room but if your lordship prefers not to see them this morning I will explain—"

"Oh no, you won't," Catherine said, pushing the door wide. "Lord Hawksmoor..." She stopped.

At one end of the ballroom was an easel set up by the long windows. An artist was painting quickly, almost feverishly. Some distance away, on a small stage, stood Ben Hawksmoor. He was naked but for a diaphanous union flag draped low around his hips.

Catherine stared, blushed and felt a wave of heat consume her entire body. She was mortified. How could she feel aroused by the sight of Ben Hawks-moor, here, in full daylight, in his own ballroom, with her chaperone in attendance? And yet...aroused was precisely what she felt. Hot and disturbed and stirred up—and very, very angry.

"Benjamin Hawksmoor!" Lady Russell said loudly from behind her. "Yes, I recognize you!"

Catherine wondered which bit of Ben her god-mother could possibly be recognizing.

"Catherine!" Lady Russell snapped. "Avert your eyes."

Catherine frowned. It was difficult to know where to avert them. She looked away, only to catch a glimpse of the curve of one of Ben's buttocks as he dropped the flag and reached for his robe. The painter sighed querulously.

"Really, my lord. These interruptions are becoming intolerable."

"My apologies, Hilliard," Ben drawled. "I will be but a moment. Pray excuse me."

He came toward them. "Lady Russell." He bowed. "It is a great pleasure to see you again, ma'am. And Miss Fenton!" He took Catherine's hand, a dangerous twinkle in his hazel eyes. "What could possibly induce you to step inside this house again, remembering what happened last time?"

Catherine snatched her hand away. Her heart was racing. "I have come to remind you of your engagement for a duel in five days' time," she said sarcastically. "It may have slipped your lordship's mind, but you have not yet named your seconds."

Ben's smile deepened. "So I have not. And have you named yours?"

"Miss St. Clare and Lady Russell are to act for me," Catherine said.

Ben smiled at Lady Russell. "I rue the day that you decided to be on the opposing side, ma'am!"

"Catherine is my goddaughter," Lady Russell said, trying and failing to suppress an answering smile, "and I understand that you have upset her."

Ben shrugged self-deprecatingly. "I fear I have, ma'am. I wish to marry Miss Fenton but she has taken against my suit. If you could see your way clear to championing my cause–"

"Just a minute!" Catherine cut in. She was outraged. "How dare you try to engage my godmother to support you? Have you forgotten, my lord, that the

reason I challenged you was because you threatened
to ruin my reputation?"

"Quite right," Lady Russell agreed. "You are a
scoundrel, Benjamin Hawksmoor, and I fully support
Catherine in her bid to put a bullet through you."

Ben laughed. "Have you told her what a good shot
I am, ma'am?"

Lady Russell sniffed. "I have not. I do not seek to
influence her decision." She paused. "I would give a
monkey to know how you escaped the French that
time, though, Hawksmoor. I could have sworn you
were surrounded."

Ben laughed again. "If your goddaughter has her way,
ma'am, that will be a secret I will be taking to my grave."

Catherine stepped forward. "Fascinating as these
reminiscences are," she said frigidly, "I wonder if you
might name your seconds, my lord, and then we may
leave you to your business." She glanced across at where
the artist was pacing the floor, a deep frown on his face.

"Of course," Ben said politely. He drew closer to
her, so close that Catherine could feel the warmth
emanating from his barely-clad body. "My cousins
Gideon and Samuel Hawksmoor will act for me in this
matter."

"Thank you," Catherine said coldly.

"Gideon Hawksmoor?" Lady Russell said disgust-
edly. "You might as well choose a chanting parson!
Can you not do better than that?"

"Aunt Agatha!" Catherine burst out. "You are supposed to be on *my* side!"

Ben was laughing openly to see her annoyance. "Your

godmother is an excellent judge of character," he said, "and she has always liked me, have you not, ma'am?"

"That is nothing to the purpose," Catherine snapped, before Lady Russell could reply and make matters even worse. She drew herself up. "We are leaving. Good day, my lord."

She was halfway to the door when she paused, overcome by a sudden curiosity. "By the by, my lord, which historical character are you supposed to be representing here?"

"King Edward the Confessor," Ben said unblushingly. "He was a saint."

"Very funny!" Catherine said. "Could they not find a more appropriate model?"

"My dear Miss Fenton," Ben said, "the pictures sell like hotcakes. Every lady wishes to have me in her bedroom."

Catherine bit her lip, feeling the awareness run between them. She could see he was remembering having her in his own bedroom. And how could she not be disturbed by such memories, and by the tempting promise he had made:

*You will not find me disappointing when we do things properly...*

"Then every lady is welcome to you," she snapped. She turned on her heels and swept out, but she heard his laughter following her down the corridor.

"Aunt Agatha," she said, once they were back in the carriage, "how *did* Lord Hawksmoor evade the French that time?"

Lady Russell's eyes gleamed. "Through cunning.

And nerve." She patted her goddaughter's hand. "You like him, do you not, Kate?"

"No!" Catherine said. She cast Lady Russell a sideways look. "But you do and although I hate to admit it, you are a good judge of character."

"The boy has charm," Lady Russell conceded.

"And arrogance," Catherine said bitterly.

"His father was a vile man," Lady Russell said. "I always thought that Sarah Hawksmoor did a splendid job bringing Benjamin up on her own. It must have been intolerably difficult for her."

"What happened to her?" Catherine asked.

There was a pause. "She died of a fever," Lady Russell said, a little gruffly. "As soon as Benjamin got his first army pay, he arranged for her to leave London and take a small cottage in the country. But it was too late." Lady Russell gave a long sigh. "Her health had been weakened by years of suffering. The first winter she caught bronchitis and a putrid fever and was too weak to recover."

Catherine swallowed hard. With her own longing to create a loving family, she could feel all too sharply what the loss of his mother must have been like for the young Benjamin Hawksmoor. She had been the only one who had been there for him through the years of his childhood. And then he had lost her, too.

"They always said that Hawksmoor tried to kill himself in the Peninsular because he was mad and bad," Lady Russell said, "but I think he was half-crazed with grief."

Catherine was horrified to feel the tears sting her throat.

"And you are right, Kate. I do like him," her god-mother added. "Have you ever wondered how he managed to touch the hearts of so many people? For all that arrogant swagger, he can still talk to barrow boy and regent alike." She laughed. "Unlike his cousin. A more pious, self-serving creature than Gideon Hawksmoor would be difficult to find!" Her eyes gleamed. "Can't wait to see his face when he finds a courtesan and a cantankerous nabob's widow in his entrance hall talking about a duel! Priceless!"

# CHAPTER EIGHT

It is the duty of a lady to be accomplished in all the feminine arts and practise until she excels at them.
—*Mrs. Eliza Squire,* Good Conduct For Ladies

"THERE ARE TWO...LADIES...requesting the pleasure of your company, sir."

Sam Hawksmoor turned over in bed and gave a heartfelt groan. The previous night had been a hard one, involving several bottles of claret. He had been supposed to meet Ben at the Cocoa Tree, but his cousin had failed to turn up and instead Sam had fallen into even more disreputable company. He had literally gambled the shirt from his back and had wandered home in the early hours feeling the winter cold with only his jacket to protect him.

Earlier that morning he had heard Gideon leaving to spend some time at his club, followed by Gideon's wife, Alice, and their daughter Chloe on their way out to shop in Bond Street. He had relaxed back against the pillows, savoring the peace of the house and planning a morning of blissful sleep. And then...

"Sir," the butler said again, with rather more urgency, "the ladies—"

"I don't know any ladies," Sam said, muffled.

"No, sir," the butler said, suavely urgent, "but one of them is the sort of female you *do* know, sir…."

Sam shot up in bed. A memory swam to the surface of his mind; a barque of frailty perched on his lap the previous night, feeding him grapes and nibbling sweetly at his ear. He felt slightly sick. Surely the silly girl had not come *here* to find him…. The butler had said two women, so perhaps she had brought some old Covent Garden abbess with her…. Oh, the humiliation of being so poor that he was obliged to reside with his brother….

Somehow, without him really noticing, the butler had ejected him from his bed and, with the help of Gideon's valet, was easing him into his clothes. Sam let them fuss about while his mind ran hither and thither like a trapped mouse. What had he promised the lightskirt the previous night? If Gideon had to buy this one off as well, he would be furious. It was only three months since the last one.

He was relieved to find that when he reached the hall, the females were nowhere to be seen. Gideon's butler, with his customary aplomb, had tucked them away in the drawing room. He was not ready to face them, but a scared glance at the clock suggested that Alice and Chloe might return at any moment for luncheon. It would be disastrous if they arrived home when he was speaking with a couple of lightskirts. Now *that* was something Gideon would never forgive….

"Lady Russell and Miss Lily St. Clare," the butler announced, throwing open the drawing-room door, and Sam suffered another paroxysm of shock so great that he tried to reverse straight out again, but was thwarted by the butler closing the door smartly behind him.

He did not recognize the older lady but it was clear that she was no bawdy-house madam. There was an imperious tilt to her chin and a martial light in her eye that belied her diminutive stature and rather eccentric gown of peacock-blue with purple turban. She fixed Sam with a sharp look.

"Mr. Hawksmoor? Mr. *Samuel* Hawksmoor? We were hoping to see your brother."

Sam was left with a feeling of inadequacy at not being Gideon.

"Beg pardon, ma'am, but my brother is from home," he stuttered. "I understood from the butler that you wished to see me?"

The elderly lady nodded. "We have business with you as well as with Mr. Gideon Hawksmoor." She extended a hand in a rather grand gesture. "I am Lady Russell."

Sam took her hand and resisted the impulse to bow over it. "Delighted, ma'am."

"And this," Lady Russell said, "is Miss Lily St. Clare."

Lily St. Clare stood up and put back her veil. Sam swallowed nervously, his Adam's apple bobbing desperately as he took her hand. He had always carried a torch for Lily when she had been married to Lord Cavanagh and now that she was the fallen society beauty, he thought she looked thinner, sadder and even more alluring. As he took her hand, and felt himself tingle all over at the contact, he realized in some indefinable way that Lily St. Clare was way beyond his star and always had been. She was not like Paris, a hard-as-diamonds beauty who would trample on anyone and anything who came between her and her goal. Lily was softer, sweeter, and to Sam infinitely more attractive.

"Ah...Lady Ca...I mean, Miss St. Clare... How..." He cleared his throat, caught Lily's eye and felt himself blush to the roots of his hair. "How may I be of service?" he managed to stutter, with what he recognized was a woeful lack of aplomb.

"We are here," Lily said, smiling at him with ravishing charm, "as the seconds appointed by Miss Catherine Fenton, Mr. Hawksmoor."

"That's right!" Lady Russell said with an enthusiasm that Sam found quite intimidating.

"Seconds?" he repeated. "Beg pardon, madam, but I have no notion to what you refer—"

Lily sighed. "I suppose that your cousin, Lord Hawksmoor, has not told you? Miss Fenton has challenged Lord Hawksmoor to a duel, sir. He named you and your brother Gideon as his seconds." She frowned slightly. "He did mention that Mr. Gideon Hawksmoor might refuse to act for him, but that you would certainly support him. So..." She made a slight, deprecating gesture. "We are here to discuss the arrangements for the duel with you."

"Miss Fenton... Duel... Named Gideon... Seconds..." Sam pressed a hand to his brow.

He did not know anyone named Catherine Fenton. He wondered if she was a courtesan. And if he understood Miss St. Clare correctly, the girl had challenged Ben to a duel. But that could not be right. No woman, not even a barque of frailty, would do such an outrageous thing.

"Beg pardon, ma'am," Sam said again, with increasing desperation. "Bad head this morning, don't you know. I misunderstood you there. Thought you said a young lady had challenged m'cousin in a matter of honor."

"She did," Lady Russell said. There was a hint of severity in her voice. Clearly she had tired of his lamentable slowness. Sam felt very stupid. And he had no wish to make a fool of himself before the very lovely Miss St. Clare. Sam went hot all over again as his mind dwelled most inappropriately on all the lovely aspects of Lily. He wrenched his thoughts back to the matter in hand. Both ladies were looking at him as though he were a slow top.

"A duel," he said, running a finger around the neck of his shirt to help ease his breathing. "Must be some mistake, ladies. Not even my cousin would do something so...so...extraordinary."

"Your cousin has no choice," Lily said crisply. "Miss Fenton has challenged him on a matter of honor and if he refuses she will brand him a coward."

"Coward," Sam said. "I see." For the first time, he felt a small stir of sympathy for Ben. Whatever his cousin was, he was no coward.

"And Gideon, you say," he continued. "Did my

cousin *truly* name Gideon as his other second?" This, Sam thought, was beyond belief. Ben had plenty of other friends as reckless and rackety as he. Any one of them would stand his second and think it a great joke. If he had named Gideon, however, he must have been suffering delusions. Either that or the lightskirt was trying to extract money from him. Perhaps she had threatened breach of promise and had called Ben out in pique when he had refused to wed her. And now Ben was hoping that Gideon would pay her off to avoid scandal tarnishing the family name.

"He did," Lady Russell said, nodding. "It is here in a note he sent me this morning." She took it from her reticule and read aloud. "I confirm that I would like to ask my cousin Gideon to act as my other second but I fear that his disapproval of me is so great that he may refuse me in my time of need…."

"He must have been drunk when he wrote it," Sam muttered. "And the least he could have done was to tell me."

Lily shrugged prettily. "I doubt that Lord Hawksmoor was taking Miss Fenton's challenge seriously at the time, Mr. Hawksmoor. But that will change soon." She glanced at Lady Russell. "Lady Russell has suggested that if Lord Hawksmoor has any doubts about either Catherine's intentions or her proficiency with a pistol, he should go to Colonel Acheson's establishment in Bond Street and watch her practice."

"P-p-practice?" Sam spluttered. "My dear Miss St. Clare—"

"If one is intending to put a bullet through a man," Lady Russell said with unimpaired calm, "it is kinder to practice so that one may hit him entirely where one intends."

Sam swallowed hard at the thought.

"If this is a matter of money then I am sure we can come to some accommodation," he said cautiously. At all costs he wanted to avoid involving Gideon, whose fury would, he felt, be utterly incandescent at this evidence of Ben's latest outrage. He started to shepherd the ladies toward the door, opening it for them himself and trying to usher them into the hall with more haste than manners.

"If you leave me your direction then I shall speak to my brother and be in touch," he continued.

"Mr. Hawksmoor, I think that you quite mistake the situation," Lady Russell said, standing her ground. "This is not a case of some poverty-stricken demirep trying to make a quick fortune from your family."

Sam flushed. "I assure you, ma'am, I had no intention of suggesting—"

The front door opened.

"Miss Fenton," Lady Russell continued with superb disregard for the new arrivals, "is the richest heiress in London. Your cousin has insulted her, Mr. Hawksmoor, and must now pay the price."

Sam turned, caught sight of his brother, sister-in-law and niece, and made vague panic-stricken flapping gestures with his hands.

"Lady Russell, Miss St. Clare…"

"Miss Fenton fully intends to carry out her challenge and demands that Lord Hawksmoor meet her in this matter of honor," Lady Russell finished.

"Samuel!"

The chandeliers quivered with the force of Gideon Hawksmoor's righteous wrath. He was a short, portly man clad in the most irreproachably tasteful morning dress. His expression, however, was violent.

"Samuel, what the deuce do you mean by introducing women of ill fame into this house—" he began.

"Sir!" Lady Russell drew herself up. "How dare you!"

"Samuel," Gideon bellowed. "Explain yourself."

Miss Chloe Hawksmoor, a lively debutante of nineteen, peered out from behind her father's bulk and gave Lily a little wave. "How lovely to see you again, Lily! We have all missed you—"

"Chloe!" Gideon was turning purple. "Be silent! Samuel—"

"Dear me." Mrs. Alice Hawksmoor, a woman with a sharp face and a long nose for scandal, stepped forward. "You will make yourself ill, my dear." She laid a restraining hand on Gideon's arm. "Chloe, go to your room. Gideon, stop bellowing. You will injure yourself. Samuel—" Sam jumped "—you had better explain yourself."

"Please excuse us," Lady Russell said, taking Lily's arm and shooting Gideon a look of deep dislike. "We will leave you to explain matters to your brother and his family, Mr. Hawksmoor."

"Leave me?" Sam looked around wildly. "But, Lady Russell, Miss St. Clare, please do not go—"

"Lady Russell?" Alice Hawksmoor's nose quivered

like a terrier. "I beg your pardon, ma'am, I did not recognize you. Nor did my husband." Sam saw her pinch
Gideon's arm sharply. "Did you, Gideon?"

"Ouch! No!" Gideon drew himself up. "My apologies, my lady—"

Lady Russell looked disdainful. "It is of no conse-
quence, Mr. Hawksmoor. If you cannot be civil to me
when you did not know my identity, I doubt I wish to
speak with you when you do. Besides, you have been
unconscionably rude to Miss St. Clare. I think it would
be best for us to leave your brother to acquaint you
with the matter in hand."

"Good day," Lily said serenely. She gave Sam a
smile that made his knees tremble. "Thank you for
your kindness, Mr. Hawksmoor."

"A pleasure, ma'am," Sam muttered. He bowed to
Lady Russell, who was watching him with a somewhat sardonic gleam in her eye. Alice took his arm
in her talons.

"This way, Samuel," she said meaningfully.

It seemed to Sam that without any conscious action
on his part, he was inside the drawing room with the
door firmly closed and both Alice and Gideon ranged
before him in an attack formation that would have
done credit to Lord Nelson. He closed his eyes.

"Well?" Alice said, with arctic calm and one hand on
Gideon's arm as though she were forcibly restraining
him. "We await your explanation with interest, Samuel."

Sam spoke very quickly, as though in doing so he
might make it through the gathering storm without
injury.

"Our cousin Benjamin has done something to upset a Miss Catherine Fenton who is an heiress and who has called him out on a point of honor and he has named both Gideon and myself as his seconds…."

Sam sensed rather than saw Gideon swell alarmingly and color up until he resembled a pomegranate, but then, as Sam thought there was no way he could be spared his brother's wrath, Alice spoke very quietly.

"Benjamin has some connection with Miss Catherine Fenton?"

Sam opened his eyes at her tone. "I believe so," he said cautiously.

"Hmm." Alice strode across the room and turned to face him with a sudden and frightening *swish.* Sam jumped back.

"And she has called him out."

"I…um…yes."

"Outrageous," Gideon hissed. "Foolish, reckless chit! She will be ruined—"

"Be quiet, dear," Alice said quickly. "You are not listening properly. Miss Fenton cannot be ruined. It is not appropriate. Not when she has eighty thousand pounds."

Sam saw a look pass between his brother and sister-in-law. The high color faded a little from Gideon's face. "Oh, *that* Miss Catherine Fenton," he said.

"Quite so, my dear," Alice said. "You will have remembered who Lady Russell is now?"

"Of course," Gideon said. "A nabob's widow."

"And worth—probably—another fifty thousand. She is Miss Fenton's godmother," Alice said, pressing her fingers together excitedly, "and she has no children of her own...."

Gideon sat down rather heavily. "And there is some connection between Miss Fenton and our cousin Benjamin," he said, his tone a mixture of speculation and avarice. "I see."

Sam stared at him in perplexity. "I have already told you," he protested. "Ben has offended Miss Fenton, insulted her. She detests him."

"A misunderstanding," Alice said quickly. She swept past Sam, and rang the bell vigorously. "I feel sure that this is, of course, nothing more than a big misunderstanding that we may overcome."

"Of course," Gideon murmured.

"Benjamin has upset Miss Fenton in some way," Alice continued, a soulful look in her eyes. "A romantic disagreement, perhaps. But the breach between them may be healed. I have always said that it was time our cousin settled down and found himself a respectable bride."

Sam goggled. "You have?"

Alice ignored him. "And Miss Fenton is very... suitable. Not from the top rank of society, of course, but then—"

"Neither is Benjamin," Gideon said.

Alice gave him a wintry smile. "I see you are quick to understand me, my dear. That is good. So how may we assist our cousin?"

"Assist him in what?" Sam said.

Alice gave a snort of disgust. "Samuel, you are not attending. It is the role of the seconds in any matter of honor to seek a solution without bloodshed, is it not?"

"Well yes," Sam said, "but—"

"And it seems there has been some disagreement between Miss Fenton and our cousin Benjamin?"

"Well yes," Sam said again. "As she has called him out, I imagine they have had quite a *big* disagreement."

"Precisely," Alice said. "And I feel sure it is of a romantic nature. What else could it be, where Benjamin is concerned? So I feel it is important that as his seconds, you and Gideon assist him in…ah…helping the course of true love to run smooth—"

Sam snorted and hastily turned it into a cough. "Beg pardon, ma'am, but you are speaking of *Ben* here. Don't think true love enters into it."

Alice looked cross. "You are so cynical, Samuel. I am trying to promote a match here."

Sam stuck to his guns. "I cannot conceive it in *any* woman's best interests to marry Ben, ma'am."

Alice glared. "It is your bounden duty—with Gideon, of course—to secure a happy outcome for your cousin and to assist in smoothing out this situation peaceably. Now—" she sat down and drummed her fingers on the arm of the sofa "—how is this to be achieved?"

"We must get them together and act as arbiter in the situation," Gideon said thoughtfully. "As you say, my dear, it is our bounden duty." He turned to Sam. "Samuel, I cannot accept our cousin's request to act as second." He plumped out his chest. "I am a responsible citizen and dueling is, after all, illegal. However, I will write to Miss Fenton in the strongest possible terms to try to persuade her to see the error of her ways."

"I am sure that she will be delighted to hear from you, Gideon," Sam murmured, wondering whether his brother's pomposity might bring a second challenge from the apparently volatile and unpredictable Miss Catherine Fenton.

"And then we shall bring Miss Fenton and our cousin together," Gideon continued, warming to his theme. "You must persuade our cousin to attend our winter ball next week, Samuel. It is imperative that he be there."

Sam's mouth, already at half-mast, now dropped all the way. "You—want—Ben—to—come—to—a *Ton* ball?" he gasped.

Gideon glared. "Was that not what I just said?"

"Yes, but—" Sam rubbed his head hard "—you hate Ben—"

Gideon puffed out his cheeks. "That is putting it a little *too* strongly, Samuel."

"And," Sam continued, "you have always said that he is a degenerate reprobate."

Gideon's crimson color was starting to rise again. "Yes, yes. Well a man can change his mind."

"Ben will never do it," Sam finished. "He says that *Ton* balls bore him."

He saw Gideon glance quickly at Alice.

"I don't care how you do it," Gideon barked, "just make sure that he is there. I want to talk to him."

Sam straightened his shoulders. "I have a few things I'd like to say to him myself," he said, "if it comes to that."

"Good!" Gideon snapped. "You bring Benjamin and I will persuade Miss Fenton to attend and we shall see what can be done."

"COULD YOU TELL ME WHAT WE ARE doing here, my lord?" Price's lugubrious tones just reached Ben's ears. The butler was speaking through six scarves and the turned-up collar of an overcoat. Despite that, he looked chilled to the bone, his face sunken and gray, and a drop of fog crystallizing on the end of his nose.

"Certainly, Price," Ben said cheerfully. "We are engaged in reconnaissance, for as we know—"

"Time spent preparing one's ground is seldom wasted," Price finished for him.

"Exactly." Ben wriggled forward on the frozen earth, pushing aside some of the rotting vegetables and piles of paper that obscured his view. They were in an insalubrious alleyway behind a very famous gunsmith's in Bond Street, and in the candlelit cellar beneath the shop, Ben knew that Miss Catherine Fenton was practicing her pistol shooting. He could see her now through the grating in front of him. And he did not need the shooting master's comments of "Very *good,* miss!" or "Excellent shot!" to tell him that he was in deep trouble. Miss Catherine Fenton could shoot the center out of a playing card at fifty paces.

Catherine was wearing scarlet this afternoon and

her upright little figure was stiff with determination and defiance as she aimed time after time at the heart in the center of the playing card. A whimsical smile played about Ben's lips. He had no doubt that she was picturing him standing there and that her outrage over his behavior gave an even steelier resolve to her shooting.

The strange thing was that with each new thing he learned about Catherine, his admiration for her grew. When he had decided to marry her for her money, he had known very little about her. He had desired her and he had certainly coveted her fortune, and in his ignorance he had thought that that was sufficient. He had tried to deny the deeper need that seemed to draw him constantly to her side. But then she had shown him the real Catherine Fenton, a young woman of extraordinary courage and resource who was not prepared to fall in with his plans. And that revelation had gained not only his respect but also something more exciting and unpredictable. He could feel it now as he watched her steady herself and take aim yet again. Her face was composed, her gaze cool as she measured the distance to the target. And in that moment he wanted her so much; he wanted her coolness and her passion, her strength and her generosity, because he sensed somehow that with her he could be so much better a man than he could ever be without her.

The only stumbling block was that she despised him.

He stood up, rubbing his gloved hands together.

"Damn it, Price," he muttered. "She's a crack shot. I wasn't sure whether it was just bravado on her part."

Price shuffled forward and took his place at the grating. After a moment, Ben heard the sound of another shot and then a sigh from Price.

"One might truthfully say, my lord, that you are now at a considerable disadvantage," he said.

Ben was stung. "Dash it, Price, it's not as though I am a bad shot myself."

"No, my lord," the butler agreed, dusting a stray cabbage leaf from his trousers, "but Miss Fenton is a lady. If you can remember that and yet still manage to shoot her then you are even less of a gentleman than people imagine."

Ben grinned. "Thank you, Price."

"I am merely outlining the problem as I see it, my lord."

Ben offered him a hand to help him to his feet. "So if that is the problem, Price, what is the solution?"

Price huffed thoughtfully. "The solution is to erase the threat."

Ben was genuinely shocked. "Erase Miss Fenton before the duel? Whatever can you mean, Price?"

Price let out a long sigh, his cloudy breath mingling with the fog. "I was not suggesting that you eliminate Miss Fenton before the contest, my lord," he said reproachfully, "merely that you remove the threat of her injuring you."

"Difficult," Ben murmured. "I have the impression that she would like to injure me quite a lot."

"Yes, my lord." Price drove his hands into the

pockets of his great coat as they started to walk back down the alleyway toward the main thoroughfare of Bond Street. "That being the case, you must do what you have to do to persuade her. Apologize, withdraw your proposal…"

Ben sighed. "That way I will lose Miss Fenton and her money, Price."

"I beg your pardon, my lord," Price said, "but you never actually *had* them, did you?"

"I will look a coward."

"Better than looking *dead,* my lord."

Ben thought of the lethal fierceness in Catherine's eyes as she took aim. "True."

"And then, perhaps," Price said, "you might woo her properly. If you still wish to marry her that is, my lord."

Ben gave a shout of laughter. "Woo her? She would as soon entertain a man-eating tiger as she would my suit, Price."

The butler permitted himself a tight smile. "That is certainly a drawback, my lord," he agreed, "but scarcely an insuperable one."

"I am glad that you believe that to be the case," Ben said dryly. He clapped his butler on the shoulder. "Thank you for the advice, Price. I am for Brooks's. I will see you later."

"Your cousin Samuel," Price said, "delivered an invitation to Mr. and Mrs. Hawksmoor's winter ball today, my lord. He stated that Miss Fenton would be attending."

Ben stared. "He delivered an invitation for *me* from Alice and Gideon?"

Price nodded. "Apparently Mr. Gideon Hawksmoor sees it as his duty to achieve a reconciliation between yourself and Miss Fenton, my lord."

A slow smile broke across Ben's face. "Does he, indeed? Well, I'll be damned. Never thought to throw my lot in with Gideon, but if it is the only way to marry Catherine…"

"Just so, my lord," Price said.

## CHAPTER NINE

> If a gentleman asks a lady to step aside with him
> from the company then it is generally accepted
> that he is a scoundrel and up to no good.
> —*Mrs. Eliza Squire,* Good Conduct for Ladies

CATHERINE SMOOTHED her evening gown of palest
green muslin beneath her velvet cloak, and seated
herself in the carriage. She burrowed beneath the traveling rug, seeking the warmth of the hot brick for her
toes. Her feet, in their flimsy evening slippers, felt like
blocks of ice.

She had not wanted to attend Mrs. Alice Hawksmoor's winter ball that night. When the invitation
had arrived—suspiciously late—she had been
tempted to throw it in the fire. Mr. and Mrs. Gideon
Hawksmoor had never been more than civil in the
past, certainly not flattering her with a handwritten
note positively begging her to attend their little party.
Besides, she knew that Ben had nominated both his
cousins as his seconds for the duel and she had misgivings about setting foot in Gideon's house under
such circumstances.

Catherine was feeling blue-deviled anyway, but her anger with Ben was mixed with nervousness now as time crept toward the morning appointed for the duel. She was not sure that she could injure a man in cold blood, no matter how much she felt he had wronged her.

In the end it had been Lady Russell who had persuaded her to accept the invitation. She had pointed out that sitting at home for another long, dark, quiet winter night was a recipe for madness. Taking dinner up to her father's room, Catherine had been forced to agree. Sir Alfred was still confined to bed with a sick fever and seemed to care little for anything. When Catherine had tried to question him on the state of her business affairs, he had simply looked blank and turned away.

So Catherine had swallowed her misgivings and had asked Lady Russell to be her chaperone for the night, and that redoubtable lady had dusted down an ancient ball gown that Catherine recognized from a magazine dating to the 1770s. There was a turban to match, adorned with pheasant feathers.

"I did not care for Mr. Gideon Hawksmoor when we met the other day," Lady Russell said now. "He is a rude man who was most uncivil to dear Lily. But if he is the only alternative to a night of boredom," she added, patting her feather-sprouting turban with approval, "then I suppose we must just make do." She huddled deeper beneath the fur-lined carriage rug. "My, my, but I hope they have some hot negus waiting or I shall be obliged to decamp to the nearest hostelry."

Catherine pulled back the curtain from the window. The freezing fog that had plagued the country over the last few weeks had lifted during the day, giving way to clear skies and a hard frost, but now that night had fallen again it had descended like a blanket once more, shrouding the city in this grim, gray pall.

"I think," Lady Russell said, shivering, "that you should call off this nonsense about the duel, Kate dear. You would not be able to shoot a house in this murk, let alone a man. And if the fog does not defeat you then the cold surely will."

Catherine sighed. She knew Lady Russell was right. They would end in a ditch if they even thought of setting off for Harington Heath, and once she and Ben had taken twenty paces from one another they would not even be visible. The whole idea was un- workable.

She sighed again as she peered through the carriage windows. "Well at least Lord Hawksmoor will not be present this evening. He and his cousin detest one another." She shivered. "Will this fog never lift? This has been the gloomiest winter I can recall. I hear that the river is frozen now and they are holding a fair on the ice."

"That sounds rather fun," Lady Russell said. "If I were not so old and prone to the rheumatics I think I would attend."

THE HAWKSMOORS HAD MORE than made up for the darkness outside by decorating their ballroom with the brightest collection of paper lanterns Catherine had ever seen. The heat was tremendous.

"Gracious," Lady Russell said disagreeably, forgetting that she had been complaining of the cold only five minutes past, "it will be like dancing in a greenhouse!"

Their hosts were waiting to greet them. The press of people seemed very great for a ball in the Little Season. Catherine could not see how so many could fit in the house. They took their places in the reception line and edged forward slowly.

"What a crush!" Lady Russell said, fanning herself with her pheasant-feather fan.

Catherine stepped forward to greet Mrs. Hawksmoor.

And stopped dead.

There, flanked by his cousins, stood Benjamin, Lord Hawksmoor. *Hiding behind a pillar so I should not see him,* Catherine thought wrathfully.

And in a split second, she realized just how neatly she had been outmaneuvered.

It had never occurred to her that in the interests of the family fortunes, Gideon and Ben would throw their lot in with one another. What a naive little fool she had been.

Meeting Ben's sardonic hazel gaze, Catherine shivered in her satin slippers. Now, when it was too late, she could see exactly what had happened. Gideon and Alice Hawksmoor had fancied her thousands in the family. In this one matter their interests exactly coincided with Ben's and, for the sake of eighty thousand pounds of nabob money, they were prepared to join forces.

Ben had once told her that everything had a price.

Lady Russell poked her in the back with her fan. "Catherine! What the deuce are you up to, gel? Have your unmentionables fallen down?"

"Did you know about this?" Catherine hissed back, gesturing toward the reception party.

Lady Russell shook her head. "Outgunned, forsooth!"

"We'll see about that," Catherine said.

She moved forward. She had no choice. There was a press of people behind her, a huge crush who were starting to gossip about the reconciliation between Mr. Gideon Hawksmoor and his cousin, the notorious Lord Hawksmoor. They all wanted to see Ben with their own eyes, in case he did something outrageous. They wanted to see him in case he did not. They just wanted to see him.

Their voices rang in Catherine's ears. Their excitement was tangible.

Gideon was wreathed in smiles, a contortion that he appeared to find difficult to sustain. Alice bore down on Catherine with suspicious warmth.

"My *very dear* Miss Fenton! How glad we are that you could attend our humble soiree!" She dug Chloe in the ribs with her fan. "We *are* pleased to see Miss Fenton, are we not, Chloe?"

Chloe shot Catherine an apologetic look. "Of course we are, Mama." She gave Catherine a hug and whispered, "I am *so* sorry, Catherine. I do not know what has come over Mama! She is not usually so gushing."

"What can you two girls be whispering about?"

Mrs. Hawksmoor demanded, with horrible archness. "Girlish secrets, eh, Lady Russell?"

Lady Russell smiled thinly.

"You must meet my uncle Samuel," Chloe said, dragging forward a young man whom Catherine instantly recognized from Ben's rather less respectable ball a few weeks before. He looked both uncomfortable and out of place, and his evening dress was a size too small. Every so often he would ease a finger around the collar as though it were choking him.

"And," Chloe continued, with the air of a magician producing a rabbit from the hat, "this is my *wicked* cousin Benjamin, Lord Hawksmoor." She beamed. "Generally Papa refuses to let me meet him. He says he is a dashed scoundrel."

"Miss Fenton," Ben said, as smooth as silk. "What a great pleasure to see you again."

Catherine caught Gideon and Alice looking at her with the indulgent gaze of relatives who have already bought the wedding presents.

Ben took her hand in his and raised it to his lips. A concerted sigh from the ladies behind her in the receiving line *whooshed* past Catherine's ears. She removed her hand from his grasp very quickly before he could feel her tremble.

"Oh, you have met cousin Ben before!" Chloe was saying with delight. "Well, that is famous!"

"Oh yes," Catherine said. She smiled at the younger girl. "But I fear your cousin is overrated, Chloe. I believe he uses his dangerous reputation to hide a rather more dull reality."

"Miss Fenton," Ben said, the amusement deepening in his eyes, "you wound me."

"Not yet," Catherine said sweetly, "but I still have every intention of doing so soon."

Somehow Alice had drawn the two of them to one side behind a huge arrangement of ferns, away from the curious gaze of the other guests.

"Miss Fenton," she said, "Gideon and I heard about the disagreement between yourself and our cousin—" here she tried to give Ben an affectionate look, which did not quite work due to her total lack of sincerity "—and we are so very sorry to think that there is this misunderstanding between you when there could be fondness—"

"A very deep fondness," Ben said soulfully. He kept his eyes on her face. "You know how much I esteem you, Miss Fenton."

"You see!" Alice said quickly, as Catherine opened her mouth to demolish his pretensions. "Lord Hawksmoor has the greatest respect for you—"

"And admiration," Ben repeated. Catherine could see the glint of mockery in his eyes. "Dear Miss Fenton."

"Dear Lord Hawksmoor," Catherine said with equal aplomb, "you have a brass-faced disregard for the truth."

"Excellent!" Alice cried. "An excellent start. A frank exchange of views. I knew the two of you would be able to settle your differences if you would but converse together."

"Of course we may," Ben said. He bowed. "Miss Fenton, may I, before witnesses, offer you a full apology for the unintentional insult that led you to challenge me? It was entirely my fault. I withdraw my comments and apologize most sincerely."

Catherine glared at him. "There was nothing *unintentional* about your insulting proposal, sir!"

Ben smiled. "I was overcome by a desire to wed you, Miss Fenton, overwhelmed—"

"By my fortune, sir." Catherine snapped the struts of her fan together with a sharp crack. "I appreciate that."

"It was a mistake," Ben said, shamelessly smiling into her eyes. "I am sorry."

Catherine bit her lip. "If you make a full apology and withdraw your proposal, does that mean I cannot challenge you?" she asked.

Ben's gaze was wicked. "I fear not, Miss Fenton."

Catherine sighed. "How very provoking."

She felt irritated to be so neatly manipulated but she also felt a certain relief. If she was to have revenge upon Ben Hawksmoor, then perhaps spoiling his physical form was not the right way to do it. She would need to think of something else.

Alice had clearly assumed that the matter was settled. She made a shooing gesture with her hands. "Benjamin, take this delightful young lady away and dance with her now, and Miss Fenton—" her sharp brown gaze fixed reproachfully on Catherine "—do please give Lord Hawksmoor a fair hearing!"

Ben offered her his arm. Catherine glanced across at Lady Russell but she had struck up conversation with an ancient general whose medals indicated that he had served in India. She made a flapping movement with her fan that Catherine interpreted as permission to accept Ben's offer to dance. Catherine thought that she was looking at Ben with entirely too indulgent a gaze.

"A fair hearing," she said softly, as he escorted her onto the floor. "This is a conspiracy of thieves! Until this moment I would not have believed that you would throw in your lot with your cousin, Lord Hawksmoor, even to gain eighty thousand pounds."

Ben covered her hand with his own, a gesture that thoroughly confused her senses. "Both Gideon and Sam felt they were honor-bound to try to effect a reconciliation between us, Miss Fenton." Ben smiled. "Naturally they cannot possibly be aware just how low your opinion of me is, or they would never have imagined such a thing would be achievable."

"At least they have saved your worthless skin," Catherine said sweetly, "for now."

Ben smiled. "I appreciate that you are still angry with me."

"How perceptive of you! I do not think that this—" Catherine struggled to frame her words and keep her anger within check "—this concerted attempt to persuade me of your honorable intentions will achieve anything other than to make me entirely furious that you will stoop to *any depth* to achieve your aim!"

"You should take it as the measure of how much I want you, Catherine," Ben said gently. "I would enlist the help of the devil himself to help me win your hand in marriage."

Their eyes met. Catherine was the first to look away.

"You want no more than my fortune," she said stubbornly.

Ben's hand tightened over hers, compelling her to lift her gaze to his again. His hazel eyes were brilliant. "That is not true. I do want the money—I have admitted that from the start—but I want you as well. You know how much." He made a slight gesture. "I do not lie to you," he said. "I am a fortune hunter, but an honest one."

The music was striking up now for a waltz, not the decadent whirl that had been playing in the house in St. James's but a stately and respectable dance that not even the patronesses of Almacks could have taken in disapproval. Ben held out a hand to her and, after a moment, Catherine rested her other hand gingerly on his shoulder and they started to circle the floor, keeping an irreproachable distance from one another.

"I have another reason for wishing to persuade you into a betrothal and away from a duel," Ben said. "I confess it freely. I watched you practice at Colonel Acheson's. You are a fine shot."

Catherine raised her gaze sharply to his. She slipped slightly on some candle grease and his grip on her waist tightened. When she regained her footing, he resumed his previous distance.

"Are you afraid of me then?" she asked lightly.

"I am afraid of what you might do to me," Ben said dryly. "Was it your grandfather who taught you to shoot, Miss Fenton?"

"He arranged for me to have lessons," Catherine said. "He felt it was important for a female to be able to defend herself." She looked at him. "Do not forget, my lord, that I was born in India. Life was a great deal less certain there than it is in London."

"My life would not have been so certain if you had exacted your revenge," Ben said feelingly. "What else did Sir Jack teach you, Kate—other than to cheat at hazard?"

Catherine glared. "I do not cheat!" She met his speculative gaze and her frown softened into a reluctant smile. "That is, he *did* teach me how to cheat, but on the occasion that you saw me play against Lady Paris, I won fair and square."

Ben laughed. "I never cheat either."

"And you never lose."

"Never before now." She saw his face go still. "But I do believe, Miss Fenton, that in you I may have met my nemesis."

There was a note of humor in his voice and when Catherine looked up and met his gaze, the smile he gave her was, for once, devoid of mockery. It gave Catherine a scandalous sensation of intimacy.

"I know you have spiked my guns with your apology," she said slowly, "and now I cannot shoot you. I think I would not feel so angry if I thought that a single word you had spoken was sincere."

For a second, his hands tightened on her body and she felt the heat through the thin muslin of her gown.

"You misjudge me," he said. "I made a mistake in attempting to persuade you to wed me the way I did, and for that I am truly sorry."

"A man of your stamp should never marry," Catherine said. "With you, there will always be other women, will there not, Lord Hawksmoor? And there is very little that binds us together."

She saw, from the sudden and shocking flash of expression in his eyes, that he was thinking of the time she had been in his bed and of the pleasure and intimacy they had found there. For a short while they had been bound together as close as true lovers and she had thought it might last forever. The memory still stirred her soul.

"Do you really believe that?" he asked.

"That you would be unfaithful?" Catherine stubbornly avoided his eyes. Her tone was bitter. "Of course. You can scarcely flaunt the most notorious courtesan in London as your mistress and expect me to believe otherwise."

Ben inclined his head. "Touché. Yet you were betrothed to Withers and you cannot have thought that he would be faithful to you."

"I did not think it for a moment," Catherine said. "That betrothal was none of my choosing and I broke it as soon as I could. It is another reason why I would never accept another forced match."

"So in marriage you demand the man of your choice and that he love you and be faithful to you?"

"Exactly, my lord," Catherine agreed. "And I do not believe that you fit any of those conditions, do you?"

Ben laughed. "Two out of three would not be bad. I can promise to be faithful." He bent his head so that his words were for her alone. "With you in my bed, why should I wish to stray? You are all I want. You must know I burn for you."

Catherine's breath caught in her throat. Her whole

body ached with awareness. She wanted him, too. "Do not—" she whispered.

"And I could be the man of your choice. You know you are tempted."

Another couple circled close and Catherine bit back the retort that had sprung to her lips. She wanted no one else to be party to this conversation. But it was dangerous. Ben was right—she was tempted. He made her want things she had sworn to forget. That night in his bed, and the tangled sheets, and the taste of salt from his skin and the scent of him… She closed her eyes against the memories.

They danced for a little in silence. Catherine was all too conscious of the brush of his leg against the thin muslin of her gown, the warmth of his hand on her waist, the sudden, shocking contact of his cheek against her as he fleetingly and most improperly held her very close for the final turn of the waltz. The music ended. A ripple of applause ran around the room. The dancers split, mingled, chattered. Catherine felt Ben steer her away from the crowds toward the relative privacy of the window alcove.

He leaned down and spoke in her ear, his breath stirring the tendrils of hair that escaped her ribbon.

"Come into the library with me. I want to talk to you properly."

Catherine looked at him. She shook her head. "A young lady does not step aside with a gentleman on so flimsy a pretext, my lord."

"Very well." Ben smiled a challenge. "Come into the library with me. I want to kiss you improperly."

Catherine laughed. She could not help herself. "You have a boundless conceit, my lord. And the answer is still no."

"Conceited or not, you would miss me were I no longer a part of your life. Marry me, Kate. It is what we both want."

The words, softly spoken, stung Catherine because they were so painfully close to the truth. She turned away from him to look blindly through the steamy panels into the dark fog of the garden. The chill from the window matched the chill in her heart.

Could it only be a mere few weeks since she had first met Ben Hawksmoor? The notion seemed absurd, for somehow his presence was knit so tightly into the fabric of her life now that she did not see how she could banish him without it tearing away some part of her existence. She wrapped her arms about herself. This was ridiculous! In the beginning she had imagined herself in love with him but she was past that folly now; older, wiser, beyond a craving for the love and intimacy she had so foolishly sought in his bed. And no matter what he said, and the strange sense of recognition she felt for him, there was no deeper bond between them. Their worlds were oceans apart. He wanted her for her money first and her body second and love came nowhere. So she could never marry him.

And yet… And yet if Ben were to walk away here and now, and she were never to see him again, then her life would be somehow darker, less rich and exciting, less full of promise. She need not marry Algernon Withers now, of course; she could find a good man, the sort of man Lady Russell assured her was still left in this world, and she could wed him and be content. But she would never see Ben Hawksmoor again.

A sudden knot of tears caught in her throat and she swallowed it, angry with herself for such weakness. She had to speak, and quickly, had to tell Ben that if he left she would never miss him, that he could walk away now and she would rejoice, that she would never marry him. The idea was absurd, insulting.

But she had thought not long ago that if she married Withers, she would barely be alive, living only in the half light. She had thought that the rest of her life would be dull and flat and lifeless, and she might as well be dead. But she could never imagine feeling like that with Ben. Never.

He was standing behind her and he put his hands on her shoulders, and she felt warm and secure and at the same time fearful and elated.

"Kate?" His question was a whisper.

She was so close to agreeing. She knew all his faults. She knew he did not love her. He had apologized to her for it on the day she had so painfully told him of her own feelings. If she accepted him now, it would be with her eyes open and in the knowledge that she would never be able to change him. But he did not love her. And that was an end to it.

"I am sorry," she said. "I cannot."

Ben had been so wrapped up in Catherine's response to him, so certain she was going to agree, that he had not even countenanced the possibility of refusal. All his attention had been focused on Kate and the fact that he wanted her to accept his proposal. He wanted it unbearably. He ached for her to agree.

He had felt the slight trembling in her body, had seen the hesitancy in her eyes, seen her lips part on a breath and known in his deepest being that he was within a second of achieving his heart's desire. And then the light had gone from her eyes and she had spoken, and the frustration and the misery slammed through Ben so hard he could not speak.

Frustration he could understand. He had just failed to secure a fortune. It had slipped, tantalizingly, through his fingers yet again.

His misery was less explicable and he was afraid to analyze it.

His gambling instincts prompted him to one last throw of the dice. He caught her hand. "Then there is something that I must say to you before we part. I beg you to step aside into the library with me."

He could see she was reluctant to do so. She did not trust him. The thought made him feel even more heartsore. But why should she? He had given her precious little reason to do so.

"Please," he said. "I promise not to touch you, Kate, but I *must* speak."

She nodded slightly, turned away and picked a path through the crowded ballroom, pausing to speak to Lady Russell as she passed. Ben watched. He knew she was telling her chaperone everything so that Lady Russell would know where she was going and exactly when to interrupt them. His lips twitched. He admired her strategy.

He waited five minutes before he followed her. It felt like an hour. When he entered the library, she was standing before the fire, very straight, her arms folded in a gesture that dared him even to draw near to her.

"Well, my lord?"

Ben stopped. He had been intending to do precisely what he had promised he would not—take her in his arms and overcome her resistance with his desire. He knew she was scarcely indifferent to him. It was a weakness and he could use it against her.

Yet when it came to it, he did nothing of the sort.

"Kate," he said. "I have never told you how sorry I am for the way that I misjudged you."

He stopped. She was looking at him with a mixture of incredulity and suspicion, and suddenly it seemed imperative if he were never to see her again that she would think him not completely lost to a sense of honor. He cleared his throat.

"It is true that I was told you were unchaste, and also that our previous encounters had led me to believe that it must indeed be so, but…" He paused. "That is no excuse for the unpardonable way that I behaved. To exact revenge upon you in so uncivilized a way…" He shook his head. "I am sorry."

Catherine made a slight gesture. She was looking stunned.

"You have refused my suit and I will not press you to wed me again if you do not wish it," Ben continued, "but I do beg you to tell me if you should be with child. If you are, then I promise to do all in my power to help you—"

He stopped again. He had never in his life imagined that he would say such a thing. He had never wanted to take such a responsibility. A part of him still did not. When he had proposed to her earlier, it had been because of the money and because he wanted to make love to her with a desperation that was driving him insane. It had had nothing to do with some misplaced notion of chivalry. And now a part of him wanted her to tell him that he need not concern himself, there would be no child, he need make no stupid, selfless gestures, she did not require his support, and another part of him urgently wanted to bind her close to him and never to let her go. And that was the bit that was so terrifying.

He saw the hot color flood her face. She looked very young, as she had in that moment after he had realized, too late, that he had just taken her virginity. He knew it must be difficult for her. Such intimate matters were never discussed and yet she had recovered from her shock now and drawn herself up very straight.

"I am not *enceinte,*" she whispered. "My courses…" She swallowed, folded her arms more tightly about herself. "I have had my courses as I usually do."

She tried to turn away from him but Ben caught her shoulders and forced her to face him. "Catherine—"

She looked up. There was grief and puzzlement in her eyes, and a mixture of relief and sheer, brutal misery. The shocking contradiction of what he could see there turned Ben's heart to ice even as he acknowledged that he had no idea how he himself felt. His strongest instinct was to reach out to her, to hold her close to the warmth of his body, to tell her that everything would be all right. He would make it right. Hell, he would give her ten children if that was what she wanted, he would give her *anything* she wanted if it would only banish that desperate confusion and unhappiness he could see in her face.

But he had left it a moment too long. Catherine's eyes went blank and she took a small, careful step away from him, shaking off his touch.

"It is for the best," she said, and her voice cracked a little. "I know that."

Ben knew it, too, in his head.

"So that is that," he said slowly.

"Yes," Catherine said. "We need never see one another again. But I do thank you for your apology and your offer."

The candlelight fell across her face in bars of pale gold, light and shadow.

"When we were in the ballroom I was so very tempted to accept your proposal," she said. "But were I to do so I would be making the same mistake again. I would be looking to you for the things you cannot give me. And when I could not change you, I would be unhappy."

Ben looked at her standing there, so beautiful and so proud. In that one reckless moment, he found he was tempted to offer her whatever she wanted, but even as he thought about it, he knew that there would always be something lacking. The one thing that Catherine needed, the thing that she deserved, was to be loved as much as she could love. And there he could never match her. The scars of the past, the fear, the disillusion, the self-interest that was in him, made him a poor choice for a woman with such generosity of spirit. And yet in his selfishness he wanted her so much.

He took her hand.

"I do not want to lose you," he said softly. "Give me one last chance to show you that you could be happy with me. Allow yourself to be tempted. Come with me to the Frost Fair tomorrow night."

Her eyes were very wide and dark. She touched the tip of her tongue to her bottom lip.

"That would be very irresponsible of me." But he could see from the gleam in her eyes that his suggestion had intrigued her.

He laughed. "True."

"What, precisely, are you wishing to tempt me to?"

The blood roared through his body at the thought of all the temptations he wished to place before her. He drew her closer. "I wish to show you that marrying me would be…" He paused.

What would it be? Vibrant, exciting, fulfilling… Would be enough to satisfy her? He did not know.

"Foolish? Reckless to the point of madness?" A faint smile curved her mouth. "I wish you were not so difficult to refuse, Ben Hawksmoor."

"Then do not."

He gave her no time to reply. His mouth came down on hers hard, his hand sliding into the softness of her hair, holding her fast.

He lost control from the first moment. The heat that had been building between them consumed him, the passion he felt for her blazing through all sense and all reason. He could not remember ever feeling such desperation and driving need. They were both panting when he finally broke the kiss and let her go.

"I will go to the Frost Fair with you tomorrow," she whispered.

He held her fast. "I want the whole night, Kate."

She laughed. Her lips were only an inch away from his. "It will take you that long to convince me?"

The passion and need fused within him as he looked into her face. He could not breathe. He felt the fear and elation of having one's heart's desire so close within reach and yet… And yet she was drawing away from him now and her face was grave.

"I promise nothing beyond my company," she said. "I need to think." She smiled. "Pray do not trouble to escort us home. Lady Russell and I are well able to take care of ourselves."

At the door, she turned and smiled at him, as though driven by some compulsion she could not resist, and the excitement slammed through him again in a breaking wave. She was a challenge, a torment, the biggest gamble he had ever taken in his life. And he might win the biggest prize—eighty thousand pounds and the privilege of never being cold, or hungry, or poor ever again. He might even start to feel truly safe for the first time in his life.

And in addition he would have Catherine.

His heart constricted. He did not wish to hurt Catherine. He would do his utmost not to do so. He sensed somewhere deep inside that she could make him a better person if only he would open all those dark places to her light.

But that was dangerous, sentimental thinking. With Catherine's money he would be safe and that would make him happy. He would treat her well even if he could not love her. That was all there was to it. It was quite simple.

And Catherine had given him that chance.

The game was on again.


"AUNT AGATHA," CATHERINE SAID in the carriage on the way home, "if a young lady wishes to spend an evening with a gentleman, what would be the advice of her chaperone?"

Lady Russell was buried so deep beneath the rug that she was barely visible. "You know full well, Kate," she said, "that any chaperone worth her salt would tell you it is simply not done."

Catherine sighed. "I suppose not," she said.

"On the other hand," Lady Russell said, "a chaperone who has seen as much of the world as I have would tell a young lady not to waste any opportunity that life provides unless she wishes to end a bitter old maid."

Catherine turned her head and looked at her.

"It depends upon what you want," Lady Russell continued. "What *do* you want, Kate? A conventional upper-class marriage?"

"No," Catherine said. "I want someone who wants me." She knitted her gloved fingers together. "Last year, before Papa gave Lord Withers permission to address me, I had a number of suitors who paid court." Her voice took on an impassioned note. "None of them wanted *me*, Aunt Agatha! Some wanted to marry me because I was pretty, others because they thought I might be biddable, or rich, or simply because I was a young debutante. I do not believe that a single one of them even saw me as Catherine Fenton, let alone wanted me for myself!"

"I think that Withers did," Lady Russell said somberly.

"No," Catherine said. "He wanted to turn me into something else, something I was not. He wanted an obedient wife, bent to his will." She shuddered.

"And Ben Hawksmoor?" Lady Russell's voice was gruff but kind. "Do you think he truly wants you for yourself?"

"Yes," Catherine said. She laughed. "And he wants my money."

Lady Russell drew one hand from beneath the fur-lined rug and patted one of Catherine's gloved ones. "You have no illusions, do you, child?"

"Not anymore," Catherine said, but she spoke without self-pity.

"Do you love him?"

"I…do not know," Catherine said. She remembered

with a faint pang of regret the innocence of her previous feelings for Ben. She had tumbled into love with him with a schoolgirl's naiveté and what she felt for him now was very far from that. "I told him that I would never wed a man who did not love me," she said, "but now I am wondering if I ask too much. Maybe desire, and liking and respect and admiration…" Her voice fell. "Maybe those can be enough. Better to play the hand fate deals me than to end with nothing."

Lady Russell was shaking her head. "You deserve the best that a man can offer you, Kate."

"But if I *do* love him," Catherine said, "then that might have to be enough for the two of us."

In the flickering light from the carriage lanterns, Lady Russell's face looked grave.

"Can it be enough?"

"I do not know," Catherine said again, honestly.

"Then you need to spend that time with him," Lady Russell said. She squeezed Catherine's hand. "Go and find out."

# CHAPTER TEN

An engaged couple, except in the presence of a
chaperone, are never under any circumstances
permitted to sit together, walk together or spend
any time together.
—*Mrs. Eliza Squire,* Good Conduct for Ladies

LILY ST. CLARE WAS VERY TIRED that night. She had
already seen four clients that evening when Sarah
Desmond burst in, her eyes bright with excitement
and cupidity.

"There is someone downstairs who is asking for
you, my love. He requested you by name and is willing
to pay a fortune for your favors!" Sarah opened her eyes
very wide, as though this were some splendid thing
instead of the one thing that made Lily feel even more
cheap and corrupt and degraded than anything else.

"Who is it?" she asked.

Sarah frowned slightly. "He gave his name as
Lander. I have not seen him here before but if his
money is good, he might become a regular for you!"

Lily sighed. She could not refuse, of course. Sarah
had been good to her in her own way, taking Lily in

when everyone in the *Ton* except Catherine had turned their back on her. And it was not a bad life in the sense that she was not cold or hungry or poor. She had many material comforts. What did it matter if she had no self-respect left at all?

Lily hated herself for what she had become. Once she had been so innocent—as innocent as Catherine—but now she had lost count of the men she had been with. Sarah did not understand, of course. She thought Lily should be pleased that the men were all hot for her and that they paid so well for their pleasure. She was waiting now, looking a little cross at Lily's lack of enthusiasm. So Lily painted a smile on her lips and fought down her repulsion.

"I am eager to make his acquaintance," she murmured, and Sarah smiled.

While Sarah went to fetch the client, Lily went to her closet listlessly to wash the previous man's scent from her body and pinch some color into her pale cheeks. She reentered the bedroom to find the man already waiting for her, and her insides curled with horror to see who it was.

"Good evening, my dear," Algernon Withers said.

Lily had always disliked Withers. She sensed some malevolence in his attitude to Catherine and marveled that her friend, so much stronger than she, had been able somehow to escape his grasp. But dislike was not an excuse she could give for refusing him, so when he requested that she strip for him and lie on the bed, she did as he asked with no demur, trying desperately to hide her shudders of disgust, but with sickness in her heart.

It seemed that Withers was in a hurry. He was already fully aroused as he joined her on the bed. That suited Lily well since her flesh was already crawling at his touch and she wanted nothing so much as to be rid of him. He entered her with no preamble and with one violent thrust that had her biting her lip to prevent herself from crying out in pain, but then to her surprise he slowed the rhythm, drawing out his own pleasure for what seemed like an unbearable time. He caressed her breasts as he drove into her and she made all the required sounds of enjoyment, but she thought he did not really hear her. There was an intent expression on his face, a distance in his eyes as though he were thinking of something—or someone—else.

Suddenly he gripped her thighs and forced himself inside her so hard that she could not suppress a scream. She struggled, but it was too late. His hands had moved from her breasts to her throat, squeezing tightly. Through the buzzing in her ears, Lily heard him groan aloud as he came in violent spasms. There was a mist before her eyes now as everything distorted and slipped sideways and the darkness closed in. She thought she understood, now that it was too late. For in the final seconds of consciousness, she heard him say the name Catherine.

THEY FOUND HER BODY TWO HOURS later. Sarah Desmond had been checking the clock and hoping that the client would pay extra for overrunning his time. In the end she had decided discreetly to interrupt.

Her screams brought Connor running from the hall

and the whores and their customers rushing from the adjoining bedchambers to see the naked tumbled figure of Lily St. Clare. It was far too late to do anything to save her. The window was open and her murderer had fled.

BEN AND CATHERINE WENT DOWN onto the frozen river at Three Cranes Stairs, her hand tight within his as he helped her down onto the ice and paid the waterman the three pennies toll for both of them. From Blackfriars Bridge the river had looked unfamiliar, like a broad silver ribbon gleaming in the moonlight. At water level it was still strange, a landscape of jagged pinnacles and great slabs of ice frozen at tortuous angles. Above them the sky was a deep, dark blue and the stars were scattered like diamonds on velvet.

"It feels a little warmer tonight," Catherine said, raising her face to the edge of the breeze. "The air smells different."

"It won't melt," Ben said. "Not tonight."

Their feet crunched on the cinders the watermen had placed underfoot. Catherine slipped her hand through the crook of Ben's arm and stayed close to his side. There were people everywhere; city merchants and their families wrapped up in their Sunday best, looking plump and well fed, and ragged children thin and pale with cold and hunger. But there was a gleam in the eyes of rich and poor alike, and a feeling of excitement in the air.

"I grew up not far from here," Ben said suddenly. He was looking north of the river where the warehouses pressed close to the bank. "There was a place called Angel Alley where we had a room." His face twisted. "Ill-named, as it turned out. Unless it was intended as a shortcut to heaven. Hundreds died of the fever in those streets."

He turned away and in the bright moonlight Catherine saw an expression on his face she had never seen before. It looked like grief. He had said that they had a room. One room on a narrow street that led to the grave for hundreds of children like Ben. She shivered.

"How old were you then?" she asked.

Ben looked at her. "I don't usually talk about it."

Catherine stood her ground and waited, and he smiled. "But I will tell you, Kate Fenton. As long as you don't go to the penny presses."

Catherine could not tell if he was serious or not. "Well," she said, "if I am short of money in future I may consider it."

Ben started walking toward the tents pitched on the center of the river.

"My father threw my mother out of the house before I was even born. She came back to London. It was where her family came from. But they did not want to know her. There were already too many mouths to feed. Once I was born she had to go back to work."

They walked slowly. The moonlight was pouring down, transforming the icy scape around them into a magical wonderland. Children ran past calling and tumbling on the ice. Some had devised makeshift skates. Others were pulling each other along on sacks or trays, pressed into service as sledges. The air was full of their shouts of delight.

"We lived in Angel Alley until I was twelve," Ben said. "Mama sold old clothes to make us a few pennies and later she became a laundry woman. She would work all night, collecting laundry from the houses of the nobility—the sort of people she might once have moved amongst had things fallen out differently."

"Your father—" Catherine began, but she saw Ben's expression shut down. "I never knew him," he said. "You will know that he refused to acknowledge me."

"But your uncles found you and sent you to Harrow School." Catherine had read this part of Ben's life in one of the many penny sheets that Molly the house-maid had asked her to read to her.

"My mother thought it was the right thing to do," Ben said. He cast a sideways look at Catherine. "I hated it. They all called me a bastard, every day, to my face, and I could not refute it. So instead I behaved very badly." He laughed. "And have been doing so ever since." He smiled. "I suppose that you enjoyed school, Kate?"

Catherine squeezed his arm. "Yes," she said. "I loved it. I had been lonely before, being an only child, growing up abroad. Some of the other girls teased me, of course, because I came from a family of nabobs, but I did not care because Lily befriended me. I was not very clever but still I enjoyed belonging somewhere."

Ben nodded. "It is very lonely to feel you have no place."

There was a row of tents close ahead of them now with streamers flying from the pitched roofs.

"Lord Wellington For Ever," Catherine read. She laughed. "One cannot argue with that!"

"They are mostly drinking shops," Ben said. He smiled at her. "Would you care for a glass of wine with spices, Kate? It would keep you warm."

"It is more likely to make me drunk," Catherine said. Just the fumes floating on the frosty air were making her light-headed. "Even so, it sounds rather nice."

They found their way into the dark interior of the Lord Wellington. A few rickety tables and chairs had been placed on the ice, around a brazier whose smoke rose straight through a gap in the top of the tent. Catherine took off her gloves and warmed her hands on the glowing coals. The landlord brought a glass of spiced wine for her and a pint of ale for Ben. She took a tentative sip and felt her eyes water as the spirits hit the back of her throat.

"Oh! It has gin in it!"

"How on earth would you know that?" Ben inquired. "I thought debutantes were permitted only lemonade."

"I daresay," Catherine said, "my grandfather—"

"Of course." Ben took a long drink of the ale. "The sainted Sir Jack. What a dreadful influence he has been on you."

Catherine giggled. "I had school to teach me how to be a debutante," she said. "My grandfather taught me things he thought would be useful."

"Like drinking gin?"

"He said that people would try to tell me what to do, what to eat and drink, what to say, what to wear," Catherine said, remembering with a jolt of nostalgia that was half pain, half pleasure. "And he told me that the true Kate Fenton should be a real person who could think for herself, not a creature fashioned by someone else."

Ben took her hand. "Then he would be proud of what you have become, Kate."

Catherine smiled. "Thank you, my lord."

"Call me Ben," Ben said. "If we are to be betrothed—"

"When we are betrothed I will call you by your name," Catherine said severely. She sipped more of her wine and felt its warmth spread through her limbs. "I imagined," she added, "that you were never a man who sought to wed unless it was for money."

There was a silence. Ben's hand was warm in hers and suddenly she was very aware of his touch.

"That is absolutely true," Ben said, "much as it pains me to admit it so bluntly."

Catherine gave him a very direct look. "Why should it pain you? You have not hesitated to tell the truth before now."

Ben raised her hand to his cheek. She could feel the roughness of his stubble against her fingers. "Because it does not reflect well on me, does it, Kate? And although I do not usually care what men think of me, I find that with you…" He hesitated. "It is the most damnable thing, but I want you to see the best in me. I want to *be* better for you."

The brazier hissed and crackled in a sudden gust of icy air. Around them the voices of the other drinkers rose and fell but Catherine did not hear them. She was trapped by Ben's words and the look in his eyes. She knew it was the closest thing to a declaration of love that she was ever likely to get from him.

She drained her glass, suddenly reckless. "Then you had better show me what you are good at and win me a prize in the shooting gallery!" She dragged him to his feet. "Come on!"

Maybe it was the wine, but as they stepped out of the tent, the night seemed brighter and more vivid than before. There were stilt walkers teetering past, and fire-eaters, jugglers and sword swallowers. Ben bought her a bag of hot roasted chestnuts that tasted sweet and smelled delicious, and some gingerbread that melted in the mouth. He tried to tempt her to ride on the boat-shaped swing called the high flyer but Catherine was content to stand and watch and listen to the screams of those who were braver than she. True to his promise, Ben shot the bull's eyes on the archery butts and won a small carved wooden sheep with Lapland Mutton inscribed on a board about its neck. When he presented it formally to her, Catherine threw her arms around his neck and kissed him. He tasted of chestnuts, and she sensed in him a hesitation before he put his arms about her and kissed her back.

"I'm sorry," she said, drawing away, puzzled.

They stood looking at one another in the middle of the shining river. Ben shook his head slightly.

"I am the one who should apologize. It is simply

that I had sworn not to touch you unless it was your desire." He looked very grave.

"Well," Catherine said, feeling a little reckless, "I would have thought that you would realize from my actions that it was." She saw his lips curve into a smile and then she was in his arms again and he was kissing her very thoroughly indeed. She could feel from his hands and the way that he held her that he wanted her very much. And when he let her go his words echoed that thought.

"I do not take a great deal of persuasion, do I?" Ben said, and she thought he sounded rather rueful. He caught her hand and drew her close to his body again but he did not kiss her. "I do want you rather a lot, Catherine," he said. "You must know that by now. And you also know most of my faults."

"I know your virtues as well," Catherine said, "although perhaps to call them virtues is putting it a little strongly."

"What could those possibly be?" Ben asked.

"That you are honest about the things that matter," Catherine said thoughtfully, "and that there are people you do care about, no matter what you pretend."

"You are thinking of Clarencieux," Ben said, and there was an odd note in his voice.

"Not entirely," Catherine said. Her eyes were fixed on the sign above the Lord Wellington. "You were an officer in the army. You must have taken responsibility for your men, shown them leadership. I have heard that you were very courageous."

"Reckless, more like," Ben said. He sounded bitter.

"And I did not lead my men. I was a maverick. I think they sent me away on the most dangerous missions in order to keep me from leading anyone else into my sort of madness."

Catherine frowned. "Were you trying to kill yourself?"

"No. Not deliberately. But I did not care whether I did or not."

The faint, plaintive music from a fiddle came to them on the night air. Over in one of the frozen boats, couples were dancing a reel. They started to move toward it, walking slowly.

"But despite that," Ben said, "I think the army was the place where I most felt I belonged. When my father died and I had to come back to England to prove my right to inherit, it almost broke my heart."

"Why did you do it?" Catherine asked.

"For myself I did not care," Ben said. There was anger edging his voice now. "They could have called me *bastard* to the end of my days and I would only have laughed at them. And there was nothing to inherit but the title. My father had drunk all his substance away years ago."

"Your mother," Catherine said, suddenly understanding.

"Yes," Ben said. His hand tightened on hers so much it almost hurt. "I had waited twenty-seven years to prove that she was not just a lord's mistress, to be taken and discarded at his whim. I had to do it for her."

Catherine felt shaken at the passion in his eyes. So there had been one person in his life that Ben

Hawksmoor had loved and he had lost her. She looked across at Angel Alley, glowing white in the moonlight, and thought of the little boy growing up with a mother who was driven to go out to work all night just to keep the two of them from starving. She tried to imagine all the things Ben must have had to do to keep body and soul together and wondered if she would ever dare to ask him to tell her about it.

"You went to court," she said, remembering the legal reports in the papers from several years back. "It must have cost a fortune."

Ben smiled suddenly. "It cost every penny I earned, Kate, from all those dubious ventures that the papers are always reporting."

"The portraits you model for and the places where you eat and the goods you endorse…" Catherine looked at him. "It always seemed most singular to me that the tailors would pay *you* to wear their clothes rather than vice versa!"

"I seldom have to pay for any of the things I wear," Ben said. His smile was lopsided. "I have sold my very soul, Kate, to pay for my legitimacy."

"No," Catherine said. "You have paid to have that legitimacy recognized. You said yourself that you did not care what people said of you, only of your mother. So you have paid the highest price for her."

"It seemed the least that I could do," Ben said, "when she died to keep me alive." He slanted a look down at her. "And I am not so altruistic, Kate. Do not give me credit for that. The fact that I now have the title and the notoriety makes me a far more bankable property. Everything can be turned to making more money."

Catherine shook her head. "It all seems madness to me. And were we to wed everything would be different for you—"

Ben made a slight movement and she held him at arm's length. "No, wait! I said *if* that were to be the case, what would you do then? If you were rich and had no need to make money anymore?"

"I do not know," Ben said. He sounded vaguely surprised, as though he had not even thought about it. He smiled. "I could turn to politics, I suppose, take up my place in the Lords…"

Catherine smothered a laugh. "I would give my fortune just to see their lordships' faces!"

Ben stopped, looked at her. "What would you like our life to be, Catherine?"

"I do not know either," Catherine said honestly. "I have always wanted to travel, or perhaps to live in the country. But," she added, "I do know one thing and that is that our future would not include Lady Paris de Moine."

Ben drew her close and laid his cold cheek against hers. "One day I will tell you about Paris, Kate, but I do not want it to be now. I never loved her. She was never my mistress. I swear it. Can that be enough for you now?"

"I do not know," Catherine said again. She felt tired and heartsore all of a sudden, and her feet were turning ice-cold. Whatever Ben said, Paris had been a part of his life, an important part, and that could never be changed. She was human enough not to wish to live with that and yet if she wanted Ben, if she loved him, then she had to accept this, too.

They walked on, arm in arm, along the City Road, as the Thames highway had been named. Ben bought her a hot mutton pie and another mug of spiced wine and they drank and talked and danced the reels until the stars spun overhead and Catherine's head spun, too.

"Almacks was never so much fun," Catherine said at the end of the last dance, when exhausted and glowing, she collapsed into Ben's arms. "What do we do now?"

"We get married," Ben said.

Catherine turned. There behind them, stood a little church made from blocks of ice. Father Frost's Chapel, the name on the signboard said. Beside it was a printing press.

"For the marriage certificates," Ben said.

Catherine laughed. "Father Frost looks like a hedge priest," she said, pointing to the benign-looking individual in a dirty surplice who stood at the door, nodding as though in an extreme state of inebriation. "I'll wager he is no priest at all, or if he is, that the church defrocked him years ago! This cannot be legal."

"Then," Ben said, "you need have no concerns over plighting your troth to me."

Catherine stared at him. "You mean it," she whispered.

Ben's smile was wicked. "Do you dare?"

Catherine straightened her spine. She was aware that she was rather drunk herself, not unlike the benignly smiling priest.

"Of course I dare! It would only be in jest!"

Ben raised his brows quizzically. He held out a hand. "Then come with me."

The tiny chapel was lit by lanterns and glowed warm. There was a slab of ice for an altar with a rather fine bronze cross upon it. The men who worked the printing press doubled as witnesses.

"I know who you are," one of them said squinting at Ben in the dim light. "You're that Ben Hawksmoor, you are. Better be careful, mate." He jerked his thumb at the priest. "You'll be leg-shackled right enough. He's the genuine article. Curate of Southwark, making some money on the side."

Catherine could not decide if the priest was illiterate or not. Certainly he recited the entire marriage service from memory and did not use a prayer book once. When the moment came for someone to give the bride away, Tom, one of the printers, nipped around to Catherine's side while Jim, the other one, acted as groomsman. At the end they both signed the register.

"You may now kiss the bride," the priest said, smiling gently.

"Thank you," Ben said. For a moment he looked at her, smiling, and then he pulled her close and kissed her until she was dizzy.

The printers applauded enthusiastically.

"Let's go home," Ben whispered.

They stumbled out of the ice chapel, arms entwined, the good wishes of the printers and the priest ringing in their ears. Outside the cold air stung Catherine's cheeks and she shivered within her velvet cloak.

"If I had had no money," she said suddenly, "would you still have wanted to marry me?"

As soon as the words were out she wished she could un-say them, wished with all her heart that the ice would crack and swallow her so she need not hear either Ben's lies or the truth. Her cheeks burned with the horror of what she had just done. She waited, nerves tensed, for his reply.

"Since you are an heiress," he said, "the question need never arise."

And that was all.

He loosed her and stood back and she could see in his face the regret and the pity she had hoped never to see again. The marriage certificate crackled in her pocket, nestling beside the carved sheep. She told herself it did not matter. It was not legal, the priest had probably been defrocked if he had ever been a priest at all. She could go home and pretend it had never happened.

She turned away. "Let us find another ale tent before we leave," she said. "I turn cold and maudlin with it."

They went back to the Lord Wellington but they did not sit down this time. It felt like time to go. The fiddler still played as wildly as ever, the high flyer still swung through the silver night and the skaters still whirled and spun, but for Catherine the light had gone out of the night. She drained her second beaker of wine and placed it down on the counter a little regretfully.

"I must find the equivalent of a ladies' withdrawing room before we go back," she said. "If there is one."

Ben pointed. "There is a tent over there. They will probably demand several pence!"

Catherine looked at the little tent and the huge woman who stood guard pugnaciously in front of it. "I will not argue," she said.

"I'll wait here," Ben said. He pushed his ale away and watched her walk away across the ice. He knew now how this night would end. He would take Catherine back to Guilford Street like the most irreproachably well-behaved suitor, kiss her cheek and wish her a good-night as though the hedge marriage had never happened. And then he would lie awake suffering the twin torment of wanting her and fearing that she would never now be his. For in his honesty that night lay the seeds of his own downfall. And yet how could he have been anything other than honest with Kate? He wished now that he had lied and told her he loved her. But she deserved to know him exactly as he was, with all his failings and precious few virtues.

He waited. A minute went by, then another. The pugnacious woman at the front of the booth stood with arms crossed, unmoving. How long, Ben wondered, did it take a young lady to visit the withdrawing tent? Five minutes? Ten? Surely not, on such a cold night. He paid the landlord and started to stroll across the ice toward the tent. The huge woman shifted from one foot to the other. She had a brazier in front of her but she looked as though she were carved from a block of ice.

"Gents is over there," she said, jerking her head.

"I am waiting for the young lady," Ben said.

"Wait away," the woman said indifferently. "It makes no odds to me."

The brazier flickered. The cold seemed to be seeping into every cell of Ben's body now, working its way up from his feet like a slow poison. Surely Catherine would come out in a moment? Surely she had not run from him here, now, knowing she could not make a future with him and never wanting to see him again? He would have seen if she had left the tent for it had been in his view for the whole time. She could not have run away unless she had crept out the back….

Muffling a curse, he sprinted around the back of the tent, his feet slipping on the ice in his hurry. The canvas had been cut. He stood still, fingering the jagged line where a knife had run all the way down the panels. And then he heard the muffled scream. Away across the river, where the ice piled up beneath the span of Blackfriars Bridge, he could see Catherine. And she was not alone.

At first Ben could not see the identity of her abductor but then the shadows shifted and the moonlight fell on the face of the man who held her. Algernon Withers. The fear clawed at Ben's throat as he started to run, slipping, scrambling, falling so hard he winded himself, entangling himself with the skaters, who shouted with annoyance and alarm,

picking himself up, driving himself on as he saw
Withers drawing closer and closer to the Queenhithe
steps. The fear pounded through his body with every
beat of his heart.

"Catherine!"

He had been intending to shout Withers's name but
it was Catherine's that came out, a half-strangled gasp
that nevertheless was enough to cause Withers to check
slightly and glance over his shoulder. Ben was inex-
pressibly relieved to see that Catherine was conscious
and she was making it very difficult for her captor,
hampering his every step with her struggles. She did
not scream again and Ben could see that Withers had
one hand clamped over her mouth as he dragged her
on.

He was not making for the steps. There were two
boatmen manning the planks there and because
Withers was keeping in the shadow of the bridge they
had not seen him. Ben wondered whether he would try
to haul Catherine up onto the quay some other way,
use one of the icebound boats, perhaps, but then he
saw the man turn and a knife flashed at Catherine's
throat, and Ben stopped moving as all the blood
seemed to freeze through his body.

"Hawksmoor!" Withers's words seemed to echo
off the ice in the gloomy netherworld beneath the
arches. "Stay where you are!"

"Let her go!" Ben yelled. He was desperately
hoping that some of the boatmen would hear, but this
wide expanse beneath the bridge was hidden from
view by the peaks and turrets of the ice slabs that had

piled up here, and was cut off from all sound. They were alone in a frozen world.

Withers was backing toward the hulk of a boat tied up on the quay. Behind him a rickety wooden ladder led up from water level and it was clear to Ben that he intended to force Catherine up there and onto dry land. Ben could see her face, pale and petrified in the shadowy moonlight, and see the blade that menaced her.

"Let her go, Withers," Ben shouted. "You'll never get away—"

Catherine gave a small yelp, cut short, and Ben was horrified to see a dark line of blood trickle down her neck. He was a mere thirty yards away and he tried desperately to calculate how quickly he could cover the ground. Not fast enough. It would take Withers a mere second to strike. Except that Withers did not want Catherine dead. He had always wanted her alive.

As Ben started to move, he saw Catherine's foot slip from the rotten treads of the ladder. Her cloak entangled itself in Withers's legs and he stumbled. Ben was only ten yards away now and everything seemed to happen so slowly. He saw Catherine reach out and grab the rope hanging frozen from the deck of the ship beside her. With a huge effort she wrenched the icy line from the deck and swung it across with all her strength. It hit Withers squarely in the stomach and he let her go, doubling up with a grunt. Catherine tumbled from his grasp and fell sprawling on the ice, and the knife skittered away along the side of the icebound ship.

Ben reached Catherine's side in one leap. He did not care what happened to Withers as long as she was safe. He was shaking as he reached out to her. "Kate—"

Catherine was pale but her grip on his arm was strong. "I am well," she gasped. "Don't let him get the knife! He will kill you!"

Ben spun around but Withers reached the knife first. Even as Ben strained every muscle, he saw the other man's hand close about the hilt and he turned with a roar of triumph.

There was a crack as sharp as a gunshot. A fine lacing of lines ran out across the ice more quickly than a man could run, and a black ribbon of water appeared beside the stern of the boat. Withers staggered, fell back. There was a sickening sound of splintering ice and Withers fell.

One of the watermen had noticed what was happening at last. With a shout he picked up his boards and started to run across the ice toward them, gesturing to his colleagues to follow.

Ben hesitated for only a moment. He lay down on the breaking ice and grabbed the waterlogged sleeve of Withers's coat. He pulled hard. Withers's head came back up from under the ice and he coughed, shaking the water from his eyes. Ben tried to grip his arm, to pull him out. But Withers was pulling away from him, drawing back, determined to wrench himself from Ben's grasp. And all the time the ice was breaking up, creaking and cracking below them as the current ran strong beneath.

"For God's sake, man," Ben yelled, "take my hand!"

The glare in Withers's eyes was malevolent as he stared up from the ice. "Not you!" he said. "You let my half brother die at Bembibre. You saved Clarencieux but you let John die! So don't save *me* now!"

Ben felt so shocked that for a moment he did not move. And in that second he saw the glint of the knife below the water and Withers's hand came up with the blade pointed straight at him.

There was a cracking sound from above and a shower of ice dusted Ben's shoulders. He tried to catch Withers's wrist to grab the knife from him, but the ice started to break beneath him and it tipped him perilously off balance. He staggered and fell. Withers slipped back, his body disappearing beneath the ice and then Ben could see him no longer as the current took him and swept him away.

## CHAPTER ELEVEN

A woman who has given herself up to the pleasures of physical gratification is in no way respectable, nor is she a lady.
—*Mrs. Eliza Squire,* Good Conduct for Ladies

THEY WERE IN THE HACKNEY carriage and Catherine was wrapped in Ben's cloak and he had his arms about her, but she could not stop shivering. Although she had not fallen in the water, she felt as cold as though she had been dipped in the icy river. She could feel that Ben was shaking as well, both of them transfixed by the horror of their experience.

When the first of their rescuers had come upon them, Algernon Withers's body had vanished, carried away by the breaking ice. The knife had sunk without trace. Catherine had listened while Ben had told the men that there had been an accident; they had been trying to reach the steps when the ice had started to break. The watermen shook their heads in grim pleasure. They had seen it all before.

"Once the ice breaks and the current gets you..." one man said. He shook his head again and all his colleagues looked grave. "You're a lucky man, my lord, that it did not take the two of you away as well as that Withers cove…."

Catherine had begun to realize that Ben could not go anywhere without people recognizing him. There had been a crowd about them already, wrapping them in blankets, helping them over to the brazier on the quay to keep warm, offering food and pouring more spiced wine down her throat. They were good-natured and friendly and all seemed to think Ben was a personal friend because they had read about him in the penny press. A couple of river policemen had come along from the docks to hear Ben's story again and bemoan the dangerous nature of the Thames even when it was frozen. One of them had bashfully offered one of the Frost Fair handbills for Ben to autograph because he wanted to give it to his wife.

"She will be fair disappointed to have missed seeing you, my lord," he had said with a grin.

Ben had promised to be available to give a full report of Withers's death. More people had arrived wanting to talk to him and shake his hand, but Ben begged them to summon a hack, which they had done with a good grace. They'd sped Ben and Catherine on their way with wishes of good health and good luck.

And all the time, Ben had not let go of Catherine for a moment, but had held her close, trying to warm her cold body with his own even colder one.

Now, alone at last, she burrowed deeper into his embrace.

"Thank goodness! Those good people were very

kind but I thought we should never be permitted to get away."

Ben kissed her hair. "I am sorry. I tried to leave as quickly as I could."

"Do not apologize." Catherine smiled in the dark. "I doubt we should have had so much help, been so thoroughly warmed and fed, were it not for the fact that every one of them wishes to be able to say that they helped the famous Ben Hawksmoor this night."

Ben laughed but sobered abruptly. He grasped her hands. "But you, Kate... Are you sure you are not injured? When I saw that he had the knife at your throat I thought—" He stopped. "He did not want to kill you," he said in an odd voice.

"No," Catherine said. She shivered convulsively. "He wanted me alive."

Ben slid his arms about her again. "I think he was obsessed with you. He needed to possess you."

"Don't," Catherine said, and her voice broke. "I understand that now. He wanted me and I thwarted him and so he became even more determined to take what he could not have."

Ben rested his cheek against hers and for a moment they sat in silence.

"Thank you," Catherine said. "Thank you for saving me."

Ben laughed. "Selfish as I am, my sweet, not even I would have stood by and let him carry you off."

But his arms hard about her gave Catherine another answer and she reveled in it.

"I heard Withers say that you let his brother die,"

she said hesitantly. She freed herself a little so that she could look at him. "What did he mean, Ben? Was that why he hated you so much?"

Ben shifted slightly to settle her more comfortably in the crook of his arm. "I am not sure, Kate, but I think it must be."

"Lady Russell told me she had met Withers's brother," Catherine said, remembering. "She said both he and the father were very wild." She frowned. "I know Lord Withers's father died years ago but I have never heard him speak of a brother."

"He mentioned Bembibre," Ben said slowly. "He said that I had saved Ned Clarencieux's life—and let others die. And it is true that at Bembibre that is exactly what I did."

Catherine could not see his face in the darkness of the carriage but she could hear the note of despair in his voice. She held him tightly, instinctively offering comfort.

"What happened?" she whispered.

It was a moment before Ben replied, and when he did he spoke dispassionately, as though he were reporting something that had happened to someone else, not something Catherine suspected was etched so deep in his memory that nothing could ever shift the nightmares.

"I was serving with Moore's troops in Spain at the end of 1808 when the French came after us at Valladolid. We knew we were hopelessly outnumbered and had to retreat. It was late in the year and the road was hard and the mood of some of the men turned sour.

They ravaged the villages we passed through, drinking, whoring, looting... They lost all their discipline."

Catherine could not help but catch her breath. "Did you... Were you there?"

"No," Ben said. "I told you I was a maverick, working on my own. I had been sent from my regiment to join the rearguard as a messenger. They were holding the French off as best they could and doing a fine job of it, unlike the rabble of foot soldiers ahead of them. I was on my way back, taking dispatches from Crawfurd and Paget up the column to Moore. When I reached the village of Bembibre I found two hundred of our troops had been left behind. They had found a wine cellar and were so dead drunk they could not stand. Their commanding officer had abandoned them, left them there. Amongst them were men that I had once commanded, including Ned Clarencieux."

Catherine made a small sound of despair. "Ben..."

"I could not save them all," Ben said. "The French were so close behind and I had despatches for Moore that I could not risk losing. Besides, what could I do, one man against a closing army? Ned was as sick with drink as the rest of them. I pulled him out and I had to leave the others to die. Withers's half brother must have been amongst them."

For the first time that night, Catherine felt the hot tears soak her cheeks and the sodden material of Ben's cloak. She had not cried when Withers had snatched her, had not cried when she'd thought Ben was going to be killed, had not cried when Withers had died. But now Ben's words pierced that icy calm with all the things he had left unsaid. How was one man to make a decision like that and to bear the memory of it for the rest of his days? And yet she knew that in war men were called on to make such decisions all the time and had to live with the consequences.

"It was not your fault," she said fiercely. "You were not the one who abandoned them. You could not have saved them all!"

"I may not have given the order but I still left them," Ben said. "I chose to help Clarencieux and I left the rest, knowing they would die. If Withers's half brother was one of those left behind, he might well believe that Ned had no right to be the only one to live." He sighed. "I will make inquiries, see if Withers had a relative who served in the Peninsula. If they had different fathers, it would account for the fact that I did not recognize his name."

Catherine didn't say anything. She knew that any words of hers, even given in comfort, could make no difference to what he felt. It had not been Ben's responsibility and yet he had felt the weight of that choice keenly and would never forget it. She curled as closely to him as she could to give him comfort. She was starting to feel warm and sleepy now, but something still nagged at her mind. Algernon Withers might well have been responsible for Clarencieux's death and have wanted to punish Ben for what he saw as his part in letting his brother die, but where did that leave Sir James Mather? Was he simply an unfortunate casualty of the whole affair, a man Withers had known and chosen randomly to be the victim when he framed Clarencieux out of hatred and resentment? Catherine's mind was cloudy with sleep now and she let the matter slip away.

She was in fact asleep when the hack drew up in St. James's Place and Ben carried her into the house, but she stirred a little in the warmth and the light. He put her gently down in the hallway but kept his arms about her. His breath stirred her hair.

"I have told the hack to wait a moment," he said, "in case you choose to go home to Guilford Street, Kate." He smiled. "But you are my bride—if a hedge bride at that. I almost lost you once tonight and do not wish to let you from my sight."

Catherine smiled sleepily. She was remembering the expression on his face when he had thought Withers had stabbed her. He had looked so white, so desperate, stricken with fear…. He had never said that he loved her but she thought now that she did not need to hear those words when she had seen all she needed in his face.

"Nor do I wish to go. Please send the driver with a note for Lady Russell, lest she worry about me."

"She will worry all the more," Ben said dryly, "when she hears you are Lady Hawksmoor."

Catherine's lips curved again. She was smiling and yawning at the same time. "I think not. She likes you, Ben Hawksmoor, and I have always trusted her judgment."

"Congratulations, my lady," another voice said, and Catherine jumped to see the very correct butler she had met previously. He was smiling.

"This is Price," Ben said, and Catherine smiled back at him.

"Good evening, Price. I am very pleased to meet you again." She yawned. "I do beg your pardon. It seems I am so tired I cannot keep awake."

"Some hot water, my lord?" the manservant asked, but Ben shook his head. "In the morning perhaps."

He picked Catherine up again but halfway up the stairs he stopped, put her on her feet and started to kiss her. She wrapped her arms about his neck. He shifted so that his hard thighs were suddenly outside hers and pinned her against the wall with his body. His kiss was deep, his tongue tangling with hers, teasing, promising, possessing. Suddenly she felt wide awake and very aroused.

"We can't stay here." Ben's voice was harsh. "Come with me."

They were in the bedroom she remembered, with the huge peacock-blue bed.

"That bed covering," she said, "will have to go."

Ben laughed. "Whatever you say, sweetheart."

Catherine looked down at her clothes. "I have no maid. I will need your help."

"With pleasure." There was a hardness in Ben's eyes, a hunger as he looked at her now. It shocked her and excited her, too. Beyond measure. She knew that this time there would be no stopping.

"You carried me over the threshold," she said, remembering.

"Because you are my bride." Ben smiled, a slow smile. "To my surprise, I find I like that thought rather a lot, Kate. It is a revelation to me."

Catherine reached up to touch his cheek. "Then you had better make me your wife in deed," she whispered.

THIS TIME HE WANTED EVERYTHING to be perfect.

Ben had placed Catherine softly, almost reverently, in the center of the big bed, and now he leaned down and kissed her. She slid her hands over his shoulders, smoothing the material of his shirt beneath her palms, then locked her hands about his neck and kissed him back.

He broke the kiss and straddled her, touching her cheek and the line of her jaw with gentle fingers. She opened her eyes and they were soft and smiling. He felt lost in that look, lost in a way he had never experienced before and for a moment it held him still, but then she reached out to him again, sliding her hands up his arms beneath his shirt, pushing it back from his shoulders so she could touch his bare skin. He shivered at her touch, spellbound. No woman had ever been able to do such a thing to him before. Her power over him was almost frightening.

"Catherine... Sweetheart..."

He shook his clothes off and threw them on the floor, then turned back to her and dealt as ruthlessly with her own until she was naked beneath him. He traced the line of her breast with one slow movement of his fingertips. She arched to him then, her hands gripping his upper arms, and made a sound halfway between a gasp and a cry. He caught her about the waist and drew her up against his own nakedness, kissing her fiercely, letting her sink back onto the bed only so that his mouth could follow the path his fingers had taken down her throat to her breasts, to tempt and tease, and then lower still, to the soft skin of her stomach.

He propped himself on one elbow and studied her face. She looked flushed and heated as though with a fever. Her eyes were half open, dark and slumberous with arousal.

"I want it to be good for you this time," he said.

A half smile curved her lips. "It was not bad last time…."

She reached out to him but he whispered, "Not yet," and saw her eyes close and felt her body soften as his mouth touched the warm, tender skin of her inner thigh.

He moved higher, lifted her to his mouth and deliberately flicked his tongue to the hot, moist core of her.

She cried out, her whole body convulsing immediately, moving beneath his hands. He waited until she had stopped, had fallen back with a gasp of pure shock, and then he dipped his tongue into her again. Again she cried out, this time a sound of desperation and passion mixed, and he held her hips down and slid up at last to rest the painfully swollen tip of his penis just inside her. He kissed her breasts, sucked on the nipples and felt her body tense about him as she raised her hips to try to draw him deeper inside.

"Ben… Please…"

Her eyes were closed, her breathing quick and her damp hair spread across the white of the sheets in a lustrous cloud. He tangled one hand into her hair and brought his lips down so that they barely touched hers.

"Open your eyes."

She looked at him. Her gaze was dark and unfocused.

"Once before I disappointed you," Ben said. His voice was rough. "I hope you are not disappointed in me so far."

A smile lit her eyes. "Will it add to your conceit if I admit I am not?" she whispered.

He did not answer, except to smile, and then he could resist no longer and slid inside her with one sleek thrust. He heard her quick intake of breath and knew that this time it was not from pain. She was tight and slick and his body ached unbearably, the need building within him. He had concentrated so hard on her pleasure that he had tried to ignore his own body's demands for release. Now, as she ran her hands down over his buttocks and gripped him hard, he almost lost all control. He withdrew a little, resisting the demands of his senses and the pressure of her hands, then slid back in long, slow strokes. Braced on his forearms, he watched her, watched the blush that stung her skin, the changing expressions that chased across her face, the way her breasts rocked so exquisitely with each thrust. She whimpered and squirmed. He watched the slide of his penis inside her, felt the quiver of her belly, and tried not to think about what he wanted and only to give her pleasure.

Within a minute she was begging. "Quicker… Aah…" Her body contracted as he maintained that slow, steady pressure. "Ah, Ben, quicker please…"

"Slower," he said, schooling the increasingly desperate clamor of his own desires. "Slower is better."

He saw what looked like a flash of temper in her face. Innocent Kate, *temptress Kate,* did not like being told what to do. He smiled with the satisfaction of possession.

She rolled him over so suddenly that he was utterly unprepared, and slid down hard and deep on top of him. He knew at once that he was going to come. He could not control it. His mind shattered and he gave a shout, holding her hips hard as he forced himself upward, his entire body shuddering with the strength of his release. He heard her scream, felt her body close even more tightly about him and then they were tumbling over and over, down into the dark and the flame. Ben savored it, waited, then let the pleasure ebb slowly, so slowly, and felt the peace take its place as he held her close to him.

WHEN CATHERINE CAME ROUND she was lying in the curve of Ben's arm, her head on his shoulder and his other arm lying across her stomach in careless possession. The sheets were tossed to the four corners of the bed, her hair had knots in it and she was cold. She wriggled her way beneath the covers and propped herself on one elbow to look at Ben. He was not asleep. He turned to meet her eyes and in his was an expression of stunned surprise. It made her want to laugh. Along with disbelief and exultation, and a rather wicked sense of enjoyment, stunned surprise just about summed up how she felt.

"I liked it," she said, and felt even more wicked to admit it.

His hazel gaze was hot and sleepy at the same time. "I'm so glad that you were not disappointed."

"How could you disappoint me?"

There was a moment of stillness and once again, as at the Frost Fair the previous night, Catherine wished she had not spoken. He had disappointed her. He had not said that he loved her.

Then he moved. His legs shifted, sliding over hers, pinning her down.

"You owe me something for that trick you played at the end," he said. His mouth came down on her breast.

Catherine gasped. "Did you not like it?"

His hands started to roam over her skin, urgently claiming every curve.

"Oh yes, I liked it, sweetheart. I liked it very much."

Catherine lay wantonly still, allowing him to touch her wherever and however he wanted. The hot shivers coursed through her veins. She parted her thighs to his questing fingers and felt him stroke her intimately. He kissed the base of her throat and the underside of her breast, and Catherine gave a little moan. There was an ache low in her belly. She recognized it now, recognized the need that made her reach out to him in turn. His penis, long and thick, felt smooth against her thigh, but when she tried to turn to him, he brushed her hands aside and pushed her gently back so that he could continue the relentless caresses that were invading her mind and igniting her body. The urgency built within her as he stroked and caressed, until his knowing hands caused her body to arch and shatter, but even in the moment of release she felt an ache for him to be inside her.

She opened dazed eyes and whispered, "Are we equal now?"

His smile was full of masculine satisfaction. "Not yet."

He lowered his body over hers, nudging her parted thighs wider and settling between them. She tilted her hips up and then he was within her, taut and tense. She could feel the tightly controlled strength of him, the heat, the hardness, and when her lips parted on a groan of sheer pleasure, he bent his head and trapped her in an endless kiss.

His possession of her was complete. His body held hers still beneath him. She was his alone.

At last he started to move, pushing deep then withdrawing, gradually more forceful until she was clinging to him and wrapping her legs about him, her little cries smothered by his mouth. She knew she was going to come at once and she wanted to rebel, to show him that he did not have that power over her, but it was too late. The wave broke over her, tumbling her helplessly in a storm of sensation, her body clenching about him.

It was only as her hazy mind drifted over what had happened to her that she realized that he had not stopped. He was still moving gently, maintaining a rhythm that once again threatened to draw a response from her still-shuddering body. Catherine's eyes opened wide in shock.

"Again?"

He nodded. His face was tense and dark, set hard with desire. She could see the iron control he was exerting. Then he shifted his weight a little and reached down to rub his thumb gently over the sensitive core of her. Catherine's body jumped to his touch. She drew in a sharp breath. It seemed impossible, unimaginable, that he could demand another response from her, and yet even as she thought it, she could feel the heat start to build. This time, she swore to herself, she would take him with her. If she surrendered, he would, too.

He lowered his head to her nipples, devouring her, setting her on fire. Her body strove to match the rhythm of his, reaching out to capture him and match the demands he made with those of her own. She could feel the heat ripple beneath her skin, the sensations building toward a climax. And then, suddenly, he withdrew from her, lifted her, turned her over so that she was on her side amid the twisted sheets. Confused, utterly aroused, she turned her head to look at him and saw he was as aroused as she.

But before she could question, he moved. Spreading her thighs he penetrated her again, lying behind her, sliding into her, his arms clasped about her. One of his hands cupped her breast, toying with it in his palm. Catherine pushed back instinctively against his hips and her entire body shivered with ecstasy as the deep rocking sensation claimed her, this time deeper, harder and more deliberate still. She felt his lips on the nape of her neck. He nuzzled her hair aside so that he could run his tongue down the slope of her shoulder and the damp heat of it hardened her nipples still further against the stroke of his palms.

He raised her onto her knees and his hands moved

to hold her hips still as he thrust now without restraint. Her mind whirling, her body shaking and heated, Catherine reached out to grab the end of the bed to steady herself. She felt even more wantonly exposed and open to him now. Her breasts trembled with each thrust. Her hair was tumbled about her shoulders, her thighs spread, her body shuddering at his invasion. She braced herself against the end of the bed and let the sensations take her, drawing him in, meeting his passion with her own.

One of his hands came up to knead her breast and she thought she would melt with the wanting. A moment later he had slid his hand across her belly, down to the point where his body joined hers. His fingers delved. Catherine tried to squirm away from his touch but his other hand was on her hip, holding her still. She wriggled, trapped, tormented as his body impaled her and the caress of his fingers drove her to madness.

Captured by the inevitable spiral of desire, Catherine knew she could resist no longer. She surrendered with a wild cry as her mind fractured and her body was finally released from its exquisite torment. She felt Ben's body spasm as he ground into her even more fiercely and then he, too, gave a shout and they both fell down among the sheets and the peacock-blue coverlet, abandoned, exalted and still entwined.

BEN LAY AND WATCHED Catherine sleep. He was falling in love with her more with each passing moment and at last he luxuriated in the feeling. He felt excited and happy but more than anything he felt warm and safe— and rich. His fears had receded beyond the edge of his mind. For once, he was sure, he could sleep peacefully. He wrapped his arms around Catherine and lay against her back, feeling the way that her body curved itself against his and how soft and tender she was in sleep. He kissed her hair and felt his heart swell with thankfulness. And then he, too, slept.

## CHAPTER TWELVE

Not all affairs of the heart may have a happy outcome and if a lady is unfortunate enough to be
disappointed in love then as a woman of good
manners and education she must simply put the
matter behind her.
—*Mrs. Eliza Squire*, Good Conduct for Ladies

IT WAS DARK THIS TIME when Catherine awoke, and for
a moment she lay on the edges of sleep, warm,
cocooned in happiness, safe and at peace. Then the
sounds that had woken her penetrated her mind again
and she sat bolt upright in bed. The space beside her
was empty. Ben had gone, and from downstairs came
the sounds of voices raised in urgent distress. Catherine grabbed a robe, tied it about her with unsteady
hands, flung open the bedroom door and ran down the
stairs.

She had expected to find her father there full of
outrage and anger with the news of her elopement, but
it was Lady Russell who was in the hall, wringing her
hands and talking at agitated speed. Ben was there, and
Price the butler looking less than his usual impassive self.

"I cannot think how to tell her," Lady Russell was saying. "They were friends—so close! Catherine was the only one who did not desert her when she was disgraced." She saw Catherine and stopped abruptly, and for a long, dreadful moment there was silence.

"Catherine," Ben said. He was looking dazed. "I am so sorry—"

"What is it?" Catherine's gaze went from his face to that of her chaperone. All the warm, happy, peaceful feelings within her started to drain away. She grabbed Lady Russell's hands and could feel her trembling.

"Aunt Agatha? Tell me! What has happened?"

She had never expected to see Lady Russell cry. She simply was not the sort of woman to do so. Yet there were tears in her eyes now. "Oh, Kate," she said brokenly. "I am so sorry. It is Lily. She is dead. They think it was Withers who murdered her."

THEY BURIED LILY A WEEK LATER in a sad little ceremony in a cemetery at Saint Day's Church. The fog had lifted for good now and it had been a beautiful, clear, cold winter's day. Lily's family had not attended and Catherine had hated them for it. They had cast Lily out in life and in death it was as though she had not existed at all. There had been so few of them in attendance—herself and Lady Russell, Sarah Desmond and Connor, sniffing into a large gentleman's handkerchief. It seemed that he had loved Lily, too. Ben had escorted her. The press, excited with the scandal of Lily's death and smelling a wonderful news story, had tried to interview him afterward but he had put his arm about Catherine to shield her from their stares and had refused to talk to them at all. Catherine had been surprised and deeply relieved.

The following days had passed in something of a blur. She was aware that Ben was working with someone called Bradshaw to investigate all the loose ends of Withers's criminal dealings. One of the other clients in the brothel had identified Withers as the man he had seen going into Lily's chamber that night and he must have gone straight from there to follow Catherine to the Frost Fair. She was so angry that Withers had drowned before she had learned of Lily's death. She wanted to rail at him with all the pent-up fury and loss inside her. She wanted to be the one to kill him.

Lady Russell had asked her lawyer, Mr. Churchward, to look into the financial side of Catherine's affairs. With Sir Alfred Fenton still sick, or pretending to be, and both her other trustees dead, Catherine knew this was all they could do. Ben did not speak to her of it but she sensed the tension in him, though he was constantly by her side during the day and held her close to comfort her at night when her grief threatened to break her heart. But even though he was there for her, Catherine felt that he was slipping away in some sense she found difficult to define. Sometimes she would feel his gaze on her, dark, unreadable, and she would know he was thinking of the money and panic would threaten her.

And then, one afternoon in February, Ben came to seek her out as she sat in the drawing room with Lady

Russell, her embroidery idle on her lap. She looked at his face and saw immediately that something was wrong.

"Is it my father?" she started to ask. "Or Maggie?"

But Ben shook his head. He looked at Lady Russell and then back at Catherine. He looked grim and gray.

"Mr. Churchward has sent a message," he said. "He asks to see us straight away."

They took their leave of Lady Russell, who made Catherine promise to send to her at Grillons Hotel as soon as she could, and took the carriage to Churchward's chambers in Holborn. The streets were clear now and the ice was melting. Each day another great chunk of it broke away in the Thames, creaking, straining, crushing boats and bridges before it. The snow was melting to a dirty gray.

Ben held Catherine's hand, but she sensed that he was far away.

"Everything will be all right," she said, although she was not sure whether she was trying to reassure him or comfort herself. "Withers may have borrowed some money from my trust fund, I suppose, but Papa will not have let him do anything too dreadful. I am sure of it."

Ben did not answer, and looking at him Catherine thought he was fighting a battle with himself. She thought she understood. She had had money all her life and so had never had to face the desperate struggle for survival that had shaped his entire existence. Yet she hoped, prayed, that the love she was sure she had seen in him would be strong enough to keep him by her side. But she was terribly afraid that it would not.

Mr. Churchward did not keep them waiting. He ushered them into his dusty office and saw Catherine to a chair, all the while offering his sincere condolences on Lily's death and the disarray of Catherine's own business affairs.

Ben did not sit, but strode across to the window as though he could not bear to be entrapped in the room. Catherine wanted to draw him to her side but he did not come close. He did not even look at her as he paced back and forth across the floor. A hard, hot, miserable weight settled in Catherine's stomach as she waited for Churchward to speak.

"I have been talking to the bank on your behalf, Lady Hawksmoor," the lawyer said. "With your father sick and your other trustees dead—" he cleared his throat "—well, it seemed for the best that someone should take control." He shook his head, as though he was overcome for a moment by the sheer untidiness of the situation. "I am sorry....really very sorry indeed, that matters have come to this."

Ben made an abrupt movement as though he had no patience for chatter, and Churchward hastily moved on. He cleared his throat again and shuffled the papers on the desk.

"Please, Mr. Churchward," Catherine said, unable to bear the tension a moment longer, "I know...I suspect...that there has been some irregularity with the funds. Lady Russell has warned me to prepare myself for the fact but I would prefer it if you were to tell me the precise details."

"Of course," Churchward said. "Of course." He

looked quite hopeless. "I am sorry to have to tell you," he said, "that we now have the evidence that Lord Withers and, I believe, your father, have robbed your trust funds of all but a few hundred pounds."

Catherine closed her eyes briefly. She could feel all the blood draining from her face, leaving her light-headed with shock. She had been prepared to hear of Withers's criminality, but her own father? Instead of protecting her interests, he had cheated her. He and Withers together had stolen everything that her grandfather had left for her.

"My father…" she said faintly.

"I am sorry," Churchward said again. "There is very little left."

Catherine looked across at Ben. He was standing by the window as though carved from stone, un-moving, unspeaking. It was almost as though he had not heard a word. The silence was unbearable and Churchward hurried to fill it.

"We believe," he continued, gabbling a little now, "that Sir James Mather uncovered the deceit and Withers killed him to keep the matter quiet. We cannot be certain of your father's part in the affair until he has recovered his health and is able to answer questions."

Catherine put her hands up to her white cheeks. "But you think that he knew?"

Churchward steepled his fingers. "Of the fraud, very probably," he allowed. "Of the murder—" he shifted uncomfortably "—well, we shall have to bide our time and see."

"He must have known," Catherine said again. "He

must have been in league with Withers all along. Clarencieux was framed because Withers hated him. But Clarencieux was also having an affair with Maggie and my father knew of that. It was their joint revenge." She felt stricken.

Once again she looked across at Ben. There was an odd blindness in his face, some sort of disintegration, as though a part of him had been torn away. And then, just as Catherine could bear his silence no longer, he set his jaw and sketched a bow.

"Excuse me," he said and walked out of the room without another word. Catherine heard Churchward's astonished gasp. "Lady Hawksmoor—"

Catherine shook her head. Somewhere inside her she had always been prepared for this final loss. She knew that Ben had wanted her and the money together, and now the money was gone. So he had gone, too. But the reality of it was almost too painful for her to bear. She tried desperately to blot it out, afraid that once she allowed herself to feel, it might destroy her.

"Thank you for telling me the truth, Mr. Churchward," she said trying to keep her voice even. "No doubt I shall require further details in a little while but for now I think I had better return home to speak with my father as soon as he is sufficiently recovered to face me."

"Can I do anything to assist you, Lady Hawksmoor?" Mr. Churchward asked. He was looking almost as pale and shocked as Catherine felt.

"I should be grateful if you could procure me a hack to take me home," she said. "I imagine that my husband has taken the carriage."

"He will be back," Churchward said. He looked desperately anxious but Catherine knew well enough that his words, offered in comfort, could not be true.

"I doubt it," she said.

She stood up and smoothed down her skirt with a very deliberate gesture. "Thank you, Mr. Churchward," she said again. "I appreciate your sentiments but I suspect I have only myself to blame. I think I have always known in my heart that this might happen. Lord Hawksmoor always was a fortune hunter and where there is no fortune…" She let the sentence hang.

Somehow she managed to get out of the building without breaking down. The black carriage with the Hawksmoor crest was still out in the street, but there was no sign of Ben. Catherine drove back to St. James's. It did not take long. She was cold now, shivering and shivering as though she had an ague, and her throat was sore with the effort of keeping the tears at bay.

She knew before she set foot inside that Ben was not there. The house was quiet and Price, his face wreathed in worry lines, confirmed that Ben had not yet been home.

Catherine took a hackney to Guilford Street and on the way she thought about Ben and her brief marriage and the fact that it was over before it had barely started. The tears were running silently down her face now and, though she tried to brush them aside, she did not seem able to stop. Little by little, the ice in which she had tried to encase her heart was melting and the pain was almost unbearable.

As soon as Lady Russell had warned her that her financial affairs were in difficulty, she had been afraid that it would come to this. Ben had given her comfort and support in the time since Lily's death but she had known it did not mean he loved her. He had never made any secret of the fact that he wanted her but it was her money he really loved. She had asked Ben on the ice that magical night if he would have married her if she were poor, and he had not answered her. In that failure to answer was all the truth she needed. It *had* mattered to him. He had just proved it. He had seen her lose her fortune and he had walked out without a word. He had simply never been strong enough to step out of the shadows of his past. He needed the security that money could buy and she could not give that to him now. So he had gone.

She had lain in Ben's arms and had known exquisite pleasure at his hands, and had loved him and given herself to him without reservation. She had thought, foolishly, that her love might be enough for both of them. There had been a moment there in Churchward's office when she had hoped with all the love that was in her heart that this would be true and Ben Hawksmoor would prove to be a better man than he had always claimed to be. She knew now a fraction of how he had suffered as a boy, all the fear and the deprivation and the poverty. She knew how much he had done to keep his mother safe when his father had abandoned them. He had saved her life when Withers had attacked her and she had seen with her own eyes the courage he had shown attempting to save Withers himself, a man he hated. There was so much good in him. Just not quite enough.

She had trusted herself to him, believing that Ben might not love her but he would never deliberately hurt her. But he had. He had wounded her so deeply now that she was afraid she could never forgive him. She closed her eyes. There was such a fine line between love and hate. She had loved Ben and he had let her down. She knew she was not feeling quite sane— Lily's death had grieved her deeply and now this latest tragedy had broken her heart. She had loved Ben and now she almost hated him for what he had done.

The carriage drew up in Guilford Street, and Catherine paid the driver and walked slowly up the steps. Tench was waiting for her at the door with the slightly nervous look that all the servants seemed to be wearing these days.

"Miss Catherine… Is it very bad, ma'am?"

"I think so, Tench," Catherine said. "I must go and speak with my father. Is he awake?"

"Aye, ma'am," Tench confirmed. "He is in the study, though he takes no food nor speaks to no one."

Catherine nodded. She went into the study and closed the door.

Sir Alfred was sitting before the fire and he did not move as she came in, did not even appear to have heard her. Catherine went around and took the chair in front of him. His chin was sunk on his chest but he raised his eyes and looked at her.

"They tell me that Withers is dead," he said.

"He is," Catherine said.

Sir Alfred nodded. He did not seem interested.

There was a silence. "Why did you do it?" Catherine asked suddenly. She felt angry but she felt empty, too, as though everyone she had ever felt she might depend upon had shown themselves to have feet of clay. "Why did you take all my trust fund?"

She looked around at the opulent furnishings. They had all the trappings of wealth, but not for long now.

"Did you not have enough for yourself?" she asked, the anger burning through her tone now. "Did you feel so deprived that you had to take what was mine—what my grandfather worked for and left to me?"

"It would not have mattered," Sir Alfred said suddenly, "if only you had married Withers. You would never have known. All he wanted was you."

"He wanted to take everything you had," Catherine corrected. "Not because you had done anything to him but simply to show you that he could. He was drunk with the power of it all, Papa, mad with laudanum. He would have stopped at nothing."

Sir Alfred's gaze slid away. He did not reply.

"He killed Lily," Catherine said. "He killed Mather and he killed Clarencieux." When her father did not speak she leaned closer. "You *knew?*"

Sir Alfred nodded slowly. "I could not stop him. You said it yourself—he was mad. He did these things because he could. It was nothing to do with me."

"It *was* to do with you!" Catherine burst out. "You connived with him because of Maggie." She shook her head. "And he took Maggie, too. Does it not appall you, Papa? That you could be so weak and let him take so much?"

"He did not take you," Sir Alfred said. "You were strong."

Catherine's mouth twisted but she did not reply.

"What will you do?" Sir Alfred asked suddenly. "What will you do to me? I have stolen your inheritance."

There was a silence. Catherine had been thinking about this in the carriage, and in the midst of her misery and despair, she knew that no matter what he had done, nor how weak he had been, he was still her father. She could not betray him to the authorities.

"I am sure," she said, speaking slowly, "that the bank will accept that we were both deceived by Lord Withers. After all, you are my father. No one would imagine that you would deliberately set out to cheat me. Although you were one of my trustees, you were fooled. Withers tricked us all."

Sir Alfred looked up, a spark of light in his sunken eyes. "You would do that for me?"

"No," Catherine said. "But I would do it for John and for Mirabelle."

"Agatha will look after you," Sir Alfred said. "She will see you are not left penniless."

"I do not wish her to," Catherine said, suddenly fierce. "I can work, Papa. I have done so little all my life that now perhaps is the time for me to discover just what I *can* do." She looked at him. "And I suggest that you do the same. People depend upon you, Papa."

She went out into the hall. Soon, she knew, she

must write to Mr. Churchward and ask him, at his earliest convenience, to meet with her and her father to discuss all the details of their financial plight. She would make it clear that Sir Alfred should be absolved of blame. Then she needed to write to Maggie and ask her to return home with the children. Now that Withers was dead and her dependency broken, there might be a way forward. She would also have to speak to the servants, make arrangements to close the house if necessary.... There were so many things to sort out. Her head ached just to think of it.

But first there was one very important thing to do. She thought of Ben and all the anger that was in her, all the misery, fused into one hard pain in her heart.

She took the waiting hackney to Grillons, where Lady Russell met her and wrapped her in her arms and held her until she was able to speak. Catherine told her godmother all about the fraud and about her father and finally about Ben. She had thought that Lady Russell would be angry, but her godmother simply held her hand and looked at her sadly.

"I thought he loved you," she said. "I thought he loved you enough to stay."

Catherine shook her head. "He may have loved me a little but he loved the money more." She straightened up.

"I called him out once before," she said, "but this time I will go through with it, Aunt Agatha. He has broken my heart. He will meet me for this. I am going to challenge him and this time I am going to kill him."

## CHAPTER THIRTEEN

If a lady and gentleman have a sincere regard
and respect one for the other then the right and
just outcome should be a happy marriage.
—*Mrs. Eliza Squire,* Good Conduct for Ladies

WHEN SAM ARRIVED AT SALTCOATS that afternoon, he
found Edna embroidering in the parlor. There was no
sign of Paris.

"Madam is upstairs," Edna said in answer to his
inquiry. "She is lying down. She is not feeling well."

"I will go up," Sam said.

Edna shook her head. "I would not do that, sir. She
wishes to see no one."

Sam chewed his lip. "I will go up to her anyway,"
he said.

Edna shrugged and bent over her embroidery. Sam
knew she thought he was a fool.

Paris was indeed on her bed, but she was not asleep.
Her eyes were wide open and she was staring into the
shadows. The marks of the chicken pox were starting
to fade now. Her skin looked creamy pale, her hair dark
spun gold and her eyes a deep mysterious blue. Sam felt

his heart lurch. He could not be indifferent to her physical beauty even when he thought her an utter shrew.

"Paris?" he said. "What is it? Edna told me you were feeling ill. Should the sickness not be receding now?"

Paris sat up abruptly and glared at him. "What, are you a doctor now, Sam Hawksmoor, that you can treat the chicken pox? How should I know why I am feeling ill?"

"I am sorry," Sam said mildly. "May I fetch you anything? A glass of water? Some food?"

For a moment, Paris looked as though she was genuinely about to be sick at the thought of food. Then she swung herself off the bed and stood up, swaying slightly.

"You can take yourself off," she said. "I need nothing from you. I am going back to London tomorrow."

"It is probably a little too soon—" Sam began.

"I need to find Beaufoy," Paris said. "I must make him marry me."

Sam blinked. He began to wonder if she was running a fever. It did not seem like the best moment to tell her that the Duke of Beaufoy's guardians had taken advantage of her absence to hustle their young charge out of London and harm's way.

Paris started to drag a portmanteau out from under the bed. She looked at him over her shoulder.

"Are you still there? Why? I told you to go."

"I will go in a moment," Sam said.

"Good," Paris said viciously, "because I get tired of you always doing everything I tell you, like a lap dog."

Sam gritted his teeth. He did not know why he was prompted to try to help her. Probably it was as Ben had once said—he wanted to see good in everyone, to believe that even this tart with a heart of ice had some redeeming features even though he had not found them yet.

"Paris," he said, "tell me what is wrong—"

"There is nothing wrong!"

"Yes there is!" Sam grabbed her arms. It was the first time he had ever touched her. In response she pummeled his chest and kicked his ankles, rather ineffectually since he was wearing boots and she had slippers on. With a noise of frustration, she wrenched herself away from him and swept everything from the top of the chest of drawers. Sam watched the white jug and bowl smash to jagged pieces. The water from the jug started to drip between the floorboards.

"That will bring the parlor ceiling down," Sam said. "It has been there since 1526."

"What do I care?" Paris shouted.

Edna, summoned by the crash of breaking china, had come running up the stairs. She looked from Paris to Sam and raised her eyes heavenward.

"She is always like this when she is in a temper," she said. "It's the spots, you know. The itching drives her to madness."

"No it isn't the spots!" Paris shrieked. She looked from one of them to the other and Sam suddenly saw that her eyes were full of angry tears. "How would you know, you stupid old woman? It isn't the spots! It isn't! It isn't!"

Sam looked at Edna. Edna was looking at Paris like a woman who has instinctively realized something very surprising and very interesting.

"Oh, my good lord," she said faintly, and sat down on the bed.

Sam felt confused. He spread his hands. "Will one of you please tell me—"

"I am having a baby," Paris said. She stood defiant, hands on hips. "I am *enceinte*. Of all the damnable disasters! I must find Beaufoy at once." She bent to the portmanteau again. "Help me with this, will you?" she ordered Edna.

Sam put both of them to one side and lifted the case onto the bed. "Is it Beaufoy's child?" he asked slowly.

Paris looked scornful. "What does it matter if it is his or not? I can make him marry me or at least pay."

"He has left town," Sam said. "His guardians have packed him off to the north. You will never find him."

Paris's blue eyes narrowed with fury. Sam prudently stepped out of range.

"Then I shall get rid of it," she said. "Drink gin, take a hot bath…"

"You can't do that!" Sam felt horrified. He stepped closer to her. "You mustn't do that, Paris."

"There is not enough hot water and no gin," Edna said.

"Then go and find some!" Paris shrieked.

Edna went, her footsteps clattering down the stairs. Sam was not sure if she had actually gone to heat a kettle or whether she was merely keeping out of harm's way.

"It will be all right," he heard himself say. "Everything will turn out."

"I am quite well," Paris said in a hard voice. She looked at Sam. "Do not even think of offering to look after me, Sam Hawksmoor. I would not have you if you were dripping in jewels."

"I was not planning to," Sam said.

"Good," Paris said. She rubbed her hand across her face. "Are you going now? Because I need to think. And I don't want you here whilst I do it." She paused and looked at him. "How is your cousin?" she asked suddenly.

"He is married," Sam said.

Paris's blue eyes narrowed to slits of fury. "I knew it. That puling little debutante! Very well. He has sold out on me. Now it is my turn."

BEN WAS DREAMING. He was on a quay and before him the wide expanse of the river stretched as far as the eye could see, rippling and gleaming into infinity. It was dawn. In his dream state he knew that Catherine would be on a ship that sailed at first light. Already that light was strengthening and he had to find her.

The quay was packed. He pushed people from his path, single-minded, desperate. So many faces, so many people who were not Catherine. He could not bear it. He had to find her because he knew he had failed her somehow and he could not stand it. He was terrified that he was too late.

Then he saw her. She was standing with her back

to him, but after a moment she turned and looked at him, and then he faced the greatest fear of them all, the dread that she would repudiate him—walk away, as he had walked away from her.

He took a step toward her and reached out.

But she was slipping from his grasp like a wraith, retreating from him and he could not hold her. He strained with his very fingertips to touch her….

And awoke with a start to find someone standing beside his bed. It was morning—of which day, he could not be sure—and the light was streaming in and hurting his eyes, and he knew he stank of stale spirits.

"Your cousins are here to see you, my lord."

Price was looking at him with disgust, as though he were some sort of specimen on a slab, and Ben could not blame him.

The truth of what he had done hit him directly between the eyes. He had walked out on his wife. He had left her, no doubt destroyed her. He was no better than his father.

He gave a groan and rolled over.

"Your cousins, my lord," Price said, implacable.

Ben opened his eyes.

"Which cousin?" he inquired.

"Both," Price said succinctly. He was already on his way back to the door, ignoring Ben's comment that he wanted to see no one.

Gideon was hurrying across to the bed, his hand outstretched. "Cousin!" His nose wrinkled as the smell of the brandy struck him and he recoiled. "We came as soon as we heard," he said. He sat down on the end of Ben's bed, in his sober attire looking rather like a priest come to administer the last rites.

"You did the right thing, cousin," he added. "I hear Miss Fenton has lost all her money. It is the *on dit* all about town. And since you could argue that you were not legally married to her, you have no responsibility and were quite right to walk away."

"You're a bloody fool," Sam said, striding across the room and fixing Ben with a glare that would have withered a cactus. "How could you do it, Ben? Only met the girl once but she was the bravest, sweetest, kindest—"

"Be quiet, Sam," Gideon said sharply.

Ben hoisted himself up against his pillows. His mouth felt most unpleasant. Price was hovering just beyond the bed curtains but he offered nothing, no hot water to wash, no cold water to drink, no bag of ice for his head... Damn it, Ben thought, there should be plenty of ice to be had at the moment. It was a poor do that his butler would do nothing for him. But Price's disapproval had always been a serious matter. And now Price had plenty to disapprove of.

"Sam's right," Ben said heavily. "I have been a confounded fool."

"Worse than a fool," Sam said with blistering contempt. He took a step forward. "You are a coward, Ben. You once told me you cared for no one but yourself and now I see the proof of it."

The lines of irritation on Gideon's face deepened. "That is nothing to the purpose. We are here because Miss Fenton has reissued her challenge, Ben. She demands that you meet her for the duel she previously canceled."

Ben put his head in his hands. He felt sick with self-disgust. What had he done? He could barely remember that moment in the lawyer's office. He had heard Churchward's words and seen the look in Catherine's eyes as she'd turned toward him. He had seen her despair and the appeal there. He had seen the love in her eyes and had felt utterly inadequate, unable to match her. And suddenly all the specters of his youth had been there to mock him, rising up to taunt him that he was no longer safe, they would hunt him down, they would win in the end... He would be penniless again, he would *die* from it, the way his mother had done, coughing the last of his miserable life up in the poorhouse. In that moment, he had been unable to breathe and had blundered out into the street looking for somewhere to run. Eventually—much later—he had found himself by the river and had reeled in shock into an alehouse. Catherine's fortune was gone. Her father had betrayed her and she had nothing. And he had left her to face that future alone.

Price must have found him and brought him home. He struggled to sit upright. The remnants of the dream still clung to him. There was only one thing worse than dying in poverty, and that was losing Catherine. He could admit that now, now that he had dreamed of her and lost her all over again.

"I must go to her," he said. He felt breathless, panicked. "I need to apologize. I need to explain."

He was reaching for his clothes when the expression on both Sam and Gideon's faces arrested him. For the first time in his memory, both his cousins looked the same. They were both looking at him with pity.

Sam shook his head. "It's too late for that, Ben."

Ben straightened. "But it can't be! If I just apologize—"

"Miss Fenton never wants to speak to you again," Gideon said. He made a slight gesture with his hands. "Naturally you do not need to meet the challenge she has issued. Just ignore the girl. She does not matter."

"Yes, she does," Sam interrupted hotly. "Ben has behaved like an absolute blackguard and the one thing he has to do now is give *his wife* the opportunity to put a bullet through him! So stop calling her Miss Fenton, Gideon, because she is Lady Hawksmoor and Ben has a responsibility to her and he is the worst sort of scoundrel for walking out on her!"

Gideon waited until his brother had finished and then continued talking as though Sam had not spoken at all. "There is nothing the girl can do. She is ruined now, both financially and because her reputation has been compromised. It is unfortunate, but—"

Ben hit him and Gideon's words gurgled into silence.

"Thank God you did that," Sam said gruffly, "because I was about to kill him."

"What can I do, Sam?" Ben appealed desperately.

Sam turned to him and Ben took an instinctive step back to see the ice in his cousin's eyes.

"Nothing," Sam said. His face was set into hard lines. "I used to admire you, Ben Hawksmoor, but now I think you are no more than a fool."

Ben caught his sleeve as he turned away. "But you will act for me?"

"Aye, I will," Sam said, "and Gideon will, too." He ignored the strangled noises of disagreement coming from his brother. "But that will be an end to it, Ben. After that I never want to see you again."

DAWN CAME SLOWLY to Harington Heath. The moon was on the wane and slipping from the sky in the west as the sun came up, pale and cold.

Catherine's coach was already there. As his carriage drew level, Ben could see her standing talking to Lady Russell. She was wrapped deep in a velvet cloak, and her face was serene and calm. For a moment Ben stared at her—his beautiful Kate, so strong and so proud. Then she sensed his gaze upon her and turned her face away.

"Come on," Sam said grimly. It was the first time he had spoken to Ben on the journey. He swung the carriage door open and let in a blast of morning air. Ben shivered as he jumped down. Gideon followed, still grumbling that he had been roped into this fiasco at all.

Ben looked around him in the growing light. It was a desolate enough place, the low scrubby bushes frozen hard with hoar frost and the thin grass icy beneath his feet. They were the only people there. Ben thrust his hands into his pockets in an ineffectual effort to keep them warm and asked himself whom else he had expected to see. No one would be mad enough to be strolling around this godforsaken place at dawn on a February morning.

There was one other carriage present and Ben guessed it contained the physician Sam had promised would be present. This piece of information had not filled Ben with confidence. Now, as the inhabitants of the coach started to descend, he stared. As well as a sparse, sandy fellow whom he took to be the doctor, there was Churchward the lawyer and Price as well.

Ben stared in mounting horror. He turned to Sam.

"Have you been selling tickets for this?"

He thought his cousin almost smiled. "They insisted on coming," he said.

"Sam," Ben said urgently. "I mean to do the right thing. I mean to delope."

Sam shook his head gently. "Of course you do. But you might be dead by then." He gripped Ben's coat suddenly. "You must tell her, Ben. Tell her you love her. Tell her the truth before it is too late and you lose her forever."

*Tell her the truth before it is too late....*

Where was he to start? With the fact that he was an utter and complete fool who had lost the only woman he had ever loved because he was so afraid of losing the material things in life? Now he knew that there were some things so much more important. He could see so clearly now—now it was too late.

He grabbed Sam's arm.

"You are right. I must speak with my wife."

All the way in the carriage, Ben had been planning what he would say to Catherine when he got the chance. To apologize...to try to explain... It seemed so lame. And so fortuitously timed as a last-ditch attempt to prevent her from shooting him. And now it seemed he would not have that opportunity anyway, for as he strode toward her, Lady Russell stepped in front of her and barred his way. Over her head—Lady Russell was very small—he could see Catherine. Her face was intent and serious. She did not even glance his way.

"She will not speak to you," Lady Russell said. "I am sorry, Hawksmoor. She needed you and you broke her heart. It is too late."

After that, matters took on the stuff of Ben's nightmares.

Sam was pacing out the ground. Gideon and Lady Russell went off to inspect the pistols.

Somehow—Ben was not sure how he got there— he was facing Catherine across an expanse of open ground. Sam offered him a pistol. He saw it was cocked and took it carefully, keeping it pointed at the ground. Lady Russell was speaking, saying something about the signal to fire, but he could not hear her. He felt a leaden dread inside that had nothing to do with contemplating his approaching death and everything to do with all the things he wished he had told Catherine when he had had the chance.

"Wait!" he shouted.

Lady Russell stopped speaking. She did not look affronted, merely curious.

"I wish to speak with my wife," Ben said. "I insist." He took a step toward Catherine and she immediately raised her pistol to point it directly at him.

"Stay where you are!"

Ben stopped. "Give me leave to speak," he shouted. "Consider it the last words of a condemned man, if you must."

He thought that Catherine almost smiled, but it could have been a trick of the dawn light.

"Speak then," she said after a moment. "You have one minute."

Ben was silent for a moment. What to say when this minute was all he had to gain his heart's desire? What to say when the woman he loved was pointing a pistol at his heart?

"I love you," he said. It came out too quietly and he shouted, "I love you!"

Nobody moved. Clearly that was not enough.

"I loved you on the night of the Frost Fair," he shouted, "but I feared the past more. I thought that because you were rich—" He paused, cleared his throat. He thought of all the elegant words he might have used, but they would not come now. "I thought that because you were rich it was safe to love you!" he bellowed. "And when it was all taken away I was afraid!" He straightened. "I admit it. I was a coward. I let my fear win. But now…" He gasped for breath. He was losing his voice. "Now I love you so much I care nothing for whether we are rich or poor, wanting only to be with you and keep you from harm. I know I can be a better man with you than without you, Catherine. Give me the chance to prove it. Give me that time—" His voice broke.

He wanted to run toward Catherine, to beg her to listen, but then something moved behind him and he spun around. A man was crouching in the bushes directly behind him, and as Ben turned he saw it was Algernon Withers. Withers had a pistol and it was aimed straight at Catherine. Ben heard Sam give a shout of warning and he straightened up, moving deliberately into Withers's line of fire.

Withers's bullet took him through the arm and the pain was like a red-hot brand that made him feel a little faint for a moment. He staggered, his hand going to his sleeve where a stain had started to spread. Withers had run, and Ben could see that Sam was not going to be able to catch him as he vanished into the scrubland. Gideon was not even trying to join the pursuit.

The doctor was hurrying toward Ben over the frozen grass, but then Ben saw Catherine behind him and he ceased to notice anything else at all, could see only her. She was running toward him now, dropping her pistol on the grass, her hair streaming out behind her as she ran. He could she was crying, the tears pouring down her cheeks. When she reached him, he pulled her into his arms, regardless of the blood, regardless of the pain.

"Ben!"

He held her close and felt the frantic beating of her heart, and put his cheek against the softness of her hair and felt a huge thankfulness, for he had been afraid that he would never hold her in his arms again.

"I thought I had lost you forever!" Catherine gulped. "I am so sorry. I swear I would not have killed you, but I was so angry and sad and lost, and then I saw Withers's bullet hit you—"

Ben cradled her head and held her so tightly he

could feel her tears soak his shirtfront. He was shaking, too.

"Sweetheart, I understand. Everything is all right." He tilted her chin up and kissed her. "Tell me you love me," he demanded.

"I love you," Catherine said. A spark of humor came into her voice. "You saved me from Withers again. I think I shall have to keep you close after all."

She smiled, rubbing the tears from her face. "Are matters even between us now?" she asked, as once she had done when she was in his bed.

"No," Ben said. "Not until I tell you again how much I love you." The elegant words he should have said earlier were coming back to him now, and more besides.

"I have been a fool," he said. "I am so sorry, Kate. I should never have walked away from you. If you trust me now, I swear I will never, never let you down again." He broke off, suddenly aware that a large and very interested audience had gathered about them.

"Do you mind?" he demanded wrathfully. "I am trying to declare my love to Catherine."

"Well," Lady Russell said, "we heard all your other declarations of love, Hawksmoor, so I do not see why we should miss this one. Besides, the surgeon requires to bind your wound, but pray do not let that put you off your stroke!"

After that, things became somewhat hazy for Ben. Catherine held his good hand and Lady Russell poured most of the contents of her brandy flask down his throat while the doctor bound a makeshift bandage about his arm. They were all walking slowly—and a little drunkenly in Ben's case—toward the carriages when there was the rumble of wheels on the road and a coach came clattering to a halt beside them.

It was a most fashionable silver equipage that had suffered somewhat on the country road for it was spattered with frozen mud.

The door swung open. And Lady Paris de Moine appeared in the aperture.

WHEN THE CARRIAGE PULLED UP Catherine was feeling tired, relieved and happier than she had ever been in her life before. It was as though the temporary madness that had possessed her since Lily's death had lifted and she was at last able to see past all the horror and loss to the possibility of the future. And then the coach had stopped and Paris had appeared and looked at her in that frightful sneering way that Catherine remembered from the night at Crockford's.

"Well," Paris said. "Lady Hawksmoor! So you did not kill your husband after all. I am glad, for I have such a lovely surprise for the pair of you."

Catherine saw Ben raise his head and his eyes meet those of his cousin. Sam blushed and Catherine realized what he had done. *He* was the one who had told Paris about the duel and brought this down on them.

"This is all most affecting," Lady Paris drawled. She took the coachman's hand and descended the steps as though she were about to greet the Prince Regent at a Carlton House ball. She was dressed all in white with a fur-trimmed cloak and diamonds. Her sharp blue gaze swept over them all, lingered a little on Catherine, then fastened on Ben's face. Catherine felt him go still and knew, with a flash of insight, that like her he was afraid. Not of what Paris might say but of the damage it might do to the two of them when they had barely begun to rebuild a fragile love and trust.

He had sworn that he and Paris had never been lovers and Catherine had believed him. And suddenly she knew, with a powerful rush of love and conviction, that Paris could do her worst and it would make no difference. Ben loved her and only her, and nothing could change that now.

"I am desolate to disturb your idyll, Benjamin," Paris said, "but there is something that I think you should know."

Ben sighed. "Like the wicked queen in the fairy tale," he said softly. "Why must you come now, Paris, to try to spoil everything?"

Paris smoothed the white satin of her cloak over her stomach. "Because I am your mistress, Ben," she said, "and I am pregnant."

It seemed to Catherine that the whole world was still and quiet. Ben had gone very white. His grip on her hand was painful.

"Do not, I beg, try to pin that on me, Paris," he said, "when you know it cannot be my child."

"No one will believe that, Ben," Paris said. She was smiling. "The whole world knows you to be my lover. If I say this is your child, who will not believe me?"

Catherine took a step forward. "I will not," she said. She glanced up at Ben's face and spoke only for him. "If I do not believe it, does anyone else matter?"

They stared at one another for a long moment.

"Sweetheart." Ben's words sounded choked. "I swear—"

Catherine put her fingers to his lips. "You need not. I trust you. I always did."

"You stupid, naive child," Paris began, but Catherine turned her back on her very deliberately and a moment later it was Sam who spoke.

"Paris, enough." His voice was low. "Do not do this. You know it will do no good."

Paris glared at him. From the shelter of Ben's arms, Catherine could feel all the hatred and malevolence in her. Slowly Paris's gaze circled around the group and pinned itself on Gideon Hawksmoor. "Then," she said slowly, "it seems I must tell the truth for once. Mr. Hawksmoor, what can you tell everyone of the real identity of my child's father?"

Catherine heard Ben's swift intake of breath. Sam had frozen, his incredulous gaze going to his brother. And Gideon had turned a strange milky-white.

He started to gabble. "It's a lie, I swear it, she always lies, she never tells the truth, I had nothing to do with it, don't tell Alice, I promise it was not me, it is not my child!"

And then, to everyone's amazement, he ran away across the scrubby ground and disappeared down the road that led to town.

SIR ALFRED FENTON WAS a conventional man and, with his wife back at his side in Guilford Street and his daughter married and preparing to move to the Hawksmoor estate in Yorkshire with her husband, he could almost convince himself that the terrible business of the previous months had never occurred.

Algernon Withers had not been apprehended and it seemed probable that he never would, but the grave robbers' activities continued unabated across London and Sir Alfred shuddered sometimes to think of the man behind them. Catherine had been true to her word and had told the banking authorities that her father had been ignorant of the fraud, so he had no difficulties to contend with there. His business had even begun to show a profit for a change. And Lady Russell had set off on a tour of the Western Isles of Scotland, wanting to travel a little closer to home now that her goddaughter was to be settled in the north.

And then, one evening in April, Maggie had returned from a trip to Madame Tussauds waxworks with the children, and everything had changed.

Sir Alfred was in his bedchamber, preparing for a most pleasantly anticipated evening at the house of his mistress in Chelsea. His cravat had been starched into firmness, his coat was padded with wadding to fill out his shoulders and his shoes had a discreet heel to increase his stature. He looked a fine figure of a man and he had no doubts that Rosabelle would tell him so, too.

He heard his family return, for John was shouting and the baby was wailing, and Sir Alfred's head was already splitting from the noise and he could not wait to be gone. He went out onto the landing and observed his wife standing at the bottom of the curving stair. The nursemaid was holding the bawling child, and her face was drawn and tired with hunger and exhaustion.

"We have not eaten the whole day!" John was saying to Tench. "Mama went off with a strange man and barely showed us the exhibits at all. I was so bored and I am so hungry now."

Maggie turned when she heard Sir Alfred's step on the stairs. He looked down into her face and felt a huge sense of shock. Gone was the pretty wife who had recovered from her laudanum dependency. She was flushed and was trembling a little, and her eyes were feverishly bright. She held out her arms to him and Sir Alfred felt a wave of revulsion. He actually took a step back. He could not banish the vision of her the time he had seen her standing in that very place, broken and desperate, prepared to sell her body for a bottle of laudanum. And thinking of it, he could feel the red heat of anger fill his brain, breaking down all the defenses he had built against the truth. The mother of his children was a whore. She had debased herself with Withers before and now it seemed she had done exactly the same thing again.

"Darling!" Despite the embarrassed gaze of the servants, she ran up the stairs and embraced him. She smelled of sweat and perfume. "I missed you!"

Sir Alfred released himself with deliberation and held her at arm's length.

"Take the boy to the nursery," he said to the maid, "and see that he is fed and put to bed. The baby, too."

He turned back to Maggie and suddenly he did not care about the astonished stares of the servants. "Who was this strange man with whom you spent the day?"

"He was only someone we met whilst we were looking at the exhibits," Maggie said. She fidgeted with the stitching on her gloves. She did not meet his eyes. "He was a visitor to London so I offered to show him about a little."

"You are all goodness, my love," Sir Alfred said politely.

Maggie had turned a little pale at his tone. She started to chatter but Sir Alfred did not hear her. His mind was far away, making connections, noting the febrile excitement in his wife's manner, which surely had no natural cause, for it was the stimulation caused by the laudanum that had always preceded the crash in her spirits. He wanted to grab her reticule and search for the bottle there and then.

"I am going out," he said abruptly, cutting across Maggie's words, and he left his wife standing dumbstruck in the hall.

IT WAS DARK AND DANK in the graveyard of Saint Crispin's church. Sir Alfred picked his way carefully through the headstones and skirted an open grave that yawned like a scar, awaiting its load in the morning. The gravedigger's hut was set against the wall, shielded by yew trees, in the shadow of the church. The door was not locked. Sir Alfred put his hand to the knob and turned it silently.

It took a moment for his eyes to adjust to the deeper

darkness inside and in that moment he thought he had made a mistake and that Withers was not there at all. From the beginning, when Withers had taken to sponsoring the body snatchers' vile trade, he had liked to go out with them, liked to watch as they broke open the graves and dragged the fresh corpses out. He had boasted of it to Sir Alfred sometimes, telling him the tales deliberately to turn his stomach and make him almost retch with fear and disgust. Sir Alfred knew it had been part of the means by which Withers had broken his spirit. And it had worked. He had been a weak and ineffectual partner in Withers's crimes.

As he hesitated, Sir Alfred heard a sound, the striking of flint, and he screwed up his eyes against the flare of the lantern. Withers was sitting in a corner of the shed, a knife lying idly by his hand. He got to his feet.

"I knew it was you," Withers said. "What the hell are you doing here?"

"I needed to see you," Sir Alfred said.

"You stink of cologne," Withers said disagreeably. "Did you wear it to try to attract that wife of yours back to your bed? I heard she had come back to you."

"No doubt she told you herself when she met you today," Sir Alfred said.

Withers just laughed. "Perhaps she did, old man. You know what she is like. Can't live without me, eh, one way or another."

Sir Alfred felt odd and light-headed. His mind was full of flashing pictures of Maggie on her knees before this man begging for laudanum, offering herself in return. The man he had sold his own flesh and blood to. He could tell that Withers had an absolute contempt for him because he had left the knife discarded on the floor as he moved across to open the door and look out on to the graveyard.

"The body snatchers may come tonight," Withers said over his shoulder. "Or tomorrow for certain. I thought we might go across to Saint Day's and disinter that little harlot Lily St. Clare and sell her body to the quacks."

The buzzing in Sir Alfred's head increased. Without conscious thought, he took his pistol from his pocket and brought the butt of it down on the back of Withers's head. The man crumpled slowly, quietly to the floor.

Sir Alfred stood still for a moment, blinking. In the end, it had been easy. He should have done it long ago.

After that, he worked quickly and as silently as he could. He scooped Withers up, panting with the effort—the scoundrel was heavier than he had thought, and he was very unfit—and placed him in the rough wooden coffin that was on the table. Withers was still breathing, though he was unconscious. The coffin wood was cheap and soft, and it splintered as Sir Alfred forced the nails through the lid. A pauper's coffin, but he knew the nails would still hold.

It was hard work dragging the coffin out into the graveyard and he was afraid of the noise, but no one came. Saint Crispin's was traditionally a pauper's church and no one really cared whether the body snatchers dug the corpses up or not. The poor were legion. There were always more sick and dying to populate the graves.

Sir Alfred tipped the coffin into the empty grave, then took the spade that was leaning against the wall of the hut and went back out to cover it with earth. He thought that he could hear a faint noise now from within Withers's wooden prison, the sound of fingernails scratching against the lid. He smiled grimly to himself and shoveled all the harder.

THE BODY SNATCHERS DID NOT come that night, but they did come the night after, just as Withers had predicted. Seeing a freshly turned grave, they knew there was the very thing they wanted—a brand new corpse. Even so, they were somewhat surprised when they broke open the coffin.

Algernon, Lord Withers, had certainly not rested in peace. Contorted, struggling, he had evidently been trying to fight his way out when he had suffocated to death.

For a long moment, the shadowy figures stood about his grave, leaning on their shovels, laughing. Then the ringleader reached down into the coffin to drag the body out.

"Never mind, lads," he said. "We can still turn a profit from him."

CATHERINE WAS LYING in her husband's arms in the big bed in their chamber at Hawksmoor. The fine plaster of the ceiling above them was peeling from the winter damp, but a fire roared in the grate and they were wrapped up tight and warm. She turned her head against Ben's shoulder and smiled sleepily at him. Hawksmoor was all they had now and it would take an inordinate amount of work to make the place serviceable again, but then as Ben had reminded her, she had once said that she wanted to live in the country and now she had her wish. In truth it did not matter to them where they were, as long as they were together.

The press had been astonished when Ben had announced that he was retiring from London, but the Prince Regent had kissed Catherine with rather more enthusiasm than Ben had liked to see, and had wished them luck. There was always a new scandal for the penny prints anyway, most of them provided by Lady Paris de Moine. She had named Gideon Hawksmoor as the father of her child, had taken him for every penny she could, and then had eloped with her coachman.

Catherine watched the firelight play across the walls and snuggled closer to Ben as he shifted her within his arms and started to kiss her. His hands were caressing her very gently now and she moved to the pleasure of his touch. But before they made love, she knew there was something she had to tell him, one last thing before they could close the book on the past and look forward to rebuilding Hawksmoor together.

"Ben?"

Her husband made the kind of halfhearted sound of acknowledgment that meant he would far rather kiss her than talk. Catherine put a hand against his bare chest and held him away from her.

"Ben…"

"Mmm…" He was kissing her shoulder, nibbling at her skin so that the soft shivers of excitement ran down her spine. Catherine tried to concentrate.

"Ben, there is something we have to talk about."

Ben stopped kissing her, sighed and raised his hazel gaze to hers. "Yes, Catherine?"

"When Aunt Agatha called here last week on her way to Scotland," Catherine said, "she told me that she wished to settle some money on me." She held his gaze. "Since Papa had been unable to fulfill the marriage contracts, she said that she thought it was only right and proper that as my godmother, she should do so."

Ben had gone very still. His eyes were dark.

"How much did she offer?" he asked.

"Thirty thousand pounds," Catherine said.

She held her breath. Ben had rolled away from her now, propping himself on one elbow as he watched her face.

"And what did you say to her?" he said.

Catherine fidgeted with the edge of the sheet. "Well, I said that I would discuss it with you, but…"

"But?"

Ben raised one dark brow. Catherine thought that there was amusement in his eyes but she could not be sure.

"But that I thought you would tell her that we did not want her money, because…"

"Because we had one another and we needed nothing more?" Ben gave a great shout of laughter and pulled her back into his arms. "That woman is as cunning as a fox!"

Catherine pressed against the warm reassurance of his body. "What do you mean?" she asked.

Ben brushed the hair away from her face and bent to kiss her gently. "Only that when Lady Russell was here on her way to Scotland last week she took me aside and offered me a marriage settlement for you of thirty thousand pounds," he said. He looked down at her and Catherine's heart turned over to see the love in his eyes. "I was going to tell you tonight."

Catherine raised her hand to his cheek. "And what did you say?" she whispered.

"I told her that I would discuss it with you." Ben laughed. "But that I thought that I knew what you would say."

"That we did not want her money, because we had one another and we needed nothing more?"

"That's right," Ben said. "I have all I ever want here in my arms, Catherine. I love you. What does the money matter to me when I have you?"

Catherine slid her hand around to the nape of his neck and drew his head down so that she could kiss him.

"I love you, too," she murmured. "I knew that was what you would say. What does the money matter, now that I have you?"

# REQUEST YOUR
# FREE BOOKS!

## 2 FREE NOVELS
## FROM THE ROMANCE/SUSPENSE
## COLLECTION PLUS 2 FREE GIFTS!

**YES!** Please send me 2 FREE novels from the Romance/Suspense Collection and my 2 FREE gifts. After receiving them, if I don't wish to receive any more books, I can return the shipping statement marked "cancel." If I don't cancel, I will receive 4 brand-new novels every month and be billed just $5.49 per book in the U.S., or $5.99 per book in Canada, plus 25¢ shipping and handling per book plus applicable taxes, if any*. That's a savings of at least 20% off the cover price! I understand that accepting the 2 free books and gifts places me under no obligation to buy anything. I can always return a shipment and cancel at any time. Even if I never buy another book from the Reader Service, the two free books and gifts are mine to keep forever.

185 MDN EF5Y  385 MDN EF6C

| | | |
|---|---|---|
| Name | (PLEASE PRINT) | |
| Address | | Apt. # |
| City | State/Prov. | Zip/Postal Code |

Signature (if under 18, a parent or guardian must sign)

### Mail to **The Reader Service:**
**IN U.S.A.:** P.O. Box 1867, Buffalo, NY 14240-1867
**IN CANADA:** P.O. Box 609, Fort Erie, Ontario L2A 5X3

Not valid to current subscribers to the Romance Collection,
the Suspense Collection or the Romance/Suspense Collection.

**Want to try two free books from another line?**
Call 1-800-873-8635 or visit www.morefreebooks.com.

* Terms and prices subject to change without notice. NY residents add applicable sales tax. Canadian residents will be charged applicable provincial taxes and GST. This offer is limited to one order per household. All orders subject to approval. Credit or debit balances in a customer's account(s) may be offset by any other outstanding balance owed by or to the customer. Please allow 4 to 6 weeks for delivery.

**Your Privacy:** Harlequin is committed to protecting your privacy. Our Privacy Policy is available online at www.eHarlequin.com or upon request from the Reader Service. From time to time we make our lists of customers available to reputable firms who may have a product or service of interest to you. If you would prefer we not share your name and address, please check here. ☐

OB07

$\mathcal{L}$ord Hawksmoor is the
Lord of Scandal—celebrated by
the pampered and paupers alike!

Scandalous and seductive, Hawksmoor is a notorious
fortune hunter. A man women want to bed—and men
want to do away with. Now he has tasted the woman of
his dreams, Catherine Fenton, and he will do anything
to make her his.

Though heiress to eighty thousand pounds, Catherine
is trapped in a gilded cage, and duty bound to a man
she detests. The ton has woven a fantasy around Ben,
Lord Hawksmoor, that any woman would find hard to
resist, but she senses there is more to the man behind
the glittering facade.

She believes he can rescue her—but has she found her
hero, or made a pact with the devil himself…?

**Nicola Cornick takes you on a journey through
the glittering world of Regency England
in her delightful new novel!**

ISBN-13:978-0-373-77211-7
ISBN-10: 0-373-77211-4

50699

9 780373 772117

EAN

S

**HQN**™

We *are* romance™
www.HQNBooks.com
$6.99 U.S./$8.50 CAN.